The Reluctant Princess

The Charm City Hearts Series, Book 1

By

M.C. Vaughan

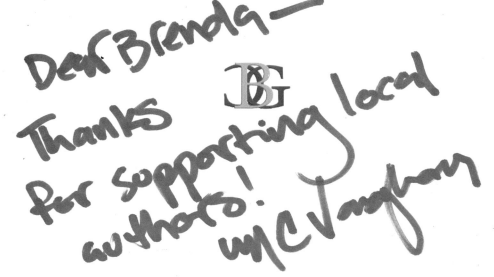

Dear Brenda —
Thanks for supporting local authors!
M.C. Vaughan

Champagne Book Group
www.champagnebooks.com
Copyright 2018 by M.C. Vaughan
ISBN 978-1-947128-64-4
February 2019
Cover Art: Trisha Fitzgerald
Produced in the United States of America

Champagne Book Group
2373 NE Evergreen Avenue
Albany OR 97321
USA

Dedication

To David—my first reader, my biggest fan, and my heart.

One

February snow swirled around Zara Kissette as she hoofed it to her day-job in midtown Baltimore. She was happy. Well, happy*ish,* which was why she should have known the universe was about to punch her square in the lady junk.

That was the kind of relationship she had with the universe, after all.

As she approached the corner of Eager and Cathedral Streets, the crossing signal switched to red. Traffic whipped past as she sipped her frothy coffee from Zeke's. A total splurge, but she was rewarding herself for her recent Grade-A adulting.

She'd paid her bills, restocked her art supplies, and acted like a consummate professional during yesterday's meeting with the gallery owner. Honestly, it had gone *way* better than she expected. Afterward, she'd tucked her portfolio in her studio, avoided eye contact with intimidating blank canvas on her easel, and proceeded to check her email every five minutes for the notification about the show.

Her belly flipped. If she landed a coveted slot in the Schwarz Gallery's showcase, *that,* right there, would be her career's turning point. She'd have proof she was more than a disciplined hobbyist. Even better, gallery sales would mean she'd be able to honor the deal she'd made with her parents.

She stuck out her tongue to catch a fluffy snowflake. Her painter's block would melt away with a vote of confidence like that. Wouldn't it?

Her cell buzzed in her coat pocket. She fished it out and peered at its paint-speckled screen.

Eleanor.

Zara sighed and accepted the call. "Hey, listen, if this is about studio rent, I sent the check."

Not *quite* a lie. She'd slipped the late payment into a mailbox fifteen minutes ago.

"No, dear." Eleanor sighed. "There's been a fire."

Zara dropped her coffee and ran.

~ * ~

Fifteen minutes later, she trembled in her combat boots as she stood on the threshold of her studio. Acrid, plastic, smoky odors tightened her throat. In the far corner, Eleanor scribbled notes on a pad on a clipboard. The older woman's untamed silver hair strained away from her head in stark relief against the blackened walls.

"Eleanor," Zara said, "what happened?"

Her mentor lowered her clipboard. "I'm sorry, dear."

Zara stomped into what had been her beautiful, curated space. She turned like a lathe and drank in the destruction. Drenched watercolors peeled from the walls. A sketchbook, smeared and bloated, drowned in a puddle. Her palette bled colors across the worktable. Even the big blank canvas, now covered in soggy soot, was ruined.

The coffee she'd drunk threatened to back up on her, and she clapped a hand over her mouth. If she'd eaten breakfast, for sure she would have lost it too. "Was it the radiator? I told you it kicks out an obnoxious amount of heat."

"No." Eleanor pointed to the ceiling with the nib of her pen. "The marshal said it was an electrical fire that started there and burned through this corner. You can see where they punched additional holes to confirm nothing is smoldering. We're lucky the sprinkler system kept it contained."

"Lucky?" Zara's gaze focused on the charred mountain next to Eleanor. It had been the stack of the paintings she'd shown John Schwarz and her tidy collection of brushes, paints, and paper stock. A compact, 'eggs-in-one-basket' location.

"Poor choice of words on my part, Zara." Eleanor's glasses' chain swooped against her cheek as she cocked her head. "I meant it could have been worse."

"Nobody was hurt, right?"

Eleanor shook her head.

"Good." Zara shuffled through a puddle toward the remnants of her portfolio. She lifted the scorched corner of an abstract entitled *Gut Punch*. It broke off like a wilted petal.

Her heart crumpled.

Eleanor slipped her glasses from her nose and dropped them to her chest. "You've had a shock, but, as the building manager, I need to talk business for a moment. To inform you of the next steps."

Zara thumbed a rebellious lock of dark hair behind her ear. "Go for it. I'm already numb."

Eleanor nodded and sidled next to her. Zara sensed her mentor wanted to throw a hug around her, but she didn't want hugs. Hugs would squeeze tears from her, and she was determined to keep them sandbagged deep, deep down. Crying was pointless. It never restored what you loved.

Zara shifted away from Eleanor, who cleared her throat.

"Per the lease agreement, the Tower will coordinate and pay for repairs to the wiring, the wall, and the floor." Eleanor slapped the clipboard against her thigh. "I'll contact our insurers today to get the process started and hound them to rush it through so you're back in your space as soon as possible. You'll also need to file a claim through your business insurance provider to get a check to replace your materials."

"Got it." Zara sucked air between her teeth.

File a claim against the policy she'd allowed to lapse, because food had been more important than insurance.

Maybe her roommates could help lighten her mood. If not, they'd at least commiserate. She held her phone at arm's length and clicked off a few pictures texting them to her roommates along with the message, *"This is *my* day. #FML."*

"Are those for your insurance company?"

"I guess?" Zara groaned. The reality of her financial situation was pretty grim. "It'll cost me at least a thousand dollars to replace my stuff."

A cacophony of text tones burst from her phone, signaling her roommates' replies hurtling back: a camera shutter click for Grier, a violin scale for Brooke, and applause for Melinda.

Zara glanced at the screen.

Wait!

An e-mail alert was mixed in with the emoji-riddled texts. Zara brought the phone closer to her face. The message was from John Schwarz, the gallery owner she'd met with yesterday.

She launched the e-mail, trying to scan the whole message at once, unable to read the words fast enough. Before her vision blurred and her breath hitched, she'd read good words like *invite*, and *participate*, and *contract*. She'd also caught bad words like *weeks*.

Her vision grayed at the edges, and she couldn't get enough air. Zara crouched and put her head between her knees before she fainted.

Eleanor pressed a broad hand to Zara's back. "Oh, Zara, it'll be okay. The fire is unfortunate, but you could use this. Make lemonade—"

Zara waved her phone over her head. "No pep talks. Will you read this e-mail to me?"

"Of course, dear." She plucked it from her Zara's grip and read aloud. "Dear Zara, thank you for coming to my gallery yesterday." Eleanor lowered the phone. "You met with John? Why didn't you tell me?"

Zara laced her fingers behind her head. "I didn't want to jinx it."

"I'm surprised he didn't mention it to me either, since I'd put in a good word about you." Eleanor raised an eyebrow and continued reading.

"I wish you hadn't done that. I want to earn this on my own."

"Don't be silly. My word may open a door, but it's your work that would earn you a place at the table. Now, shall I continue?"

No point in arguing with Eleanor. "Yes please."

"I liked what you had to say with respect to your vision and process. You could be a good fit for the gallery. We'd originally spoken about the New Artist Showcase in June, but it's your lucky day, kiddo, because an artist dropped out of our 'Phoenix' exhibition. We're hanging in five weeks—"

Zara barked a noise halfway between a sob and a laugh. A laub? A saugh? Whatever it was, it hurt her throat.

"I'd love to include you. I'd need three pieces for the exhibit." Eleanor squatted next to Zara and nudged her. "What wonderful news! This will be your first gallery show, won't it?"

"It would be." She closed her eyes against her wrecked studio. "If my paintings weren't pulpy cinders."

Eleanor rubbed a small circle on the flat spot between Zara's shoulder blades. "You can't pass this up. You simply can't. It'll open dozens of industry doors for you."

"I know." She rose and raked her fingers through her hair. Deep breaths, like her Gramma had taught her when she had low-key panic attacks. This wasn't an open-ended invitation. If she turned it down, there was no guarantee Schwarz would extend it to a future show. She needed this for all kinds of reasons, but mostly to satisfy the deal she'd made with her parents.

"The fire was fate," Eleanor said. "The show is named 'Phoenix,' after all."

Canvas, stretchers, paint, and brushes—she'd have to replace it all, but her credit was wrecked. How would she earn enough money to replace her materials and paint three pieces in five weeks? Pieces worthy of a prestigious show?

Well, there's always…

A plan surfaced. A plan so perfect, so nauseating, it must be right.

No. Not that. Anything *but that.*

She sucked in a chest-bursting bucket of air.

Oh, God. Do I still have the dress?

There was one speedy way she could make the bundle of cash needed to replace her art supplies.

Two

Brendan Stewart rolled his neck. He was certain this meant surrendering his man card. Didn't matter. A dad's gotta do what a dad's gotta do.

"Okay, Pinterest, let's see what you've got."

He keyed in his daughter's favorite cartoon princess, "Ravenna from *Rising*" and "party ideas," hit return, and boom. His browser loaded with a billion different ways to make his daughter's fifth birthday party epic.

He slogged through the pictures. Elaborate cupcakes, costumes, party favors—all of which appeared to be homemade. What kind of free time must these people have? Even if he didn't have a monster deadline in a month, he'd refuse to spend hours of his free time on stuff like this. His days with Emma were already cut in half.

Nah, he'd buy as much as he could, stock up on the best Party City had to offer, and maybe go overboard on the balloons. Emma loved balloons almost as much as she loved candy.

Now, what the hell would a dozen little girls do during the festivities?

He scratched his neck and yawned.

Kid parties were the worst. There's the party for the kids, but the parents have to hang out because they happen to have kids the same age. Most of the parties Emma'd been invited to this year involved the same conversations—*Are you Emma's older brother? You're her father? You look so young!*

Because he was young. Most of these parents had a good ten years on him.

Maybe he'd hire some entertainment to take the strain off parental small talk. Like a magician maybe? Or a clown? He shivered. No. Definitely not a clown.

He opened another browser tab and searched up children's party entertainers in Baltimore. Hmmm…a face painter could be fun. The third link was for one who dressed like a princess. Bingo. As soon as the site loaded, Brendan widened his eyes. The face painter, Zara, could be Ravenna's twin. Authentic black-and-purple hair, glacier-blue eyes, porcelain skin, and Ravenna's signature scowl. Her austere website could use an overhaul, but never mind the site's design. This girl was *perfect.*

He had to hire her.

After he clicked the 'Contact' button, Brendan typed the details of the party and shot the note off into the ether. Not a bad night's work—he'd ordered the food, decided on the decorations, and had feelers out for the entertainment. Time for a beer.

Eh, who was he kidding? Time to get back to coding. Those queries weren't going to write themselves.

Before he could move from the couch to his workstation, his e-mail alert chimed. Zara had gotten back to him.

Hi there—

Got your note. I'm available. The charge is $200 for 90 minutes and includes a gallery of photos after. If you want to book me, Venmo a 50% deposit to the account below, and Ravenna will be there.

—Z

No hesitation. He paid the deposit and texted the link to her site to Jess.

Adorable! Jess wrote a few minutes later. *I'll kick in half.*

Huh. That was unexpectedly generous of his ex.

Thx, but I've got this.

When is it, again?

Sighing, he texted back. *2 weeks—Sunday, 2/11 @ 1:00 p.m.*

Jess notoriously double and triple-booked herself. But come on. This was her daughter's birthday. Unlike last year, for the sake of Emma, they'd agreed to co-host one party instead of separate events. They'd chosen this date *weeks* ago.

Pulsing dots. They disappeared, and reappeared. Aw, hell. This was no good. Whenever Jess started and stopped texts, she was about to drop a bomb on him.

Oh no! I thought it was the next weekend since that's closest to her actual birthday. I'm away for her party. ☹ Booked a sponsored blog post for a spa.

He clutched his phone and ground his teeth together. A fucking *spa?*

Jess, you *have* to come.

It kills me, but I can't. Signed a contract. Her private school's expensive, Brendan. I have to pay for it somehow.

His hurled his phone across the room, and it crashed into wall.

Good. He wouldn't have to deal with the follow-up texts she'd shoot his way throughout the night.

Have to pay for it somehow…

What a load of horseshit. They split the cost fifty-fifty. Besides, she pulled down ten grand a month in ad revenues alone. He should know—he'd developed her site. This trip was probably a freebie rendezvous with her selfie-happy boyfriend. Couple of pictures of their feet on the boardwalk, hints she was dating someone new. Lather, rinse, repeat. This kind of nonsense was all Jess seemed to publish since Brendan put the legal clamp down on posts about their daughter.

He stood, shoved the chair away, then paced toward the stairs of his Federal Hill townhouse. He had to burn off some of this irritated energy. Damn, *Jess's me-first* attitude picked at every scab he had about their relationship.

Splitting up and disentangling from the fat cash cow her blog had become had meant sacrificing control over the work he chose to do. He'd given up independent contract work and had settled into a salaried job with benefits. Emma's EpiPens alone were a nightmare without decent insurance. He'd get back to freelancing someday, but for now, he needed a guaranteed flow of money to keep things steady for his daughter.

In his bedroom, he tackled the enormous jumble of laundry he'd meant to put away for the past week. He yanked a Ravenna towel free, almost toppling the whole pile of clean clothes to the floor. As he folded the towel in thirds, and in thirds again, he wished with everything he had that the princess would help Emma have a happy birthday.

Three

The cherry red Mercedes ferried Zara through the streets of Federal Hill, the centuries-old residential neighborhood hugging Baltimore's Inner Harbor. The car purred to a halt in front of the townhouse bearing the address of her gig.

"That," Zara said and jerked her thumb over her shoulder, "is a shit-ton of balloons with my face on it."

Grier cut the engine and peered through her roommate's foggy window. In the front garden, a vast bouquet of silvery orbs strained against their tethers. One more, and they'd probably uproot the black iron address plaque to which they were tied.

"Oh my God." Grier snickered. "It is. You resemble her even more in this new wave of party merchandise. Especially now you've streaked your hair with purple again. It's pretty amazing."

"What's amazing is how lucrative it is to be a dead ringer for Princess Ravenna of Everly."

"At least she's the most gothicky princess. Jewel tones suit you. Think about it—her costume could have been pastel pink."

Zara shivered. "Bite your tongue."

"What I enjoy most about shooting these parties," Grier said as she checked her chirping cell phone, "is your unparalleled acting skill. If I didn't know better, I'd say you actually like kids."

"I don't *not* like kids." Zara flipped the passenger sun visor down and checked her makeup in the mirror. "At worst, I'd say I'm neutral. They're fine when they aren't manic balls of soul-sucking neediness. It's the parents who get to me. I can't deal with the ooey-gooey 'kids are special snowflakes' mentality most of them have."

"Yes. Parents should tolerate their children, not celebrate them."

"That's not quite—"

"Oh." Grier glanced up from her phone. "Andrew texted to ask if I can help him with a wedding next weekend. I need more nuptials to round out my portfolio. Do we have any more kid parties, or is this the last gig before you re-hang up the face paints?"

"Yes, thank the sweet baby Jesus." Zara dabbed a tissue at the overdone eyeliner on her lower lids. "Five done, one to go. Two hellacious weekends, but a girl's gotta make that paper."

"I can't believe your parents wouldn't lend you money." Grier shoved her phone into her coat pocket.

"I didn't ask. They'd use it as an opportunity to highlight how stupid and chancy my career is. Except they'd call it a hobby and enroll me in community college business classes so I can help them run their inn when I retreat home."

"Solid vote of confidence there."

"Right?" Zara reapplied the dark berry stain on her lips. "Can I borrow your Bluetooth speaker thingamajig? I broke mine last weekend."

"Yep." Grier snatched the sleek blue amplifier from the depths of her backseat. "Gimme your phone so I can sync it up."

Zara handed her crackled black device to Grier.

"OMG, Zara, you can't have nice things." Grier poked icons until she found the Bluetooth settings. "What did you do? Use your phone as a hammer?"

"I walked into a spider web. Fear happened. Arms flailed and phones flew."

"One hundred percent correct reaction. So, do you want the normal play list?" Grier scrolled through the music on Zara's phone. "Or a different one?"

She squinted at the screen.

"Wait, why do you have Britney Spears's 'Work Bitch'? I thought you didn't listen to music recorded after 1997."

"It gets me pumped at the studio." Zara clunked open the passenger door. "Come on. I have to hurry and sneak in before the birthday girl arrives."

"I'm judging you so hard right now."

"Yeah, yeah." Zara butterflied her hand at Grier. "I've seen your Top 25. Abba, much?"

"Abba is crazy good. You're not sophisticated enough to appreciate their music."

Zara unfolded herself from the car and dropped the train of her jade gown to the ground. She twisted and tugged her leather breastplate down a few inches. The damned thing had shifted position on the way over and mashed her chest flat.

The costume must have been designed for a B-cup Ravenna, at best. While Zara's cups runneth over. Still, she was grateful for the corset-like piece of armor. It did double-duty, desexualizing her a little, and providing a much-needed shield in the chilly February air. Stiff nipples at a children's party was *not* the look.

"Oh, much better." She sighed once she seated the breastplate where it belonged. "I bet I have bruises."

"What about me? I am such a pack mule whenever we do these parties." Grier wheeled a crate stuffed with Zara's face-painting supplies behind her. The speaker was in her other hand, and a chunky camera hung around her neck.

"I'd offer to help, but princesses don't hump huge crates around." The rear car door creaked when Zara popped it open.

She lifted Ravenna's double-sworded belt from the backseat and buckled it around her hips. Once the belt was in place, she sheathed the gleaming, thin-bladed prop replica swords.

"I would think swords are a bad idea at children's parties." Grier snapped a photo. "For obvious reasons."

"I'm a stickler for authenticity. If Princess Ravenna of Everly carries swords, then so must this humble impersonator."

"I worry you'll chop a kid's arm off if she tries to hug you."

"I wouldn't. Probably." Zara arched an eyebrow. "But I might spank a kid with the flat of the sword."

"Hey, do you have plans after dinner tonight?" Grier trailed Zara as they made their way along the tidy fieldstone path to the front door.

"Yeah." She yawned. "My studio's usable again. I'm hitting Pla-Za tonight to buy canvases and oil paints."

"Oils?"

"Yep. Didn't I tell you? I'm not feeling the watercolors anymore. They seem weak, and if I have learned anything, it's to..." Zara ticked off her fingers, "...one, get business insurance, and two, use more durable materials. I'd fucking sculpt in steel if I could weld."

"If you change your mind, Melinda and I are watching a bunch of movies that pass the Bechdel test."

"Thanks." Zara gathered her skirts before climbing the steps to the glossy red door. "But I need to concentrate on work."

Before she could ring the doorbell, the front door swung inward. A heart-stopping heap of dimpled handsome filled the doorway.

~ * ~

As soon as Brendan Stewart clapped eyes on the princess on his stoop, the iceberg of tension in his chest melted. It had drifted into place two weeks ago when his *OMG-so-busy-traveling-meetings-*

meetings-meetings ex-wife, Jess, bailed on the party for Emma.

He'd gone overboard with the party prep to compensate, and a real, live Ravenna had become his Hail Mary. Now that she was here? He wanted to go back in time and buy himself a beer.

Ravenna had migrated from the two-dimensional cartoon world and landed on his front stoop. Man oh man, he loved her in 3D. How had he not noticed those pouty lips in her pictures online? The woman in front of him blinked, and the thick fringe of her eyelashes kissed her creamy cheeks.

They stared at each other. *Did Ravenna always give off a sexy vibe?*

Something low and primal tightened in his groin, and he began a silent mantra: *Focus on her eyes...focus on her eyes...focus on her eyes...*

"Um..." The princess raised a thick black eyebrow. "Is Mr. Stewart home?"

"Right here." He smiled and tapped his chest. "I'm Brendan. Come on in."

He pressed himself to the side to allow her room to enter the house. As the face painter princess crossed the threshold and passed him, her skirts caressed the floor. *Don't stare at her ass, don't stare at her ass, don't stare at her ass.*

"Wow. You...really resemble Ravenna."

"That's kind of the idea." She swished around and stuck out her hand. "I'm Zara Kissette, children's entertainer by day, starving artist by night."

He grabbed hold. Her fingers were long, tapered, and calloused, and her grip was firm. She eyeballed his stubble and rumpled plaid shirt. Might've been a good idea to shave and iron.

"Hi, I'm Grier." The second woman clumped into the house, towing a stubborn plastic crate behind her. He hadn't noticed her behind Zara on the porch. "I'm the photographer and party grunt."

"Can I help?" Brendan released Zara and stood aside to give Grier and the crate room to pass.

"What a gentleman," she answered. "Thank you, I've got it. But I'll be happy to give you my coat."

She shrugged off her red trench and stuffed her gloves into one of its sleeves. He took it from her and hung it in the foyer closet. Cold clung to the material. The princess, Zara, hadn't been wearing a coat. She must be freezing. Should he offer her coffee or tea to warm up?

When he turned back around, the two women were whispering to each other.

"You look familiar," Grier said. "Do we know each other?"

"I don't think so." He forced himself to keep eye contact with Grier. She was cute, but Zara was in a different league. A dark-haired, edgy league.

"I'm sure we've met at least once. I have a memory for faces. Professional hazard, but I won't torture you with twenty questions. The princess and I have a job to do, after all."

Zara narrowed her eyes at her friend, then asked Brendan, "Is the birthday girl here?"

He almost didn't hear her question over his silent *don't stare* mantra.

"She's out with my mom." He glanced at his watch. "They're due home in ten minutes." He dipped his gaze to her cleavage. *Whoops.*

"What about your wife?" Zara crossed her arms over her breasts and tilted her head.

"Ex, actually." He stuffed his hands into his pockets. "She's not coming."

"Oh, that's...hmm." She untangled her arms and darted her gaze around the house. "So, where do you want me?"

Where don't I? He riffled his hair. *Christ, Stewart, get it together.* "Follow me."

Hopefully she couldn't tell she'd flustered him. He wasn't normally this goofy about attractive women, but he hadn't mentally prepared for this scenario. He was in dad mode. All the other women who'd be here today were either relatives or married moms.

Not exactly potential flirting opportunities.

Probably didn't help he hadn't been with anyone since the divorce. Who had time? Dadding, work, and the gym absorbed his undivided attention. Or it *had*, right up until five minutes ago when this scorching woman entered his house.

Now, he could barely focus on anything besides the princess.

He had to squash that, and quick. Today was about his kid and making her feel special. Besides, the princess was here to do a job. He'd bet the last thing she wanted was a dad hitting on her at work. One thing was for sure—it would be nice to run into Zara out in the city sometime.

"So," Brendan said as he approached the end of the hallway. "I went nuts with the decorations."

He'd strewn hundreds of Ravennas on every surface in the family room. Banners, balloons, streamers, tablecloths, plates, cupcakes, and even a Ravenna pull-string piñata.

"Nah. This is rad. Your daughter will love it. Is that me, over there?" She pointed to a breakaway table in the corner, next to a picture window that overlooked a manicured yard.

"Yeah. Is it okay?"

"It's spiffy. Thanks." She maneuvered the table around a bit. "I like to create a flow where a line of kids can wait, hop into the chair to be painted, then exit without bumping into another kid right away."

Grier rolled the crate over, and Zara bent forward to free the lid.

Brendan replayed his mantra and stared at a cluster of balloons in the upper corner of the room. He had to, otherwise his gaze would slip to wildly inappropriate geographical highlights on Zara's body.

"Any predictions for which face paint design your daughter will want?" Grier unfurled a banner then taped it to the front of the table. Twenty portraits of face-painted children dotted its surface.

Brendan knelt in front of the table and peered at the pictures. "I'd bet the house on Ravenna." To Zara, he said, "These are cool. Are these your designs?"

"I'm taking light readings," Grier said to no one in particular and went as far into the opposite corner of the room as she could.

"Yes." Zara spilled her brushes on the table. "Grier gets the credit for the photos, but the designs are mine. Some are more inspired than others, and I always mix in non-*Rising* characters. A few girls are over it and want Wonder Woman or Maleficent. I'm dying for a girl to choose Frida Kahlo, but no takers as of yet. The boys always want Spider-Man or Ninja Turtles. Not much for the little dudes in *Rising*."

"I wouldn't say that." He thumbed the cleft in his chin. "I liked it. The message about loving yourself and not hiding what makes you unique is pretty powerful for kids."

"I thought the message was that marriage can be great, but shouldn't be everyone's end-goal."

"Both, when you think about it." He rose from his crouched position. Her quick, efficient hands organized the table in the blink of an eye. Watching people who were good at their gigs fascinated him, as did the gleam of her black nail polish, another perfect copy of the Ravenna look.

"I'm sure a Ph.D. candidate has written a thesis on it by now." Zara pointed a brush at him. "By the way, if I create a masterpiece on your daughter today, can I add her to my catalog?"

She smiled. The brightness of it blinded him. He wanted to get a smile from her again.

"Definitely. Anything I can help you with?"

Eagle-level boy scouting, Stewart. If he stayed busy, maybe he could clamp down on his urge to hit on the princess. This was not the time or the place. His five-year-old was about to skip through the door. Yet, here he was, laser-focused on Zara's perfect plum of a bottom lip.

This woman shut off the controlled, logical part of his brain.

"Um..." Her gaze flitted around her table. She snatched up a plastic container and held it out to him with a paint-splotched hand. "Could you fill this with water?"

"Sure." He took the cup and forced himself to ratchet his pace down to a mosey into the kitchen. The struggle to appear relaxed was real.

Zara called after him. "Are you a gamer? Or an evil genius plotting to take over the world?"

"What?" He glanced over his shoulder to see what prompted the question. Ah. She was staring at his workstation. It took over what had once been a breakfast nook. His heart swelled with pride at his home HQ.

Four enormous monitors formed a concave command-center, and several devices dotted the desk. Sleek bundles of cables dripped toward a computer tower below the desk. He'd taped a dozen of Emma's colorful butterfly, flower, and Ravenna drawings to the wall around the set-up.

"I game, but that's my office. I'm a software developer."

"Impressive." Zara lined her brushes up and arranged her paints in rainbow order. "By the way, do you have party music planned? I can play the *Rising* soundtrack. Unless you're sick of it by now."

"It's perfect—Emma loves it," Brendan called over the water rushing from the kitchen spigot.

"*Rising* on repeat, then."

"I'll try not to sing along." He returned to her station and held out the container. The moment stretched and slowed as her cool fingers grazed his. He knew it. The cold temperatures had gotten to her. He wanted to take her hands between his to warm them, to warm her.

Instead, he let the moment pass.

"Thanks." She settled the water among her paints, her eyelashes a thousand tiny whips on the curve of her cheeks. "What happened to your hand?"

He glanced at his raw knuckles. "I, uh...got into a fight with a wall."

Why the fuck did I admit that?

"Ah." She laughed. "Who won?"

"The wall. The wall always wins." He took stock of her table.

"Need anything else?"

"Nope." She placed her hands on her hips. "I'm ready to paint facial masterpieces."

A zillion conversation topics slipped through his mind, but they were all ridiculous and inadequate. Because all he really wanted to ask this princess if she wanted to get a drink, get a meal, or get naked upstairs.

Jesus, did he need a cold shower? Yeah, it'd been three forevers since he'd been anywhere close to alone with a woman, but now was *not* the time for lust. A dozen kids and his family were seconds away from arriving.

On cue, a staccato honk sounded outside. His mom. They'd prearranged the weirdo honk as a signal.

"That's the birthday girl." Brendan glanced toward the hallway. "Can you make a big deal out of meeting her?"

"It'd be my pleasure."

The way her mouth shaped the word *pleasure* was almost too much. He hightailed it away from her, scrubbing the impure thoughts from his brain, and slapped on his dad cap on tight.

~ * ~

Zara picked up her skirts and minced to the middle of the family room, ready to play her part in his little girl's fantasy. Pinned to this spot, she drank in the way Brendan's rangy form loped down the hallway, like invisible rope was tied to his hips, drawing him forward.

Grier's digital SLR camera *thunked* next to Zara's ear.

"*Those* shots are for my personal collection." Grier held the camera aside and craned her neck. "Can you believe that guy's a dad? With that ass? If you can tell it's a fine ass through cargo shorts, you know it's a piece of art."

"He's okay." Zara ramrodded her spine to mimic the regal bearing of Princess Ravenna of Everly.

"Okay, huh?" Grier trained her lens on Zara. "Then why do you act like you want to lick him?"

"Shut up." She tucked a twist of raven-purple hair behind her ear. She'd admit nothing. And clean-cut dads in cargo shorts and polo shirts were not her type. Terse guys with arm cuffs were her normal speed. "Why are you so chatty with him, anyway?"

"Chatty? This is my gracious socialite training. I am full of etiquette, whereas you normally utter four words to the dads at these parties. Methinks you have a tiny crush."

"Don't be ridiculous."

"So, why'd you ask Hot Daddy if I could take a picture of his daughter for your poster?"

"Brendan. His name's Brendan."

"I don't care. He's still Hot Daddy. This is your last party, right? You've earned what you need to replenish your palette. Why would you need more face painting pics?"

"It slipped out." Zara gulped a lungful of sweet air. The whole house tasted of sugar. "Now, zip it. Here they come."

"Emma Bear." Brendan's voice, rumbly and rich, flowed from front door. "Close your eyes. I have a surprise for you, sweetheart."

Sweetheart. An endearment wrapped around an anchor. Her mother had sprinkled it throughout the conversation they had earlier this month, when Zara phoned to share the happy news about the Schwarz Gallery invitation.

That's nice, sweetheart, but I don't think it'll matter, will it? The year's almost up, and it's time for you to start paying back the tuition we loaned you. We're expecting you to move home and work it off at the Inn. Your bed's waiting for you...I don't understand why you're fussing, anyway. You can still paint in your free time here. The Beach Gallery always shows local artists' seascapes.

Zara clasped her hands and pointed rigid elbows out to the side. Yes, this was Ravenna's pose, but it helped stop her from dry heaving at the thought of painting imaginary seagulls swooping across a rosy sunset.

"What is it, Daddy?" a small voice asked.

"You'll see, Em."

Brendan reappeared, arm flexed around a sprite whose eyes were squeezed shut. The little girl was cute, but it was hard not to stare at how his blue shirt strained to contain his bicep. He pressed a finger to his full, kissable lips and winked at Zara.

Grier steadied her camera and snapped away.

A woman with a honey-colored bob—the grandmother, Zara guessed—captured the moment with her phone.

Brendan knelt and deposited three feet, nine inches of girl in front of Zara's skirts. From what she could observe, Emma was made of sugar, spice, and forty pounds of wild, curly, waist-length hair. Not to mention amazing style—the kid wore a tie-dyed, long-sleeve shirt, a purple tutu, and black mini-combat boots.

"Can I open my eyes, Daddy?" She clutched a Princess Ravenna of Everly action figure.

He made the "okay" signal with his thumb and forefinger. For a second, they locked gazes, and Zara couldn't breathe. She and Brendan were in cahoots on a delightful surprise, and the fizzy joy it caused shocked her to her core. Almost to the point where she'd forgotten her cue.

Whoops.

"You may indeed, Emma Stewart of Federal Hill," Zara said.

Emma blinked big moon eyes.

Zara held her breath and prepped for the weepy shrieking these encounters produced.

"Hi." The girl fluttered her tiny sausage fingers. "I'm Emma."

"Greetings, Emma." Zara peered down her nose, maintaining her royal stance. Kids normally lost their minds at this point, but Brendan's daughter furrowed a brow and planted a fist on her waist.

"Are you for real?" the little girl asked.

Zara folded herself with a dancer's grace until she stared into brown eyes flecked with green and gold. The same color as Brendan's. "Of course. Why would you doubt it, little one?"

Emma inspected Zara's face. She gasped when she glimpsed Princess Ravenna's delicate port-wine seashell birthmark, the Mark of Everly. Before each performance, Zara used her finest sable brush to paint this tiny, intricate symbol on the tender spot between her left cheekbone and her ear.

Emma's eyes went wide, and she dropped her Ravenna doll. "Eep!" The strangled noise escaped the little girl.

"You appear to be quite excited, Emma."

Emma bounced on her toes and her curls jangled like yo-yos on elastic strings. To settle her, Zara clasped the girl's shoulders and rubbed her thumbs along Emma's avian bones.

"I'm excited to meet you too."

Emma threw her arms around Zara's neck and squished her cheek next to hers. "I love you."

As Zara's heart melted a few degrees for the kid, Emma coughed. Right onto Zara's face. A small puff of air. Nothing liquid, or phlegmy about it. Obviously, the kid had just infected Zara with Hantavirus.

"Sorry, sorry, sorry." Emma squeaked and covered her mouth.

"Don't let it trouble you, little one." She kept the Ravenna veneer buckled on tight, but she yearned to dunk her face in antibacterial gel. It would suck hard if she got sick. She'd have to skip teaching at the retirement home for a week because she couldn't risk infecting the residents, which meant her grocery money would be down the drain.

No sense worrying about it now. Time to concentrate on today's job.

"Emma, may I paint your face?" She led Emma to the poster with the design options.

"Brend?" The grandmother said. "I'll set up the snacks in the kitchen."

"Thanks, Mom."

She smiled at Zara. "Nice to meet you, by the way. I'm Robin."

"Princess Ravenna, at your service." Zara bowed. To Brendan, she said, "I'm sure you want a design as well. Maybe a lion? Or a bear?"

He laughed. "No thanks."

"I want this, please." Emma jabbed at the Ravenna design.

"Excellent choice." Zara helped Emma into the chair. "Now, do you promise to hold still?"

Emma nodded and folded her hands in her lap. "You're pretty."

"Why thank you." Zara smiled. She surveyed Emma's face, identifying the perfect place to start. "Ready? Here we go."

Zara lifted a brush, and her shoulders relaxed.

The brush brought peace.

Lost in the paint, she dipped the brush into the deep purple pot, slanted Emma's face a fraction to the side, and went to work. This was always the best part of these parties. No matter what medium she chose, the act of creating, of making an interesting image, satisfied her like nothing else could.

She rested the tip of the brush at the bridge of Emma's nose and swept upward in confident strokes. A seashell unfurled over the expanse of Emma's forehead, followed soon by ribbons of color curling across her temples. Zara swapped the brush for another tipped in silver shimmer, and then another covered in black, layering highlights and shadows to give depth to the design.

Behind her, Grier clicked and clunked to document the transformation.

In three minutes flat, Zara painted a masterpiece on her wriggly canvas. Time for the finishing touches… She fixed a series of adhesive gemstones across Emma's cheekbones and a final, larger one above the bridge of her nose.

"Here you are, little one." Zara picked up an elaborate hand mirror from her array of party props and showed Emma the results.

"I'm handsome." She nudged the emerald on the apple of her cheek.

"You sure are, sweetheart." Brendan's voice came from close behind Zara, low, intimate, as if he'd whispered in her ear. Heat collected at the nape of her neck and oozed, thick and languorous, down her spine.

She stiffened.

"Sorry." He placed a steady hand on the naked patch of her back, right above the band of the breastplate. "Did I startle you? I didn't mean to sneak up on you. I wanted a closer peek at Emma."

Sparks erupted into fire where his palm pressed against her exposed skin, and the fire spread along Zara's neck and to her cheeks. Her ears must be melting from her head.

She cleared her throat and glanced at him with her peripheral vision. "It's fine. I'm fine."

She was not fine. She was about a million degrees hotter than fine.

He dropped his hand, but didn't leave. Zara willed him to go away to give her a chance to tranquilize the reaction her body had to him. With him right here, her body temperature couldn't cool. Grumble. Why wouldn't he go away?

"Em, be sure to sit still to let it dry," he warned.

Zara busied herself by cleaning her brushes. She swirled the purple-tipped brush in the water, clouding the clear liquid.

The doorbell chimed.

"My friends are here!" Emma scrambled from the chair and sprinted toward the front door.

"Be right back." He jogged after Emma.

"Zara." Grier snapped a few pictures. "You're blushing."

"Fuck off." Zara stabbed the wet paintbrush into a thick pile of paper towels.

"Well, well, well." Grier laughed. "I've hit a nerve. You *do* have a crush on Hot Daddy."

"Fuck off twice." She glared at the camera lens, imagining Grier's unblinking eye on the other side.

"You should ask him out."

Murmured greetings and high-pitched giggles swirled down the hall.

"I'm titling these shots *Besotted*." Grier snapped more pictures of Zara.

"Can you act like a professional, please?" She clasped her hands and resumed a majestic pose. The partygoers would tumble into the family room at any moment.

"I will. As soon as I am a professional."

Emma reappeared. She spread her arms wide. "Guys, look! It's Ravenna!"

The passel of little girls following Emma squealed like

teakettles. The energy of it blew Zara back a pace. It had taken her a dozen parties to understand that this moment was the kid equivalent of meeting a squee-worthy collage of your favorite actress, athlete, and president.

"Welcome," Zara announced in a voice an octave deeper than normal, "to Emma's fifth birthday party. To celebrate, you may choose a face-paint design."

Slightly terrified by the number of children popping up around her, Zara gestured to the poster in front of the table. Wide-eyed girls clustered around it, each shouting their choice of design.

The doorbell rang, and a few seconds later two young boys and their pixie of a mother joined the party. Brendan greeted Pixie with an ursine hug and an enormous smile.

What was this twist in Zara's gut all about?

Someone small tugged on her skirt. A girl with a fine curtain of bright blonde hair lisped, "Can I be Ravenna?"

"Of course, little one." Zara patted the seat of the chair. "Hop up here."

Over the next half-hour, she cycled through the children and produced four Ravennas, Wonder Woman, a butterfly, a puppy, and two Teenage Mutant Ninja Turtles.

She was impressed she hadn't screwed any of them up, considering the constant furtive glances she shot toward Brendan and Pixie.

As Zara cleaned her brushes, the opening strains of the *Rising* anthem trickled from the speaker. The girls mimed Ravenna's blocking from the famous questing scene, extending their arms on the same lyric, pretending to throw shadows and darkness at their enemies. Emma caught her father's shirttail and dragged him into the fray, and he didn't hesitate. In fact, it appeared as though he might be leading the little girls through the choreography.

Zara chuckled at the sight of this grown man enthusiastically dancing with a gaggle of tiny children. His ease with them made her heart happy. Most of the dads at these parties tended to busy themselves with the practical set-up stuff, and then hang back in the corner on their phones.

He flicked a glance her way, and crap, he'd caught her staring at him. As the song came to a close, he eased next to her. The warmth from his body skimmed her skin.

"You did a nice job," he said.

"Thanks." She dabbed a brush against a paper towel. "I'll knight Emma next, and then we'll take pictures."

"Gotcha." He scratched the back of his neck, showing off his triceps. "Do you want me to do anything?"

Zara's flesh prickled.

Yeah. I want you to kiss me until I can't think straight.

What the hell? Where had *that* come from?

"No." She cleared her throat. "Thanks though. Whoops, there's the end of the song." She killed the music app on her phone and emerged from behind the worktable. "Children," she said, "gather 'round. We're here to celebrate Emma's birthday."

"Yeah." Emma pumped her tiny fists in the air. "I'm five."

The kids collected in a wiggly group in front of her. Zara glanced at Brendan. With his arms crossed over his chest, his biceps, triceps, and Jesus Christ, *all* of him bulged against his sleeves.

The soft-bellied models she'd sketched during freshman year's The Human Body class were nothing like him. If those guys had resembled the man in front of her now, she would've gone to class more often.

She shifted her attention to Emma and unsheathed a sword.

"Can I hold your sword?" Emma asked.

"No." Zara shook her head and tapped the little girl's shoulders with the blunt blade. "I dub thee Lady Emma. Lady Emma, I call you to my service. Will you be brave?"

"Yes," she shouted. "Can I hold your sword now?"

"Nope." Zara knelt next to Emma and winced when the breastplate's stiff leather dug into her hips. "We will, however, pose for a photo."

"Okay." Emma threw herself at Zara like she expected to be caught. Which she was, but still, that was weirdly trusting of the little girl. As they cuddled for the pictures, Zara caught the scent of strawberries from Emma's untamed ringlets.

Grier snapped a few shots, then called over the other children and arranged them so their painted faces were visible.

"Now," she shouted over the restless children, "on the count of three, yell, 'monkey feet.'"

Half of the giggling children did as they were told. Grier's flash fired a few times, and she reviewed the pictures on the camera's display. "Got it."

"Okay, kids, who's ready for a game of pin-the-tail on Kilda?" Emma's grandmother asked. Kilda was Ravenna's horse.

"Me!" the kids yelled and scattered.

"Emma." Zara held the little girl's shoulder. "I must take my leave now."

"Why do you have to go?" Emma's lower lip puffed out. "I don't want you to."

"Everly needs me. I will always carry you in my heart." She smoothed a curl from Emma's face. "It has been a pleasure to attend your party."

Emma wrapped her arms around Zara's neck and squeezed. Whoa, this tiny girl was refreshingly free with her affection and zero percent shy. For a second, she let herself sink into the embrace.

"Thank you for coming to my party, Ravenna."

"You're welcome, little one."

Emma let go and scurried toward the basement to join her friends. Zara rose, brushed her skirts, then started toward the table to tidy up.

"Hang on, Princess." Grier touched Zara's sleeve.

She did not trust the impish expression on Grier's face. The first time she'd worn it, they'd crashed a senior's rooftop party and gotten footless drunk on Jungle Juice, a deadly strong grain alcohol and fruit punch cocktail. Lucky for them, Melinda had abstained and had gotten them home safe. Zara darted her gaze around the room. Lots of fruit punch, definitely no booze. What was Grier up to?

"Emma's Dad?" she called across the room. "Let's get a shot of you and Ravenna."

He raked his hand through his hair. "Okay."

"You're such an asshole," Zara said from the corner of her mouth.

Grier winked.

He stood next to Zara. "Like this?"

"Closer." Grier held the camera in front of her face. "Now, Princess, hook your arm around his."

If Zara could transform into Ravenna and command the princess's magical powers, she would, without question, throw shadow daggers at Grier's head.

Instead, she wrapped her arm around Brendan's. Oh. Was he smuggling bowling balls under his sleeves? He gazed at her and smiled, and the heat pooling in her belly all afternoon rushed everywhere. No way he'd miss the stupid exuberant blushes now.

"This is like a prom photo, isn't it?" he asked.

"I didn't go to prom." She glared at Grier and mouthed, "I'll kill you."

"Smile, Princess," Grier said.

The flashbulb blinded her.

"Nice." Grier reviewed the picture on the back of her camera, shoulders quaking. "Total keeper. I'll start packing up."

Zara let out a long, measured breath and unwound from Brendan, hyperconscious of the way the polo's cotton buffed the palm of her hand. Besides Grier, the two of them were alone in the family room.

"That's pretty much it for the whimsy, except for this," she said, fished around in her skirt pocket.

Aha, there it was. She held her fist out to him, palm up.

"What is it?" he asked.

"A miniature. Here." She opened her fingers. The tiny portrait she painted of Emma as part of the standard party package lay in the center of her palm. "It's a keepsake for Emma. Or you, I guess."

"Wow." His fingertips kissed her palm as he took the portrait. He shifted the tiny likeness, inspecting its intricacies. "Did you paint this?"

She tipped her lips up into a smile. "I did. I based it on the picture you sent when you booked me."

"I didn't expect this." He glanced at her and flashed the dimples. "You must hear this all the time, but you have a gift. How did you capture Emma's personality without even meeting her?"

Wow, those dimples. There goes the swoony. Is it hot in here? Stupid eleven million layers of dress and leather are making me sweat.

Zara plucked at the linen peeping above her leather breastplate to encourage a breeze to cool her heaving chest. "You like it, then?"

God, would the flush in her cheeks stop? She must look like she has scarlet fever.

"I love it." He nestled the portrait among the photos on the mantelpiece.

Whomever, whatever sculpted his ass deserved first place in the show.

"Uh, rad," she muttered. She shifted her gaze to his rounded shoulders. Nope. Didn't help. The way his muscles strained the stitches of his shirt made her blood pound faster.

She redirected her view toward the safe, non-Brendan direction of the kitchen. The bobbed mom mafia hovered near the veggie tray. One of them, Pixie, clutched a carrot stick and beamed at them like she'd stumbled across a double rainbow.

"So, Zara…" He scratched the nape of his neck.

Pixie's smile grew wider. Was she elbowing his mother to get her attention? Ugh, what was it with her? Why were they staring? Whatever. Zara had to escape this foreign land stuffed with sugar and kindness.

"Time to go. While the kids are downstairs, it's time to pull my Cinderella routine and disappear. We'll get our stuff and catch our carriage home."

"Hang on." He touched her elbow, setting off the glitter bomb on her insides. "I wanted to ask you something."

Four

"Can I carry stuff to the car for you?" Brendan buried a hand in his pocket and pinched his leg. Hard. For being a total chicken shit.

"That's what you wanted to ask me?" Zara raised a thick eyebrow. Those bright blue eyes of hers scanned him, like she could see his soul, his heart, his DNA. Fingers crossed—not his dirty thoughts.

"Yeah. You have a big crate. It must weigh a ton. Can I carry it?" He rocked on his heels. Choking noises erupted behind him. Had to be Monica. Ten minutes ago, his sister-in-law informed him over crackers and crab dip that he'd be the biggest tool in the shed if he didn't ask out the princess who was clearly into him.

He'd said he couldn't because his big deadline was in two weeks. Monica punched him in the shoulder and told him to man up.

Her female intuition must be off, though, because the princess seemed confused by his offer to help. Wait, no. She was frowning. Not confused, then. Annoyed.

Oh, Christ. He was screwing this up. It had been nine years since he'd asked a woman out. What the fuck did he know? He had the romantic skills of an eighteen-year-old and had spent the past sixty seconds eyeballing Zara like a certifiable psychopath.

He wouldn't want a dude staring at Emma like that when she grew up.

Jesus Christ, Stewart. Stop thinking about Emma. You're asking a woman out. Agh. This is why it's ridiculous for you to date when you have a kid.

"No, we're okay, thanks." Zara waved him off.

Grier shoved the crate toward him with her foot. "Speak for yourself, Princess. Please, take this monstrosity to the car."

"Happy to." He tugged the handle. It barely budged, and he yanked hard to get the thing rolling. What'd they have in there, an anvil? He had no clue how these women heaved this stuff around without snapping in half. As they entered the foyer, he disentangled

Grier's trench coat from the other guests' puffy parkas.

"Thanks, Good Sir…" She slanted her head toward him. "What did you say your name was?"

"Brendan."

"Good Sir Brendan."

Zara glared at her friend, who smiled back.

Aw, man, they were having a whole conversation with their facial expressions. Be nice if he understood it too.

Grier punched her arms into the sleeves. "I'll edit the pictures, upload the best of the batch within a week, then send the link to you. You can download them, or buy prints from the site."

"Cool."

He opened the front door and ushered the two women ahead of him. The salty breeze off the bay caught Zara's hair, making the black and purple strands dance in the air and along her back. As they clattered along the short walkway to Grier's car, he couldn't tear his gaze away from the way the velvet cupped the rounded smoothness of Zara's backside.

Grier popped the trunk. "The monster lives in here."

Brendan heaved the crate into its cluttered confines. There had to be something he could say, some funny or interesting conversational nugget that would impress Zara and open the door to a date.

He came up empty.

"Thanks. Hey, Zara, you want to throw your stuff in too?" Grier yelled to the princess.

"Yep." She tilted forward, and the sweet swell of her breasts bubbled higher. She unbuckled her sword belt, and the blades jangled together as she chucked it into the trunk next to the crate. "Thing's been chafing me today."

She rubbed her hips.

His balls ached. If she bent over again, he'd need to go for a brisk walk before re-entering his house.

She fixed her gaze on him. "Hey, so there's one more thing."

Bright and shiny hope burst in his chest. Maybe she was asking him out? That would rule. Then he didn't have to risk making an ass of himself. "What's that?"

"Our payment?" she asked.

He winced. "Ah, sorry. Of course. I meant to give it to you when you arrived."

Please let her not misinterpret the way I said that.

He extracted an envelope from his pocket and handed it to her. "Thanks again. Emma will never forget today."

"You're welcome." Zara grasped the envelope.

For a moment, they held the packet at same time, and he could've sworn a current zipped through the paper.

Now or never. She was beyond sweet to your kid, she's smart, and she's hot. You'll regret it if you pass this up.

"Zara?" He released the envelope. His pulse drummed in his ears, drowning out the hum of city traffic a few blocks away.

"Yes?" She tucked the envelope under her breastplate.

Speak, Stewart. "Would you like to go to dinner sometime?"

She didn't answer. Not good. He prepped himself for disappointment as she bit her lip, her perfect, kissable bottom lip.

Please let her shoot a yes his way.

~ * ~

"With you?" Zara laced her fingers together to hide the shakiness his invitation had caused.

"That's the idea." His face relaxed. The fleshy, concerned crinkle between the slashes of his dark eyebrows ironed itself out, and then he grinned.

Oh, that grin. She was already good friends with that grin. If it grew any wider, the dimples would appear. After the dimples would be the gleaming whites of his teeth, and if they made a repeat appearance, she'd be lost, unable to say no.

Time to shut this down.

"Uh, thank you, but..." She bit her lip, fumbling for a gentle way to say, *I'm way too busy, you've got a kid which is outside of my comfort zone, and I can't spend the brain space on this.*

Which, fine, was like tipping over the king in chess after an opponent makes his first move. But what else could she do? A divorced dude with a kid fell firmly in the Can Not Deal column of her life. If anything, saying no was the kindest option.

His lips flattened, causing a twinge in her belly. That wasn't fair. She didn't want to be the reason any unhappiness parked itself on his face.

"She'd love to." Grier slammed the trunk shut. "I'll start the car. Take your time making plans."

Heat flooded Zara's cheeks, and sweat trickled down her neck despite the cold bite in the air. "I'm sorry," she said to Brendan. "We need to have her evaluated."

"Oh come on, like you don't want to go out with him." Grier opened the driver's door

The car rumbled to life. Exhaust chugged from the twenty-year-old tailpipe.

He raised an eyebrow and half-smiled. "Your friend thinks we should go out."

"Grier is fond of posing people in pleasing tableaux. Whereas I tend to skew abstract."

Brendan angled his head. "I can't tell if that's a yes or a no."

"It's a…"

He flipped on his heart-melting smile, and her 'no' evaporated. No matter what her priorities, she couldn't refuse a chance to bask in his smile for a whole meal. Sketches had been as difficult as yanking staples from frames with her fingernails lately, but in the scant hour she'd been near him, she'd wanted to draw, create, and paint non-stop.

"Yes." She sighed the response.

"You don't sound sure."

He curved toward her. A gust of wind played between them, tugging his shirt. She glimpsed flesh the color of summer sand. A black triangle peeped from above his waistband too. Ink? On this All-American boy? Intriguing.

Goddammit. The whole trajectory of this thing might've been different if he'd tucked in his shirt.

"I'm sure. It's just…my schedule is bananas." She caressed the hollow of her throat.

"Me too. How's Wednesday? It's the first night I have free."

She furrowed her brow. "Valentine's Day?"

"Is it?" He laughed. "You must think I'm a coming on strong."

She lifted her shoulders. "No, just masochistic."

"We can go another day." He ran his hands through his hair.

Poor guy was obviously nervous, which set her at ease. "No way. Valentine's it is. It'll be delightfully awkward. I'll text you later?"

"Absolutely." He glanced toward his shoulder at his front door. "I'd better go. It's cupcake time in there."

"Oh, yeah. Kid chaos requires all adults to keep it contained."

"See you later, then." He caressed her bicep, a quick kiss of a touch that sent a ripple through her arm and set her heart pounding.

Brendan walked backward for a few steps, then turned on his heel and entered the house. This view was almost as good as his smile. Her fingers itched for charcoal to capture his purposeful stride on paper, but she'd have to settle for locking it in her memory.

He turned and waved before he disappeared into his house. Once the door closed, she let out a breath, and her pulse slowed to a normal beat. Was she *actually* going on a date with him? She'd never tried on someone like Brendan. He had no man-bun, brushy beard, visible piercings, or detectable *ennui*.

This was so not planned, which made it so un-Zara.

She opened the Mercedes's passenger door and settled herself into its warm leather embrace.

"When are you going out with him?" Grier asked.

She elbowed her. "You're such a bitch. You're lucky I don't have my swords."

"Exactly why I waited until you put them in the trunk."

~ * ~

A half an hour later, Zara and Grier wove through the clotted downtown traffic to their townhouse on Eager Street. Sunset gilded its brick face.

"There's a spot." Zara pointed to a gap among the cars along the curb. "Thank God it's close. I'm not a fan of trudging around in this getup."

Grier docked the Mercedes with an efficient swoop of the wheel.

"Tonight's your night to cook dinner, isn't it?" She shut off the engine. "I want to finish the wedding from last weekend before editing Hot Daddy's daughter's birthday party."

"I wish you wouldn't call him that." She waited for a lone car to chug by before she gathered her skirts and slipped out.

"Is he a daddy?" Grier climbed their stoop and unlocked the front door. Sweet violin strains flowed toward them from Brooke's room.

"Yes." Zara pushed past Grier and into their entryway.

"Is he hot?"

"I guess."

"Please." Grier settled her camera on the console table and draped her trench on the coat tree. "He's Gosling-level hot. Thus, your guy has been christened Hot Daddy."

"He's not *my* guy." Zara pivoted and presented the corset laces to Grier. "Dinner'll be ready in an hour. Can you untie me? Princesses don't cook chili."

In her bedroom, Zara shucked off her princess garb and zipped it into a garment bag. She shoved it in the deep dark no man's land of her closet, behind her graduation robe and an awful pink paisley raincoat her mother sent her. She changed into her standard uniform of jeans, combat boots, and a vintage concert T-shirt. Today's tissue-thin classic featured My Bloody Valentine.

Oh Brendan Stewart. Why do you make my belly tumble?

On a whim, she clasped the locket she'd inherited from her gramma around her neck. She hadn't worn it in ages, but it hadn't lost its luster.

Zara stomped down the stairs, the tones of Brooke's violin practice providing bold and bright background music. *She's busy. Good. I need uninterrupted 'thinky' time.*

In the kitchen, she opened the bi-fold pantry door.

"I have a date on Valentine's Day," she muttered to the cans she pulled from the shelf. She clutched the heavy load to her chest. "This is baffling."

She clamped the jaws of the can opener into the can of tomatoes and let it spin. A jagged metal seam opened along the edge and revealed the tender red contents.

She blew the hair from her face.

"He's a nice guy," she said to the cans. "But..."

Zara wasn't a Valentine's kind of girl. She preferred her hearts bloody, her love tragic. Not sugared and shiny and possible.

She chopped an onion. Tears leapt to her eyes. She tossed the shattered bits into a frying pan with the beef and clicked on the flames.

No. He's not possible. The very opposite of possible.

As she batted the pesky thought away, she snorted. Like she even *had* free time right now. Maybe someday she'd have a few minutes to address the molten situation Brendan had triggered in her.

Today was not that day. She had a deadline. The Schwarz Gallery show could be the toehold she needed in gallery shows. If the show went well and she sold enough pieces, she'd be able to honor the deal she'd made with her parents. If she blew it, no matter how much she hustled, the chance she'd get invited to another show before June was pretty slim.

Zara slid a store-bought pan of cornbread into the oven to warm. To the pot, she added the rest of the ingredients and sprinkled pungent spices on top.

She sighed. Why was the right thing to do always the hardest?

After dinner, she'd text him to cancel. She'd have to deny herself the pleasure of his company. Her career was more important.

"I wish I'd met him at a better time," she said to the bubbling pot.

"Who're you talking to?"

Zara jumped. "Jesus, Brooke."

Brooke had cat-footed it into the kitchen.

"Sorry." She stood next to Zara. "*Kurwa*, it smells good in here. Yay for real food!"

"I wanted something hearty." Zara lowered the flame. "Are you finished practicing?"

"Nope." Brooke wiggled her fingers at Zara. "I'm giving these babies a dinner break. You cost me five bucks, by the way. I bet Grier you'd make buttered noodles for the millionth time."

"I'm sure you can cover the loss now that you've got a side job. How is it, by the way?"

"Fantastic! Thanks for hooking me up with it." Brooke's wide smile tipped upside-down. "But it's cold. Would they let me pose on an electric blanket?"

Zara laughed. "I can see the title now: Still Life, Nude, with Electric Blanket."

"For real, I might have perma-stiff nipples."

"I… Don't have a response. Dinner's ready. Can you get Melinda and Grier?"

"Mel's not home yet."

Grier threw open the heavy wooden basement door and emerged from its depths. The sharp smell of photo-developing chemicals clung to her hair and clothes. "I'm here. Brooke, can you believe it about Hot Daddy?"

"Hot what now?" Brooke asked.

Zara sighed.

"You didn't tell her?" Grier smoothed her hair from her forehead. "If he'd asked *me* out—"

"Zar, a dude asked you out?"

Grier sniffed the air. "What's burning?"

"Shit. The cornbread." Zara creaked open the oven door and extracted a smoking square pan. The alarm screeched above their heads. "Somebody get that, please?"

Grier jumped on a chair, rotated the alarm off its base, and freed the battery. "With recent events at your studio, Zara, you should be more careful."

"Dammit. Must've set the temperature too high." She flipped the pan upside down and dumped the cornbread onto the cutting board. She shaved off the burned bits with a bread knife. "Most of it's edible."

"Uh-oh," Brooke said.

"Uh-oh what?" Zara asked. The women bustled around the kitchen, dishing out food, pouring drinks, and taking their seats.

"Carbs mean you're stressed. What's it this time? Parents or rent?"

"Both." Zara shrugged, faking nonchalance. "No biggie. I'll power through."

It is a biggie. It is a big, gigantically huge biggie.

"Liar. It's neither of those things. Hot Daddy's got you hot and bothered." Grier pried the cork from a bottle of red. "Because this mood of yours can't be about money. I've told you I'd cover your rent. Same goes for each of you, if you find yourselves in dire straits."

She leveled the rest of the table with her hazel-eyed gaze.

"You're not paying my rent." Zara frowned. She didn't like this topic of conversation, but she liked talking about Brendan less. "You already pay more than us, Grier."

"I pay more because I took over the basement. Stop changing the subject."

"Where'd you meet a guy?" Brooke raised an eyebrow.

"Paying my own way's important to me." Zara had kept the deal she'd cut with her parents a secret. Grier would try to foist money on her, but charity would violate the spirit of the agreement. Zara always kept her word and never accepted favors she had no hope of reciprocating. "Financial independence equals artistic independence. Anyone who subsidizes me would be entitled to an opinion about what I do. I can't make art that way."

"So, guys, have we put a pin in this Hot Daddy situation?" Brooke asked.

"I don't care about your art." Grier pointed her spoon at Zara. "I care about *you*. If I were to pay your rent once in a while, I wouldn't expect you to cater to my tastes. I'd be your patron."

"That worked super well for Michelangelo and the Pope."

"I love you to bits, Zara, but you're not Michelangelo."

"You shouldn't give a fuck what other people think." Brooke threw her arms wide and upended her bottle of water. "Oops. Sorry."

She righted the bottle and mopped up the spill with her napkin.

Zara flipped her ponytails over her shoulders. "Big talk from a girl who hasn't told her parents or brother about her nude modeling. Oh, and have you introduced your guy—what's his name, Jason?—to the family yet?"

"Hey now. He's not my guy. He's *a* guy."

"Hi honeys, I'm home," Melinda called from the foyer.

Brooke leaned back in her chair until she'd poked her head past the kitchen archway. "Zar met a guy we're calling Hot Daddy."

Melinda appeared, and her glasses fogged in the kitchen's warmth. She shoved them to the top of her head, causing her spiral curls to fan out on either side of her head.

"Where'd you meet him?" Melinda asked Zara.

Zara groaned and dove into another piece of scorched cornbread.

"At the party today," Grier said. "He's the birthday girl's dad.

He's a distractingly attractive, full-on man, who asked Zara to dinner. On Valentine's Day."

"Shut up." Melinda plopped into the empty seat. "That's hilarious. Does he know you hate love?"

Zara flipped Melinda the bird. "I don't hate love. I don't have time for it."

"Who doesn't have time for love?" Brooke asked.

"Let me grab my camera." Grier backed away from the table. "I have pictures we can ogle."

"No, Grier. Sit." She didn't want the others to view Brendan through Grier's lens. Zara wanted to paint the picture. She took a deep breath to calm the fizz in her heart.

"Brendan's an archetypical All-American boy." She twisted her low ponytails. "Except, he's not a boy. All-American man. Dark hair, brown eyes with gold swirled in. Cheekbones. Dimples. Unbelievable smile. Kind—was helpful to me, and he really loves his daughter. His clothes are kind of generic, but from what I could tell, he had a good build. Like, actual muscle definition."

Her hand flexed as she recalled his softball-sized bicep under her palm when they'd posed for pictures, and oh, that tantalizing glimpse of his abs was tough to forget too.

"Holy shit." Brooke slapped the table. "You want him."

Warmth washed over Zara's face, and her scalp prickled. She was desperate to fan herself, but wouldn't give Brooke the satisfaction. "I do?"

"Devil's in the details." Brooke helped herself to more chili. "Meaning, you provided a fuck load. You don't notice that many details unless you're attracted to him. Or Sherlock Holmes."

"I'm an artist. I catalog details. You, for instance, have a zit on your forehead."

"You're not redirecting this. That was an asshole thing to say, by the way, but I forgive you." Brooke rested her chin on latticed fingers. "If you're worried it'll be awkward, maybe you and Mel and Nathan can double date."

Melinda shook her head. "No go. I have rehearsal so Nathan and I are waiting 'til the weekend."

"Staaaahhhhhp it." Zara waved her arms. "I decided to cancel."

"The hell you will." Grier flicked Zara's shoulder. "As your best friend, I can't let you do that to yourself. You like him."

Of course I like him. I have eyes and a heart, but the better question is—why does he like me?

Grier turned to Brooke and Melinda, "He was *so* into Zara. He hovered, offered to get things for her, found ways to touch her. He even carried our stuff to the car. Totally adorable. And when he asked her out? I died. Dead."

"I have no time. He probably got divorced a minute ago, which is a mountain of baggage by itself. Then there's his kid. Can any of you picture me with a ready-made family?"

"No." Melinda slipped her glasses down to the tip of her nose and narrowed her dark brown eyes at Zara. "Aren't you skipping ahead? He didn't ask you to marry him."

Sweat beaded on Zara's upper lip. "Can we not talk about me for maybe five minutes?"

"You're blushing." Melinda glanced at Grier. "He didn't ask her to marry him, right? Did I miss that part?"

"No." Grier laughed and roped her flyaway hair into a bun. "It's dinner. Definitely no proposals."

"One date is not jumping into the deep end, Zar." Brooke's green eyes crinkled at the corners. "You can dip your toes in, take a swim in the shallow end. An adult swim."

"I don't see the point. I'd never stick with a guy in his situation. Besides, the clock is real. I've got two part-time jobs, and I've got to create three more pieces for the gallery exhibit, which means a ton of studio time." Zara rubbed her forehead. "My schedule's too tight for fun."

"That's what she said." Brooke cackled.

"Brooke," Melinda said. "That's not how that joke works. Zara, sweetie, you should make the time. You obviously have a crush."

"Ooh," Grier said. "Besides, you said your paintings are shit."

"I didn't say they're shit." Zara played with the locket resting against her breastbone. Her meal sat like a fat anchor in her belly. "I haven't had any ideas since the fire, is all. I'm not sure what that has to do with anything."

"Sorry. I can see how the connection is fuzzy." Grier steepled her hands. "Hard truth here—your well's dry. You work. You sleep. You lock yourself in your Tower and torture a canvas until you need to leave for work or sleep. Everything you do is planned to the minute. You've got no time to consume new experiences, or messy emotions, or reflect, and it's killing your creativity."

Could that be the problem? She couldn't express herself because she had nothing to express?

Time slowed for Zara as her roommates nattered on about what she should do. She let her mind drift to her normal source of inspiration, the one she'd revisited often these past seven years.

Have I made peace with it?

She breathed deep and fingered the smooth silver locket dangling from her neck. For the first time in forever, she pictured her grandmother and didn't visualize the wisps of hair, the sunken eyes, or the waxen skin hanging on her frail frame toward the end. Instead, Gramma was smiling, the way she had when she'd painted a landscape *en plein air*. A thick quilt of warmth, sweetness, reassurance, yellow, and the scent of the sea wrapped around her soul.

Well, fuck.

That mental visit with her grandmother almost always made her want to weep. Today, though, she was okay. This was a problem. She wasn't sure who she was without her deep, dark brokenness.

"Hang on, guys." Zara pressed black-lacquered thumbs to her temples. "I'm having an epiphany, and it's giving me a migraine."

"About?" Grier asked.

"You might have a point."

"Does that mean," Melinda said, leaning forward, "you're going on this date with Hot Daddy?"

"Brendan." Zara hunched her shoulders. "Yes. I am. One date."

A thrill shot up her spine.

"Yaaaasssss!" Brooke said. "Turn *up*. Get crazy."

"Sweetie." Melinda drummed her fingers on the table. "Can you make us a promise? On your date, don't do those creepy things you do with new people."

"What? What do I do?"

"You stare without speaking." Grier yawned. "It's like talking to a gargoyle."

"Or," Melinda said, "you ask deep, personal questions."

"I do not."

"Zara, honey…during Orientation weekend, you asked about my scar."

"I wanted to draw it. It's fascinating, and it's huge."

"I'm aware, since it's on my chest, but polite people don't talk about other's health histories right away or ask if they can draw it. My advice? Keep it in check with this guy, who, for the record, you should hook up with. He's clearly gotten under your skin."

Zara removed the elastics from her ponytails and ran her fingers through her hair. She couldn't deny he'd gotten under her skin. Evidence—he'd been on her mind nonstop since she met him. True, she could never be in an actual relationship with a dad, and she wouldn't sign on to take care of a kid. The idea made her laugh. Maybe the fact that he *had* a kid made him the perfect choice for this.

"Your collective prescription to my artistic constipation is to go on a date and get some ass." She made eye contact with each of her giggling roommates.

"Yup." Grier drained her beer. "Let's make it official. Motion for Zara to get some ass?"

"I second it." Brooke raised her hand.

"All in favor?" Melinda asked. Four hands shot in the air. "Motion approved."

Melinda pounded the table with her omnipresent mini-Maglite.

Zara's phone bleated at her from the counter next to the stove. She left the table, snatched the phone, then glanced at the number.

"Ah, hell. You guys, I've gotta take this."

Five

Zara slipped away from the kitchen and into the shadowed front room. What could Mama want? To tell her for the millionth time this was a stupid, dead-end pursuit?

She glanced at the giggling roommates she left in the kitchen, gratitude inflating her.

Since they'd met as college freshmen, they'd constantly cheered each other on and encouraged each other's artistic pursuits. Each of them had buoyed Zara's self-confidence when yet another gallery denied her participation, or when she didn't place in a juried show. If she didn't have them, she might've given up and slouched back to the shore.

Lucky for her, she did have them.

She glimpsed her frowny reflection in the entryway mirror, took a deep breath, then accepted the call. Zara extracted her locket from where it rested against her heart and worried it. The oval's smooth silver coolness soothed her.

"Hi Mama. How's life at The Sandcastle?"

"Fine, just fine." Her mother's drawl, the one Zara had worked to evict from her own speech patterns, lazed through the phone. "Listen sweetheart, I couldn't leave things the way we did this morning."

She froze. This was new. Mama was apologizing?

After a few beats, she cleared her throat. "Where are you? I can hear the tide."

"On the veranda. A bad storm rolled through an hour ago, and I wanted to check on the chairs." The crashing waves faded as Zara's mother must have headed inside. "We upset you this morning, and I'm sorry."

Holy shit!

She'd said it. Mama actually said 'I'm sorry.'

Zara's heart rate sped up, and she steadied herself against the foyer console. She'd hungered for an apology for years, but she never expected it. That was a fairy tale. Her parents weren't wired to make amends with anyone besides guests at The Sandcastle.

"Um…okay."

"We didn't mean to hurt your feelings. You know Daddy and I've never understood this art stuff of yours. We were talking during lunch today, and we worked out a way to come to your event."

Double holy shit. Another first.

"Are you sure?" Zara's knees gave, like a wet bucket of sand had thumped her from behind. Donna and Robert Kissette, in Land's End's finest threads, circulating among art show people in all their curated glory.

Crazy pants.

If her parents were there, though, she wouldn't enjoy the night as much. Instead of indulging in champagne and cheese cubes, she'd serve as their docent. Most of her time would be spent explaining and defending the work in the show. She couldn't handle it if they came, and saw, and dismissed it.

"You said it was important, didn't you? We should be there. Aunt Sophie'll mind The Sandcastle so we can come. March 14th, isn't that right?"

"Yeah. March 14th." Zara hugged the phone to her ear. Maybe she wasn't giving them enough credit. This could be an olive branch, a sign they were coming around to accepting what she wanted to do with her life.

"I'd hoped you'd be pleased."

She pictured her parents congratulating her with pride etched on their faces. This particular fantasy was one she'd never allowed herself before. It was too indulgent, too impossible. She had scars from their indifference.

Then again, they'd never arranged time off for her events before…

God, what if they really were coming around?

"I can't even tell you how glad I am you can make it." She bounced on her toes, and her mind spun into planning mode. "Maybe we could get dinner beforehand? There's a great restaurant up the street from my house."

"Sure, hon."

"Okay." She massaged her jaw muscle. She wasn't accustomed to multiple hours of smiling and chitchat. After Emma's party, dinner, and this happy news, her face would ache for hours.

"Sweetheart, while I have you on the line…"

"Yes?"

"The weekend after your event is St. Patrick's Day. We're

booked solid. I'd love it if you came to the shore to help us out. You could ride home with us and maybe stay for a bit. The summer job fair's two weeks later. We'll need help interviewing for staff for the busy season."

Zara closed her eyes and dropped her chin to her chest. It took every bit of her willpower to stay upright. She eyed the thick foyer carpet Grier's parents had just second-hand gifted them. Perfect for plummeting to the floor and curling into the fetal position.

Of course it was a *quid pro quo*. It'd been stupid of her not to sniff out yet another attempt to corral her into working at The Sandcastle.

"That won't work, Mama."

"I don't understand. It's after your show, isn't it?"

"Yes, but—"

"But what?"

Zara's lips blew outward with her exasperated sigh. Did she have to remind her parents of the terms of their deal again? Her indentured servitude was *not* a fait accompli.

"The year's not up, and I have a life and jobs here. I can't take off for a weekend."

In the street, a police car chirped its siren. The chirp grew into wail, stopping their conversation until the car flashed around the corner and toward downtown.

"Goodness, what was that?"

"Police car. It's gone now."

Her mother sighed. "What kind of life do you have there? You're barely getting by. I'm proud of you for trying, but you've got everything waiting for you here. A job, free time, no bills. Your room's the way you left it. We didn't touch a thing."

Zara's stomach clenched.

"How many times are we going to have this conversation?" She peeked through the curtains on the front window, spying on the street traffic. Freezing rain spiked down from the clouds and ricocheted off the generous sidewalks in front of the house.

"I suppose 'til you see sense. Or June. Whichever comes first."

"Oh, Mom, I love you and Dad, but if you're using it to guilt me into moving to the shore early, I'd rather you skip the show." Zara slammed her phone on the console table, adding another fracture to its face. After three cleansing breaths, she shoved it into her pocket. Something rustled and stopped the phone's progress.

Brendan's money.

The crisp bills burned a hole in her pocket. She had to get to the art supply store. Now.

~ * ~

Zara beelined to Pla-Za Artist Supply, dropped a couple of hundred dollars, and caught the Circulator to the Bromo-Seltzer Arts Tower. The shopping bag crinkled against her knees the whole ride, raising the hair on the nape of her neck.

She had a plan. She'd recreate, in oils, the images that had garnered Schwarz's invitation. Why had she been making this so hard? If those had caught his eye, she'd replicate them. No problem. She had snaps to reference. Should be easy.

The empty Tower lobby reeked of lemony linoleum polish. She sneezed, while waiting for the ka-chunky slug of an elevator.

Why did her mother *always* have to remind her that opportunity had taken its sweet time to knock on her door, and a job was waiting for her at The Sandcastle? Fueled by fresh prickles of irritation, she stomped up the seven flights of Tower stairs. Her enormous plastic shopping bag whacked her in the back the whole way.

The first time she'd climbed these stairs, there hadn't been much of the other residents' artwork scattered along the walls of the stairwell. Now, paintings, sketches, and photos crowded the walls. The breadth of their collective skill should've been inspiring and make her want to attack the canvas. Sadly, nope. The gleaming genius siphoned Zara's confidence, until she convinced herself she was only producing clumsy strokes and half-baked ideas.

A medium talent, at best.

In the sanctity of her studio, she dropped to her knees and yanked the biggest canvas from her trove of supplies. Her grandmother would've wagged her finger at Zara. Oils had been Gramma's paint of choice, and she'd been a devotée of do-it-yourself.

"Hon," she would say as she carefully measured mineral spirits, "always take care to mix your own paints and stretch your own canvases. Don't use any pre-made stuff. Get an idea in your head first, then match the canvas and the paint to it. Otherwise, the materials make the first decisions for you."

Zara ripped the shrink-wrap from the primed canvas. She slapped it on the easel and wound the crank until the easel's jaws clamped onto the canvas's frame. After she squirted the mixed oil paints onto a plastic palette, she grabbed a new sable-tipped paintbrush.

Normally, she loved this part. The bright blank of the canvas was full of potential, full of challenge. Not today. Today, the emptiness sneered at her.

She jammed the brush into a pile of color and hoped the brush would whisk away the tension in her shoulders. Maybe her problem wasn't a lack of inspiration. Maybe she'd just been overthinking everything. Zara had zero clue how this painting would turn out, but she was full-throttle going for it. Come hell or high water, she'd have a painting by morning.

All night long, she worked color into the canvas. Guzzled black tar coffee. Power-napped when her eyelids went on strike. In the dawn's early light, rolling the barrel of her paintbrush between her thumb and forefinger, she evaluated the result of her frenetic effort.

It's...

She made the noise again. The barky *saugh* or *laub* or whatever it was.

The painting's fucking awful.

Zara hurled her brush at the canvas, and it bounced the brush right back at her. The bristles punched her square in the breastbone, leaving a crimson splotch behind.

"This is my favorite shirt," she shouted and splatted her palette in the center of the painting, smearing it around.

Her stomach lurched, and she fell her to her knees. The urge to vomit was real.

The paintings aren't coming. Nothing is good. I'll never create anything good ever again.

An emotional avalanche kicked off in her heart. She needed to stop it. She couldn't give in and allow it to sweep her away in an indulgent cascade of sobbing self-pity. What good would it do? It wouldn't help her summit, blast through, or tunnel under this Everest-sized blockage in time to create the pieces needed for the exhibit.

Zara cradled her head and breathed.

This was why she shouldn't take her parents' calls twice in a twenty-four-hour cycle. The stampede of irritation they let loose was impossible to herd. *New rule. No talking to them until after I finish the new paintings.*

She flashed back to one of the times she'd supernovaed at her parents. They'd changed her ninth grade electives from the art cluster of classes to business. She'd discovered the switch when she received a copy of her schedule in the middle of swampy, thick-aired August.

After her parents met her blowup with passive faces and eye rolls, she'd retreated, raw-throated and sniffly, to her grandmother's room. She'd wanted a hug as big as the dunes. Plus Gramma always had a stash of caramels.

Instead, the soft-spoken woman had given Zara advice.

Gramma passed Zara a tissue and parked herself on the soft,

flowered bedspread. Her greater weight caused the mattress to dip, tipping Zara into her. She'd thrown an arm around Zara and patted her on the head.

"There'll be times, more'n a few, when you're gonna feel boxed in. Painted into a corner, if I'm being funny. Anyways, I've been there. There are only a couple of things you can do if that happens. You can try to punch your way out, but more often than not, all's you get is bloody knuckles. Second way's to see if there's a side door you might've missed. Or the third option, the one that works for me most of the time, is to ask for help."

Zara smiled. Her grandmother could steer her to sanity, even from the great beyond. Not that Zara believed in mystical hoo-ha, but still.

She slid her cell phone from her back pocket, clicked open the messaging app, then launched a fresh message. Brendan's name was at the top of her list of contacts.

She wasn't sure if she was opening a side door or asking for help.

Maybe both?

~ * ~

Across town, Brendan released the trigger on the miter saw he'd been using to cut two-by-fours. The shrieking blade ground to a halt, its jagged steel teeth grinning at him. He pushed his safety glasses on top of his head and wiped sweat from his brow with the edge of his tank top.

Jesus, Mike's garage is hot.

His phone buzzed against his butt.

Zara had texted, *Dinner on Wednesday... What time?*

He punched the air and waited a few respectable seconds before replying. He'd back-burnered any distracting daydreams about the princess while he worked with dangerous power tools. Now, here she was, in his hands. So to speak.

7 OK? he texted.

Rad. Where?

Her enthusiastic response boosted his confidence. No point in playing coy and delaying a return text. That wasn't his style, anyway. All in from the get-go was how he rolled.

Not sure yet. Location preference?

Anywhere I can get to on the Circulator.

That narrowed down the options, but he could work with it.

Any food allergies or dislikes?

Allergies?

Brendan slapped himself in the forehead. *Sorry. Play date question. Do u have any, tho?*

Nope, none. No dislikes either.

Done. Will let u know where soon as I make the res.

Can't wait, Brendan Stewart.

Brendan yanked his safety goggles free and twirled them by the elastic strap. *Can't wait.* Amazing how those words pumped him up and dropkicked job stress off his chest.

For the ten hours he'd been at his desk, he'd been copied on a barrage of snippy e-mails among the company's higher-ups. Each distraction cost him time, and all he wanted was to be left alone to code. He especially didn't want to be an audience to a virtual pissing contest, but a start-up project was all hands on deck, day-in, day-out. Cost of doing business when you're on the ground floor of an innovative idea that could set him and Emma up for the future.

Still. 'Reply All' could go fuck itself.

None of the job stuff mattered at the moment, because Zara couldn't wait for their date. Two years ago, hell, two *weeks* ago, he would've laughed at the idea of dating. Would've said he was too focused on keeping Emma's world stable.

That was before he'd met a woman who flipped a switch in his body that had been off for ages.

Brendan's older brother, Mike, shouldered his way into the garage carrying two bottles of Loose Cannon beer. His beefy build came from days in the auto shop and home improvement projects. Those projects were where some of Brendan's muscles came from, too. Mike had a to-do list a mile long and paid Brendan in food, drink, and advice.

"Here you go." He shoved a bottle toward Brendan. "What's that grin for? You can't love framing walls that much."

"Nah." Brendan eased himself onto the stool next to the workbench, legs splayed. "Making plans for Valentine's Day."

"For real?" Mike clinked bottles with Brendan. "Good for you, man. She serious?"

"No, I only met her yesterday."

"The princess from Emma's party? Monica said you eye-fucked this girl the whole time."

"Monica said I eye-fucked a girl?" Brendan raised an eyebrow.

"She said flirting." Mike shrugged. "I read between the lines."

"I guess I was." Brendan stuffed his phone into his pocket. "I asked her on a date before she left."

"For Valentine's Day? Aw, son." Mike planted his hip against the workbench. "You're hopeless. First girl after your divorce, and you take her out on Valentine's? This should be your practice run. Here's a tip—you don't have to get married at the end of the date, even if you knock her up."

"I'm aware."

"Promise me you'll cut loose, Brend."

"I'm loose, I swear." He surrendered. "This is a start, that's all. I'm ready to find someone who's got my back and—"

Mike scowled. "I've *always* had your back."

"I was about to say someone who's got my back and shares my bed."

"Oh. Gotcha. Yeah. Can't do that."

"Plus, it'd be good for Em to see me in a healthy adult relationship so she knows what one looks like. It'll give her a better shot at one when she's older." He guzzled a healthy amount of his beer. "Not that I plan on introducing any women to her right away. This one's tricky because Em already loves her."

"Too soon to worry about any of that, dude. Stop living in here." Mike tapped his skull with the mouth of the bottle. "Hey, how's work?"

Brendan grunted. Since he was ten years older, Mike was both a buddy and a junior dad. Since they'd covered dating, job updates were typically next on the list.

"That good, huh?" Mike asked.

"I'm busting my ass. Since I'm working for a start-up offshoot of the company, management is finding its feet. Stress levels are through the roof. I'd leave, but I haven't caught wind of any full-time remote gigs like this. If I'm in an office, Em'll have to go to aftercare." Brendan sighed. "I hate the of idea losing that time when she's with me."

"Thought you were going to start your own company?" Mike gestured at Brendan with his bottle. "You almost finished with my site, by the way? I can't wait to start using an online scheduler. Everything got fucked up yesterday because Troy spilled coffee on the book at the front desk and we couldn't read who was coming in for what."

"Another week, maybe." Brendan scratched at his hip. "My side jobs add up to a good twenty hours a week as-is, but making them my only gig? No can do. I'd have to rustle up a dozen new clients of the same size, or four or five big ones. Tons of risk to it and no fringe benefits."

"Except you'd have control of your day and the work you do. Like with me and the shop. It'd suit you."

Monica poked her head into the garage.

"Hey, is it okay if Emma has a grilled cheese? I'm making dinner for the kids. It's not *paleo*," she said. "But it's organic. It won't cause a riot between you and Jess, right?"

"Nah, go for it. Em loves grilled cheese."

"You want one? You could use some fattening up." Monica evaluated his midsection.

"Why, I'm too cut?" He flexed his biceps.

Mike flicked him in the forehead.

"Is that a yes or a no?" she asked.

"Two please and thank you."

"Be ready in ten." She closed the door behind her.

"Hey, Monica said Jess wasn't at the party. Things okay with her?"

"Not bad. Not great either." Brendan took a big slug from his beer. "Doesn't stop her from asking me to do handyman shit around her house. She's stressed and taking whatever sponsorships come her way. Her blog traffic is dwindling and she's scrambling for content but her readers don't care about her diet, or workout routines, or places she travels. Even though it's been two years, she still hasn't figured out the right direction to go, and blames me and the rules I insisted on during our settlement. Like I'm a fucking bad guy for wanting to keep our daughter's bedwetting habits private."

"Jesus." Mike furrowed his forehead. "Wait. Should I use a tarp the next time Emma sleeps over?"

Brendan laughed. "That's your takeaway? No tarp. I'll pack a GoodNite."

"A what?" Mike blew across the top of the bottle, producing a low groan.

"How do you have two kids and not know what a GoodNite is?"

"Monica deals with the middle-of-the-night stuff." He drained his beer and chucked the bottle in the recycling bin in the corner. It clattered against the other empties.

"There might be a big chunk of fatherhood you're missing."

"Doubt it." Mike grabbed the shop brush and tidied the sawdust into a neat pile on the workbench. "She should give it up and get a regular job."

"For her sake and Emma's, I wish she'd get her certification to become a therapist. It's what she was working on before Emma happened. She'd be good at it, too. The thing she enjoys most is dissecting people's behavior. What sucks is she wouldn't even consider it unless her site stops paying the bills. She likes being Internet-famous too much."

"You two are like polar opposites. I don't know why you ever got hitched."

The kids' laughter pealed through the closed foyer door.

"Sure you do." Brendan glanced in the direction of the sound.

"Plenty of people have kids but don't get married."

Brendan smirked. "Yeah, but they weren't trying to uphold a golden boy image."

"Some golden boy. If Mom and Dad knew half of what you got up to…"

"They'd never believe you."

He swept the sawdust into a dustpan and carried it to the trashcan, making sure to spill at least half of it on Brendan's leg.

"Real mature." Brendan laughed, brushing it from his jeans.

"What'll Jess do if you get a girlfriend and can't drop everything to help her out?"

"Complain on her blog. In all caps." Brendan grinned. "But ask me if I care."

~ * ~

A few hours later, Brendan hustled Emma into the tub at home to wash off play date sweat and ice cream stickiness. After brushing, braiding, and reading bedtime stories to his sleepy-eyed girl, he tucked her in and headed downstairs to log on at work. Five minutes later, he re-tucked her into bed when she shuffled from her room, clutching Ravenna, and claimed she needed a drink of water.

By the time she truly settled in for the night, the kitchen clock glared nine-fifteen.

Aw man. Emma would be a basket case in the morning when he woke her for school. His kid needed at least twelve hours of sleep a night or she was grumpy for the rest of the day. There was a reason he'd nicknamed her Emma Bear.

Brendan's office chair huffed as he dropped into it. With a few clicks, he opened the reservation website and pulled up everything available for two people on February 14th at 7:00 p.m. in downtown Baltimore.

Four hits.

He riffled his hair, browsed the reviews, and immediately struck two dives off the list. The third one held promise—an Ethiopian place. Mike had taken Monica there, and he was pretty sure they'd enjoyed it. He picked up his phone to text Zara.

Hi princess—you busy?

Nothing for a second. Then, three pulsing dots told him she was replying. He could live and die a thousand times in the seconds those tiny circles throbbed at him. A quiet digital whoop from his phone heralded a return message.

Princess? Am scrubbing paint from my hair. #busynotbusy.

Finally. Brendan let out a breath. He fat-fingered a couple letters in his reply, but his strict coding standards forced him to correct the typos. It didn't matter in a text like it would in a function or a stored procedure, but he had standards. He didn't want to come off as an illiterate goon.

Birthday party gone wrong?

Nope. I fought with a painting. It won.

He snorted, scratched his chin, and typed, *LOL. Demand a rematch.*

Already planned. Where am I meeting u tomorrow?

God, she must have lightning fingers. Whereas he had forty-seven uncoordinated thumbs. *Depends,* he typed. *Ethiopian good?*

Never had it. I'm down with trying new stuff, tho.

Me too. His groin twitched. There were lots of new things he'd be down with trying. He typed the restaurant details and hit send. *Here's the name & address.*

Oh, *that* place. Been wanting to go there. It's not far from me.

Can't wait, princess.

Me too. Signing off. Have to dunk my head in turpentine to clean the paint out of it before tomorrow.

He slotted the phone into the charging cradle on his desk, smiled, then spun in his chair. This was a full-on crush. He hadn't been this goofy about a woman for years. After the responsibilities he'd taken on in his twenties—marriage, mortgage, kid, divorce, lawsuits—he wouldn't have believed he was capable of these kinds of junior high reactions.

Then Zara, this unexpected princess, popped into his life and hit his buttons in all the right ways.

He plunked his feet to the floor to stop the spinning.

After making the reservations, he opened the remote connection to his workstation at HQ. He wanted to get ahead on his project in case the date went well tomorrow night. If that happened, and he *really* hoped it would, the following day could be a late start.

His cell lit up with a text message. Zara again so soon? Glancing at the screen, his guts clenched. It was Mike.

DUDE. Shitty Jess post alert.

Six

Zara's Tuesday obligations blurred together. She taught watercolor techniques to a bunch of retirees at the Waxter Center in the morning, bought more raw materials at Pla-Za in the afternoon, and then herded a group of half-drunk women through a nightscape design at the Wine & Paint event. After cleaning up, she stumbled home in the dark, exhausted but unable to indulge in anything except fitful, sweaty sleep.

She never rested well under deadline.

She'd spent Wednesday morning in her Tower studio, cleaning the aftermath of her tantrum from Monday, and cutting her new paints with medium. In retrospect, that had been part of the problem with Monday's mess-terpiece. She'd used paint straight from the tube. The pigments didn't have the right consistency and she'd ended up with mud.

To prove her point, she'd use this afternoon to begin an abstract with self-made paints.

Zara sat cross-legged in front of the last of her prefabricated canvases, eyes closed, divining the emotional source of her next painting. She needed to tap into a fresh vein, one that wasn't collapsed from overuse by the sad and angry girl who'd left the Eastern Shore years ago.

She circled back around to Brendan and wrinkled her nose.

"No," she mumbled to the canvas. Making him the subject of her art would *literally* be putting him on a pedestal. The whole notion of a casual fling would fly out the window.

Her traitorous heart wouldn't obey. There he was again, and again, and again. His smile. Those soulful eyes. His floppy hair. His confident stride. His manners. The way he had zero chill about the Princess Ravenna theme for his daughter's party.

Maybe she could paint sort of a tribute to *Rising*? Ugh. She'd been spending too much time with kids lately. Did she actually admire a corporate-manufactured cartoon? This was *so* not her normal dark and anxious vibe.

She lingered in front of the canvas, and a possible composition took root in her imagination.

One focused on…beginnings.

Rising had illuminated a path forward. Playing Princess Ravenna had covered the deposit, first, and last month's rent on her studio, allowed her to rebuild her arsenal of art supplies, and forced her to interact with people she never would have encountered.

Including Brendan.

She grabbed her brush and got to work.

The alarm on Zara's phone startled her five hours later. As she blotted her brushes on newspaper and swished them in turpentine, her belly bubbled with anticipation.

Time to go home and get ready for her Valentine's Day date.

~ * ~

Come on come on come on. Brendan rang Jess's doorbell a second time. He glanced at his watch. 6:15. The restaurant was twenty minutes away, plus parking. He *hated* being late. Being late sent the signal his time was more important than anyone else's, or that he didn't plan well. Either message made his skin crawl.

Jess's whiny blog post about missing Em's birthday put an extra kink in his neck, for sure.

This day had already been annoying enough, what with his project manager riding his ass about the due dates for his tasks. Yes, he'd assured her, he was still on target to get the new features done, peer reviewed, and tested on time.

All he wanted was to put normal life on pause and go have a nice dinner with an attractive, kind woman. So if his ex could hurry and let their potty-dancing daughter into the house, that'd be stellar.

He hit the doorbell a third time.

The deadbolt tumbled, and Jess cracked the door, wielding a plunger.

"Sorry," she said. "Minor crisis."

"I have to go potty." Emma ran past her mother.

"Remember to flush!' Jess yelled, then shoved a plunger at him. "Can you fix the kitchen sink? It's not draining. I tried, but…"

He sighed. Zero-point-zero likelihood she'd get a plumber out here tonight. Ten minutes here and he'd officially be cutting it close, but what choice did he have? His daughter's half-time house needed a working kitchen sink.

"Let me get my tools." He handed Emma's book bag to Jess, then about-faced and marched to his SUV to grab his toolbox. Back at her door, Jess moved aside to let him into the house and followed him to the kitchen.

Savory scents curled through the air, and his stomach growled.

"Hungry?" she asked.

"Skipped lunch."

"Stay for dinner. Emma and I are having gluten-free chicken tenders and carrot fries."

He tried not to gag. Carrot fries?

"No Kenny?" he asked.

She shifted her gaze to somewhere over his shoulder. "No. We sort of broke up. Are you sure you don't want to stay? I also made flourless chocolate cupcakes for dessert."

He could not begin to explain to her how un-tempted he was by this offering. As much as he wanted to snark on Jess and Kenny calling it quits, the smart thing to do was not to comment on it all.

"Thanks, but no." He set the toolbox next to the sink, slung his coat on a kitchen chair and shoved up his sleeves.

"Wow. What's with the tie? And did you iron that shirt?" She crossed her arms and leaned on the counter next to the sink.

Nope. Not getting into this with her.

"You have a bucket or big bowl? Something to catch the sink water." He crouched in front of the sink with his pipe wrench. "It's probably a clogged P-trap."

"There's a mop bucket under the sink."

He positioned the bucket under the plastic pipe, then fitted the wrench around the slip nut and rotated it. Murky water slopped from the pipe and into the bucket.

"While I'm here, I want to talk to you about your latest post. It was...not cool." He kept his gaze fixed on the plumbing to avoid the exasperation lighting up Jess's face.

"The spa post? Jeez, I didn't mention you guys in it."

"I still come off as an asshole." After a few more twists, the pipe came free, and the sink emptied its contents into the bucket.

"How?"

"First off, you wrote you're a single parent, but, last time I checked, we split custody."

"I'm a single parent when she's with me." She tapped her foot.

Brendan sat back on his haunches and knocked the PVC pipe against the bucket to dislodge whatever was stuck. "That's not the same thing. We back each other up all the time. Then you wrote that people don't accommodate your work schedule and you end up missing family events and milestones. You knew the dates and made other plans, but conveniently left that out. Anyone who's read the blog from the beginning knows who I am. It makes it sound like I'm deliberately planning parties when you can't be there."

"You're acting paranoid." She drummed her fingers on the counter. "*Maybe* I can see how you'd take it the wrong way. But to be fair, I was super bummed I couldn't be at Em's party. When she came home smitten with the girl who played Ravenna, I got jealous, okay? I'm human."

Her western Pennsylvania accent thickened. She must be agitated.

"You don't have to be jealous. You're her mom. Emma missed you." He stood with the amputated P-trap. "I couldn't postpone the party at the last minute. We can't put her life on pause if one of us can't be there."

"That's the thing, isn't Brendan?" Jess's nostrils flared. "You're *always* there. Mr. Safety Net."

"Is that bad?" He peered into the P-trap and reached in with a pair of needle-nose pliers and extracted a lumpy bit of chewed up plastic. "There's your problem."

She wrinkled her nose. "Please tell me that's not a mouse. I will move if it is."

"It's—or, was—Ravenna's selkie friend, Merial. In her seal form. Guess Em decided to send her to the sea?" He dropped the toy onto counter and fished a few more items from the pipe. "Teabags. Are you still throwing those in the drain?"

Jess sighed. "Yes, yes, I'm murdering the disposal."

He peered into the sink. She hadn't gotten the strainer he recommended. Not his house, not his money, not his wife. Brendan knelt to reattach the P-trap. "It's your dime."

"Thank you for acknowledging that. Since you're being helpful, can you look at the dryer? It keeps shutting off before it's fully dried a load."

He backed out of the cabinet and hit his head. "Ow. Shit."

He touched the tender spot on his head then glanced at his fingertips. No blood.

"You okay?"

"Yeah." He washed his hands and grinned in satisfaction as the water swirled down the drain. Code could be fickle. It was a nice change when something did what he wanted and expected.

"Anyway, the dryer started—"

"I can't, Jess. I've got a date."

"Oh?" She gulped like a goldfish a few times. "Good for you.

Do I know her?"

"No." He slipped into his coat. "We met at a party."

"You're taking her on a date on Valentine's Day?" she asked. "She must be special. Is she from around here?"

He snagged his toolbox. "I'm not talking about her yet."

"I told you about Kenny from day one."

Yeah, and he would have preferred it if she hadn't. "I've gotta run, or I'll be late." He walked toward the front door and called up the stairs. "Emma Bear, I'm leaving now."

"When do I get details?" Jess followed Brendan. "If she's spending time around Emma—"

"She isn't. Not yet. I'm sticking to the three-month rule."

Jess opened the front door. "Good."

"'Bye Daddy. I'll see you later." Emma hugged the railing spindles at the top of the stairs and smooshed her face between two of them. "Mommy, what do I smell?"

"Dinner, baby. We'll eat in a couple of minutes." To Brendan, she said, "Are you sure you can't work your magic on the dryer? Emma needs clean clothes."

"No can do, but maybe you can hang things up to dry?" He shifted his toolbox. Bailing on a chance to help his kid fell outside his norm. Then again, so did making a date with a complete stranger.

"Thanks for the hot tip." Jess rolled her eyes and opened the front door. "Have fun tonight, and any time you want to tell me more about this mystery woman, I'm all ears."

All ears and a big mouth.

"I'll see you on Sunday." He legged it to his car. 6:30. Should be able to get there with a couple of minutes to spare. Hopefully she hadn't gotten there before him.

~ * ~

"Want us to wait up for you, sweetie?" Melinda asked. She, Brooke, and Grier had hunkered in the living room with a barrel of popcorn and the *Pitch Perfect* movies.

"No thanks." Zara slung her bag on her shoulder.

"Text us if you need a rescue," Brooke said.

"Or if you're not coming home at all." Grier snapped a photo of her with her phone. "You look hot, by the way."

"Thanks. I'm coming home, but don't wait up."

"No judgment if you go home with him. Hashtag, you should go home with him."

"Whatever." Zara dragged her hat onto her flat-ironed hair. "Don't wait up."

She left the house to a chorus of smoochy noises and tromped through patches of dirty slush on her way to the restaurant. Some of the icy mess spattered her tights and soaked through to her thighs, making her shiver. Maybe a miniskirt was a mistake in thirty-degree weather. On the other hand, she wanted to show off her legs.

The restaurant lay ahead, across Maryland Avenue, glowing and cozy in the deepening night. Butterflies rioted in her belly. She was having dinner with a stranger. Not a friend, or a classmate, a coworker, or even a friend-of-a-friend. A complete stranger.

Why had she let Grier push her into this? Zara *hated* uncertainty. Even when the work didn't flow, in the studio, she was in control. Out here in the wild, who could predict what would happen?

Moored on the corner pavement, waiting for the signal to cross, Zara shifted her weight. She sucked in cold air and exhaled in short bursts to calm her nerves.

I am calm. I am zen. I am...

Brendan stood sentry under the restaurant's heavy green canopy, and her breath stuck in her throat.

I'm in trouble.

Since he was facing a different direction, she was free to stare. He'd popped the collar of his pea coat against February's bluster, lending him a cloak-and-dagger mystique. Whoa. Such an improvement over cargo shorts and a polo. He squinted in the distance, searching for her.

Delicious as he appeared, that wasn't what made her belly thrill and shove her anxiety aside. He'd planted himself there, in the cold, to wait for her. He wasn't inside, on his phone, having a drink. That spoke volumes about his character. Plus, she adored punctual people.

She jabbed at the crossing signal's button, annoyed she couldn't get to him faster.

He glanced in her direction, and dimples puckered his cheeks.

Oh, wow. I'm in so much trouble.

Zara waved. The tingle in her thighs might've been a reaction to Brendan. Or the extra time she'd spent grooming in preparation for their date. Or maybe even the distinct lack of pants between her nether regions and the wintry elements.

Could be all three, but the safe money was on him.

The stubborn traffic light finally changed, and the oncoming cars stopped, snorting like bulls in bucking chute. She bounced across the street toward her date.

"Hi Princess." Brendan angled toward her to kiss her cheek.

The brief press of warm flesh buckled her knees.

He smiled at her. "I like your boots."

"Thanks. I wasn't sure what level of fancy to go for." Zara scanned the length of her body. Her moto jacket hugged her torso, and her red mini-kilt flared underneath. Sheer, rhinestone-studded tights and thick-soled boots completed the ensemble. "I ended up practical with gothic fancy so I can run if you're a total creeper."

"I like a girl who makes contingency plans." He tugged open the restaurant door.

The exotic swirl of aromas within nearly knocked her off her feet. Onion, garlic, paprika, oregano, roasting meat, melting butter, and a few other thick, delectable fragrances she couldn't identify.

"This must be what heaven smells like," she said. Her stomach rumbled, chasing away the rabble of butterflies. What had she eaten today? Besides the butterscotches the retirees had thrust at her? Coffee and a lonely early-morning yogurt.

Brendan loped toward the wild-haired hostess, and Zara imagined how she'd sketch him on a sheet of double-sided Bristol paper. The rough side, definitely. The sharp planes and angles of his body demanded the rough side.

"Follow me," the hostess said as she gathered menus. "Our upstairs dining room is this way."

"Ladies first," he said and slipped his hand over Zara's jacket until he found the small of her back and encouraged her forward.

A geyser of champagne feels bubbled up her spine.

She swayed through the crowded dining room, doing her best not to bump into the moony couples occupying tables sandwiched into the small space. She followed the hostess to the stairs at the back of the dining room.

Uh-oh. The tight staircase meant they'd need to climb single-file. Given the sheerness of her tights and the shortness of her skirt, there was an excellent chance Brendan would see her ass. As her boot hit the first step, Zara's face heated, but she carried herself with as much grace as she could muster.

The hostess placed the menus on an intimate table in the corner, next to the window. "Your server will be here soon. Enjoy your evening."

"Mind if I take the gunslinger seat?" Zara ducked under the strap of her messenger bag as she removed it and hung it on the chair by the wall. "I prefer to watch the room."

"Be my guest."

She unzipped her jacket. Before she could shed it, Brendan drifted behind her and tucked his fingers under her collar.

"Let me help." He peeled it from her, and his knuckles skimmed down her arms. She trembled, which was just so embarrassing. How long had it been since anyone had touched her like that?

"Are you cold?" he asked. He draped her jacket on her chair, then pulled it from the table for her.

"A little." *Liar.* "But I'll warm up."

She settled herself on the polished wooden chair and allowed him to scoot her in, and tried not to stare as he unbuttoned his coat.

Tried, but failed. Her eyes grew hot with her non-blinky state. Wait, was *this* what her friends meant? Was she gargoyling right now? Oh, man, she was. Zara twisted her ring around and around. She should speak, but the words coming to mind were trite or porny.

It sure is cold tonight.

Nice shirt. Much better than the polo. It fits you well.

Forearms are sexy.

Your silver watch is gorgeous. Is it an antique?

Are your lips as soft as I imagine?

I've never gone on a date with a guy wearing a tie.

Said tie buckled as Brendan sat and rested his arms on the table, covering his half of the oak square. His rolled-up sleeves revealed thick, corded muscle.

The flickering candlelight danced in his eyes. "When I asked you out, you mentioned we might enjoy a shared sense of awkwardness."

"I did." Her shoulders relaxed. Thank God he took the lead in the conversation.

"Think we're there?"

"Definitely."

"Welcome to Dukem," their waitress greeted them. "My name is Adina. May I bring you anything to drink?"

"After you." He gestured toward Zara.

"Oh." She shook her head to clear the Brendan-induced glaze from her brain. "This is new to me. Can you make any recommendations?"

"If you like lager, Bedele is tasty, or our robust stout. Many people also enjoy the sweet honey-wine, *tej*, to complement the spice in their meals."

"*Tej* for me," Zara said.

"I'll have the stout, and a water, please."

"Of course." Their waitress shifted her gaze between the two of them. "May I see your ID?"

Without hesitating, Zara fished her wallet from her bag and slipped her driver's license free. The waitress scrutinized it for a few seconds before returning it.

"And you, sir?" she asked Brendan.

He raised an eyebrow, but complied and wrangled his wallet from his coat's inner pocket. He flopped it open, and as he held it up for the waitress, a photo of Emma grinned at Zara from the plastic picture flap. He may as well have dumped a bucket of ice in her lap.

After the waitress disappeared, he chuckled and wedged his wallet into his coat.

"I haven't been carded in forever."

"How old are you, anyway?" Zara folded her arms on the table.

"Guess."

The candlelight made it impossible to guess accurately. She squinted and, channeling the age-guessing boardwalk carnies who scammed money from tourists every summer, she said, "Anywhere from—" she wobbled her hand, "twenty-five to thirty-five?"

"Jesus Christ, I look thirty-five?"

"A *hot* thirty-five. Does that make it better? I assumed you were Emma's way older brother at first. Then you said you were her father, which made sense because you were wearing the dad uniform."

"The dad uniform?"

"Polo shirt, cargo shorts, and sneakers. All of you wear it, even in winter. It changes sometimes. Like, jeans instead of shorts, or mandals instead of sneakers."

"That's what American men wear. It's not a dad thing."

"There's nothing *wrong* with it. Anyway, I thought you might be one of those baby-faced men who never ages, like Paul Rudd."

She patted his forearm. He had *really* great forearms. What if she squeezed it? Would that be creepy? Wait…was *she* the creeper? Zara pulled her hand away and sat on it.

Brendan thumbed his chin and narrowed his eyes at her.

"I'm twenty-seven. I'll be twenty-eight in April."

She pressed her fingertips to her forehead. "You were twenty-two when Emma was born?"

"Yup. While I was up to my elbows in diapers, my friends were getting tanked in Fell's Point."

"Wow. I never would have guessed you're only two years older than me. You've got a house and a kid and I've got…Ramen."

He laughed. "Plenty could change in two years."

"Well, I won't have a kid. *That's* for sure." She winced. "Sorry. That came out super-judgy. Your kid is adorable, but I don't plan on having any."

Why? Why did I say that?

"How can you be sure?" His chair creaked as he shifted away from her.

Proceed with caution. There had to be a way to explain her stance without bagging on his choices. Right?

"Same way you were sure you wanted kids, I guess? Kids are okay, but I don't see myself taking care of other people, tiny or otherwise. It takes over your whole life. Doesn't leave room for your own aspirations, unless you plan to ignore your kids. I'm a product of the latter—being ignored, I mean. I'm afraid I'd repeat those mistakes. No thanks."

Oh my God, will you hush your mouth? Zara held her face, hoping her cool palms would extinguish the embarrassed flames licking her cheeks.

Brendan's big watch scissored off the silent seconds.

"It's tough, absolutely, but it's gratifying." He shrugged. "Having Emma...well, it didn't happen the way I would have planned. But I'm happy, and I wouldn't change anything."

He glanced at the menus lying prone along the edge of the table.

"So, we should figure out what we want."

"Good idea." Zara picked up a laminated menu and studied the unfamiliar words, grateful for the distraction. Dithering among the choices, she drummed her fingers on the table. Without any frame of reference, how could she know what she'd like? Trying new things could be amazing, but there was a healthy chance she'd end up disappointed. Then again, she could game the system and try as much new stuff as possible. There was bound to be at least one item she liked.

"They have combination platters. Do you want to split one? We can try some of everything."

Brendan read the description. "I'm game."

He placed his menu on top of hers, and they exchanged shy smiles.

A car horn blasted outside for an eternity.

Okay, it would be *fantastic* if the waitress came back now.

Was this a normal conversational lull, or an uncomfortable silence? *She* was uncomfortable. Panicky, if she was being honest. She'd never mastered the art of small talk. Her parents had honed their ability to converse with tourists about anything. That trait must skip a generation, because here she sat, twiddling a loose thread on her cuff, casting for a neutral topic.

You will make eye contact and have a normal, grown-up conversation with him. You will ooze intelligence and ask interesting, appropriate questions. You will NOT do the gargoyle gawker thing.

"Brendan Stewart." She released the thread and peered into his gorgeous brown-and-golds. Okay, she was talking and making eye contact. So far so good.

"Yes, Zara Kissette?"

"I have scant information about you." She tried not to stare at his lips, which, at the moment, were curved in a smile.

"Which is why we're on a date. To get to know each other. Do you have any burning questions you'd like to ask?"

"Why did you and your ex split up?" She clapped a hand over her mouth. What was *wrong* with her? This was not small talk. This was big talk, *huge* talk, but she was so busy trying not to stare, she'd abandoned her filter.

Shit, shit, shit.

Across the dining room, a waitress fumbled a wineglass, and it shattered against the floor.

"Jumping straight to the deep stuff, huh? I figured we'd cover jobs, favorite movies, bands, novels..."

"Yes. Good idea." She tucked her hair behind her ears. "Those are much better icebreakers. I'll go first."

"Zara, it's—"

"Okay, so, jobs," she said. "I'm an art teacher at a senior center and an instructor for Wine & Paint events, and the occasional children's party entertainer when I'm desperate, but my real job is visual artist."

"You don't—" He shifted in his chair.

The unstoppable words tumbled from her mouth. "My favorites. Movie, *Addams Family Values*. Band, Throwing Muses. Literature, anything by Edgar Allen Poe, but you asked about novels... So, if I'm trying to impress people, I say it's *Jane Eyre*, but it's really *Flowers in the Attic* by V. C. Andrews."

She took a breath and straightened the napkin on her lap. Blood pounded in her ears.

"Any more revelations?" he asked. "I don't want to interrupt you."

"I'm done." Breathless, she wheeled the saltshaker around on its bottom. "Did that shed any light on who I am?"

He laughed. "Well, you're a nervous talker."

"True," she said, and the salt slipped and scattered white grains across the table. Out of habit, she gathered a few to throw over her shoulder, but he covered her hand with his. Heat snaked up her neck, across her cheeks, and to the tips of her ears, and her heart kicked against her ribs. If she reacted like this to a casual touch, what would happen to her if they kissed?

"We have a band in common too."

He rubbed his thumb along the fleshy spot below her index finger. Zara's entire being focused on that square inch of skin.

"We do?" *Where was the waitress with the drinks?*

"Yep. It's endearing you're ashamed of your taste in books but not your terrible taste in movies."

"What?" She threw her hands in the air. "How dare you? That movie is an under-appreciated classic. I live for Wednesday Addams."

The waitress arrived with a tray laden with friendly beverages and negotiated her way around Zara's flailing arms.

"Do you have any questions?" Adina asked as she set their drinks on the table.

"Many, many questions." His eyes gleamed in the quivering candlelight as he gazed at Zara. "We'd like the Dukem Combination number six."

"Excellent choice. Spicy or mild?" the waitress asked.

"What do you prefer?" he asked.

"Spicy, always," she answered. Never mind the heat already fanning across her chest from his unbroken attention.

"Spicy it is." He gave the menus to the waitress, who disappeared toward the back of the restaurant.

He raised his blocky pint glass. "First, a toast."

Zara lifted her chilled *tej*. Condensation clouded the glass, and its surface was cool in her grasp.

"To trying new things."

She clinked her glass against his, then tipped her *tej* toward her lips. The sweet liquid cascaded over her tongue, and she trapped it, savoring the taste before swallowing.

A deep crinkle appeared between his brows as he stared at her.

Maybe we both do the gargoyle thing.

He wiped a foam mustache from his lip with his napkin "It's interesting you wanted to discuss my divorce on our first date."

He said first date. First date implies there will be others. Does he already want another date? Flattering, but how will I find time to... Stop. Get out of your head. Talk to the handsome man, gargoyle.

"Sorry." She ran her fingers through her hair, pulling it taut, letting go once her fingers reached the ends. "I've recently discovered I ask new friends awkward questions. I'll reciprocate, though. Hit me. Open book, right here."

"Glad you're fair, but it's fine. I don't have a problem telling you about the divorce. Big picture, we broke up because of our daughter."

"Oh." Zara sipped her wine to prevent herself from asking awkward follow-ups. "I've heard kids can mess with a relationship."

"I didn't mean it that way." He chuckled. "Emma's the best. No, my ex and I were rocky from the start. Honestly, we probably would have split no matter what. The real issue was we couldn't get on the same page about important parenting stuff. You sure you want to hear this?"

No, but I have zero good conversation ideas. "Yep."

"My ex is a blogger. She wrote about our family in amplified, excruciating detail. Like, if Emma was constipated, she'd make it seem like the poor kid hadn't gone for a week and we were on the verge of taking her to the ER before Miralax kicked in. She said it was funnier to exaggerate."

Zara wrinkled her nose. "Doesn't sound funny."

"I agree." He gulped his beer. "I didn't want our lives broadcast on the Internet, but oversharing made her happy during a time when not much did. As she got popular, it also brought in a decent amount of money. Paid both of our salaries for a year, which, I'm not gonna lie, was nice. So, I might've been able to make peace with how she portrayed me. Em, on the other hand…I'd been asking Jess to reel it in, give our daughter space to be a kid without the world reading every detail. And then…"

He ran his thumb through the condensation gathered near the lip of the glass. Tension vibrated off him. The set of his jaw, and his hooded eyes were fantastic. If they were in her studio, she'd be up to her elbows in charcoal trying to capture him in two dimensions.

"…I got call from the police saying my two-year-old's photos were found on a pedophile's computer."

"Oh, whoa." She blinked away her artist's gaze and snapped back to what he was saying, instead of how he was saying it.

"Exactly. Time to shut it down, right? No more posts or photos of our kid on public sites. Except Jess didn't agree. Said she couldn't help what sickos do. I strongly disagreed. Ultimately, the only way I could set some ground rules around posting about Emma was to divorce and build it into our custody arrangement."

Zara searched his face. "That's bleak."

His lips wobbled in a tentative smile. "It's all good. Worked out for the best."

"What's her blog called?" She dragged her fingertip through the salt and flicked the grains over her shoulder.

"*The Messy Jess*. Have you read it?"

"Nope. I'm not a blog person. Or a web person. Too much trollage and bad vibes. Plus my Mom was always commenting on my posts when I had social accounts. Wasn't worth the aggravation."

"Totally agree. Privacy is underrated."

Zara grinned and fingered the lip of her wineglass. "Have the other women you've dated read her blog? That has to be strange for you, if they have."

"You, miss, have asked your fair share of questions this evening. My turn. Why'd you agree to go out with me? A mid-thirties," he said, winking, "divorced father?"

"Because you asked, and you're a looker."

Ah Jesus. Maybe I should ease up on the wine.

"I am?" His eyes widened.

"Come on." She touched his arm. "You know you're hot."

"I do?"

The waitress arrived with a tray full of dishes. She settled a platter in the middle of their table. Dollops of colorful food decorated various parts of the flatbread underneath, like a giant palette of deliciousness. Next came a woven grass basket, then a smaller dish filled with steaming towels.

"Have you eaten in the Ethiopian tradition before?" the waitress asked.

"No," they said in unison.

"Allow me to explain. We don't use forks or knives. This," she lifted the lid on the basket, "is what you use to eat. Tear off pieces of the *injera* and use it to pick up the *wot*, the *tibs,* the cheese, or the vegetables."

The waitress's hand hovered over each food as she named it.

"Also, if you're with family or good friends, it's an Ethiopian tradition to feed one another. This is called *gursha*, and is a sign of respect. If someone offers *gursha* to you, you must accept. It's rude to refuse." The waitress eyeballed the level of liquid in their glasses. "Would you like another round?"

"Could I have another *tej*, please?" Zara swabbed her hands with a towel. The wet heat and rough texture soothed her skin.

"Nothing for me. Thank you," Brendan said.

The waitress nodded and bustled away.

"So, this 'I'm hot' thing…" He dragged a steaming towel along each digit.

His hands were beautiful, big and strong. What would they feel like on her body? Her stomach quivered. There goes that imagination of hers again. Honestly, it was both a blessing and a curse.

She cleared her throat and continued, "Women must hit on you regularly. Like the one at your daughter's party who wouldn't leave you alone."

He smiled. "This woman who was into me... Was she blonde? Short hair?"

"They were almost all blonde, but yep, short hair."

"She's my sister-in-law, Monica."

Oh. "She is?"

"Yep. She cornered me and said I'd been ogling you the whole party, so I should ask you out."

"I'm sure you're dating lots of women."

Zara took another drink. "No. Been a little while, actually."

They locked gazes, and the naked vulnerability in his eyes softened her heart. With his scrunched shoulders and lowered lids, it was obvious he was nervous. Why hadn't she seen that before? Some finely honed observational skills she had. Too caught up in her own anxieties, she'd never considered he might also be outside his comfort zone. She drifted toward him, wanting to put him at ease. Couldn't help it. If he crooked a finger she'd climb over the table and sit in his lap.

Bet the restaurant would frown on a public display like that, so she busied herself with tearing a piece of *injera* free and pinched a wad of red stew.

"Well, *I* didn't catch a single ogle." She popped the packet into her mouth. Garlic, onion, and fire erupted on her tongue, and her eyes glassed over with spice-induced tears.

"How is it?" he asked.

She gulped half her water to cool the lava in her throat. "It's making me cry, but I love it. How's my make-up? Do I look like a tragic raccoon?"

"Nope. Still beautiful. I'll give the greens a try." He ripped *injera* free of the round. "Mind if we circle back around to you agreeing to meet me tonight because I'm hot?"

"That's not the *only* reason. I'll have you know I contain multitudes."

"I'm all ears."

"I got an offer of representation from a gallery. It's an important, potentially life-changing thing. They've asked for three pieces for an upcoming show, but the pressure is giving me brain cramps." She tapped her temple. "I'm blocked, and I'm over-thinking everything. I figured if I went on a date with you, I'd be distracted and wouldn't stress about painting for a couple of hours, which could free my subconscious to work out some kinks."

The waitress refilled Zara's empty glass with more wine and left them alone.

"So you're using me as a distraction."

"Yes. No. Well, yes. Yes and no, but mostly yes." She picked up canary-colored potatoes. "Listen, I'm a terrible conversationalist. Save me with another question."

"Okay…" He dragged his bottom lip between his teeth, and Zara almost melted from her chair. "Since you're an artist, who's your biggest influence?"

The potatoes stuck in her throat and she guzzled her wine to help surf them down. "My grandmother."

"That's sweet." He grinned. "Do you get to see her often?"

"No, uh…" She clutched the stem of her glass. "She died seven years ago."

He brushed her knee under the table. "Aw, I'm sorry. I didn't mean to—"

"It's okay." She willed the heat pricking her eyes to disappear. "I like to remember her. She was my soft place to land when things were tough. I was an oddball kid, and my parents couldn't handle me. Gramma got me, gave me my first set of pencils on my tenth birthday, and that smoothed things out."

"Sounds like you were lucky to have her."

"I was." She bit her lip.

He tore at the *injera*. "What about your parents? Do they live around here?"

"No, thank God, but they keep trying to get me to move back home. They want me to help them run their inn on the Eastern Shore. That's where I grew up."

"You?" He raked his gaze over her. "Are a beach bunny?"

She snorted. "Hardly. I never fit in with the beach scene. It operates on island time, whereas I'm more frenetic. Plus I explode into sunburn if I'm not coated in SPF 50. I didn't have much of a chance to go to the beach anyway. Tourist season equaled working season."

"How'd you end up in Baltimore?"

"Art school. Drawing, painting, creating…it completes me, if that makes any sense? But I needed more education than what the schools at the shore could offer. My parents still don't get why I'd refuse a steady job running a family business to chase an elusive art dream."

"Maybe they want stability for you. I've only been at it a few years, but it's natural to want what's best for your kids."

The ice was thin here. Her roommates knew to stay away from this particular topic, but Brendan blundered right into the middle of it. There had to be a way to explain this without invoking her normal explosive, irritated temper. "Their idea of what's best for me is way different from mine."

"And what's that?" he asked. "That's not a challenge. I'm just curious."

"Spending as much time as possible in my studio, creating." She straightened, sitting tall in her chair. Certainty settled in the cells in her body, the way it always did when she fantasized about clocking time in the Tower. "I can't have an emotion without trying to capture it in a picture. The urge to sketch, paint, to create... It's in my bones."

"Sounds intense. You sure it's not arthritis?"

She wagged her finger at him. "You're making fun of my passion, Brendan Stewart. Dangerous move. And you? What gets under your skin?"

"I'm pretty easygoing."

"I find the people who say that usually have an enormous trigger button."

He drummed his fingers on the table. "You've got me. There's one thing that bugs me. My ex not showing up for our kid. Em feels loved, but she still needs her mom to be around more. Jess has it in her head that she'll make it up to her later, but what if Em doesn't want her around at that point?"

Zara pursed her lips. *The ex again.*

Her roommates would beg her not to over-think this. They'd remind her tonight was supposed to be a cotton candy escapade. Nothing deep, but Jesus, she sucked at keeping things light. They'd already covered his ex-wife, Zara's dead grandmother, and, bonus, her mommy and daddy issues.

"Well." She steepled her fingers. "Speaking as someone whose parents never showed up for the stuff that meant the most to me, I can testify it's an unfortunate parenting style."

"It's not a parenting style. It's being shitty." He pushed his sleeves up, and the material bunched further around his biceps.

Whoa. She wanted to lick his forearms. Instead, she drained her *tej*.

"I can't argue with you."

She swept her gaze over Brendan's chiseled features and the

swell of his shoulders under his shirt. Why was she fighting this? She'd throw his baggage in a closet and pretend it didn't exist—the kid, the divorce, and the messy state of his ex-ness—and keep things breezy.

While she was at it, she'd squash her warm and fuzzy feelings for him. Yes, he was kind, and grounded, and had a cute sense of humor. None of which were the reasons she was here. Her ass was parked in this chair because of the way he made her breath catch and her skin sizzle.

She'd focus on the hot. It would be her guiding star toward the shallow end.

"Here, let me feed you," she said, pinching a morsel of the spicy chicken stew. "What did the waitress call it?"

"*Gursha.*" He raised an eyebrow.

"Prepare for a *gursha*, Brendan Stewart."

He opened his mouth and cupped his hand under hers as he took the bite. His warm breath tickled her fingertips as she withdrew.

His lips look so soft.

She shifted in her seat and clasped her thighs together.

"Your turn." He ripped *injera* free from the round. "Which was your favorite?"

"Everything was fantastic." Her gaze circled the food. "You choose."

He mixed the beef *tibs* with the greens and raised himself from his seat for a better angle. Despite his care, he knocked into the corner of her mouth.

"Sorry." He brushed at the spot with his thumb.

A shiver skated up her spine.

"Thank you." She washed the bite down with honeyed wine. "Do you usually treat your date like an empress? FYI, I wouldn't mind a cluster of peeled grapes. Unless you want to fan me with ostrich feathers?"

"I'd love to. Speaking of empresses, and therefore princesses, I've been wondering—"

"How'd I get to be this charming?" She batted her eyelashes at him. *Hmm. I should definitely throttle back on the wine.*

"Obviously you were born with it. Your level of charm can't be learned. No, how'd you start playing Princess Ravenna?"

"Have you looked at me?"

"Yes." He leaned forward. "As much as possible."

"Oh." She flushed, nervous fingers knotting and twisting in her lap.

His unvarnished interest sent her blood pounding through her veins. Showing interest without any subterfuge—giving another person the power to inspect you and maybe say *no thanks*—took some goddamn balls. With the meal almost over, it would be time to go, but she didn't want to part company.

Zara stopped picking her nails under the table. She glanced across the table at the smiling heap of handsome, and oh, there had to be a reasonable way to keep him with her.

Brendan's gaze flicked to the left. "I see the waitress. Do you want dessert?"

"I would, but I'm stuffed. Maybe we could get coffee, or a drink, or…"

"I have an idea." He traced the soft skin of her hand.

Is the back of the hand an erogenous zone?

"I'm listening." She scooted forward. If she wasn't careful, her breasts would end up on the platter, which would be too on the nose.

"You said you live close by, didn't you? Let's get dessert to go; I'll walk you home."

Home? Where giggling roommates with prying eyes lurked? The three of them were probably staked out on the couch, waiting for her, eager to dissect the details of her date.

"No, not my house." There *was* a private place where she could keep him to herself. Bonus, it would be easier to maintain this as fling situation if she didn't have to factor her friends' opinions.

"Of course." He straightened his tie. "I wasn't trying to…"

With her heart pounding against her ribs, she said, "Let's go to my studio. Mind walking me?"

Seven

The outside air cooled Brendan's flushed skin. After the close confines of the tables, and the workout his heart got whenever he touched Zara, he needed to chill. That was a tall order when his body wanted to wrap itself around hers.

From the moment he spied her in her tiny skirt across the street, his thumping blood had washed away the thousand tiny stresses from earlier in the day. Not that he'd spend a second thinking about them now. No, he was taking Mike's advice and shutting down his dad side.

Tonight, Brendan was just a man.

"Which way?" He held open the door.

"Hang a right," she said as she joined him on the sidewalk. "It's a mile from here."

He laced his fingers with hers, and his back stiffened. Stupid, stupid muscle memory. His body hadn't unlearned this stuff since he split with Jess. Like he was on autopilot—walk around with a woman, hold her hand.

He couldn't hesitate now. That'd be worse.

Zara folded her hand around his, her fingertips fitting into the divots between his knuckles, then tugged him south toward the city center.

Stop over-thinking things, Stewart.

"Do you walk this way by yourself?" he asked.

"All the time. There's where I teach the retirees." She knocked her elbow toward the Waxter Senior Center, a red-bricked building anchored by a round turret. She pointed toward the Pla-Za Art Supply store across the street. "I buy my paints and canvases there. If I'm going from my house to the Tower, I hop on the Circulator. Unless it's jacked up. Then I hoof it."

"Doesn't seem safe." He boosted his shoulders, milking his six-two frame for all it was worth. "I'll get an Uber."

"Are you kidding? Cathedral Street is one of the safest streets in the city. My guess is the churchy name keeps the bad juju away."

"But you're so…" He glanced at the top of her slouchy gray winter cap.

"I'm so what?" She angled her face toward him and pinned him with those bright blues. "Feisty? Scrappy?"

He sifted through words, rejecting *naive* and *easy target*.

"Small." There. Small was an indisputable fact.

"I'm not small. You're…large." She popped him on the shoulder. "At five-six, I'm medium, and I'm freakishly strong."

As they marched past a series of shuttered shops, he scanned the shadows. "I've lived here my whole life, and I wouldn't let my mother walk around here on her own."

"*Let?* You wouldn't let her?"

Yeah, that sounded bad when she repeated it back to him. "I mean, I'd offer her a ride."

"Well, aren't you gallant." Zara laughed. "It's fine. A couple of blocks from here is dicey, but this way's fine."

"Trouble from a couple of blocks can migrate. I'm not a nut for thinking you need to be cautious in burned-out parts of Baltimore." He tightened his grip on her hand.

"Thank you for your concern, but I'm good. I do this all the time. Especially in October. I like to pay homage to Edgar Allen Poe's grave."

"Edgar Allen Poe's buried around here? Huh. I didn't know that."

"Are you kidding me? His grave is over at Westminster Hall. It's a minute from here." She quickened her pace and dragged him along the gum-speckled streets. "The fact you've never seen it is a tragedy we are rectifying this second."

Within a few beats of their feet, a gothic brick church erupted from the dark. Its illuminated spire stabbed upward into the hazy February night. In contrast, commercial buildings soared toward the sky, as though they were keeping the rest of downtown Baltimore's bustle at bay.

"There." Zara gestured through the iron rails of a locked gate. A tidy graveyard lay within. Brendan sat the carrier bag of desserts on the sidewalk and stood behind her, hoping his body blocked the biting wind.

"Wow. That's crazy it's right there." He hovered his face next to hers. God, he could get drunk on the citrus and lavender scent of her hair.

"A mystery person used to leave a rose and a bottle of cognac on the grave on the anniversary of his birthday." Her voice had dropped to a reverent hush. The monument's white marble gleamed in the garden lights within the cemetery. "The deliveries have stopped. Nothing for the past couple years, now."

She wrapped her gloved hands around the top spokes of the railing, then bent to inspect the monument. In the process, she'd bumped her ass squarely against his hips, and if she shifted, the friction would make him lose his mind.

Concentrate, Stewart.

"You weren't kidding when you said Poe was your favorite, were you?"

"Of course not. He's the godfather of Goth." Zara released the fence. She tilted her head, maybe to read the monument? The curtain of her hair slid away, exposing her neck.

Did she want him to kiss the smooth, creamy patch between her nape and her jacket? He'd be thrilled to oblige, but if he was reading her wrong, she'd bolt.

Settling for something in between, he traced the cord of her neck that ran from the divot behind her ear to her collarbone. "What's your favorite story of his?"

"*The Tell-Tale Heart*." Her chin nudged her jacket as she glanced over her shoulder at him. The corner of her lush mouth quirked into a smile. Oh, he was gone.

This was an invitation. Had to be.

He cupped her shoulder and waltzed her around to face him.

"These lips." He caressed the alabaster column of her neck and ran his thumb along her bottom lip. "I've wanted to kiss these lips since I found you on my doorstep."

She relaxed against the iron fence and let it hold her upright. "So what are you waiting for?"

"I have no idea."

The moment his lips touched hers, the outside world fell away. The sweet give of her generous mouth tightened his body with need. He cradled the base of her skull to protect her from the unyielding metal behind her, then closed the last sliver of space between them.

Delicious. She was honey and spice and woman.

He broke the kiss, smiled, then pressed his lips to hers once, twice more.

"That was nice," Zara murmured.

"I can do better than nice." His hands drifted to the twin streams of purpled hair coursing down her shoulders. "I have a thing for women who appreciate literature."

"Then, you should see my bedroom. Stacks and stacks of

books."

"Well, now you're talking dirty."

An ambulance siren chirped to life and quickened to a full-blown wail. She stiffened and broke their body contact. *Damn.* These empty arms of his were chilled by her sudden absence.

The emergency vehicle screamed past them.

"I startle easily. C'mon," she said. "My studio's a few blocks away."

"Lead the way."

If she'd said it was on the moon, he'd follow.

~ * ~

"This is me." Zara jerked her thumb over her shoulder, indicating the trim, clock-topped skyscraper behind her. His electrifying kiss still tickled her bruised mouth.

Brendan tipped his head back to drink in the full fifteen stories of the Bromo-Seltzer Arts Tower. "This is your studio?"

"Well, not the whole thing. See those two windows on the corner of the seventh floor? That's my studio."

She spun her jangle of keys on her finger, caught then, then squeezed until the jagged metal bit her palm. Her buzzy bravery from the restaurant evaporated. Was she really bringing him here? Into the Tower? Into her inner sanctum?

This wasn't the plan. This was *never* the plan. She was a worship-a-guy-for-ages-and-hope-he-notices-me kind of girl. Definitely not a take-a-man-home-on-the-first-date kind of girl.

Not a girl. Woman. I am a woman these days.

"Wanna see?" she asked. "It's kind of a hole-in-the-wall, but I love it. Don't get too excited."

"Too late." He grinned and held the plate glass door open.

Inside the building, she nudged the button to prompt the elevator. He would be the third person she'd ever allowed inside her studio. Eleanor had shown her the space, and Melinda helped her install the giant wall easel when she first moved in. Now, Brendan.

The elevator doors slid apart to welcome them, and Zara poked the 7 button. The elevator bounced a bit as it slouched upward, and the doors *whuffed* open on her floor. Artwork tiled the hallway, big splashes of framed color against the neutral gray walls.

"Are any of these yours?" Brendan asked.

"No." She gestured toward the empty swath next to the door to Studio 7-2. "That's where I *would* put my stuff, if I weren't a coward."

"You've got a show coming up, and you don't want people to see your work?"

"I'm ridiculous that way," she confessed. "For a year, I've been hauling my portfolio to galleries, hoping they'd bite, but I haven't put anything on the walls here. People blurt their opinions, and it ruins the vibe of the whole thing. Especially the works-in-progress."

"I do that with complicated web projects. It's because I suspect the code sucks. Like if I hide it, or skip the peer review, I can figure out what's wrong before anyone else notices."

The keys fell from Zara's grip, clattering on the floor in front of her studio.

Was *that* why she hadn't participated in the Residents' Showcases? Was she afraid they'd find her art juvenile or boring? So much so she'd risk sacrificing helpful feedback?

Oh, Gramma would kick her ass if she were alive.

Zara swept up the keys and slipped the right one into brass doorknob. As she dragged open the teak door, the fug of oil paints, linseed, and newspaper greeted them. A smoky undercurrent had settled into the normal mix of smells, changing the bouquet for the better.

"So, this is my home away from home. Word of warning though, the radiator's temperamental, and it can get hot in here." She flicked the light switch inside the door. The overheads flared to life, illuminating the studio's sparse contents.

Besides her tools of the trade, she'd also hauled in whatever paintings and sketches she could find at home. Not because she loved them, but she had to do something to mute the optic white paint the fire restoration team had slapped on after fixing the fire damage.

Ugh. It had to be seventy-eight degrees in here, at least. If she opened the window, the arctic temperature outside would freeze them out. Better to strip off layers instead.

She unzipped her moto jacket and draped it across the back of the studio's single rickety chair, positioned next to a repurposed card table. Removing the jacket helped, but sweat threatened to break out on her upper lip. Perspiration was not a look she was shooting for.

"Wow." Brendan thumbed the buttons on his coat apart. He revolved around the room, scanning the drawings pinned to the wall with the neatness of a butterfly collection. "This is amazing."

Her stomach fluttered. She'd braced herself for the possibility he'd joke his five-year-old could do the same thing. That particular joke was a favorite between her parents. They didn't understand her pursuit of an art career, and they *really* didn't understand abstract art.

Admiration was a welcome surprise.

Letting out a pent-up breath, Zara asked, "Think so?"

"Absolutely. I'm kind of impressed and jealous. It's audacious to believe in yourself enough to chase a dream like this. I respect you going for it. Now's the time for it, too. You have to go for it before you've got obligations to other people."

"I'd go for it no matter what. It's like breathing to me. Feel free to wander."

He strolled from image to image and she catalogued his details as he circuited the studio. His jeans were tight in the right places, his biceps strained against his sleeves, and his facial hair straddled the line between sexy stubble and scruffy scientist. He filled the small room, what with his broad shoulders and thick legs. Every part of her was aware of his presence.

I've got a man in my Tower.

Sparks shot through her veins as she busied herself with the radio in the corner. She struggled to find a station playing romantic, treacle-free tunes. Static... News... Bubble-gum pop... Hair band... Hardcore hip-hop...

There.

Van Morrison, courtesy of the local college radio station. With their freeform platform, the next song might be by a Swedish folk waif or a neo-death metal band. She'd chance it.

Brendan's arm brushed her shoulder as he passed on the way to her worktable. A ribbon of warmth unfurled down her arm and across her chest. Being around him might give her the best, sweetest heart attack possible, if she didn't pass out from the heat in the room first.

He threw his coat on top of hers and placed the bag of desserts on the table. "Where do you want to eat?"

"I've only got the one chair. So, maybe..." Zara peeled off·her long-sleeved T-shirt, leaving her in her snug, paint-speckled tank top. "A picnic?"

She caught him staring at the bits of the cherry blossom tree tattoo peeping above the edges of the tank top. Her belly thrilled. She knew a hungry look when she saw one.

"A picnic?"

"Yeah. You, me, and the food, on the floor."

"Love it," he said. "Do you have a blanket?"

"No, but I'll improvise." She unspooled many feet of canvas from the bolt she kept in a corner and cut it free with her utility knife. After flapping the canvas a few times, she laid it on the shiny hardwoods under the wall easel.

"A renaissance woman." He unpacked the desserts and offered her one.

"Thanks." She folded herself to the floor and hooked her legs to the side. Brendan sat on the wrinkled canvas next to her.

As they ate in silence, Van Morrison crooned about gypsy souls.

What was this weird pause all about? Conversation had been flowing; now they were mired in this sticky, awkward silence. Was it her? Was she doing the gargoyle thing?

Well, screw that. There would be no gargoyling. She would fight her default routine—observe, process, and produce a painting later. Tonight was about living in the present. Like, right now, his lips shone with baklava, and she wanted to know how he tasted.

"Here," she said, offering a spoonful of her tiramisu. "*Gursha.*"

"I can't refuse, right?" Brendan leaned toward her and planted his fists on the floor to balance himself. She glided the spoon into his mouth and his Adam's apple bobbed as he swallowed the bite.

"Thank you," he said. "I'd return the favor, but I finished mine."

He was fixed to the spot, and his arms were pillars holding up the roof of his chest. Those lips, his lips, were a breath away from hers.

It was now or…

Hot and cold swirled in her gut, creating a soupy mess.

Not yet.

Zara jumped to her feet to pace off her jitters.

This was nerve-wracking.

She wanted him in a way that was scary. If she got her wish, tonight would end with him on top of her. Or vice versa. Or both?

She needed to sit with that for a minute, absorb it, and own it.

Except while she was absorbing and owning her unbelievably strong attraction to Brendan, she'd left him hanging mid-kiss, hadn't she? She couldn't hide that her feet had iced over for a second, but she could distract from her hesitation.

"So, I need an opinion." With shaky fingers, Zara snapped on the two floor lamps flanking the behemoth wall easel. They threw a perfect imitation of sunlight on the work-in-progress she'd begun earlier. "Any thoughts on my latest stab at artistic greatness?"

She orbited the room, giving him space, but circled back and stopped behind the still-seated Brendan. She forced herself to stare at the floor. Otherwise, she'd misinterpret every twitch and head tilt.

"Um." He buttressed his torso with back-stretched arms. "I don't know anything about art."

"That's okay. Hit me with your first impressions."

The background of the banner-sized canvas was a perfect, glossy black. Miasmic of jewel tones clouded the bottom of the canvas then resolved into sharp lines curling upward. A lonely amethyst filament forked to the top and kissed the border.

He considered the work, hunching with his hand clamped over his mouth.

He must hate it.

Unable to contain herself, she said, "I can't decide if it's a just started, done, or terrible."

"Nothing's ever really done, though, is it? Done's determined by the go-live date."

"Go-live?"

"Sorry. Techie term. Go-live means a website, or a new feature of a site, goes live to the user. What I mean is that nothing is ever finished to the satisfaction of the creator. I've got a huge deadline in ten days, but if I didn't, I'd tweak the work forever." He straightened his legs and his big boots lay dangerously close to her knees. "Deadlines get the thing out the door."

Jesus. He'd nailed it. She never declared a painting done. She worked on it until she had to turn it in for a grade or submit to a juried show. Had that been her problem this past year? Too much time freedom to work toward perfect?

She massaged her temples and closed her eyes. Having multiple epiphanies in a short span of time would give her an aneurysm.

"Hey, you okay?"

"Yeah. Grappling with big ideas. That's all."

"Well, since you're busy grappling, can I throw away your trash?" He pointed toward her empty container.

"Yes, thanks. Can's in the corner, next to the mini-fridge."

When he returned to their picnic spot, Brendan inspected the big canvas. She was surprised he didn't go cross-eyed, as close as he was to the image. "I like this, by the way. I'm not sure if I was clear about that. It reminds me of the Hubble's photos of other galaxies."

What? Galaxy photos?

She cupped her hands around her neck and stared at her work with fresh eyes. *Shit.* He was exactly right. Her painting was basically a space snapshot anyone could buy off an Etsy site.

She wanted to rip the canvas from the easel and slash it with her utility knife.

"Out of everything, these portraits are my favorites." Brendan, unaware of her quiet existential crisis in the corner, had wandered back to the card table. He gripped its edges, and the weight he put on it made the legs tremble.

"Really?" Zara stuffed down her mounting sense of inadequacy.

At the table, she lodged herself next to him. Distraction would be nice right about now. Especially distraction in the shape of his warm, solid, oak of a body. If she gave him her best shove, she was sure he'd stay upright, and she'd tumble backward.

"These aren't even the finished products," she said. "These are the rejects."

He studied one of an elfin blonde girl with big green eyes. "They're still enchanting. I'm not a man who uses the word 'enchanting' in everyday conversation."

"They're so *easy*. I'm not sweating a thousand decisions for the hour or two it takes me to paint them. They're pretty pictures of little girls. Nothing important."

He scratched at the whiskers on his jaw. "I wouldn't say that. Emma's portrait is important to me. It's hanging on the wall next to my computer. I love it, and I would've paid extra for it."

"That makes me happy." She cast a sidelong glance at him, and her body hummed with awareness. "And I'm not a woman who uses 'happy' in everyday conversation."

"Your talent is special. Why don't you branch into family portraits? There's a huge market for them. It'd be easy to set up a site to—"

"Hell no." Zara shivered. "I prefer to avoid family dynamics. Too much drama, weird tension, and the expectation everyone will be sweetness and light in the painting. Total non-starter for me. The gallery's the right path for me."

"Duly noted, but these rejects are still gorgeous. Maybe you could blend the best of both worlds."

She picked up a portrait and tilted it in the studio light.

Nope. I don't see what he sees.

She dropped it to the table. "These are commercial, sappy pieces. Like the painting equivalent of a Hummel figurine. There's no self-expression. I can't imagine putting them in a real art show."

"Who cares what fits under the 'Real Art' label?" He stood tall and turned toward her. "If people like them, and want to look at them, isn't that something to be proud of?"

"Well, shit." She blew at the stubborn lock of hair blocking her vision of him. It lifted and flopped back in front of her eye. "That's the nicest, most encouraging thing anyone's said to me in years."

"People should only say nice things to you." He tucked the hair behind her ear. His hand lingered, and he brushed his thumb along her jawline.

She nuzzled into it, the friction unspooling thick tendrils of heat through her body. Finally, they'd returned to where they'd been on the street in front of Westminster Hall. Why had she been afraid of this? Anything that focused her restless energy and produced this buzzy tingle couldn't be a bad idea.

"Please." She arched an eyebrow. "Tell me you're not stopping there."

"Your wish is my command, Princess." He unraveled her arms, then tipped her face up toward his. Soft, strong lips explored hers, contrasting with the sting of his raspy jaw.

God, yes. Soap, beer, and a hint of aftershave overwhelmed her senses. She threaded her fingers through his wavy hair and coaxed his head closer, opening her mouth to taste him. Honeyed cinnamon and heat. More. She wanted more. Kissing wasn't enough.

Touching, pressure, skin—that's what she needed.

She smoothed her hands over the firm muscle of his back, kneading as she went. His starched shirt whispered under her palms, and beneath the shirt she found hard, ridged muscle. The earlier sparks in her veins must've been pumped into her pelvis because her hips had a mind of their own. She slid against him. Couldn't help it. Was he as turned on as she was?

A smile graced her lips.

No denying he was turned on. Not unless he'd hidden a flashlight in his pants.

"Tonight's ensemble is better than your dad uniform, but this," she said, catching the knot of his tie, "should come off."

"I agree."

Zara worked the knot, loosening it until she could slither the tie free from his collar. An easy job, and once the tie was gone, Brendan curled toward her, leaning, invading, but also bracing her with his arms belted around her waist.

She didn't worry about falling. Brendan would take care of her.

"Zara." He cradled her face in his palms. "You're beautiful. I'm lucky to be here with you."

"You don't have to feed me lines."

"I'm not." He planted another kiss on her tingling lips. "Just stating facts."

Sincerity beamed from the depths of his gorgeous brown eyes.

She broke eye contact to dip her fingers into his waistband. "Well, thanks. You're beautiful too, but I need to see more to be completely sure."

"I like the way you think."

"Good," she said, tugging on the undershirt and oxford snuggled tight against his hips. The clothes rustled loose, and there…oh, right there. A flash of his skin. She dragged her nails along his waist then burrowed her hands beneath his undershirt and upward toward his chest.

"I can make this easier." Brendan shucked his shirts and tossed them to the ground.

Her breath gushed from her. *Oh, sweet Jesus.*

She was no stranger to the male body. In her art school classes, she'd sketched and painted dozens of them. There'd also been a few boys in her personal past. Emphasis on *boys.* They were striplings, soft-bellied kids. Not men like this.

This was new.

"Can I touch you for a minute?" she asked. "That's not too weird?"

"Be my guest."

He was a landscape she was meant to explore She stippled her fingers along his rounded shoulders and up the cords of his neck. Emma's name and birthdate were tattooed high on his bicep, and the top of a black triangle on his hip. Otherwise, his flesh was unmarked.

She circled around him. Unable to resist, she traced the column of his spine down to where it curved to an ass unfairly hidden beneath his jeans.

"That tickles," he growled.

"Not sorry."

She returned to his front, lightly dragging her fingernails against his waist, and stopped where the wide v-muscle dipped into his waistband.

One night to study this man would not be enough.

"How?" she asked, resting her palm on his chest. Thick, sinewy mounds of muscle shifted under her touch. Was he flexing his pecs, or was his heartbeat high-fiving her?

"How what?"

"How can you be a dad and have a body like this?"

"Good genetics and a shitload of CrossFit."

"I see."

"I'm feeling underdressed."

"Well, we can't have that."

She allowed him to help her shed her thin tank top, leaving her half-nude in her lacy black bra. Friction from his palms ratcheted up the already steamy temperature in the room, and whoa. The smile on his face as he studied her, like she was some exotic creature, perked her nipples to the edge of pain.

Yes. This was the oblivion she'd been seeking. Getting lost in want and desire was shoving all of her anxieties to the side. She and Brendan were the only two people in the world, and all that mattered was getting closer to him.

He hauled her to him. "You're going to get tired of me saying it, but you're beautiful."

"I doubt I will." She arched toward him. "Touch me, please."

"Since you said please..." He cupped her breasts and swept his thumbs over the taut flesh hidden by the frills. Lowering his face, he hopscotched kisses along her collarbone, neck, and cheek, coming to rest next to her ear. Each time his mouth connected to her skin, she was one step closer to liquefaction.

Her breath hitched, and oh God, w*hat was happening?*

She wasn't this animal-passion person. Her history involved lots of quiet fumbling in the dark, keeping a lid on her voice, worrying more about what other people thought than what she was feeling. That wasn't an issue in the Tower. Here, there were no prying eyes and ears.

They were isolated, and there was freedom in being alone together.

He eased her bra cups down and flicked her nipples with his tongue, alternating, taking the buds of flesh in his teeth. Under his attention, they hardened to eraser nubs.

Zara moaned and caressing the length of him straining at the fly of his jeans. Promising.

"You sure this is okay, Princess?" His voice rumbled.

"Yes." She kissed him, breathless. "It's way okay."

"Do you—?"

She undid his belt, his zipper, and reached inside. Silky, smooth, hard. *Jackpot.*

He sucked in his breath. "—want to go to your place? Or mine?"

No. Out there was real. In here, in the Tower, time was suspended. Besides, she would explode if they delayed any further. "I want you here."

He growled, crushing her with a kiss that would leave a mark. Good. She wanted his mark on her body. Edging him backward, toward their picnic spot, she stroked him, eager to get closer. When they arrived at the canvas, they melted against each other, then sank to the floor.

"Help me out of the rest of my gear?" She lay back against the rough canvas.

"Happy to." Brendan knelt at her feet and worked the laces of her boots.

"They're double-knotted."

"I can handle it."

First one, then the other boot thumped to the floor.

He slinked over her body, his knees on either side of her. The broad, warm reality of him hovering over her caused her own body to flood with hot delight. He edged his hands under her, and she arched her back to let him unhook her bra and cast it aside.

"Perfect." His compliment was lost as he kissed the valley between her breasts, down her sternum, to her belly, then stopped his advance at her skirt. Each connection was a tiny spark against her skin and traveled straight to her core. By the time he explored underneath the pleats of her kilt, smoothing his palms over her thighs, she writhed under him.

Who *was* she?

Brendan hooked his fingers into the waist of her tights then slowly peeled them free, a whisper over her skin. All that lay between her and complete exposure was one tiny skirt. One by one, he worked the buttons until the panels fell to the side. He sat on his heels and his gaze roved the slopes of her body.

As she raised herself up on her elbows, her curtain of hair brushed her back. She was the tiniest reflection in his hooded, dark eyes. What did he think of her as she lay there, a pale scoop of porcelain girl, completely, totally nude?

"So, I don't usually wear underwear with tights," she said.

"Lucky me," he said.

Question answered. Dampness rushed between her legs as she licked her lips

She wanted to taste the shapes that stacked up to make Brendan. His neck muscles slanted into his shoulders and created a pyramid of flesh, leading to the thick cut of his chest sprinkled with hair. She followed the scanty trail that whorled down his abs and disappeared into his jeans.

Those have got to go.

His heavy-lidded gaze locked with hers. "Like what you see?"

"I like it, and I want it." Had she actually just said that? Admitting you wanted something, hungered for it, were *desperate* for it meant you couldn't brush off the disappointment if you didn't get it. The admission was worth the risk to her dignity. If she didn't get him, she'd howl.

"Want?" He kicked off his shoes. "Or need?"

"Both."

"Good, because I can't get enough of you." He took her breast in his mouth and sucked the tip into a rigid peak while tweaking the pearled nipple of the other.

It felt so good, so fucking good. He needed to feel something intense too. She scored his back with her nails. Shallow streaks, nothing harsh. But enough for him to remember she'd been there.

The slickness building between her legs expanded into an aching pressure. Brendan shifted and lay on his side next to her. He palmed her sex, stroked the wet seam of her opening.

"What else I can do for you, Princess?"

"Plenty." She placed her hand on his and guided him to her clitoris.

He slid his fingers along either side, gently wheeling around, causing a tingling sensation to tendril from the soles of her feet up through her heart. Her body unfolded for him, and her consciousness was laser-focused on the spot in his hands. She needed sweet release.

"How about now?" He planted a kiss on her mouth. "Do you want me? Or need me?"

She gasped as he withdrew his touch. His absence was intolerable. So were his clothes.

"Need. Need, need, need, need…"

She pushed his jeans and boxers past his ass, palming the smooth, rounded skin along the way. He kicked them off, but not before freeing a foil square from the back pocket.

"Confident, weren't you?" she asked.

"Hopeful." He tore the packet open with his teeth. "Two would've been confident."

"What does it mean that I packed three, then?"

"That you're awesome."

He rolled on the condom, and she pulled him to her, wanting to enjoy the shelter of his body. There was his cock, jutting from his hips, pressed to her sensitive, swollen sex.

This was it. The mind-blowing, mind-numbing, get-out-of-her-head sex she'd been hoping for since she saw him waiting for her outside the restaurant. Since she saw him on his doorstep, if she was being honest with herself.

He coaxed her legs further apart. She tented them and twitched her hips, encouraging him. He ground against her, slipping back and forth, covering himself with her anticipation.

He nipped her ear. "Ready for me, Princess?"

~ * ~

Her whispered, simple, "Yes," nearly made him come.

Zara's sparkling eyes searched his, waiting, anticipating. Fuck, he was a king with this woman pinned beneath him. Everything he'd normally worry about had taken a hike from his brain. Reliable, protective, good boy Brendan didn't have sex with first-time dates on the floor in a downtown building.

That guy sure as hell didn't know how good it could feel.

He eased his full length into her, and his mind went blank. Christ, their hips fit together like long-lost puzzle pieces. It had been so long—too long—and for his re-entry to be with this gorgeous woman? It was like hitting the fucking lottery.

She moaned and dragged her hands down his back. Her inner muscles gripped him, three hundred sixty degree pressure. Tender tightness spread from his root upward, outward, until his body buzzed with tension.

Scaling his arms, her fingertips scrutinized the muscles of his shoulders. She entangled her fingers in his hair and fixed him with her glacier-blue eyes.

As she squeezed her thighs around him, she whispered, "I won't break."

"Good to know," he said and covered her mouth with his.

He rocked in and out, slow, then building speed. She wrapped her eager arms around him and raised her hips to meet his thrusts. He dipped his head low, kissed her neck, and worked his way to her breasts.

Her dark pink nipples waited for him. He tongued one then the other, unhurried and worshipful. Their hardness thrilled him. She wanted him as much as he wanted her.

Zara moaned and arched her back.

I'm going to come if I don't change rhythm.

He draped her leg over his shoulder. Here, on the floor, this wouldn't be as perfect a fit. Good, because he'd never last, otherwise.

He kneaded her soft, creamy thigh as he thrust, again and again and again. Zara's breasts swayed with the motion, and she caught one, massaged her nipple, rolling the erect flesh between her fingers. Her other hand snaked down to her clit, circling, circling, circling it. Every time he tunneled into her, her fingertips brushed his cock.

Man up, Stewart. Ten minutes, at least. But Jesus fucking Christ. Look at her.

~ * ~

Zara moaned. "Oh, God, yes. There."

Her chest was warm, the skin taut. The heat flared up her neck and swirled into her cheeks. She'd become a hot, dissolving ball of need, and she thought she would come apart at the seams.

Her sighs—short, kittenish bursts—grew thinner, higher, and more desperate.

Any thoughts she had were quelled by the pressure building inside her.

He released her leg and kissed her, eating her moans. She tightened around him, digging her fingers into his flesh as the tension burst and sent spasms of gasping bliss through her body. She bucked her hips with each fresh tidal wave, calming when the pleasure faded to a swish.

She opened her glazed eyes, broke off the kiss, and held the face of this man who had pulled her to pieces and put her back together again.

~ * ~

"Did you come?" Brendan asked. He planked over Zara, his cock buried deep within her core. As she'd moaned, he'd kissed the lipstick off her mouth, leaving behind a smeared rose tint.

"God yes."

Desperate to keep going, he needed to check on her first, give her a moment to wallow in the afterglow. He smoothed a rebellious lock of hair from her face. "I can't stop staring at you."

"Let me give you a fresh view," she drawled. "I want to be on top. Lay down."

He didn't need to be told twice.

With confident hands, she wedged his eager cock at her opening and sank down. On a groan, she tipped her head to the side, and her hair kissed her breasts.

He was hard before, but with this view? Pure steel.

"Good?" she asked.

"Fantastic."

She rode him. Steady, slow, and sweet as molasses. It was everything he could have wanted. The sensations, the visuals, everything challenged his control. Her ass pillowed against his thighs each time she dropped down, and her breasts bobbed with her effort.

Yes, she was an artist, but she was also art. With her black hair, milky skin, and the overhead lights flaring, this woman was an angel— a fallen angel, who was enjoying earthly pleasures. One who was giving him one of the best nights of his life.

"Tell me what you want," she demanded, her voice ragged around the edges. A bead of sweat snaked a course between her ivory breasts.

He laced his fingers with hers to give her leverage, and they locked gazes. "You, for as long as I can have you."

Low groans spilled from her lips and she sped up her rhythm. "I…I'm going to…come again."

"I'm coming with you this time," he ground out.

Slipping his hands to her hips, he bent his legs and thrust upward over and over again. After a few strokes, a familiar electric pulsing ball of pleasure began to build in his balls. It grew bigger until he couldn't hold onto it anymore, didn't *want* to hold onto it anymore.

She gasped above him, and the dam burst. He moaned as his cock shuddered inside her, his body melting with satisfaction. Zara fell forward against him, all loose elastic and sinew, fitting herself to the contours of his body.

With her face resting on his chest, he belted his arms around her and kissed the top of her head.

"Happy Valentine's Day," he said.

~ * ~

Zara chuckled. "Same to you."

Her hair spilled across her face and onto Brendan's chest, a tapestry of purple and black. It half-hid her smile, which, at the moment, was the only part of her body she could control.

"We," he said as his fingers lazed a circle on her bare shoulder, "should do this again."

"I agree." One night with him wouldn't be enough. The pesky fun-killer side of her brain was already yelling at her. She had work to do, work that takes time to tease into perfection, and she couldn't whittle away her precious days and hours with a distraction named Brendan.

A distraction whose heart, at this minute, drummed a bluesy beat under her ear.

Her smile dimmed.

Her schedule wasn't the only issue. The tattoo on his arm was a black and white reminder of why she couldn't make a habit of him. He was a package deal. A second date could lead to a third, which could lead to many more. What was the point if she'd never sign on to share her life with a kid?

So she should not agree to do this again with Brendan.

Even if her eyes went starry when he came near.

She thumbed the raspy line of his jaw. It would be easier to say no to a second date if she didn't know sex between them could transform her into happy jelly. This was the height of unfair. She needed to fire whoever organized the order of events in her universe. The good stuff, the *best* stuff, happened at the *worst* possible times.

No matter what, they had tonight.

"Me too. Think you can go again in a half hour?" she asked, twisting what he meant by 'again.'

His fingers skated down her back and lodged on the crook of her hip.

"I could go again in five minutes. Not what I meant though, Princess. I want to see you again. Another date. Many more dates. Because I like you."

With a Herculean effort, she eased upright. He stayed within her, thick and relaxed.

Zara took a deep breath to muster the energy to turn him down. Saying yes wouldn't be fair to either of them, but mostly him. Not if she already knew this was doomed. She wouldn't mention his baggage. She'd keep the focus on her situation, and how she *had* to deliver those pieces to the Schwarz Gallery by her deadline. Which meant she couldn't make any promises about future dates.

It sounded good and smart in her head.

Before she uttered a word, he threw an arm behind his head to prop it up, and his eyes creased with his smile. His other hand stayed anchored to her hip. "God, you're beautiful."

He wasn't making this easy.

She appraised herself like she might a nude model in class—her rose-tipped breasts, her pearly skin, and her slender thighs wrapped tight to this man's hips.

"I'm not bad. Beauty comes and goes." She grazed the bumpy lines of his corrugated abdomen. "I'd rather be interesting."

"You're both." He caught her hand and kissed the calloused pads of each finger.

Her head told her to stop him, stop this from going any further…

Her heart, though—oh, her soft and crazy heart—fought her nagging brain. It told her none of the logical junk mattered, because if he could convert her into this relaxed, happy, satisfied self, she needed to give it a chance.

For the first time in forever, her heart won.

She bent forward to claim a kiss from the man between her legs.

Eight

Hours later, Zara lay wrapped in Brendan's arms on the floor of her studio, catching her breath. She'd traced the thick beams supporting the ceiling with her eyes.

"Good thing we both came prepared." She swirled her index finger around his shoulder.

"I won't be able to walk for a week, Princess."

She loved the way his voice rumbled.

"I expect you to recover by Saturday." Between jobs and custody arrangements, Saturday was the next night they both had free. "You'll need your legs."

"Sounds promising."

"If I were you, I'd be excited."

His chest rose under her as it ballooned with a deep breath. "Listen, I've gotta ask you a question."

Her adrenaline spiked. "What is it?"

He swallowed hard, and his Adam's apple bobbed in his throat. "I'm out of practice when it comes to dating. Whatever you want is okay. Do you want to stay the night at my place? My kid's at her mother's. Or I can get you home safe to yours."

"Oh." Zara bit her lip.

She pictured his house decorated in birthday party shimmer. Definitely nope. Not ready for that yet. He couldn't stay at her place. Her roommates would attempt small talk with him over coffee. Christ, Brooke would probably ask him to show her his abs.

"We should head home. To our own homes, I mean."

"Okey-doke." He kissed her head. "Clothing is a good idea, then."

"Well, if you want to be *boring*."

"Boring's not bad, but a frostbitten ass would suck. 'Scuse me, Princess." He pushed up from the floor. "I left my pants by the table. Which is a sentence I've never said before."

She peeled away from him, reaching for her skirt and tights, and he padded to his puddle of clothes. The curve and shift of his back muscles as he hopped into his jeans and buckled his belt was mesmerizing.

A shivery breath escaped her.

Oh, how her fingers tingled for a charcoal nub, a scrap of pencil, or ink. She wanted to command him to stop so she could darken her best acid-free, 64-pound stock with a sketch of his body. But his tired Vitruvian Man stretch hinted she should save her request. Another time. He slipped into his snug white tee and blue dress shirt, but he left the oxford unbuttoned.

His tie lay crumpled on the floor under her tank top. Scooping it up, she wrapped it around her neck and fidgeted with it until she produced a passable Windsor knot.

"Here," she said, "I tied your tie for you. I like the colors, by the way. Real men wear purple."

"It suits you better. Keep it, if you like it."

"Thank you." She let the material slip through her fingers and flop against her belly, then checked the time on her phone. "Oh, perfect. The bus will be here in fifteen minutes. I won't have to rush."

"I'm not sticking you on a bus. I'm seeing you home, safe and sound."

"This again?" She bundled into her coat and hat.

He held out her messenger bag. "Let me guess. You ride the bus in the dead of night?"

"All the time. I'm a big girl, and I have faith in humankind."

"Faith is crucial, but caution's good too." He riffled his hair. "But *I* can't handle wondering if you're safe. Do me a favor, and let me take you home."

She flicked off the lights and locked the door of her studio behind them.

"Okay," she grumbled. "But only as a favor to you. *Not* because I need you to."

"I'll take it." The elevator ride shushed them to the lobby, and Brendan requested an Uber. "Address?"

Hesitating for a second, she finally spit out her address on West Eager Street.

"Wow, only two minutes," he said. "Guess you don't have to wait long this time of night."

Out on the street, the wintry air stole her breath.

"Guess not," she said. True to the estimate, a car rolled up a few minutes later.

Opening the rear door, Brendan swept his arm, and said, "Your carriage, Princess."

"If I'm a princess, does that make you a prince? Or a footman?"

"Whatever you want me to be."

She settled herself within, scooting to the side to make room for him. After he climbed in beside her, he confirmed the destination with the driver and reached for her hand in the back seat. Within a few quiet minutes they were in front of her house. *Aw.* Her roommates had left on the light. She grabbed the cab's door handle. How do you say goodbye at the end of a date like this? She'd never *had* a date like this. "Tonight was—"

"Hold that thought. Sir," he said to the driver, "wait here for me?"

The driver nodded, and Brendan jumped from his side and circled around to open her door.

"This isn't necessary," she said as he helped her from the car.

"It is for me." He escorted her to her front door. The car purred at the curb and puffed white exhaust into the night.

"Honestly, you didn't have to, but thank you. Tonight was great. Every part of it."

"I agree." Under the porch light, he planted another wooze-inducing kiss on her swollen lips, palmed her ass, and drew her in close. "See you Saturday, Princess."

He backed toward the car, but didn't climb inside, waiting for her to enter the house before he left. She twisted the key like a crank on a jack-in-the-box, hoping the slow tumble stifled the clunky lock. Not exactly sneaking in, but she didn't want to call more attention to her arrival than necessary. Despite the late hour, if her roommates were awake, they'd demand an instant replay.

Her shoulders lowered, she swung the door open, and her breath whooshed from her in relief. The living room was dark and empty. She didn't want to dissect the past couple of hours. Not yet.

Zara preferred to keep the night to herself, whole and intact.

She waved goodbye to Brendan, closed the door, then crept upstairs to her room. In the middle of the hallway, she paused. Distinct creaking noises came from behind Brooke's door. Well, now. She hadn't been the only roommate to get some Valentine's action. Wonder who the lucky guy was?

In her room, Zara changed into pajamas, the drag of fabric against her back reigniting the rough redness she'd earned on the floor. She pictured Brendan's corded body above hers and smiled.

Fatigue clutched at her, and she collapsed into her bed. Wait, her alarm. She reached for her phone to set it for 5:00 a.m. A fresh text shone on the screen. Brendan.

"Can't wait until Saturday. Sweet dreams, princess."

Before she could second-guess herself, she typed, *"They'll be sweet because you'll be in them."*

Send. Zara from a week ago would have thrown up from the sugar in those texts. Today, the sweetness tasted good.

She squinted at the red balloon next to the phone icon. Whoops. She'd missed a call from her parents. They'd left a voice mail, but... *Nah. Too tired and happy to deal right now.* She set down the phone, curled up against a pillow, and fell into a deep, dream-filled sleep.

~ * ~

As the sun rose on Thursday morning, Zara returned to the Tower. She bounced along the hall toward her studio, slipped her key in the door lock, and flung it wide.

Today, within these walls, she'd start something beautiful. The truth of it hummed in her fingers.

The space presented the familiar aromatic bouquet of paints, canvas, and solvents. Despite the radiator hissing steam, the whole vibe of the room was more relaxed than the last time she painted.

Of course, maybe *she* was more relaxed. With fluid, oiled movements, she dropped her winter gear on the floor next to the radiator and stripped to her Cocteau Twins T-shirt. She'd threaded Brendan's tie through the belt loops of her jeans to complete today's work outfit.

"Listen you." She kicked at the ancient metal heater. "I've got too much to do today. If you could chill out, I'd appreciate it."

It clanged in response.

"Fine." She flipped the latch on one of the studio's tall windows.

This morning was warmer than last night, so she could cool the room without risking hypothermia. Since she'd be working with paints and spirits today, she'd need to ventilate anyway. As the creaky window pane slid upward, invigorating air swirled around her and the sketches pinned to the wall began to flap.

She stuck her head outside to let the cold, crisp air wash over her tired eyes.

Coffee.

Ten minutes later, she sat on the floor in front of her easel, drinking a scalding cup of fresh-brewed black. There was no question. *Trouble with Hubble* had to go.

Zara set down her chipped mug and spun the wall easel's tension knobs to lower the bottom support. She yanked the painting free of the easel's jaws and crossed the room to the desolate spot where she tacked up her failed efforts. Over the years, glaring examples of what *not* to do were as helpful as any successes she had.

At her request, the fire damage restoration team hadn't bothered with this wall of the studio. The soot loaned her collection of rejected works the gothic vibe they deserved. *Hmph.* Apparently, she'd been failing hard in the week since she'd moved back into the studio. There wasn't much real estate among the tattered, pimpled sketches and paintings. That bare spot high in the corner would be perfect.

Killing a piece of art always made her queasy, but it had to be done. Otherwise, she'd waste time trying to torture it into perfection. She flipped open the lid of her toolbox and fished out the necessary tools. With the hammer tucked into her belt and a nail dangling between her lips like a cigarette, she climbed the step stool against the wall.

"Was good knowing you," she mumbled, then spiked the painting to the wall.

Now, time to work on something new. The rumpled cloth that had served as last night's picnic blanket would be the skin of a new painting. Maybe the magic from their Valentine's escapades would infuse the canvas. Grinning, she gathered it in her arms and hugged it to her chest.

Was that only a couple of hours ago?

The delicious soreness between her legs answered her.

She snapped the canvas a few times and measured off the amount of material she'd need. With her utility knife, she slashed and tore until she had a perfect, ragged rectangle. Next, she folded the canvas around the frame, stapled it to the wood, then squirted a blob of Gesso onto her palette.

Creating a blank slate of pure possibility was joyful and terrifying.

She saturated the bristles of her brush until they were fat with white then coated the canvas with a thick layer of primer. As she worked, an idea took shape, an idea full of bold color and sweeping lines. Each stroke of her brush whispered to her about last night.

About Brendan.

~ * ~

On Friday, Zara palmed the center of the big canvas. She'd built a few others, sanded them, and performed an encore round of priming and polishing. Now, their surfaces were smoother than ice cream.

This canvas was ready, but best of all, *she* was ready to paint. The idea had formed as she'd built this canvas, familiarizing herself with each warp of the wood and pucker in the cloth. The only challenge would be how skillfully her hands could translate the image into paint.

She chewed on her bottom lip.

This idea…it could be awful. Last night, locked in the Tower and waiting for paint to dry, she'd sketched a dozen variations on the same intimate theme. Try as she might to redirect her insistent fingers to other ideas, they refused. This was *the* painting, and until she exorcised it, it would haunt her.

Haunt wasn't the right word. Flirt? Yes, that was better. The idea would flirt with her, seduce her, occupy her every thought until she acted on it. And honestly, she wanted to act on it. Every time she pictured Brendan, a hot thrum rolled down her spine and circled around her hips.

For the first time in years, she wanted to paint a realistic image of people. Sure, she'd whipped up the mini-portraits for birthday parties, but those were basically on-demand doodles with zero underlying emotion.

Today would be different.

Seven years ago, she'd put away her brushes to take care of her grandmother. Then, after Gramma died, she'd reopened her kit and began an abstract, exploratory period. At the time, she'd wanted to vomit her feelings onto her canvases. Grief, anger, depression. Those emotions didn't have a form.

Abstracts were also open for interpretation, so she'd always have plausible deniability about her heart's contents. People could read into it whatever they wanted.

She queued up the *Paint NOW* playlist on her phone. She'd semi-stolen Grier's fancy speaker, so instead of tinny beats coming from the phone, Britney Spears's "Work Bitch" pounded into the studio. Zara didn't want the things detailed in the song, but she subscribed to the philosophy. You don't get what you want by sitting on your ass and hoping for it.

She picked up her beta pen, tapped it against her chin, and squinted at the canvas. The starting point was hiding in the huge rectangle trapped in the easel. Her job was to find it.

There. I'll start right there.

The work was quick. Broad swoops at first, tighter focus as she scratched detail into the skin of the canvas. She backed away and considered the outlines. Excitement rippled through her veins. Even though this was not her normal style, not her normal focus, it worked.

It was as if every inch of the canvas whispered, *Keep going.*

An hour of furious sketching later, and she'd roughed in the image she wanted.

Perfect.

Off came the lids of the mason jars containing her paints. Their familiar scent was home. It was the paint recipe her gramma had used, an invigorating mix of color, mineral spirits, linseed oils, turpentine, and oil of cloves.

Everything seemed right for a change.

Zara dolloped the paints onto her palette stepped back, then took a deep breath to fight the knot forming in her stomach.

"Please let me not fuck this up," she said to the room.

Each painting had potential to be the best piece of art she'd ever produced, or to be the worst garbage seen by human eyes. To capture what she was feeling—the explosive giddy hope that was way outside of her wheelhouse of emotions—this canvas *had* to be the best. Anything else would be a crushing disappointment.

No pressure, right?

Washing in the colors with her round brush, the figures took shape.

The ghost of them, anyway.

She squinted. It was good. Wasn't it?

Break. Whenever she lost the ability to discern good from bad, she needed a break. Zara put the brushes down, walked away, then stared out the window to cleanse her critical eye. The watery morning sunshine lit up the emerald fields within Oriole Park at Camden Yards and gleamed against the highways twisting into the city streets.

After waiting through one traffic light at the intersection of Howard and Conway Streets, she turned back to the canvas.

Relief flowed through her. It *was* good. This sparkly buzz was the same way she'd felt about the paintings that had gotten her into the Schwarz Gallery show. Unlike then, though, the buzz was strong enough to rattle her teeth.

With zero doubt in her bones, she'd bring these shapes to life with thick, bold strokes of color.

Five unbroken hours later, pounding at her door startled the brush from her grip.

"Hello?" she called and twisted her hands in the turpentine rag from her paint tray.

"It's me," Eleanor answered.

When Zara flung the door wide, her mentor proffered an

explosion of purple flowers.

"An arrangement." The older woman peeked above the enormous bouquet. "For you."

"Me?" Zara blinked. Flowers? This was a first.

Something hatched in her chest. Something suspiciously like happiness.

"Can I come in, dear? These are heavy."

Zara hesitated. Her protective gaze flicked toward the glistening canvas. Eleanor critiqued fresh work, whether you wanted her to or not. Then again, hiding hadn't been doing the trick for Zara either. Maybe an early critique would be a good thing.

"Of course." She tucked the rag into her jeans pocket and took the vase. Whoa. They were sledgehammer heavy. The immense collection of flowers tickled her cheek and smelled divine. Lilies, roses, and others she couldn't name.

Only one person in the universe would have sent these.

Warmth pooled in the soles of her feet, twined around her legs, her hips, her torso, and settled on her chest. She situated the flowers on the deep windowsill, found the envelope nestled next to a lily, then plucked it from its plastic trident.

The card read, "A bloom for each time I've thought of you since our date, Princess. Can't wait until tomorrow."

She smiled, and the warm sensation drifted up to her cheeks. It was only fair he'd been thinking about her. He'd been on her mind often enough these past two days, he owed her brain rent.

I should call to thank him.

The sharp corners of the card bit into her fingers as she reread the message.

Happiness was an ensemble she hadn't worn much in the past couple years. Did it even fit anymore? She never would've guessed this man, *so* not who she would have sketched out on paper for herself, would be the one to inspire shiny emotions.

Because the kid. The ex. The way he dismissed my intention never to have kids. The fact that caring about people means giving up your dreams.

The warmth cooled and dripped down her front like she'd been egged in the face.

"Zara Kissette," Eleanor yelled.

She dropped the card and it sifted to the floor. "Yes?"

Her mentor had sidled up to the wall easel. "What is *this*?"

"A new piece." Zara tucked her shoulders inward and chewed her thumbnail.

Eleanor retrograded then went direct, her jersey skirt billowing behind her. She stopped a hand's breadth away from the canvas, lifted her dangling glasses from where they lay on her sternum, and set them on the tip of her nose.

She sniffed and pivoted. "Zara."

"Yes ma'am."

"You did this in one day?"

Zara nodded.

"The whole thing?"

"I painted the whole thing today, but I made the canvases yesterday. The composition came to me as I Gessoed them. Why?"

"Because *this*..." She gestured at the painting. "This is your best work."

The tension melted from Zara's shoulders. "You think so?"

"Oh, honey, *yes*. The strokes are bold, thick, and passionate. Your heart vibrates in this." She hovered her hand over the surface. "John will love it."

"He won't be pissed?" Zara planted her butt on the windowsill next to the flowers. The low soughing of the breeze through the open window cooled the sweat under her arms. "I expected he'd want the pieces I showed him. I tried to recreate them, but they didn't come together. Something was off."

"No." Eleanor waved the notion away. "John knows good art, and this, Zara, is *exceptional*."

Zara hugged herself. "I hoped it was. It felt right while I was painting it."

"That's excellent." Eleanor dashed over to Zara and gripped her by the shoulders. "Have you ever experienced that sense of rightness before?"

"Yes, but it's been a long time." She glanced at the bursting vase of flowers on her worktable.

"It's the sixth sense for what's true. Memorize it. You are blessed and favored, my dear, to identify it this young. Not all artists experience it. For some, it takes a lifetime." She released Zara and smiled beatifically. "And you are such a baby artist."

"I'm not a *baby*."

"Says the pouting child. Don't take offense." Eleanor lifted a shoulder. "I was a baby until last week. Zara, I'm glad you've hit your stride this early in your career."

"Has my stuff been bad until now?" Zara asked.

"Of course not. I would never have dreamed of connecting you with John if your paintings were lackluster. He's an old friend, and I know what catches his eye. May I be honest, even if it stings a bit?"

Zara's chest expanded with the deep breath she drank down. "Hit me."

"Since you've been with us in the Tower, your creations have been workmanlike. You hit the correct technical notes, but you've had no *passion*. As though you adhered to an algorithm for creating beautiful images. Like those adorable portraits on the table. Until today." Eleanor glided to the easel. "This piece oozes passion. I can't stay away from it. It's captivating."

The air puffed from her until she was on the verge of crumpling in relief. Instead, Zara clutched the windowsill to keep herself upright.

She'd done it. Like a magician, she'd conjured the exact emotions she wanted from Eleanor. During her night with Brendan, Zara's heart soaked up their passion, which she'd taken and wrung out on the canvas. Even though she'd doubted herself, here was Eleanor, telling her she'd succeeded.

That wasn't luck. That was the power of an artist who owns her craft.

"Will this be a series?" Her mentor flicked a glance over her shoulder at Zara. "Will you produce more paintings in this vein? *Please* tell me this is your new direction. It *must* be."

It can't be. I have thrown a private moment between two people onto a huge canvas, and only one of us knows it.

"Zara Kissette, you've found your voice. You must *speak*. Whatever it is you need to do to keep producing this? Do it."

It's not so much what as it is whom.

~ * ~

An hour later, after Eleanor left, Zara ripped the nail from the canvas she'd crucified on Monday.

Enough beating myself up for my mistakes.

She laid *Hubble* on the floor. Next, she peeled down the tattered victims of the fire and sprinklers. Once the wall was empty, she scraped swatches of tape free and added them to the pile at her feet.

On the wall, the collection had appeared to be a massive amount of work. Stacked on the floor, the pile was small, which could be translated as inconsequential. Nope. Not even a little bit of truth to that, because as part of her evolution, these pieces were vital.

She *had* to spend time creating these works to achieve her current style and level of skill. They'd served their purpose, and she didn't need them anymore. These were the molted feathers of her old self. She trash-bagged them and left the lumpy sack in the corner.

With her hammer and fresh hooks in hand, she canted her head and considered the now-empty wall.

Time to shine a spotlight on what's working.

~ * ~

Later that night, Zara twisted her damp hair into a bun and checked her reflection in the foyer mirror. After her shower, she had no time to paint on her typical complicated makeup. So, here she was, off to work, half-armored in matte red lips.

Relax. It's a Wine & Paint night, not a date.

"Zar!" Brooke shouted from upstairs. "That you?"

"Yeah, but I'm leaving for work."

"Hold up a minute, okay? I have to find my shoes, and we can walk together."

"Okay." Zara pinched the bridge of her nose. She'd dodged her roommates since Valentine's Day, hoping their curiosity would evaporate. Her brilliant plan hadn't worked, and her phone had buzzed with texts more than bees in a hive these past two days. No chance she could stonewall Brooke for the ten-minute walk to work, despite her reputation as a gargoyle.

Zara didn't hash out her emotions, even if they were the shiny happy kind. 'Cause when the shiny turned to shit, and it *always* did, she'd have to endure pitying stares and pep talks. Much easier to keep her heart wrapped like a mummy, even though it was so full of shiny happiness it probably glowed.

"Hurry up, Brooke. The Winers riot if I'm late." She unhooked her keys from the rack, flipped the deadbolt, and then opened the front door. Street noise and a chill burst through the gaping threshold.

"Coming." Brooke bounded down the creaky staircase, clutching her violin case in one hand and the hem of her voluminous black skirt in the other. Her conservative fishtail braid roped its way along the front of her crisp, white oxford. Prim from the front, but as she rounded the newel post, she brought the sexy with her shirt's lacy back panel.

"New threads?" Zara hadn't seen her friend decked out in a performance ensemble since…wow, since Christmas, maybe? God, she might as well have bricked herself up in her studio at the Tower for all the real life she'd missed.

"New-ish. In addition to fattening my world-travel-savings account, nude modeling ironically pays for my symphony clothes."

Zara's own work uniform was the epitome of genderless chic—khakis and a polo shirt with the Wine & Paint logo embroidered at the breast. She gothed it up as best she could with combat boots, a chunky studded belt, and a leather wrist cuff, but there were limits to stylizing corporate gear.

"I'm dying to hear how your date went." Brooke slipped into her green puffer coat, collected her violin, then followed Zara. "We've got eight blocks for you to gimme the dirt. It must've been fantastic because you weren't home by the time I went to bed."

"Were you waiting up for me that night?" Zara closed the door and locked the deadbolt. "Sounded like you had company."

"Yes I waited, because I fucking love you." Brooke pressed a fist to her hip. "But then I got distracted. Anyway, give me details before you go all hushy. You hunker down when you're crushing on someone."

"I do?" She dropped her keys in her messenger bag and buckled it shut. She hopped from the stoop to the street and they started walking toward Symphony Hall.

"Your tell is radio silence. Like you're afraid you're gonna jinx it."

Yeah, because bad shit happens to whatever I care about. Zara wrinkled her forehead. Where did that come from? She didn't care about Brendan that deeply. Not yet. How could she?

Wait...what did she mean by "not yet?"

Argh. This was not supposed to be that complicated.

Maybe she'd spill some details, get Brooke's take on her night with him. A chat might even zap the distracting feels churning inside. Every time Zara tried to concentrate on work during the past two days, her sneaky brain kept returning to him—sifting through the warm fuzzy compliments he'd rained on her, the way her body had exploded in a rainbow of pleasure, and the chivalrous way he'd attended her.

If it weren't for his family and 'ex' situation, she might—

"Zar, come *on.* You're killing me."

Brooke would be a perfect confessor too. Grier and Melinda were too gooey, but Brooke didn't have a sentimental bone in her body. She'd cackle, tell Zara to calm the fuck down and enjoy herself for a day, a week, or whatever, and it'd be fine.

"Okay, but I swear if you make any kissy noises or utter the word '*lurve,*' I'm shutting it down."

"I won't. I swear on my brother's safety."

"Jeez, you don't have to whip out the big guns."

Zara hastened west, toward the late winter sunset unfurling orange stripes across the sky.

"I wanted to show you I'm serious. Now talk."

The deep breath Zara took cooled the back of her throat. "So, the goal was to get out of my head, right? Live a little, fill the well. Achievement one hundred percent unlocked. Being with him sparked tons of new ideas. I mostly finished a painting today. A good one."

"That's amazeballs. Isn't it? I mean, it takes you forever to paint your nails."

"It was crazy how the whole thing…" Zara undulated her arms, "…flowed. That hasn't happened in forever."

"So is it another abstract, then?"

"Uh, abstract*ish*, I guess?"

Brooke nudged her. "Cool. Now tell me about your date."

They clomped along Eager Street in silence.

You can do this. Start small.

"We went to Dukem. I recommend it. We split a—"

"Ugh, you're the worst." Brooke threw her arms wide. "Not the menu. I want the blow-by-blow *on the boy*. At least, I hope there was blowing."

Zara's cheeks heated. She couldn't plot a better lead-in or a more enthusiastic audience, but her heart rattled in her chest. "Not blowing, but…much sex. Dry spell over."

"*What?*" Brooke clutched Zara's arm and dragged her to a stop. "We thought you were painting out your frustrations in your studio until the middle of the night. This is *way* better."

She threw her arms around Zara, and her violin case slapped her back. "Ow."

"Sorry." Brooke let go. "But I'm proud of you."

Zara jabbed at the crossing signal's button. "It's weird to be proud of your friend for hooking up."

"No it's not. This is a huge thing for you." Brooke eyed her as they stepped over the dirty snow edging the curb. "*Was* it huge?"

"Groan. Don't make me regret confiding in you."

"Sorry." Her friend laughed. "I'll stop. Tell me what happened. Don't leave anything out."

"Dinner was…tactile." Zara licked her lips. "All of these casual touches, like, our fingertips brushing or he'd put his hand on mine, and he helped me take off my jacket."

"The 'can't stop touching each other' stage is the *best*, isn't it?"

"It kind of is. Each touch was like…" Zara paused, searching for the right image. "Like it lit up whatever patch of skin he grazed. By the time dinner was over, I wanted to climb on top of him."

"Whoa, Zar. This is a whole new level of detail you're giving me here. That's not like you."

"Because I'm trying to understand it, so I keep *thinking* about it. I've never had this kind of reaction to a guy, much less *this* kind of guy with his ironed clothes and steady job. When he offered to see me home safely, and he grabbed my hand out of the blue, I swear my heart skipped three beats."

"But you didn't come home. Did you go to his place or something?"

"No, I..." She shoved her gloved hands into the shallow pockets of her motto jacket. "I took him to the Tower. To my studio."

"*O mój boże!*" Brooke stopped in the middle of the sidewalk. "You haven't even let *us* in your studio. Wait, is that because your studio is actually a sex dungeon?"

"We've got to keep moving, or I'll be late." Zara looped her arm through Brooke's and dragged her along. Their feet flashed over the sidewalk's bricks. "My studio is categorically *not* a sex dungeon, but it *is* private. I wasn't sure how far things would go, but I'd been staring at the way this beautiful man's clothes hugged his body, loving the laugh crinkles around his eyes, feeding him—"

"Feeding him?"

"It's a thing with Ethiopian food, and it's romantic if you do it right. Anyway, I wasn't sure I'd invite him up. I was still trying to figure out what to do when we stopped by Poe's grave and...we kissed."

Heat bloomed fresh across her skin. The phantoms of the rough iron rails against her back, and the rasp of Brendan's whiskers sweeping her cheek.

"Yay! I mean, it's twisted it happened at a graveyard, but so you." Brooke clutched Zara's arm. "Please tell me he's a good kisser."

"He melted me. I couldn't stand up straight afterward."

Brooke kept silent for a few paces before muttering, "Wow."

The biggest, squishiest, most uncomfortable reveal was next. Zara gulped and clenched her belly muscles, the same way she did at the shore when she swung out on the rope swing, let go, and plunged into the deep of the bay.

"Yeah. That's why I decided to let him into the Tower. If his kiss could turn my brain to putty, I wondered what the rest of him could do."

"That's where you..."

"Yeah." She shuddered as a deep well of desire rippled within. "Three times."

"Holy shit, Zar! Stamina like that is a treasure. When are you seeing him again?"

"Tomorrow. He sent me flowers." Zara steamrolled over

Brooke's squeal. "I haven't talked to him since Wednesday. Every time he pops into my brain, which is every third breath, my belly rollercoaster-drops."

Her belly was the least of it. The achy, empty pressure between her thighs was a constant reminder of his absence. A gallery of sense memories played over her body—Brendan's weight on top of her, the hot sensation of his skin on hers, and the solid comfort of his arms cradling her.

She pressed her hands to her face, trying to wick away the heat. "Is it normal to be this…distracted?"

"No," Brooke said, shaking her head with such vigor her braid whipped to her other shoulder. "It's goddamned special as fuck."

"You have the soul of a poet."

"Thank you. Will we meet the new boyfriend soon? I promise I'll be gentle."

A block ahead, the curved outer wall of Symphony Hall blazed bright in the setting sun, signaling the end to Brooke's part of the walk.

Zara jammed her hands down hard in her pockets. "He's not my boyfriend."

"Why not?"

"Because one date? But mostly because he's got a kid and an ex-wife who gets under his skin. That whole look is not me. I've got enough on my plate without hitching myself to a mess like that."

"Makes sense up here," Brooke said, tapping herself on the forehead. "But the heart's a different beast. You said you're thinking about him all the time?"

"Maybe not *all* the time," Zara lied. "I mean, aesthetically, he's interesting, and I want to paint him again. He kind of made me see stars."

The liberal spread of chunky salt on the sidewalk in front of the symphony's performance hall gritted under their feet. After a minute of silence, Brooke pivoted toward her and narrowed her eyes. "Is he a jerk? Dumb? Boring?"

"No, not at all." Zara glanced at her watch. Yikes. She'd have to hustle to make it to work on time. "He has a deeply cautious paternalistic streak, but otherwise, he's lovely."

"Can't be completely cautious if he's nailing a stranger on the first date."

"Hey," she held up her hand. "Too far."

"What? It's not like it isn't true. You could have been someone who sells organs on the dark web for all he knew." Brooke shrugged. "So, my two cents, he sounds like a catch. And if this has no potential, mind if I date him when you're done? Nice guys-slash-good lays are right up my alley."

Her stomach oiled. "What the hell, Brooke?"

"Ha!" Brooke pointed at her.

"What ha?"

"You proved my point." She wagged her finger. "You don't want me to ask him out because you're on the edge of falling for Hot Daddy."

The truth of Brooke's accusation knocked the wind out of her. "His name's Brendan Stewart. *Not* Hot Daddy."

"Dodging. Admit you *like him* like him. You were about to rip my head off. Which, by the way, not cool. Sisters before misters, remember?"

Other arriving musicians drifted around them and nodded hello to Brooke as they passed. Zara waited for them to go away before continuing.

"I'm *not* on the edge of anything." She scrunched her face. "He's my muse. Nothing more. My temporary, no-strings muse."

"Go ahead and fool yourself if you need to, but what you described, Zar? The lighting up, always on your mind distraction? *That's* starting to fall for someone." Brooke patted her heart. "Trust me. I do it all the time."

Zara stood stock still as the world swayed around her. "You're wrong. I can have sex without getting all emotional about it. Besides, I can't fall in love. Not with him—not with anyone. Not now."

"It's hard to stop. That's why they call it falling." Brooke retreated a few paces toward the performers' entrance ramp on the side of the building. "You can argue with me later over ice cream, but I've gotta run."

Zara seized her phone. *To hell with Brooke's theory.* Her friend was wrong, and she would prove it.

Nine

Brendan muscled his way through the crowd at Ottobar toward where Mike stood in front of the main stage. A variety of people—pierced, tatted, vanilla, grizzled—dotted the hundred-strong audience.

He tapped his brother on the shoulder with a cold, sweating bottle of beer. "Here. They're not done the sound check yet?"

The monotonous lead singer's "check, check, check" and the band's warm-up guitar flourishes drowned out any hope of normal conversational volume.

"Not even close, bro." Mike stifled a yawn. "Can't believe I agreed to hit a show on a weeknight. Tomorrow morning's going to hurt. Hey, you ever talk to Jess about her post?"

"It came up during Wednesday's drop-off." Brendan slugged his beer. "We had a couple of minutes when I was fixing her sink. Boils down to Jess being jealous because Em worships Ravenna-slash-Zara."

"Hang on, hang on, hang on." His brother swiveled around to face him. "Why are you fixing shit for Jess?"

Brendan shrugged. "Should I leave my kid in a house with no kitchen sink?"

"Absofuckinglutely." Mike cranked his brows down. "You've gotta stop being her safety net."

"It took fifteen minutes." Brendan peered past his big brother's shoulder toward the stage. He hated this conversation every time it came up and hoped the band would drown it out.

"Doesn't matter. Fifteen here, fifteen there, adds up to a lifetime of ball and chain. With no balling. Any new chick is gonna take issue with you running to Jess's to do the basic upkeep for her."

"I'll explain I'm taking care of my daughter."

"Oh boy, what you don't know about women would fill the Bay." Mike took a slug of his beer. "Any woman'll have strong opinions about you spending time at your ex's house. Promise me you'll ponder that for at least five minutes."

"Will it end this conversation?"

"Yes."

Brendan held his hand up in the Scout's honor salute. "Then I promise."

"Good." Mike turned back to the stage.

"For what it's worth, she asked me to fix her dryer too. I told her I couldn't because I had dinner plans. She was pretty interested in that piece of information."

"Don't tell me she was jealous."

"Nah. If she was, it'd be a fucking riot. She dated Kenny for months, and I didn't say word one. They broke up, by the way. Color me shocked a long-distance relationship with someone she met at Firefly didn't last." Brendan tucked a hand into his pocket. "Jess gave me the third-degree, but I didn't say much since she's a Class-A Google snoop."

"Speaking of... How'd the date go?"

"Good." He smiled behind the lip of his bottle. As a gentleman, he wouldn't give Mike *details*, but he'd give him something.

"How good'd it go?" Mike lifted his baseball cap and ran his hand over his buzz cut.

"Great." His brother would understand.

"Nice." He elbowed Brendan. "How're you doing?"

"Besides great?"

"Great's perfect." Mike gulped his beer.

"Only thing is—"

A girl with a mane of blonde hair sashayed past and bumped into Brendan. "Oh, sorry. Did I make you spill?"

"It's all good." He siphoned a slosh of beer from his forearm.

She flashed a bleached-white smile at him. "I'm Candy."

What was happening here? He flicked his gaze past her to Mike, whose lips bubbled with a pinched-in laugh.

"Uh, hi."

"My friends and I are hanging out in the loft." She pointed above the stage, then slid her hand down his arm. "You should join us. Promise, you'll have a good time."

Without waiting for an answer, she swaggered off in her skinny jeans and stiletto boots.

"Dude." Mike snickered and bumped him with his shoulder. "What'd you do? Change your cologne? Why are women hurling themselves at you?"

"What are you talking about?"

"You're giving off a vibe. She didn't even notice me, impossible as it is to believe."

"You're married."

"Happily too. My point is, that chick only had eyes for you. Go get her number."

Brendan glanced up toward the loft. Candy stood at the railing, shifting her gaze between him and the stage. *No thanks.*

"I'm not a player. I like Zara. A lot. She's fun." Her snappy chatter at dinner, her determination about her career despite all the obstacles, her unrestrained passion in her studio, and her general take on life all added up to pretty thick blinders against other women.

Except there was still that one, inescapable fact...

He shifted his weight.

"What?" Mike asked. "There's something you're not saying."

"She said she doesn't want kids."

"Jesus Christ, a first date is way too fucking soon to dig into deep shit. Didja talk about religion and politics, too, or stick with family planning?"

"But it's a total deal-breaker. I can't have Emma getting attached to a woman and wake up one day and she's gone. That's already happened to her once. I can't let it happen again."

"*Dude.* I repeat—one date. So the fuck what if she doesn't want kids? Let yourself have fun."

"You're right." Brendan sighed. "Thing is, she was great with the kids at the party. I'm sure she'd warm up to the idea of having one in her life."

Mike side-eyed Brendan. "I re-repeat, you're getting ahead of yourself, here. At least tell me you haven't texted her since Wednesday. We've both been outta the game for ages, but I hear you gotta give it three days, minimum, before texting."

Shrieking feedback from the stage made them both wince.

"Nope. I haven't texted her since Wednesday night. Been too busy working twelve hour days."

"Good boy."

"But I sent flowers."

"Aw, bro." Mike tipped his head back and closed his eyes the same way he did when his kids accidentally punched him in the nuts and he didn't want to scald their ears with the foulest language this side of the Atlantic. "You're fucking hopeless. Did you give her a vice for your balls too?"

"That's more of a first anniversary gift." He rested his thumb and finger on his chin and glanced skyward. "Or is that paper?"

"Joke all you want, dude, but I've seen this before. When you fall, you fall like a meteor." Mike shook his head. "In case you missed the fucking on-point metaphor, meteors bust apart and burn up in the atmosphere."

"Wow, that was beautiful." Even though he teased him, Brendan's chest tightened with affection for his brawny older brother. All he was doing was looking out for him, like he had their whole lives. Little wonder Brendan looked up to him, even in adulthood.

Mike rolled his eyes. "You and what's-her-name—"

"Zara."

"You and Zara got a second date?"

"Tomorrow. She's supposed to text me the details." Brendan's phone buzzed in his pocket. He hauled it free and grinned at it. "Speak of the devil. Hold this."

He shoved his beer into Mike's outstretched hand and read Zara's text.

Still game for tomorrow? A night of entertainments and casual sex?

He wouldn't admit this to Mike, but he'd been nervous when he hadn't heard from her. After he sent the flowers, she'd texted to say thank you. Then, silence. It left him thinking the flowers were too extravagant, and she was pulling a polite fade away.

All that worry was for nothing, which was gratifying beyond all measure, considering she was the only thing on his mind yesterday. Total surprise he'd gotten any work done, what with the blood being diverted to his groin.

Absolutely, he typed.

Fantastic. Important question: how do you feel about balls?

*My own? *Great.**

Meant bowling balls.

Those are good too. Haven't been bowling since…

… his nephew's birthday party in December. Nope, not sharing that info.

…I can't remember.

B/c you're old?

We could've gone to high school together, you know. I could have asked you to prom.

Ugh, never. Unless it's like the one from Carrie. *Meet me at Mustang Alley's @ 7?*

You got it. Dinner after?

Dinner there. Fried goodness. Thanks again for the flowers. They're totally rad.

Welcome. Want to come over later tonight?

Would, but can't. Working.

K. See you tomorrow, princess.

He shoved his phone into his pocket and took his beer from Mike. Brendan rocked on his heels then glanced at his brother. Mike's thick, surprised eyebrows rode so high on his head they disappeared under the bill of his cap.

"What?"

"You're all dimples and grins, you motherfucker. You're bound and determined to get wifed up again, aren't you?"

"Someday, but not now. I'm taking your advice. This is fun only—not serious."

From the stage, the band's lead singer shouted a welcome, and the crowd cheered. As the audience bobbed around them, Mike muttered to Brendan. "Bet you a fucking hundy you bring her to Easter Dinner to meet the fam."

~ * ~

Zara dragged a thick purple stripe down her canvas to demonstrate how to paint the last building in the Baltimore skyline. She was situated in front of two dozen women seated in the lounge above a Cuban restaurant. Small desktop easels rose from the rows of tables, and canvases the size of cafeteria trays rested upon them.

Counting to ninety in her head, she waited for the group of women to catch up. In the first hour of class, she'd only counted to sixty. Now, mid-evening, they were deep in their cups and needed extra time.

Her mind drifted to tomorrow night and she almost giggled.

Bowling was genius. Minimal chance the dopey, unromantic activity would augment her uncomfortably mushy emotions. Plus, it would allow her to study how the lines of his body moved, make sure she'd gotten the lines right in her painting. Not to mention provide a solid hour of staring at his ass.

All for research purposes, of course.

"Okay, that's the last building for the Inner Harbor skyline." Zara put her brush in a cup and faced the group. "Next, we'll dab in windows, alternating between medium blue and a yellowish-white. Use the blue for darkened offices, and white where we want to show the lights are on."

"Should we mix the colors now?"

"Go right ahead. Also, feel free to get up and refer to the example." She pointed to the dry canvas from the corporate office, strategically placed next to the bar. "If you're not there yet, don't worry. I'll circulate to answer questions."

A lanky, brunette woman in the front row shot her hand up.

Zara picked her way past Coach purses littering the aisle, trying not to bump into the squashed-in tables. The woman's hair swooped across her forehead, and she'd twisted the rest into nubby ponytails.

"Did you have a question?" she asked, peeking at the woman's canvas. She'd saturated it with an inky background color and had painted in half of the buildings, but had done little else with the design.

"Yes." The woman flashed a wide smile at Zara, but it didn't reach her eyes.

The shape of her smile reminded Zara of someone...

"You said your name is Zara, didn't you?" A slice of white was visible all the way around her amber irises. "I have to say, you look just like Ravenna from *Rising*."

"I get that a lot."

Another student's raised hand at the rear of the room caught Zara's attention, but the woman in front of her kept talking.

"She's my daughter's favorite princess. She carries a Ravenna doll around with her everywhere. To school, to bed, to the bathroom. I'm worried she's *too* attached to it."

"Ravenna is popular with kids, isn't she?" Zara used her polite small-talk voice, hoping to wind up this conversation. She gestured toward the woman's painting. "Is there something I can help you with?"

"Yes, actually." The woman fingered her giant crimson statement necklace. "I was wondering... Did you by any chance dress up as Ravenna and paint faces at a birthday party last weekend for a five-year-old named Emma?"

The question rooted Zara to the spot. "Be there in a moment," she called to the student in the back. To the woman in front of her she said, "Yes, I did." She searched the woman's face. Something about her was familiar. "Were you there?"

The woman's lips thinned. "No, but I wish I could have been. I'm Jess Stewart. Emma's mother."

If looks could shove, Jess's gaze would've knocked her flat.

Zara widened her eyes. *That* was why she recognized this woman. Emma was a tiny version of Jess, except with Brendan's hair color and eyes. Zara leaned in close, artistic curiosity bumping polite social behavior to the side. Yes, there was Emma. The snub nose, the rounded cheeks, the wide smile, the sticky-outy ears...

This was Jess, from *The Messy Jess*, Brendan's ex.

Zara choked down the urge to giggle at the Dr. Suessian rhyme. A giggle fit wouldn't be mature, now would it? It would, however, be the perfect response to this whole ridiculous situation. How often does a person randomly run into the ex-wife of the guy she's dating?

No. Not dating. Remember? Not dating, not falling, not any of the goofy Valentine's, Hollywood romantic comedy, sugary pop song nonsense. What she and Brendan had was an artistic experiment.

She brushed the thoughts aside to focus on the figure in her foreground.

Mathematically, Jess could show up in a class. They both lived in Baltimore and were in spitting distance of each other's ages, but Zara never imagined she'd meet this woman in the wild. Never expected to meet her at all, honestly. Jess existed in the abstract. She had no actual bearing on Zara's day-to-day. Kind of like koala bears, or Antarctica. They were real, just not part of *her* reality.

Until now.

Jess stared at her, nostrils flared and lips curving upward, like she'd smelled something awful but was too polite to point it out.

Is she waiting for me to talk? Shit. Have I been gargoyling?

Zara offered the truest, safest thing that came to mind. "Your daughter is great."

"Thank you." Jess sipped at her plastic tumbler of white wine. "She *loved* you. Has not stopped talking about you. So I went to your princess site to figure out how to send a thank you note for making her party special. There was a link to your Wine & Paint Artist page, and I decided I had to meet the girl Emma adores."

Jess was using words like 'love' and 'thank you' and 'special,' but her icy tone didn't exactly jibe with the sweet sentiments.

"I'm glad the party was special for her."

Jess's knuckles whitened, and the mouth of her cup warped to an oval under the pressure. "It's been a constant loop of 'Ravenna painted my face,' 'Ravenna made me a knight,' 'Ravenna said we'd carry each other in our hearts,' and 'Ravenna said I could skip vegetables.'"

The cold tightness in Zara's belly washed over the rest of her. She knew this feeling, this anticipatory chill. It was the same as when she'd ridden through the haunted house on the boardwalk as a kid. In the shadows, monsters waited to leap and scream at her.

Something was coming. It was only a question of when.

"The last thing isn't true, I swear."

"I didn't think so." Jess fiddled with her lacquered bangs, tucking away invisible errant hairs. "Isn't that funny? How she's put you on such a pedestal? Honestly, I worried her party would've been ruined without me."

"She seemed to have fun."

"Oh, she *did*. She's been telling me about it nonstop. It's obvious in the pictures from the party—she's smiling or laughing in every single one. That one photo of you and Brendan is adorable. He's *such* an amazing father. He even handles the honey-do list at my house so Emma's always comfortable."

I don't want to know any of this messiness. Don't want to know her. This is too much. I've got enough on my easel without his baggage exploding into my life.

Jess drained her wine and nailed Zara with a stare. "He's a much better dad than he was a husband. He had a condescension problem. Like he knew the right way to do everything."

There's the jumpy-outy monster she'd been anticipating. Instead of shrieking or flailing or hiding her eyes, Zara twisted her lips and dug her nails into her palm. Because casual or not, it made her angry this woman was trying to smear underhanded opinions on whatever she had with Brendan.

"Why are you telling me this?" she asked. Her pulse quickened in her ears, drowning out the chatter and swish of dozens of paintbrushes against prefabricated canvases.

"I'm a big believer in sharing information if it means saving people from mistakes I've made." Jess contemplated her empty tumbler and flicked her glance to Zara. "Wish they served whiskey, know what I mean? Oh, maybe you don't. Are you old enough to drink?"

"Different people don't necessarily make the same mistakes." Two more hands shot into the in the air at the back of the room. "Anyway, I need to talk to the other students."

"I agree. You do." Jess shifted her features back to the placid, generic expression she'd been wearing five minutes ago. "My daughter will be excited I saw her Ravenna. That's what she's been calling you—*her* Ravenna."

Zara breathed hard to get air past the bands of tension constricting her chest. "Please tell her I said 'hi.'"

"I will." Jess fingered one of her spiky ponytail nubs. "I'm sure we'll see each other around."

Zara made a noise she hoped could be construed as a polite version of, "Holy balls, I hope not."

Walking away from Jess and toward another student, Zara had the distinct impression she wore a target on her back.

~ * ~

The uncomfortable plastic seat vibrated as the bus rumbled north on Charles Street. Zara was skipping the Tower tonight. Though the deadline stress was real, she had no brain for painting. Her gray matter was buzzing too hard.

Tonight's surprise peek into Brendan's past had sketched her out. Jess's vibe was way spooky. Like she'd come to size Zara up. That was goofy though, wasn't it? She was zero threat to their situation. All she wanted from Brendan was his mushy goodness. Which was why this odd inspection from Jess sucked big, fat nuggets. It had unleashed a tidal wave of emotions.

Annoyance, defensiveness, possessiveness, tenderness.

Pressing her head against the cool glass off the window, she sighed and fogged the window. *None* of this was part of the deal. At all. This was supposed to be a flingy shallow adventure.

They circled around the Washington Monument and bounced over the cobblestone street toward her stop. She rose and stood in front of the side doors as the bus's air brakes hissed and popped. As soon as the door opened, a cold blast of February air slapped her face and froze the inside of her nose.

"Christ," she muttered, hunkered into her coat and exited onto the slushy sidewalk. Empty midnight streets stretched around her. Total population—Zara and one lonely tumbleweave. Blowing out her bottom lip, she hung a left onto Eager Street and carried her keys so they poked out between her knuckles.

Why the hell had Jess come tonight? Maybe Zara should call Brendan to tell him, explain why she couldn't keep dating him? Except, *eyeroll*. The point would be what, exactly? He'd probably be in her life for only the next fifteen minutes, and—

"Boo!" someone shouted from behind her.

Zara's mind blanked, and she sprinted.

"Whoa, whoa, whoa, sweetie!" Melinda shouted. "It's just me!"

Zara puttered to a stop and turned, her heart hammering as she registered her friend's approaching face in the dark. "Fuck, Mel. Don't sneak up on me."

Melinda's Cheshire cat smile gleamed in the night, and she managed to giggle out, "I'm sorry."

"*Suuure* you are. Hence the laughing." Zara climbed the stoop of their townhouse.

"I *am*. Why are you so jumpy, anyway?"

"Because you shouted "boo" at me at midnight in the middle of the city?" Zara jammed her keys in the deadbolt to the house, twisted, and opened the door.

"Not buying it. I've done that at least three other times, and you've never run away."

She dragged her cap from her head and tossed it on the foyer table. "It's been a weird night."

"Do tell," Melinda said, unwinding her scarf.

"Brendan's ex-wife came to my Wine & Paint class tonight."

Melinda paused, mid-hang. "Well, damn. I thought you were going to say one of the Wine & Paint women blazed a fat blunt mid-class or something."

"I wish. I could've used the contact high." Zara flopped on the squashy living room couch and cuddled a pillow. "She flagged me down and introduced herself. She *deliberately* came to the class. Told me her daughter loved me, and Brendan was the bomb as a father but had been a shitty husband. The whole thing was…odd."

As Zara twiddled the fringe of the decorative pillow Grier's mother had foisted upon them, Melinda settled herself on the couch. "What's her name?" she asked and fired up her tablet.

"Jess Stewart." Ugh, saying her name was like coughing up a hairball. "Why?"

"Because we're going to unearth this psycho's history. I do this when we're casting to suss out the brand of crazy we're bringing to the table."

Melinda poked the Internet icon and typed in Jess's name. Her glasses reflected the screen's backlight and loaned Melinda's brown skin a bluish glow. *Ooh, pretty.*

What if Zara used devices as light sources and captured the alien cast they give to everything? She pinched her bottom lip between her fingers. Yeah, after she exhausted this naked people impressionist series, she could play around with modern ambient lighting.

Hang on. Did Mel say she was doing a background check on Jess? "Stop, Mel. That's an invasion of privacy."

"Nuh-uh. It's public record," she said, shrugging. "Not that it matters—there's not much to see."

She showed Zara the device.

"A couple of speeding tickets, the divorce, and a closed civil case. Nothing juicy there, either. She didn't pay a country club bill. Hashtag, first world problems." Melinda clicked the *Stewart vs. Stewart* link and scrolled. "But their divorce is more detailed than others I've seen. Look at the amount of back and forth."

Zara peeked at the entries. The jargon was beyond her, but even she could sense the discord in the bullet points. This timeline of court transactions added up to Brendan's lengthy divorce. God, it had dragged on forever.

She clonked her boots onto coffee table next to Melinda's. "He said he'd fought to set up privacy guidelines on social media to protect his kid's info online. His ex is a blogger, or something."

"Why didn't you tell me she had a blog? That'll be the mother lode. What's it called?"

Zara scrunched her face and shrugged. "Jess is Messy, or something?"

Melinda Googled and asked, "Is this it? *The Messy Jess*?"

Brendan's ex-wife's waxy smiling face peered at them from a banner at the top of the page.

"Yep. That's her."

Melinda's gaze shifted across the words. "Girlfriend is fond of caps lock. And elephants. Has kind of a potty mouth, too. It's tame as far as—oh."

"What oh?" she asked, and snagged Melinda's tablet. "Gimme."

Zara's eyes lit on the post from yesterday, titled, "Coping—My Ex Is Dating Again."

Talking to my therapist...normal...jealousy...remembering reasons we divorced...a hundred times weirder when you have a kid because a new person is in your kid's life and you have absolutely no say in it...worried about the upcoming March equinox and my depressive cycles...

"Wow, so personal," Melinda said and sucked air through her teeth. "Why would she put that out there?"

Zara rested the tablet on her lap and glanced at the ceiling. Dammit. She didn't like Jess any better, but maybe she understood her a little more. "It's a purge."

"A what?"

"A purge." Zara swirled her hands in the air. "For some people, the only way to process big thoughts and emotions is to work it out in words, or a painting, or a song—something—and make it public because there's beauty in the pain, and it might make someone else less lonely. That's what this is. She's hurting and working through it."

"Bullshit. That's what a journal is for. You write it down, and then you lock it up."

Raising an eyebrow, Zara turned toward her friend. "How are you in the arts?"

"I'm a stage manager." Melinda shrugged. "I don't have time for emotional purges. I have problems to solve."

"But you're such a marshmallow."

"You haven't seen me at work." She tapped her finger on the tablet. "So are you guys going to have tea together? Maybe brush each other's hair?"

"No, because crashing my job was creepy as fuck. If we'd been dating for months, that'd be one thing. But her angst is way premature. He and I went on one extremely enjoyable date. We're going on another date, but we aren't dat*ing*. There's no way I'm getting mixed up with him long-term."

"Why not?" Melinda elbowed her. "Sounds like he's got potential."

Zara tamped down the glittery eruption inside her that agreed with Melinda and whispered *keep him*. Logic was key here. Not squishy sentiments. Hiding her face in the pillow, she groaned into its satin fluff. "Because *kid*. Because weirdo ex-wife. After tonight, maybe I'll give him the "you're great, but this can't work" speech."

"Okay." Melinda laughed. "Big talk from such a small woman."

"Quiet, you giant."

"Whatever. You envy my height." Melinda snagged her tablet back. "Don't shun the man because of his ex. She's all bark. Poisonous, scary bark, but no bite. And definitely no one you should let get in the way of a fun romance."

Zara didn't correct Melinda because then it would become a lady-doth-protest-too-much situation. This was not a storybook romance. Not one little bit.

Ten

Grinning like a dumb puppy, Brendan threw open the second-floor doors of Mustang Alley's. When Zara texted about bowling near Little Italy, he'd pictured a dark and smoky local joint. This place was the exact opposite—sparkling lights, clean lines, and cocktails like they'd snuck a bowling alley into the bar at the Four Seasons.

Where was she?

As he glanced around, his pulse thudded in his ears, muting the rhythmic percussion of the place. Candy-colored balls popped off bowlers' fingers, glided along the boards, then smashed into stubborn lines of stocky pins.

He checked his watch. 7:05 p.m.

She wouldn't have ditched him, would she?

Damn, he hoped not. She'd been on his mind constantly since Wednesday. The way she tilted her head at him when she was listening hard, the smell of her hair, the snorty laugh she tried to cover up, the warmth of her hand in his, and her studio...

Blood rushed low. *Binary. 01000001, 01000010, 01000011.*

"Brendan." Zara's voice cut through the clutter of noise. She wove through the crowd, stocking-footed, carrying a bold pair of bowling shoes.

"You look great," he said.

"Even with the goofy shoes?" She rose on tiptoe to kiss him. A quick, mint-flavored icebreaker of a smooch. "I got us a lane. I opted for duckpins because the big balls hurt my fingers."

He chuckled.

She batted his shoulder. "You're supposed to be mature."

"I'm older." He smiled at her upturned face. "Never said I was mature. You're much shorter without your shoes."

"I'm not short. You're a giant slab of man. Who's about to get his ass handed to him." She swung the shoes around by their laces. "You know the difference between duckpin and ten-pin, right?"

"Besides the size of the balls?"

She shrugged. "So you don't know, then."

"How dare you? I'm Baltimore boy. Three balls per frame instead of two."

"Gold star. Now, go get a snazzy pair of shoes like mine." She pointed toward a pine counter in front of an exposed brick wall. "Meet me on lane two. I already ordered us a pitcher."

"Yes ma'am."

He collected a pair of size twelves from the rental counter, hung his coat next to hers, and padded toward their lane. She was perched on the edge of a bench, tugging on her shoes, then bobbed forward to tie the laces. Her slouchy black shirt drooped low, offering him an unobstructed view of the shiny red satin underneath.

He could stare at her all night.

She flipped her hair back, exposing the pale column of her neck. Gentle kisses and licks right there would prickle her flesh and make her arch her back. Memories of doing exactly that a few nights ago cranked him on all the way to ten.

Sitting up, she asked, "Find a sexy pair like mine?"

"Uh, what?"

She gestured toward the clown shoes he held. "They're even more beautiful in bigger sizes."

Right. When she referred to a sexy pair, she meant *shoes*. Had he caught a virus that made him hear dirty double *entendres* in whatever Zara said?

"I'll enter our names," she said as she rose from the bench. "Who do you want to be? Extra points for clever incognito names."

He queried his mental database of possibilities, and the only result was *Daddy*. Christ, no way. Tonight he could be anyone.

"Apollo," he answered.

"The sun god?"

"Sci-fi character. Calm exterior, passionate underneath, driven by doing the right thing even if it causes him problems. Been told I resemble the actor who plays him. Plus," he said, lifting a shoulder and grinning, "I have a sunny personality."

"Whereas I skew dark," she said and entered "Wednesday" into Player 1's name field.

He stared at her ass while she bent over the console. With this kind of distraction, the next hour of game play would feel like twenty. All he wanted was for her to come back to his place across the Harbor, but there was no guarantee she would. Had their Valentine's hook-up been a holiday-induced fluke? Was she into him even half as much as he was into her?

If not, that would definitely suck balls.

Strolling up behind her, he asked, "Care to make it interesting?"

"Oh, I always make it interesting." Zara glanced over her shoulder, and her sweater slipped down her arm. More of her tattoo peeked out, the cherry blossoms he'd glimpsed in her studio. Another thing he wanted to explore later.

"True."

"How about this," she said. "If I win, you foot the bill for tonight's festivities."

"Done." Brendan snaked his hands around her waist. "If *I* win, you come to my place after."

He hugged her closer and inhaled in her citrusy scent. She pressed her hips to his groin. Good sign of how the night would unfold. How fast could they play a game and cut out of here? He nuzzled her neck, right at the spot where her pulse throbbed, the patch of skin that made her shiver if he—

Someone cleared her throat from a few feet away, and he backed off Zara. Jesus, he'd forgotten he was in public, surrounded by eyeballs and judgment.

"Um, I've got your pitcher." A woman with thick black glasses and a mountain of zigzag hair set the beer and plastic cups on the table. "Did you want to order food?"

"You want to see the menu?" Zara asked him.

He poured two frothy beers. "Order for both of us. Your track record's good."

"Done." Zara turned to the waitress. "We'll split a couple of appetizers. The crab pretzel, buffalo chicken dip, and fried pickles, please."

"Fried pickles?" he asked.

"Good choice," the waitress said as she jotted it down. "My personal fave."

He gave Zara a beer. "Well then, bring on the fried pickles."

"Be ready in a few." The waitress spun on her heel and scooted toward the kitchen.

"Wait until you try the pickles," Zara said. "You won't— whoa!"

Her gaze snagged on his Throwing Muses T-shirt.

"Like it?" he asked.

"Love it." She ran her hand over the shirt's pristine surface. He vacuumed in his belly, loving the way her palm bumped against his tensed abs. She traced his collar and blinked big blue eyes at him. "I propose new stakes. If I win, this shirt is mine."

Brendan blew out the breath he'd been holding. "I don't know…"

Which was a lie. The minute he unearthed it from the plastic tub in his attic, this shirt was destined to hug Zara's curves. Especially when he'd put it on and it fit like a muscle shirt, a clear sign he'd bulked up since he was twenty. Back in the day, he'd been nerdy string bean, but these past couple of years of burning off annoyed energy at the gym provided excellent side benefits.

"Aw, please," she said. "I covet it hard."

"One condition. You have to take it off me."

"Deal." She nudged his plastic cup with hers to toast their agreement.

That meant she was coming back to his place, right? Tough to drink through his broad grin, but he managed.

"Now prepare to be shamed." She set her beer on the table, plucked a ball from the lineup, and positioned herself on the arrows painted at the base of the lane.

What good deed have I done to earn an evening of staring at this woman's ass?

As she walked the approach, she swung her arm wide, and the ball blurred at the triangle of pins. They exploded apart, and a downed pin spun on the boards until the pin sweeper scraped it from the lane.

"You're up," she said and dusted her hands together.

He narrowed his eyes. "You're hustling me."

"Nuh-uh." She dropped onto the seat next to him and picked up her beer. "I've been boasting about my prowess this whole time. You can't grow up on the shore without playing an obscene amount of Skee-Ball. Same skills. Not my fault you assumed you'd win."

"You're right. Glad you're competitive, because when *I* win, it'll be sweeter if you don't take it easy on me."

"Yeah yeah yeah. Let see what you've got."

"You've seen what I've got," he said and quirked an eyebrow.

"On the lane, *Apollo*."

"Either way works for me."

He rose from the bench and hefted an eleven-pound ball. Solid, heavy. Definitely going to kill it and impress Zara. He strode the boards and hurled the ball down the lane. In a blink, it collided with the pins and…

Crap.

He'd only knocked over six. Bowling required more finesse than he remembered. He straightened his spine, pivoted, and got a confidence boost. Zara was laughing, but her smoky gaze was fixed on him and only him.

A woman hadn't looked at him like that in years.

He rolled another ball down the lane and put a little spin on it. Boom. The four remaining pins drunkenly stumbled and collapsed.

"Yes!" He pumped his fist as the overhead scoreboard played an animation celebrating the spare.

"Seems we have a player," she said.

He stepped off the lane as the waitress set their food on the table in front of their bench.

"Need anything else?" she asked.

"We're good, thanks." Zara cut off a wedge of the crab pretzel and chewed it thoughtfully. "That's the best thing I've ever tasted."

He loved the way she went for whatever she wanted, with no hesitation. "Better than the Ethiopian food?"

She forked up another bite. "No...but yes? Honestly, I'm not super-picky. Any food someone cooks for me is the best thing I've ever tasted."

"Then I'll have to cook for you. I make a mean steak. Are these the famous fried pickles?" He pointed to a small boat of breaded spears.

"Yes, and they're amazing. I generally avoid eating phallic food in public, but I make an exception for those."

"Well, here goes nothing." He dipped the pickle into the side of ranch dip and bit down. The salty crunch mixed with the creamy cool of the ranch was weirdly good. "Wow."

"Told you." She scooped a generous helping of buffalo dip.

He ate another pickle. "I like trying new foods. My normal date's kind of a picky eater."

Zara's smile fell. She cleared her throat and wiped her mouth. "I'm up."

Had he said something wrong? After she knocked down seven pins and finished her frame, she seemed to drift back to her normal winking sarcasm. Maybe he was overanalyzing?

Jesus, he was terrible at figuring women out.

They swapped turns, finished the food, and taunted each other as they racked up pins. Zara's performance had been uneven after her first strike, while his had been steadier. Thanks to a mid-game turkey, she'd earned a final score of 186.

He contemplated the spread at the end of the lane. He had one shot left. If he knocked down three pins—a difficult, though not impossible feat—he'd win the game. He wanted to win too. After losing approximately one million Nice Dad games of Candy Land,

Connect Four, and Mario Kart, competition was exciting.

Plus, more time with Zara—ideally naked time—was the prize.

"Hey, Apollo," she said from the bench, "I need to tell you about a weird thing that happened at work last night."

"Hang on." He selected the yellow ball. "Let me win this game, first."

"I admire your confidence." She folded her leg up in front of her, laced her fingers around it, then held it to her chest.

He stood at the end of the lane. This was it. One, two, three steps forward, release...

Two pins.

Final score—Zara: 186. Brendan: 185.

One fucking point.

On the overhead screen "Wednesday" pulsed amid fireworks. Bummer, but he wouldn't be that guy who pouted over losing to his date. Unless it was mini golf. Then he might lose his shit. Rolling his neck, he turned to congratulate Zara, then laughed. She was busy dancing a snaky, celebratory jig.

Well, if she danced like this when she came out on top, he'd happily lose to her anytime.

"Nice moves, Princess." Brendan flopped on the bench and drained the last of his beer. "You were talking about your job? Which one?"

"Wine & Paint." She smooshed next to him, her thigh against his.

Blood thrummed low in his body. Time to speed up the getting-out-of-here process. It'd be, what, a fifteen-minute Uber? Or a twenty-minute water taxi, which would be more romantic. Yeah, he'd steer them toward the water taxi pier.

"What happened?" He kicked off his bowling shoes.

She twisted toward him, then propped her elbow onto the back of the bench and leaned her head against her hand. Clearing her throat, she said, "I wasn't sure I should mention it because you don't need to do anything, but it seemed strange not to, and it might come up elsewhere, so, here it is."

Her hesitation made him uneasy. Don't let her say she was seeing someone else. That would be an epic disappointment. But the shadows on her face meant something big.

"Here what is?" he asked.

"Jess came to my Wine & Paint class last night. Your Jess...or, not *your* Jess. Your ex."

The world went weird around the edges. His stomach dropped

from his body, through the floor, and straight into the street where Little Italy valets darting around the neighborhood probably trampled it.

"What? How?" He furrowed his brow. What the fuck? Was this a joke? Zara didn't seem the type to yank his chain. So was this a crazy coincidence, or had Jess gone full-on stalker?

Which brought him straight back to what the fuck?

Zara met Jess. Jess met Zara.

Worst of all, he hadn't been there to make sure the introductions unfolded the right way.

"She said my face painting website—mental note, take that site down—linked to my Wine & Paint profile, so she decided to come to a class." Zara gave up on untying the knots, toed off her shoes, and let them tumble to the ground.

He gripped the bench. "She went out on an Emma night."

Zara fingered the locket resting above the valley of her breasts. "Does your ex-wife always do this, or am I special? Should I expect her to pop up at random places?"

"No. I don't know. This is new to me. I haven't dated anyone in—" *Shit*. He hadn't meant to let that slip. "What'd she say?"

"Mostly that Emma's been talking about me a lot. It made Jess want to meet me in person."

Jess was doing it *again*. Prying, digging, exposing, forcing *everything* to happen sooner than it should, and much sooner than he wanted. All the frustration he'd banked during the past few years in the interest of a friendly relationship with Jess boiled up.

No fucking way was he going to let her keep doing this kind of shit.

"Jesus, Zara." He jammed his foot into his shoe, knelt, then yanked the laces. "Why'd you wait this long to tell me?"

She bent her arms, palms up. "What do you mean, 'this long?' It was last night."

"You should've called me as soon as it happened. I could have fixed it and told Jess to leave you alone."

He was being unfair, misdirecting his anger at Zara, which tripped him up all over again. Jess wasn't even *here*, and she was somehow blowing up his spot.

"Don't be ridiculous." She twisted her lips.

"Ridiculous? My ex-wife went to my girl—to your job. I'm not being ridiculous."

Did I almost say "girlfriend's job"? If that wasn't hitting the gas hard.

"Um, the tendons in your neck look like they're going to snap, which I think is kind of ridiculous. There's nothing you need to fix. I'm telling you because it's weird not to, not because I expect you to *do* anything because FYI, if I want her to leave me alone, *I'll* tell her to leave me alone. We're adults. You're not responsible for her behavior or mine."

Hot spit collected in his mouth, and he gritted his teeth. After he finished knotting his laces way too tight, he locked gazes with Zara. "I'm going there right now to set her straight."

"No, you're not." She stone-faced him.

A few seconds slipped by.

Was this the gargoyle thing she did? "Come again?"

She folded her arms and continued, "I'm *not* following you to your ex-wife's house to watch you argue with her. Not my idea of a good time. Do it, and you're heading home solo, dimples."

These leadership skills of hers were simultaneously endearing and a pain in the ass.

Scratching the back of his neck, he confessed, "Everything with Jess is…complicated."

"Clearly, but I don't think this is about you. I got the distinct vibe she didn't enjoy that Emma liked me. I read her blog and—"

Brendan groaned. Sweat prickled his back, and he dragged his hands down his face. How much had Zara read? Jess had posted dozens of anecdotes about him over the years, them of them snarky and unflattering.

What a nightmare.

His worlds should not overlap. Not yet. If he could code life, he'd have written a stored procedure on the conditions and criteria for introducing a woman to Emma, to his family, his friends, and then, finally, to Jess.

This set of circumstances was a total edge case. Everything was happening out of sequence and would throw a showstopper error, for sure.

"Why did you have to read that? I'm not the way she describes me."

"Duh, I know. And I only read the most recent stuff. It seemed smart to bone up on the woman who special guest-starred at my job. Anyway, she wrote that it's a struggle when your kids' other parent introduces 'a friend.' During the Wine & Paint night, I got the impression she was scoping me out."

A geyser of cheers burst from a party on the next lane.

Brendan rolled his neck. "I can't talk about this here. Let's go."

~ * ~

Zara walked through the door Brendan held open for her, and *bam,* he enveloped her hand with his and their fingers wove together like they'd practiced for years. He rubbed his thumb back and forth as they wended their way toward... somewhere?

Not knowing was okay. She enjoyed a good wander. It prickled her brain, gave her ideas that transformed into paintings. Tonight was nice for February, too. Crisp, but no wind, and a faint sickle moon glimmered in the black above them. Her high-heeled booties *tock-tock-tocked* against the pavement as they hurried along.

As long as they could circle back around to the flirty comfort they'd had before she brought up Jess, she'd be happy. That might not happen, though, not with the worry etched on Brendan's face. She didn't have the whole story, but this was sensitive, serious territory. Friendly flings didn't get grumpy about interfering exes. No, they laughed off this kind of drama, right?

"What's on your mind, Brendan Stewart?"

"I'm..." He squeezed her hand, "...trying to figure out how to say something."

"Thought so. You get this crinkled spot between your eyebrows when you're pondering."

"I do?" He poked the bridge of his nose.

"You do." Zara had first noticed his crinkle at Emma's party, when he waited for her to accept his dinner invitation. It reappeared at Dukem during the conversation about his divorce and showed up a third time after she blurted her news about meeting Jess.

He took a deep breath. "Okay, I don't know how to say this right, so I'm just gonna go for it. Bear with me. I like you, Princess. A lot."

Her excited heart slapped her rib cage. "I like you, too."

Oh God, she did. She *really* liked him. Why was she trying to deny it? Sure, he didn't fit within the neat lines she'd drawn for her life, but she'd never been good at staying within the lines anyway.

He'd unlocked something in her, something she wanted, needed to explore further. Physical attraction vibrated between them, but underlying that was big, blooming affection. Already, she cared about this man more than she'd expected to. Had been blindsided by it, actually.

Butterflies whipped through her as she waited for him to continue.

"I'm glad," he said. "And I don't want to scare you off."

Scare her? Anything he was about to say couldn't possibly

squash her desire to sketch him at every angle.

"Not a chance. As long as you aren't secretly a man made of spiders, we're good."

He laughed. "Scare isn't exactly right. It's more like I don't want to...overwhelm you."

"Overwhelm me how?"

He sighed. "I can't hide Jess's existence, but I'd hoped you and I could get to know each other better before she became a factor. I'm not happy you met Jess already or that we're talking about her. It's dredging up strong feelings."

"Of *course* you have strong feelings about your ex, but you don't have to get worked up. We—"

"No, Princess. I have strong feelings for *you*."

Her belly rollercoaster-dropped, and Zara stumbled over a crack in the sidewalk. She cleared her throat. "For me?"

"Fuck." He pounded the heel of his palm into his forehead.

"Was that a yes?" She loosened her hold on his other hand.

Traffic thickened as they approached the main arteries pumping cars through the city. Drivers blasted their horns, impatient with the slow progress through this two-lane part of town.

He tightened his grip and towed her across the busy street.

"It was a 'fuck.' *This* is what I meant by not overwhelming you. Jesus Christ, I'm supposed to play it cool." He exhaled his pent-up breath like dragon steam. "Give me a sec. I'll get this right."

They followed the cobblestone traffic circle in Harbor East. Spotlights blazed on a sculpture in the eye of the circle, a collection of golden metal flames leaping skyward, trapping figures within its swirling embrace. As they strolled along the street, past the posh hotels and toward the water, the city traffic shushed to a background hum.

"Okay, here's what I'm attempting to say. We're not an *us*, Princess, but we could be. I can see it. You and me, we're this great big balloon of potential." He swept his arm wide in front of them. "It's delicate, and I want to protect it."

"Oh." She squeezed his hand.

Moonlight bounced on the rippling calm of the harbor, and its murky waters slapped the hulls of the winterized boats.

"I want to keep this between you and me for a minute. Give us a chance to be whatever we'll be without outside commentary and pressure. Especially from Jess."

Zara scooched her giant bag stuffed with overnight necessities further up her shoulder. "Why does Jess worry you, anyway?"

He clamped his lips shut.

"Come on." She bumped him with her elbow. "We've declared our mutual like. That means you have to tell me things. Spill."

"Okay, okay. Before I get into it—do you want to go to a bar? Or back to my place for wine and snacks. I didn't win the game, so…"

"You had me at snacks," she said. "Now that we've settled that, please continue."

"For the record, this is way too early for this conversation," he said, "…but I'm finding it difficult to refuse you anything. I told you Emma wasn't exactly planned, right?"

"Yeah, but I'd kind of worked that out for myself. Not many twenty-two year-olds are eager to get married and start having babies."

"When we found out Jess was pregnant, and we decided to keep the baby, I had this whole blueprint of how we'd break the news to our parents. I wanted to wait and tell them all at once during graduation weekend. I already had a good job lined up and wanted Jess to come live with me here. I thought that would take some of the shock out of it for them—that we had a plan."

She pictured a younger, leaner, scruffier version of Brendan earnestly jumping into problem-solving mode.

He cleared his throat. "Jess agreed that a plan was good, but she was desperate to tell her parents we were getting married, said without that, the news would break their hearts. I was honest, told her I loved her and I wanted to get married someday, but I could only deal with one thing at a time."

Zara admired Brendan-from-five-years-ago. What would it be like to have such a firm grasp on your emotions, and what you could handle? Half the time she understood herself only after she poured her heart out onto enormous canvases in bright, bold colors.

"So why'd you get hitched?" she asked.

"Jess didn't follow the plan. She called her parents, told them she was pregnant and we were getting married. She left out the 'someday.' They called my mom and dad, who called me. My mother was crying. At the time, my choices were to call Jess a liar and refuse to marry her—even though I loved her and she was pregnant with my baby—or go along with it."

Ahead, at the end of the pier, a small crowd of people waited for the water taxi to ferry them across the Harbor.

"That's why I'm touchy about keeping what's between us, between us. When other people get involved, it corners me, puts pressure where none is needed."

Brendan said 'us' and it shot an electric shock straight into her chest.

So much for moving the needle back to flirty comfort. They'd moved another level deeper, and much to her surprise, that was kind of okay.

Except...the canvas glistening in her studio broke the "keep what's between us, between us" philosophy, now didn't it? Zara stuffed that thought down deep, choosing not to worry about it while she walked hand in hand with this man.

No, she'd wait to burn that bridge when she came to it.

Eleven

On the water taxi, Zara shivered. Despite the makeshift plastic and canvas windows and roof, there was zero protection from the frigid air.

"Here." Brendan unbuttoned his coat.

"Don't be crazy." She waved off his gesture. "I'll be fine. Keep your coat."

"I'm not *giving* it to you, Princess. I'm sharing." He hooked an arm around her waist and scooped her onto his lap. After he wrapped the woolen sides of his coat as far as they'd go, he belted his arms around her. The material didn't quite meet in the front, but snuggling against him warmed her up.

"Thanks." The curve of her head fit the slope of his shoulder like he was her own tailor-made pillow. She was hoping for another idea tonight and had a sneaking suspicion one would materialize at his house.

"My pleasure, but don't get too comfortable. Our stop's next."

A few quiet minutes later, they puttered to the dock at the foot of the Rusty Scupper, the restaurant that had anchored Federal Hill's foothills for the past thirty years. Zara and Brendan disembarked, climbed the stairs to the street, and clattered up the fieldstone path to his glossy red front door.

"I can't believe I met you only six days ago," she said as he unlocked his house.

"Feels like longer, right? In a good way." He opened the door and stood aside to let her enter. He'd left the overhead on, and it bathed the hallway in a honey-gold glow.

"Yes, exactly."

"Can I take your coat?"

"Please do." She shrugged it off and handed it over.

"Well, no wonder you were cold." He slipped her coat onto a hanger. "This thing is as substantial as a grocery bag."

Zara unzipped her booties. "Fashion comes at a price."

"Hypothermia?" He threw his coat onto a hanger, toed off his oxfords, and filed them in a cubby before shutting the closet door.

"Okay if I leave these here?" She pointed to the lineup of shoes that included a pair of Brendan's snow boots and a tiny pair of sparkly purple Uggs.

"Yep. Nice shoes, by the way."

"Thank you. I wanted to prove I own girlie shoes."

"I never doubted it. Want to get comfortable in the living room? I promise I've gotten rid of all the party decorations." A cluster of wilted Ravenna Mylar balloons shambled along the hallway. "Except for those."

"Ravenna isn't aging well, huh?" Zara smiled at her reflection in the silvery side of the balloon.

"Em made me pinky-swear I wouldn't throw them out. Total mistake. I almost pissed myself on Monday because of them."

"What?" She laughed.

"Em was at pre-K, and I'm in the kitchen, working. I got up to refresh my coffee, and they were *right there*, next to me, leering."

"Bitches." She punched a balloon in its smirk.

"Thanks for defending me." He kissed her on the hand. "Can I get you a drink? Water? Beer? Wine?"

"Wine, please. Red, if you have it."

"Coming right up." He twirled her in the hallway, changing places with her to get to the kitchen. He flicked on the pendant lights dangling above the island, woke his computer, and punched up a website. Acoustic rock spilled from the speakers.

"What are we listening to?"

"I..." Brendan lifted his shoulders. "I might have made a playlist for us. I'll face this way so you don't see me blush."

"I like that you're old school."

As he rummaged in a drawer for a corkscrew, she texted Grier. *Don't wait up. Probably not coming home tonight.*

Grier responded with party and eggplant emojis.

Zara snorted and slipped her phone into her back pocket, then busied herself in the living room, examining the scattered photos. A framed family portrait rested on the mantle above the painted-brick fireplace. There was Brendan with Emma anchored on his hip, and, based on the resemblance, his parents, and his brother, sister-in-law, and their kids.

No Jess. Must be a recent portrait.

They were wearing white oxfords and jeans. Grier would never make a family do this—her philosophy was that everyone should wear their favorite outfits so the portrait reflected who they were.

Pictures of Emma, ranging from babyhood to today, lined the built-in shelves on either side of the fireplace. Zara smiled at an adorable portrait of the little girl in a fluffy pink outfit. Affection for Brendan's daughter washed over her. In it, Emma frowned, arms hugged tight around her middle, and she stared at the camera as though she wanted to eviscerate the photographer.

"Does Emma like pink?" she called.

"Absolutely not. She acts like pink clothes are made of razors."

Zara snorted. She had the same reaction to the floral Laura Ashley gear her mother bought her.

From the kitchen, a soft pop signaled Brendan had freed the cork. The stemware clattered against the counters, and the booze glugged into the glasses.

The last picture in the lineup revealed a skinnier, puffier-haired Brendan in a school uniform, surrounded by a bunch of other gangly teenage boys.

"Did you go to private school?" she asked.

"Catholic school, all twelve years. Cathedral of Mary Our Queen, then Loyola-Blakefield." He padded into the living room.

"Is Loyola all boys?"

"Sure is." Brendan proffered a generous glass of wine. "Which may have contributed to my girl-craziness in college."

"I figure you overindulge in whatever you're denied as a kid." Zara surveyed the house. "By the way, when it isn't covered in a layer of Ravenna, you have a gorgeous home."

"Thank you. Cheers." He clinked her glass.

"Have you lived here long?"

"Five years. We moved in a few months after Emma was born." He touched Zara on the hip. "Let's sit on the sofa."

"You bought this place when you were my age?" She followed him to the squashy leather. "How the hell did you purchase a prime piece of real estate in Federal Hill?"

"I wasn't your age." The sofa gasped under his thick body. He winked at Zara. "I was younger, but I also had unbeatable motivation. As a newlywed with a pregnant wife, I didn't want to live in my super-Catholic parents' basement any longer than I had to. They loved me and liked Jess, but didn't approve of the circumstances. Their disappointment wasn't fun to come home to."

"But the *money*, dude. How'd you afford it?" She clapped a hand over her mouth. "Sorry. There's my inappropriate question habit again. Don't answer that."

He peeled her hand away and kissed the center of her palm.

"It's okay. I've come to expect them from you. It's endearing. Anyway, the short version is my parents stashed away a bunch of money for me for college. Since I didn't need it for tuition, I asked if I could have it for the house."

"Why didn't you need the money for college?" She shivered. The boat ride chilled her more than she'd realized.

"Let me start a fire." He set his glass on the coffee table and pushed up from the couch. "Warm you up."

"You don't have to go to any trouble."

"You're worth it." He knelt in front of the fireplace and opened the flue. "Besides, fire's good on a cold winter's night."

"Not always. Remember? Charred studio?"

"We're safe. I replaced the fire extinguisher last year."

As he worked, she sank further into the cozy welcome of the couch. This whole scene was bone-meltingly pleasant, one she would not have painted herself in a few weeks ago. When the fire caught, he dimmed the lamps then returned to Zara, backlit by the growing flames. *Uhnf.* The flickering shadows snatching at his face cast him in an edgy light.

She shifted her hips to ease the delicious tightness the view inspired.

"Where were we?" He slid onto the couch. Closer this time, facing her. Courtesy of the growing fire, his body heat, and the heavy-lidded expression he wore, she was warming up in record time.

First, satisfy the curiosity while he was in a chatty mood. "Your college money."

"Right. I got a full ride and only needed to pay for room and board. So I used the rest of my college savings for down payment on a fixer-upper with good bones."

"A handsome face *and* brains?" She laid her hand on her cheek and batted her eyes at him. "You're a constant surprise, Brendan Stewart."

"Don't forget the body."

"Trust me. I never forget about your body."

He raised an eyebrow.

Maybe it was getting *too* warm in here? "Did you do the fixer-upping?"

"Not by myself. I contracted out the HVAC and electrical work. Mike, my brother, helped me renovate the basics before Emma was born. Nights and weekends for six months. I'm still paying him back with projects around his house."

"It's nice that your family was supportive of you."

"Yeah, they're good people. That's what family does."

Zara shook her head. "Not my family. I don't ask my parents for help."

"Why not?"

The open curiosity on his face was endearing. Her roommates knew all about her fraught relationship with her parents, but she'd never hashed it out beyond her close circle of friends. Didn't trust people with the information. Something about Brendan was so *good* though, and he actually had a kid. His opinion on the matter would be interesting.

"Because their help comes with a bucket of judgment and a litany of I-told-you-sos. There was even a spreadsheet tracking how much I owed them. So I'm working my ass off so I can clear the balance and clip all the strings attached to the money."

There. *Whew*. And where was her wine? Confessions called for booze.

Brendan wrapped his fingers around hers. "I'm sorry, Princess. It shouldn't be like that. If you ask for help, your parents should help. Not make you beg or lord it over you."

Sparks flitted through her veins. Who knew it would be such a thrill to have a dad validate her take on her situation? One thing was for sure—Emma was a lucky girl.

"I like your fairy tale." Zara hid her smile behind her wine glass as she drank.

"It's not a fairy tale. It's reality. Help shouldn't involve a balance sheet."

"I agree, but that hasn't been my experience."

"What a mind trip. Everyone needs unconditional help. I know I needed help to make the best of my mistakes. Shit. Not mistakes."

He raked his hair. The way his forelock flopped across his forehead in a way that made her want to tackle him. Could he be anymore adorable? The art world was full of snark and irony, and Brendan's earnestness was refreshing. She could listen to him all night. Zara shifted her legs and let him continue.

"My choices led to having a kid at twenty-two. Which meant I had to replan to support my daughter the way she deserved. Marriage, house, good job, stable income. I'm proud I pulled it off."

"Did what your family did for you cut into your sense of accomplishment?"

"Nope." He smiled at her. "They gave me start-up money and help. For which I am eternally grateful, but I sweated my ass off making this place livable. I jumped on overtime to pay the bills and build my career. Their help absolutely gave me a leg up—I realize hitting a double from second base doesn't mean I hit a home run. But I also worked hard, and I take pride in that."

He plucked the empty glass from her hand and set it on the coffee table.

Zara bit her lip. "I hadn't thought about it that way."

"Speaking of thoughts…" Brendan smoothed her hair behind her shoulder, skimming his fingers on her arm. A prickling thrill pooled at the nape of her neck. "You've been on my mind, Princess."

She swallowed hard. "What a terrible segue."

"Best I could do. I've been thinking about this mouth of yours." He ran his thumb along her bottom lip. "And how I want to lose myself in it."

Brendan circled point where her two lips joined. "This is the part that kills me, where your lips hook up at the corners. Makes your mouth look like a bow."

"A gift bow?"

"Not for you." He kissed the corner of her mouth. "A hunter's bow. You shoot me through the heart every time you smile."

"Congratulations. That's the corniest thing anyone has ever said to me."

"Corny doesn't mean wrong."

Zara sucked her breath between her teeth as he zip-lined his fingers along the chain of her necklace and leapt off at the pendent nestled between her breasts.

Nuzzling her neck, he shimmied a hand under her ass to slide her down on the sofa, pressing his body against hers from hips to chest. Ooh, yes, she liked this, laying under him, weighed down by his body.

He peeled up from her and smiled. The lock of hair dangling from his forehead begged her to play with it, and the strands were liquid between her fingers.

"I've been wondering, Brendan…"

"We're not done with Q & A for tonight?"

"One more."

"This should be a doozy."

"Why'd you ask me out?"

"I hear the popular answer is 'because you're hot. But that's not why I asked you out."

"Wait. So you're saying I'm *not* hot?"

A log crackled, sending a shower of sparks heavenward.

"C'mon, you know you're gorgeous. The thing I found

irresistible? You were nice to my kid. You talked to her like she was a real, interesting person."

"Oh."

"Also, you've got the prettiest rack I've ever seen." The divot between her breasts earned a kiss from him. "I want to see more of it now, please."

"Only because you have good manners."

Zara shed her slouchy sweater, next the shimmery camisole, and left them on a puddle on the floor. She'd worn a red satin bra today. Simple, soft.

The heat from the fire warmed her exposed skin.

She threw her arm behind her head. "Better?"

"The best." Brendan sighed. He lay on his side next to her and spiraled his fingertips around her breast working her nipple into a stiff peak.

Pleasure and gratitude swirled together.

Earlier, as she painted the image of the two of them entwined in her studio, she'd wondered if she was amplifying things, making a bigger deal of their night together than it had been. The bolt of excitement rocketing through her body informed her she'd gotten it exactly right.

"I could do this all night," he murmured.

"I'll kill you if this is all we do all night."

"What else," he pinched her nipple with his lips through the satin, "do you have in mind?"

"Lots of this." She clutched his hair and dragged his face to hers. Once, twice, she flicked her tongue against his lip and he opened his mouth for her. *Yes*. The taste of him was becoming familiar and caused the same flood of happy reactions in her body.

"And this." Zara burrowed her hands between their bodies, intent on his belt.

"Wait. Let's go upstairs."

He eased off her and stood at the edge of the couch, raking his gaze along the length of her reclined body. Firelight danced along his body, and his heavy-lidded expression was inscrutable.

"What?"

"Thinking about how lucky I am. Come here."

He reached for her, pulling her upright. The moment he fixed his lips to hers, her knees wobbled. *This*. This was what she'd felt in the Tower, this happy fizz that blocked out all the noise, the doubt, the worry. In these moments, it was just the two of them.

He smoothed his hands along her hips and down, down, down,

until he cupped her ass, hauling her close against his hips.

"Where," she whispered, "is upstairs?"

"I'll show you. Hang on."

"Hang on? What are you—"

Brendan scooped her up by the backs of her thighs and she locked her legs around him. "I wanted to take you upstairs, but I didn't want to stop kissing you. Now I can do both."

He hiked her up further, his strong arms bracing her on the sides.

"I can you straight in the eyes you this way." She brushed his hair back and kissed the spot between his eyebrows then moved to his generous mouth. Suspended in his arms, she bounced to his walking rhythm. Strange, but pleasant to give herself over to his strength.

The dark wood creaked as he ascended the steps, turning as they wound upward and into the first bedroom. He kicked the door shut behind him.

He lowered her to the bed until she was seated on the edge. "I've been wanting to get you in here since the moment we met."

"Well, here I am. What have you been planning?"

"Something that involves a lot less clothing. Lay down."

Zara fell back on the cloudy comforter, mounds of it puffing up around her. Her belt was no challenge for him. Over his shoulder it went, and the buckle jingled as it hit the floor.

She tucked an arm behind her head, enjoying his progress along her body. Feathery kisses rained down on her belly, and he dipped his tongue into her navel. Goosebumps fanned over her skin.

"That tickles," she said, laughing.

One more lick before he flicked at the button at her waistband. "Laughing is not allowed. This is very serious business."

"I make no promises."

Under his deft attention, her jeans sighed open. Inch by inch, he peeled them down, tugging hard to free them from her ankles. Stupid skinny jeans. Fabulous as they made her ass appear, taking them off was harder than shedding skin.

Brendan parted her legs and her stomach fluttered in anticipation.

Please let it be as fiery this time around. On Wednesday, she'd been all heart-eyed about him. How could she not? Surprise multiple orgasms will do that to a woman. Now that she expected the heat and the fireworks, though, maybe he wouldn't be able to deliver on her sky-high hopes.

She prayed she was wrong.

He fanned his hands over her rib cage and dragged them down the flat of her abdomen until his palms rested on her thighs. Oh, good start. Sweeping his thumbs along the edge of her thong, he massaged her clitoris through the scrap of red satin.

There. She wriggled to increase the pressure against her awakening flesh, wanting more. More contact, more tension, more *him.*

Maybe, if she were lucky, he would...

"I want to go down on you, Princess."

Was he a mind reader? "Okay."

Okay? Oh for fuck's sake. He offered to do the thing I want more than breathing, and my sexy answer is 'okay?'

He slid his grip down her thighs, toward her knees, and spread her legs further apart. Chances were excellent she would fall apart from this alone.

"You have the softest skin." With firm, warm lips he kissed the crease of her hip. "Creamy, like vanilla. I want to lick you all day long."

He lapped at the top of her thigh and massaged her ass as he held her in place. Anticipation made stillness impossible. Each inch of skin he touched lit up like a comet, burning and breaking down her control until she was a squirming bundle of energy.

He kissed her mound through the satin of her thong then darted away, back to her thigh.

Stars. All she saw were stars.

"If you don't deliver soon I will lose my mind." Everything below her hips was taut with need. A few sparks from his tongue and she'd explode.

"Patience." He bit the top edge of her thong and withdrew, dragging it with him. With the last barrier gone, she was open to him, and with his tongue, he painted confident strokes along her outer lips. Fire. She was on fire, and she didn't mind the burn.

"More?" He massaged her breasts, his fingers slipping over the material that covered her pebbled nipples.

"Yes, oh please yes."

Brendan ducked back between her legs and dropped kisses along her seam. His lips lingered, firm, and oh, the point of his tongue, warm, wedged in between her lower lips. He worked it, opening her inch by tortuous, sweet inch.

With his thumbs, he massaged the outer edges of her sex, coaxing her to bloom. She was like the lilies in the bouquet he'd sent, splitting and opening in the right conditions.

"There. Oh, yes, *there,*" she gasped.

He swirled around her shy pearl, then flicked his tongue, alternating, teasing until she was overwhelmed with sensation. Electricity shot from the center of her body, radiating outward as though beams of light erupted from her hands, feet, and the top of her head.

She was close. *So close.* While he continued to work her with his mouth, he nudged her opening with his fingers. Slow at first, hooking upward to find her sweet spot inside then speeding up the rhythm.

The orgasm built and burst before Zara could herald its arrival. She settled for pulsing after math.

"You," she sighed and brushed her hair from her face, "are a wonderful man."

~ * ~

Brendan rose from between Zara's legs. A lazy smile played on her lips. Each time he earned one of her satisfied smiles, he felt like a hero.

He planted his fists on either side of her waist and kissed her sternum above the clasp of her bra.

"Lay down," she said. "You're giving me vertigo."

He did as he was told. "So that was good, then?"

"Beyond good. I don't know my own name." She rolled onto her side, facing him.

"It's Princess."

"Hardly." She raised an eyebrow. "Oral sex wasn't in any fairy tale I've ever read."

The swell of her ass was smooth under his hand. "You're reading the wrong versions. Anything else you need?"

"My brain isn't working. You have the good ideas tonight, anyway. Suggest something."

"That is a dangerous thing to say to a man in my state." He fingered the chain of her necklace where it rested on her breast. "But I'll have a light bulb moment."

"I have faith in you." Zara pinched the front of his shirt and let it snap to his chest. "Before we go further—side note, I want to go much further—you have to take off my shirt. I don't want to ruin it in the heat of passion."

"Done." He sat up and pulled the shirt off over his head.

"Lose the jeans too."

"For a person with a broken brain, you're super bossy." He unzipped and let the denim fall to the floor. His boxers transformed into a plaid dick tent, so he shucked them too. From the nightstand drawer, he yanked out a strip of condoms.

"Prepared *and* hopeful, tonight, I see."

"And you?"

"Same. Before you put that on…"

"Yeah?" He paused, teeth about to tear open the packet.

She bit her lip, hesitating. "I want you against me."

"Your wish is my command." The bed welcomed him, and his weight tipped her toward him. He slipped his arm beneath her head, allowing her to use his bicep as a pillow.

They curved together, like double parentheses.

"Like this?" He wrapped his arm around her waist and stretched his hand over her belly, hugging her to him, his erection pressing against the cleft of her ass. This simple intimacy warmed him more than the fire, eased his tension more than the wine.

"Perfect." Zara rubbed her foot along his calf, rustling the hair on his legs.

He nuzzled her hair and kissed her shoulder blade. "Your ink is amazing, by the way. It had to have hurt like a motherfucker."

"It did, and thank you."

"Is there a special meaning to it?"

"It's a painting of mine," she said. "Of a cherry tree outside my parents' inn. Anyway, the painting won first place in a regional show for high-schoolers. Winning showed me I could be a legit artist, and I decided, right then and there, to go to art school. I wanted this tattoo so I always have my painting with me."

"Who owns it now?"

"I sold it to the congressman who sponsored the show. It paid for my application and first semester of books."

He ran his fingers along the twisting trunk to its termination at the small of her back. "You must be made of cream. The roughest part of you is softer than the softest part of me."

"I have rough parts." She ground against his hard length. "What about your triangle tattoo? Any special meaning?"

"Can mean a bunch of different things to different people." He nipped at her shoulder and rocked his hips. "Trinity, or the perfect stable shape, or masculinity."

"Well, you're definitely that last one."

"Happy to show you how right you are."

"How?"

He trailed his fingers along her waist and whispered into her ear, "Get on your knees."

"Yes sir."

She glanced over her shoulder at him and he nearly came from the desire in her eyes. He ripped open the packet and rolled the condom down his shaft. Positioning himself behind Zara, he eased her legs wider and palmed the pale ivory roundness of her ass. She shimmied, encouraging.

"I'm not sure I can go slow." He swooped his thumbs across the small of her back and hooked his grip around her hips.

"Don't." She flicked her hair and locked eyes with him. "I want it fast."

Brendan sank home, and Zara pulsed around him.

This is the only place in the universe I want to be right now.

He lost himself in the movement, in her sweet softness under him. *So good, so fucking good.* He ran his hands from the dimples above her ass, up the trunk of her cherry tree, until he hit the red stripe of her bra cutting across her shoulder blades.

"Up," he said, and tugged her to him by the flimsy material.

The front clasp of the bra flipped open with a quick flick, and he slipped it from her shoulders. Over his head it went, landing in a corner. With her breasts freed, he claimed them and gently pinched her nipples. She arched her back against his chest, and he clamped his arm across her collarbone, steadying her as they moved together.

"You're going to make me come," he groaned into her ear.

She kissed his arm. "Do it. I want you to come, Brendan."

With his name on her lips he was gone, erupting, coming like a lightning bolt. He thrust again and again as the earthquakes quieted to tremors. Spent, he dropped his forehead to her sweat-slicked spine, breathing hard. When he withdrew, they collapsed side-by-side.

"So that was fun," she said.

"I'll say." After a few minutes, he kissed her on the cheek. "Back in a minute."

He slid off the bed and padded to the bathroom. After tidying himself up, he shuffled downstairs to check on the fire. Satisfied the smoldering embers would safely burn out, he poured a glass of water, double-checked the front door was locked, then went back upstairs.

Routine, but also out of this world, because he was headed back to a woman who excited and soothed him at the same time.

"Thirsty, Princess?" He grabbed the bedpost nearest her head and leaned to kiss her cheek. In his absence, Zara had put on his T-shirt, hers now, per their wager, and settled into his side of the bed. *Hmm.* He'd hoped she would stay over, but didn't realize it meant giving up his side of the bed. "Mmm-hmm." She raised herself on her elbows and took the cup from him, and he slipped into pajama pants.

"Scoot over. You're on my side."

"I don't think so. If I'm the princess, I get to pick my side. Flawless logic."

She stretched and flopped back against the pillows. How could he argue with the dark-haired beauty in his bed?

"Fine." He twisted his lips. "This time."

He lifted the comforter on the other side, climbed inside, and punched the pillow into shape. Sleeping on this side, furthest from the door, was wrong.

Settling in with Zara, and the way her body melted against his? That was all kinds of right.

Twelve

"Would I be a total glutton if I had a sixth pancake?" Zara swiveled in the chair. Her naked knees brushed the underside of the island counter. The lazy breakfast lulled her into an unusual state of calmness. The whole morning had progressed slowly. Last night's muscle-melting exercise, the million thread-count sheets, and the perfect temperature in his bedroom, meant she'd snoozed way past dawn.

Unusual for her.

Across from her, Brendan sipped coffee, wearing nothing but loose-waisted pajama bottoms and a dishtowel slung over his shoulder. Luckily, he made the best blueberry pancakes she'd ever eaten, so if he caught her drooling, she could blame the food.

"Go for it. They'll go to waste otherwise."

She forked up another pancake from the stack, slathered it in butter and syrup, and cut the whole circle into squares. Gold star to Brendan for easing them into the day with comfort food.

Her other sleepover adventures had involved scurrying away within ten minutes of waking. She figured she'd save herself and the guy the awkwardness of early morning chitchat. Except this wasn't awkward. This was a solid block of nice.

"What's on your agenda today?" he asked.

"Studio." She slid a crisp, airy bite into her mouth. A droplet of molasses escaped the forkful and landed on her exposed thigh.

A part of her wanted to stay and laze the day away, but her itchy fingers had returned. Painting was the only balm. There was an image, an idea that crystallized last night, before she fell into the deepest sleep she had in years. Brendan kept racking good guy points too. For instance? Her *reveille* had been a kiss and a cup of grizzly-bear strong coffee, perhaps the most perfect way to be gentled from a slumber.

She stifled a yawn. "What about you?"

"I missed church already." He winked at her. "I pick Emma up

144

at one. We normally eat lunch at Gertrude's and go to the Free Family Sunday series at the BMA afterward."

"What is that?"

He stretched and extended his arms in an iron cross. His wingspan matched the length of the monolithic island. Her gaze roved the shirtless planes of his flesh. She'd asked him a question, but for the life of her, she couldn't remember what.

"Free Family Sunday?" He dropped his arms. "Usually a craft relating to an exhibit. This week, we're making a lotus light. I'm terrible at it, but Emma loves going."

"You're such a good dad." Zara sipped her coffee.

He pulled the dishtowel from his shoulder and slapped it against his hand, letting the cloth slide along his palm. She wished she were that floral rectangle.

He waved her off. "It's all for smoke and mirrors."

"Yeah, I'll bet."

"So I was thinking," he said, and smiled over the rim of his mug.

"Uh oh. Dangerous."

"Jess lives in Roland Park. The Tower and your house are both on the way. I could drop you off at either place, if you like?"

"I like that idea." She glanced at the microwave clock. A glittery feeling coiled between her hips. They had time "Since it's only ten o'clock now, whatever shall we do to occupy ourselves before departure time?"

"I have a few ideas. Like—"

The doorbell rang, and Brendan furrowed his brow. He parked his mug on the counter amid the haphazard ingredients from breakfast. "Back in a minute."

Hyperconscious she was wearing only a T-shirt, fresh underpants, and a smear of syrup, she scooted off the chair and peeked around the corner as he opened the door.

"Daddy," a honey lemon voice shrieked. "Surprise!"

Zara froze.

Beyond the A-frame of Brendan's legs, stood two tiny legs attached to blinking high top sneakers. Beyond them were other, bigger legs wearing killer caramel-colored boots.

Shit. With her heart pounding, she retreated and stood ramrod straight next to the wall. Her gaze flitted around the room. She was trapped. Unless she escaped through the French doors to the deck. In thirty degree weather. Without pants.

"We had *candy* for breakfast! *Then* we went to The Donut

Shoppe!"

"Wow," he said in a flat tone. "Candy and doughnuts?"

Shit, shit, shit. Zara eyed the pantry. Possible escape plan?

No, my dignity won't allow me to hide among canned goods.

"Where are my balloons?" Emma's voice bounced off the walls, and someone shut the door. They were inside now. "Mommy got me a balloon, and I want my balloons to meet."

Okay, so, this was happening. Time to approach it with confidence.

Zara perched on a stool at the island, crossed her legs, and tried to appear as collected as a woman could while wearing only a concert T-shirt and just-fucked hair. Maybe Brendan would keep everyone penned in the foyer, and she had a chance to retain her dignity?

Little feet pounded down the hallway. Emma blurred into the kitchen and tumbled ass over teakettle, smacking into the floor. The balloon she'd been tugging behind her floated to the ceiling.

Zara bolted from her chair and knelt next to the facedown pile of curls. "Are you okay?"

Brendan and Jess hurried into the room, bringing the winter chill with them.

"Daddyyyyyyyy!" the little girl wailed.

Wincing, Zara fought not to cover her ears. Christ, it would've hurt less if the kid had stabbed her in the ear with an Exacto knife. She toughed it out and didn't reveal her discomfort. She was, after all, the mature adult here.

Sans pants.

Brendan squatted and rubbed Emma's back as her screeching arced higher, then calmed. "Em, sweetheart, you're fine."

She lifted her head, revealing a fresh pink blot on her cheekbone. Ooh, that would be some bruise. The little girl blinked big, brown eyes as fat teardrops coasted over her cheeks.

"It's you!" Emma sat up, widening her eyes. "How come you're here?"

"Uh…" Zara glanced at Brendan. "Your dad invited me over."

Emma glared at her. "Daddy would NOT be friends with Ravenna's evil sister."

"Ravenna doesn't have an evil sister," Brendan said.

Jess appeared in the kitchen, wearing a black-and-white chevron coat and faded skinny jeans.

Emma pressed back against her mother. "She's not in the movie, but Mommy read about her."

"Em." He palmed his daughter's shoulder. "Your book bag is

by the front door. Can you put it in your room?"

"Okay." She galloped away, paused in the hallway, then stuck her tongue out at Zara.

Well, then.

The moment their daughter was gone, Jess swiveled her gaze toward Zara. "Hi again."

The air in the house was freezing, but it had nothing to do with February. She willed her T-shirt to grow, but the stubborn thing refused.

"I hear you've already met," Brendan said, and crossed his arms over his naked chest.

Jealousy forked through her heart. She was *not* okay with him being shirtless in front of this woman. They had a child together, so obviously Jess had seen it all before. Which was precisely the problem. Was this a thing that happened often? Him half-naked and everyone treating it like it was no big deal? Or were they all graciously ignoring it?

"Sorry, B. I couldn't wait to meet the girl who stole Emma's heart. When the opportunity presented itself, I took it." Jess's red-lipped grin stretched wide. Zara was surprised her stunningly white teeth weren't covered in icicles. "So, you're dating the face-painter princess. How *adorable*."

If there was one thing that plucked her nerves, it was a dismissive tone. Like Zara should be embarrassed of working hard? Well, not today, lady. Not. Today. Even if Jess was remarkably put together for nine o'clock in the morning and Zara was wearing a too-short T-shirt and syrup, she could go toe-to-toe with her attitude.

"That's only one of my side gigs," she said. "I'm an artist. I've got an upcoming show."

"Really? Which gallery? I love to feature artists on my blog. I curate a weekly round-up of interesting things I've discovered, and I could slot you in."

"She's not a source of content for you, Jess."

Was Brendan talking about her like she wasn't even here? Zara cut at glance at him, but he was too busy focused on Jess to notice.

"The Schwarz Gallery," Zara said, pleased she landed at one of the most reputable galleries in the city. *Suck on that, Messy Jess.*

She clapped. "Wow, fantastic—John and I are such good friends."

Groan. Of course they were.

"I'll include you in a round-up. It always boosts John's business, and I'm sure it would help you out, too. Anything for a friend, you know?"

Who was the friend in this case? John? Had to be, because there was no way this woman had just added Zara to her friend list. Not with how her eyes iced over every time she looked in this direction.

"So, B, does this..." she gestured toward Zara, "...mean we're doing away with the rule about waiting three months before introducing a significant other to Emma?"

"The rule stands. I was supposed to pick her up from you in a couple of hours, remember? Not my fault you showed up here."

Jess grinned and tucked her chin into her shoulder. "You're right. I'm sorry, but something came up, and I need your help."

Was this real life? Was Zara watching Brendan's ex-wife fake flirt with him? The pendulum swings of this woman's emotions were tough to absorb. This fake sweetness met Brendan's irritation, and the whole thing made Zara's soul itch. The room rippled with tension, like the walls themselves held their breath as these two worked their way through the conversation.

"I wish you would've called first," he said, then leaned on the island.

"I did! You didn't answer. I left a voicemail and sent a couple of texts. I'm not sure what..." her gaze drifted to Zara, "...you were doing. I'm grateful there were no emergencies."

Heat spread across her chest and swirled over her face. Embarrassment must not mix well with pancakes because they'd turned to lead in her stomach.

"I'm sorry." He sighed. "I should have checked my phone this morning. What's up?"

Oh no, this sounded like the start of a conversation. How great would it be if she could just disappear? And if disappearing wasn't in the cards, her next most fervent wish was for pants.

"I wanted to save Emma from a boring car ride. My cousin... You remember Callie?"

He nodded, and Jess nattered on about a cousin who was flying in to scope out colleges in the Metro area. Brendan's annoyance seemed to melt away as he caught up with his ex about people they had in common.

Zara knit her brows. What happened to the angry Brendan from last night? The one who declared everything to do with his ex-wife as complicated? What she was seeing in front of her didn't seem so complicated. No, this chummy, shirtless chatting between her whatever-he-was and his ex was bizarre.

All she wanted was to get dressed and leave, but she couldn't head upstairs without drawing attention herself. *Maybe there's an apron around here I can slap on.* She searched the surfaces in the kitchen. *Nope. Dishtowels and sponges.*

"People don't stay the same, B." Jess bumped him with her elbow.

There was a bucket of flirt in that bump.

Forget pants, and forget leaving. Now the thing she wanted most in the world to cleave Jess's arm from her body.

Okay. Not really.

She sucked in her lips and bit down to pinch back the snarky insults she wanted to hurl at Jess. Was this jealousy? No. Couldn't be. She refused to be jealous of their shared history. She and Brendan didn't know each other well enough for that to make sense.

"Anything I need to know for school this week?" he asked, and pushed off the island.

"It's her turn for Show & Tell on Monday. Oh, and I couldn't wash her naptime blanket because of the dryer. It's in her book bag."

"I'll handle it. You'd better take off so you're not late to the airport." His feet slapped the hardwoods as he herded her toward the front door. "Say hi to Callie for me, okay?"

"Of course." Jess peeked around Brendan's body. "Nice seeing you again, Sara."

"Zara," she corrected, but Jess was already halfway down the hall.

At the stairwell, she called, "'Bye, Emma Bear."

"Mommy, wait. One more hug." Emma threw herself around her mother's knees.

Jess bent to kiss her on the top of her head. "Until Wednesday, sweetheart."

"Until Wednesday, sweetheart," the little girl parroted.

Brendan closed and locked the front door behind Jess.

"I'm going to get Em settled—be back in a minute," he called and disappeared up the stairs with his daughter.

She should make her escape now, but she didn't want to interfere with whatever was going on upstairs, or risk Emma overhearing an awkward conversation. Sigh. She was still trapped.

When he returned to the kitchen, carrying his daughter, he wore a soft white undershirt she just knew smelled like clean linen and aftershave.

Emma had a fresh bandage on her forehead and clung to her father. She cast shadowy glances at Zara and whisper-yelled. "Daddy, I want her to go."

"Em, don't be rude." He flashed an apologetic smile at her.

He didn't need to be sorry. She was with Emma on this one. She wanted to go, but hadn't figured out a graceful exit strategy. Awkward might be the only way.

Emma let loose an exasperated, growly groan. "I want apple juice."

"How do you ask?"

"Please."

"That's better." He plucked a short plastic cup from the cabinet next to the refrigerator, poured three fingers of juice into it, then set it on the counter. "Be careful not to spill."

"I won't." Emma clambered onto a stool.

"Did you have fun at Mom's?"

"Uh-huh." She spun around in the barstool. The leather backrest *whish-whish-whished* against the edge of the counter on each revolution. As she spun, they talked about mundane stuff. School, classmates, and swimming at an indoor pool yesterday. Nothing earth-shattering, but they were the threads of everyday life that, over time, stitch a relationship into closeness.

The cozy scene sent Zara's heart spasming in a way she couldn't explain.

Brendan's eyes blazed with affection while he chatted with his daughter. All that muscled man, leaning over the island, a happy satellite revolving around his tiny girl-star. Whereas Zara was on the edge of their universe. At best, maybe she was a comet burning brightly as she passed over the horizon.

"Want to go to the museum today, kiddo?" he asked.

"Yes." She *whished* her seat toward Zara. "But not you."

"Emma Katherine. You are being rude."

"That's okay," Zara said. She might not love the tone, but she agreed with Emma. The last thing she wanted to do was crash a daddy-daughter date.

"No, it isn't." He frowned at his daughter. "Say you're sorry."

Emma stared at Zara, expressionless.

Holy shit, Emma was *gargoyling*.

Zara bit the inside of her lips to keep from laughing. The kid had zero intention to apologize. Why should she? Some weirdo half-dressed woman was hanging out with her dad. Zara fully supported the little girl's shade.

She waved off his intervention. "Brendan, I don't—"

"Please, Zara. It's important for Emma to learn she can't be rude."

"Even if I'm not offended?"

"That doesn't matter. Come on, Em. Say you're sorry."

Emma's shoulders curled further inward. Jesus, he was laying it on thicker than Gesso. Couldn't he see his daughter's reaction was beautifully true? Why couldn't he let her just *be*?

Zara winced. The whole scene triggered her rebellious streak. He was handling this wrong, and she had to stop it. "Don't apologize to me, Emma, because you're right. I shouldn't be here. So, I'm going to go."

She scuttled upstairs to find her pants. What the hell was *wrong* with her? Why should she care how he parented his kid? Where did she get off, interfering with what he thought was right? Though, for the record, he *was* wrong. At least for forcing an apology.

Brendan followed her. "What is going on?" he asked as she tugged on her jeans. She was seriously going to have to reconsider wearing skinny jeans. They interfered with a quick escape.

"Nothing. I…I have a lot going on today."

She fumbled with the button at the top of her fly and refused to face him.

"Come on, Princess. Talk to me."

"There's nothing to talk about." She scoured the room for her bra. How had it landed under the bed? She slipped it on under his shirt—*her* shirt—and snapped the clasp. The gnarled band dug into her back, but she wasn't wasting time to fix it.

She ran her hands through her hair. That was sum total attention it would get before she left. No time for makeup, either. What a contrast with Jess, who looked like she was on her way to a classy champagne brunch.

Belt? Where's my belt? Nah. Fuck it. Don't need it. I have a ton of belts.

"I shouldn't have stayed last night," she muttered. If she hadn't stayed, she wouldn't have been here for the early arrival, and she wouldn't have to scurry away like a draft dodger.

"Don't say that. I'm glad you stayed."

Truth was, she was happy she stayed too. Thrilled she'd curled up next to this man for a solid eight hours, content and dozy in his arms. She was happy until the moment his reality came bounding through the door.

"When can I see you again?" he asked.

"Brendan, I…"

He stood with his legs apart, fists planted on his hips, and his biceps bulged. No. She would not be distracted.

"How's Wednesday?" A muscle twitched in his jaw. "I've got Emma 'til then."

"Why don't we check in?" Zara took a deep breath and let it go, slow and easy.

"Okay." He pressed his lips into a thin line.

She rushed past him. Downstairs, she zippered her feet into the booties, then yanked her coat from the closet. Its hanger clattered to the floor.

"Are you leaving?" Emma galloped Ravenna's horse, Kilda, in the air.

Brendan appeared at the bottom of the stairs.

"I..." Zara tore her gaze away from him and the crinkle blossoming between his eyebrows. "Yes."

"'kay 'bye." Emma disappeared into the living room without a backward glance.

God, that kid was awesome.

Where had that burst of affection come from? Who *was* she? Zara scrabbled at the deadbolt. Why won't the fucking thing turn?

"Here, let me." He reached past her to twist the shiny brass lock. "I'll call you, okay?"

"Rad." She kissed him, a quick peck, and tasted the sweet syrup from breakfast. "'Bye."

She sped over the brick walkways of the Inner Harbor, past the Science Center, and toward Pratt Street. Her unkind heels clicked off a steady chant of *stu-pid, stu-pid, stu-pid*. Shoes were the one thing she'd forgotten. She'd packed fresh underpants, a pair of socks, and a toothbrush, but somehow she'd blanked on day shoes. Not a walk of shame, exactly, but she wasn't proud, either.

Stu-pid, stu-pid, stu-pid.

Her cell phone rang, jangling her nerves. *It couldn't be him already, could it?*

It was local number, but she didn't recognize it. She accepted the call. "Hello?"

"Is this Zara Kissette?" The voice was familiar.

"Yes." She dodged a jogger huffing in the other direction.

"This is John Schwarz. Hope all's well with you this morning."

Oh, God, please don't change the deadline on me.

"It's...sunny." She squinted against the bright sun glistening on the Harbor.

"It is, isn't it?" He paused, and the many permutations of how his pause could end made her want to vomit. "You must be wondering why I'm calling, aren't you?"

"I assume it's about the show?"

"It is. I ran into Eleanor Jones yesterday, and she mentioned you have exciting new work. That you've been in a creative frenzy since your studio caught fire. I'd love to see what she's talking about, if you have time today?"

Shit. What did Eleanor tell him?

"Yes, of course. Should I come to the gallery, or..."

"I'd prefer it if I could come to your studio. Given how fresh it is, I wouldn't want you to haul it around Baltimore."

She rolled her ankle in a loose chink of masonry. In a blink, her phone flew from her hand and skittered across the bricks. *No, no, no!* She chased the slippery rectangle, willing it to stop before it reached the lip of the Harbor. *Phew.* The life preserver stand served its purpose and halted the phone.

Please let Schwarz still be on the line.

"Hello?" she held phone to her ear. "Did I lose you?"

That might have been the final nail in the coffin for my poor phone.

"Whoa, kiddo. Are you okay?"

"Sorry. I dropped my phone." She braced herself against the life preserver stand and rotated her ankle a few times. Seemed okay. "I'm heading to my studio now. You could meet me there, if you like?"

"Sounds great. You're in the Bromo-Seltzer Arts Tower? The building Eleanor manages?"

"Yes. Studio 7-2."

"I'll be there within the hour."

Her back went rigid. *Why, universe? Why do you wallop me with these things all at once?*

"Great," she said through tight lips. "See you there."

She hit the end icon and nudged the fresh crack in her phone. The thing would be unusable soon, but that wasn't a problem to solve today. The first problem to solve was this insubordinate shoe situation. Zara gingered toward Harbor Place to buy a pair of cheap shoes at H&M. Not because her ankle hurt—though it did—but because she couldn't take the heels calling her stupid for the half-mile walk to her studio.

~ * ~

An hour later, Zara rested against the windowsill in her studio, dressed in last night's clothes and a tight pair of ballet flats, chewing her thumbnail while John Schwarz examined her newest work. The painting would speak for itself, but she wished she'd taken the time put on makeup, or at least straighten out the gnarled band of her bra irritating her ribs.

Pay attention. She fixed her gaze on John Schwarz's balding head, which happened to be as round as one of those Ravenna balloons.

Don't do the gargoyle thing.

She picked up her nearest brush, a beauty of a double-thick Filbert.

Or the inappropriate questions thing. DO NOT ask this man inappropriate questions.

"Well." Schwarz tapped his folded glasses on his chin. "You painted this recently?"

"Earlier this week." She twirled a brush between nimble fingers. If she focused on the twirling, maybe could ignore the high tide pounding of blood in her ears.

"Tough break about the fire. Eleanor told me about it."

"Thanks."

He slipped his on his glasses and inspected the painting. "Why didn't you say anything when I invited you to the show?"

"I didn't know yet. I found out right after." The lie slithered free before she could stop it. She wanted him to think well of her, not judge her as someone who would gamble with the integrity of his show. Although, *crap.* Eleanor might've filled him in on the timeline?

She held her breath.

"The pieces you showed me during our meeting—they were ruined in the fire?"

"They were." Zara's brush slipped mid-twirl and clattered to the floor. She swept it up and returned it to the worktable. "I lost everything. I had a few other pieces at my house, but they weren't my best work. I thought I could recreate the paintings I'd shown you, but they didn't turn out right. Honestly, I was kind of in a panic and decided I needed to try something new and different."

"You're living the Phoenix story. Rising from the ashes."

"I suppose so." She needed another outlet for her nerves, so she twisted her ring around her finger. "I should have told you, I realize that now. But I wanted to have new work for you to consider. Without a full portfolio, I was afraid you'd rescind the offer to participate in the show."

Which he can still do.

"Can you complete two more pieces by the deadline? We hang in ten days."

She stopped twisting. She flashed to the composition she'd envisioned as she snuggled against Brendan in bed this morning. For sure, she had a painting in the chamber.

"Yes. They might be wet, but they'll be ready."

That third one, though...

"Good." Schwarz's eyes were magnified in the half-moon lenses of his glasses. "Because if they're as exciting as this, your paintings could be the highlight of the show."

Her knees wobbled, and she wanted to fall into a boneless human puddle in the middle of her studio floor. Probably not the most professional reaction, so she tensed her muscles in a superhuman effort to stay upright.

"The highlight?" Her voice was thin and reedy.

He nodded. "Originally, I offered you a consignment contract. But this—this is something special. I'd like to convert the offer to a representation contract. Pending delivery of the additional pieces, naturally."

She clapped a hand over her mouth to stifle a giggle, and her smile bubbled against her fingers. This was a serious business offer. A representation contract meant Schwarz wanted to broker Zara's work for the long-term. He'd be Zara's storefront, the conduit through which she could establish herself as an artist.

He smiled. "I take it you'd like the Schwarz Gallery to represent you?"

"Oh my God, yes, of course."

"Great, kiddo," Schwarz said. "Our business manager will draw up the paperwork. To be clear—you don't have any work for sale elsewhere? That's a hard line in our contract. We'd have exclusive rights to sell your work. Eleanor said you have nothing in the Resident's Showcase."

"No. I don't have anything on the walls right now."

"Excellent." He removed his glasses and slipped them into his shirt pocket. "I'll need a bio and photo of you for the program. Can you have that to me by Tuesday?"

"Not a problem." Zara would ask Grier to do the honors.

"Welcome to the Schwarz team, Zara Kissette. You have a bright future ahead of you."

She hunched her shoulders and did her best to ignore her anxious thoughts.

Only if I can hang on to my flame.

~ * ~

Zara squinted at the cobalt skies over Camden Yards from her studio window and idly ran her thumb along the new crack in her phone, testing if it would cut her. Nope. Safe to text.

After Eleanor collected Schwarz for a lunch date, Zara made

good progress on the next painting, but she had hours more work ahead of her.

No chance she was making Sunday roommate dinner.

She fired off a group text. Ordinarily she'd call to cancel, but not tonight. She didn't need to clue anyone into her stress. Her wobbly voice would be a dead giveaway.

Heyyyy lady-wives, can't make Sunday dinner. Am painting all the strokes.

Brooke responded first. *Boo. Melinda made tacos, and you were supposed to tell us about your sleepover.*

Only if you tell me about your mystery sidepiece.

Brooke texted a frowny face. *Fine. Details soon, tho. I'm thirsty for them.*

She sent another text, this time to Grier alone. *You around? Need a photo favor.*

Happy to! Now?

Grier was the best. Maybe there was grace in accepting help.

She smiled, and typed, *Nope—tomorrow. Late night here. Details in the a.m., cool?*

Grier sent the thumbs up emoji

Zara clicked off her phone, grabbed her brush, then got to work.

~ * ~

Brendan glanced at the microwave clock as he logged off his computer. Midnight. He riffled his hair and checked his phone. No incoming messages or missed calls. Hmph. He couldn't let today fade into tomorrow without checking in on Zara, not with the way she busted ass out of his house.

You up, princess?

He waited for a response for a minute, two, three, then trudged upstairs and checked on Emma. She was snoring, snuggled among sixty-eight stuffed animals.

He shushed the door closed then padded toward the bathroom. Zara's toothbrush dangled in the holder. She must've forgotten it in her hurry. Christ, she'd barely gotten dressed before she bolted, let alone packed her gear.

Not the most mature move on her part, but he couldn't blame her.

He sighed. This morning had not gone as planned. Instead of pancakes and sex, it'd been pancakes and stress. He had to talk to her, sooner rather than later. Things were bound to get more awkward if too much time went by.

It wasn't like he could change the facts of his life. He had a daughter. He had an ex. Simple facts.

Then again, not so simple. What was the best way to ease into a life where these people overlapped and it didn't give him heart palpitations? Because Zara had gotten under his skin, and for each minute he spent with her, he wanted three more.

He docked his phone in his alarm clock to charge before peeling down to his boxers. Next, he twitched the comforter aside, then sat on the cool, crisp sheets. When he flopped onto his pillow, the citrus and lavender smell of her puffed up around him.

Great. Just fucking great.

Groaning, he curled onto his side and mashed his face into the pillow. Tonight he'd toss and turn until dawn, for sure. He snapped his bedside lamp off then closed his eyes, letting his memory play back last night's highlights.

He was at the part where he was just about to slide Zara's panties past her hips when his phone chirped. Sitting up, he snatched it, then perched his heels on the side rail of his bed.

A smile spread across his face.

Hey, she'd written. *I'm up. Too much coffee + much painting = awake all night. Love what I'm painting, tho.*

His hovered his thumbs over the keypad. He had to get this right. Convey he'd boxed her in this morning, but hadn't meant to. That he was on board when she suggested they leave this as a free-range relationship and not label it or worry about what other people thought.

All through texts.

No pressure.

About this morning... He jittered his feet against the bedrail.

Yeah. Awkward. Could you sense my discomfort?

He snorted and typed, *Only a lot.*

How's Emma?

New bruise, but OK. You? Did this morning scare you off?

The dots pulsed. Eternity ticked by.

Texting sucked.

Brendan couldn't wait. He clicked on the telephone icon next to 'Princess' in the top of his messaging window. As the phone rang, he paced. His mind cleared when he was in motion.

One ring.

Two rings.

Three rings.

God, the phone sucked too. Adrenaline pumped through his chest, and he choked the bedpost to the point his knuckles blanched.

Would she let him slide into voice mail?

"Hi," she said.

Ah, there she was. Real. Breathy.

He released the bedpost and shook out his hand. He could do this. He could apologize for this morning without apologizing for the circumstances of his life.

"Hi, Princess. Do you have a minute?"

"Many. I'm literally waiting for paint to dry." The deep breath she took belied her sarcasm.

Brendan wanted to jump through the phone to be with her. He always did better face-to-face. It gave him a chance to read the other person. With Emma in the next room, though, he was on lockdown.

"Listen, I messed up this morning, and it's been bothering me ever since. My lotus lamp is shit because I couldn't concentrate."

She laughed, a sweet sound that quelled his nerves. "I thought you were calling to chastise me."

"What? No. I—"

"Come on. You're not mad I ran away? Like, literally ran?"

"I'm not *thrilled* you ran away, but I get it. Jess showing up out of the blue was a nightmare. I stayed calm for Emma's sake, but it caught me off guard. I didn't consider how weird it was for you."

"Thanks," Zara said.

"And I'm sorry Em was rude to you."

"Whoa, no Brendan. She did right to throw shade at the weird half-naked woman hanging out with her dad. It's what I would have done. Seriously, it'd be a crime to file down those instincts."

He pinched the bridge of his nose. Little soon for her to chime in on parenting choices. "I appreciate what you're saying, but—"

"Don't try to choke her spirit, is all."

Quiet roared on the phone. This wasn't what he wanted to talk about. At all. He wanted to make sure they were cool and that she understood the tricky balance he was trying to strike between dad life and dating. Not the manners he was trying to instill in his kid.

He leaned his forehead against the bedpost. "The reason I called was to explain that I'm figuring things out as I go. I haven't..."

Ah, hell. He might as well just say it.

"You're the first woman I asked out since Jess and I split up."

Silence. He glanced at the phone to make sure the call hadn't dropped. Nope, still going, the seconds ticking away. She wasn't the type to ghost, but he hadn't expected she'd be surprised into silence.

"You still there?"

"I'm here," she said, and laughed. "That's...wow. So you

really don't know what you're doing, is that what you're saying? But I have to warn you, if you're looking for me to Sherpa you through this, you're out of luck. I'm pretty clueless in matters of the heart."

He doubted that. She seemed to be doing fine.

"I wouldn't say I don't know what I'm doing. I mean, I had a plan. That's what Jess mentioned earlier—we're supposed to wait three months before introducing people we're dating to Em. Or reintroducing you, I guess, since she's already met you once."

He kicked around the room to his dresser. Better to pace and burn off this nervous energy than let her hear it in his voice.

"Are we dating?"

He should stop. Right now. Hadn't he *just* said he didn't want to scare her off? Then again, he'd never been good at listening to advice, even the advice he gave himself. "What would you call it?"

"Hanging out? Spending time together? We've only been on two dates."

"This is what people do now?" Brendan asked. "Noncommittal hook-ups?"

"Well, yeah. Reminder—two outings. A third is imminent, but still."

"Correction—we have three dates under our belts, Princess."

"Three?"

"You stayed over." He stretched out on his bed. "I'm abiding by Cinderella fairy tale rules. Dates end at midnight. So, breakfast was a fresh date. We changed clothes and shared a meal."

Zara laughed. "Okay. Fine, three times."

"The whole thing seems chicken shit."

"What whole thing?"

Brendan drummed fingers against his stomach. "The dating, but not calling it dating, so if it doesn't work out, it's all good because you weren't *dating*-dating."

"Are you calling me a chicken shit?"

"No." He twisted his lips. "Well, yes."

"Brendan Stewart, if this is how you pitch woo, you need to up your game."

"You're right. I'm rusty. I own that. But I stand by what I said." He threw an arm behind his head. "Question—are you *hanging out* with anyone else these days?"

"I can hear the air quotes."

"Answer the question."

"No, I'm not *hanging out* with anyone else."

"Do you plan to?"

"No."

"Good. I would like you to keep it that way." Brendan smiled. "Are you busy this week?"

"Work, but that's it. Why? Do you want to *hang out*?"

"No. I want to take you on a romantic date and pitch better woo. Wednesday?"

"Wednesday it is."

"Done. And Princess?"

"Yes?"

"This'll be fancy."

"Duly noted. I'll wear my tiara."

"What are you wearing now?"

"Tank top and jeans. My studio's hella hot, as per *use*."

Brendan pictured her leaning against a wall in her studio. "If it's hot, why don't you strip—"

"Daddddyyyy," Emma wailed outside his bedroom door. "I'm sick."

Oh man, midnight visits from Emma were never good. "Sorry, gotta run. Sick kid. Talk to you later." He yanked open the door in time for Emma to coat him with her half-digested dinner.

Thirteen

"Can you try to be chill about this?" Zara slipped the key in the door of her studio. "Promise me you won't be obnoxious or you can't come in."

"I will employ the genteel etiquette my privileged upbringing has afforded me, but I can't guarantee it'll work. I'm too fucking excited." Grier squealed and pom-pommed her fists. "Honestly, I'm going to pee my pants."

"Please don't." She opened the door, and her friend skipped over the threshold.

"It's so small." Grier clapped. Her supple leather gloves muffled the sound. "Melinda said it was small, but I had no idea it was such a shoebox."

"It's not *that* small." She pursed her lips. "It's a hundred fifty square feet."

"It's perfect, totally *bijou*. Seriously. Love." Grier caught sight of the worktable, and she widened her eyes. She pointed at the large bouquet of flowers overwhelming the table. "What are those?"

"Flowers."

"You're the worst. Okay, yes, flowers. From whom?"

She massaged her temples. "So shouty, so early on a Monday. Brendan sent them after our first date."

"Oh, Zara. That man has it bad for you." She stuck her nose in the middle of the bouquet. "Gorgeous. Calla lilies, roses, lisanthus, and freesia. He sent these last week? They're holding up well."

"Is that what the purple flowers are? Freesia and li—what'd you call it?"

"Lisanthus." Grier squatted, peeled off her gloves, then shrugged her giant bag of camera equipment onto the floor. "They're my mother's favorites. They're everywhere in her garden."

"In Ruxton?" Zara asked, referring to the Cushmans' primary estate. "Or in Bethany?"

"Ruxton. The gardeners can't get shit to grow in Bethany. Is there anywhere I can hang my coat?"

"Not really."

"How very Spartan of you." She folded her cashmere coat in a sloppy heap and dropped it on the floor. "I'm glad we're here. The studio and the flowers will make a stellar backdrop for your headshot. Shabby chic meets urban boho. With this natural light, I'll make you look like a goddamn goddess. Go stand by the window in the corner."

"Don't I always give off goddess vibes?" she asked, strolling into the pale shaft of light that slanted through the panes.

"More like down-three-pints-of-blood vibes. Though, I have to say, you're more vibrant these days. Kind of glowing." She covered her mouth. "Oh my God, are you pregnant?"

Zara yawned. "Zero chance. Pill plus condoms plus my PMS is kicking in *right* on time."

"Well, something's working for you." The camera bag's zippers chittered as she yanked them down. She yoked herself with her camera before she plucked her light meter from the bag's contents.

"Or someone," she muttered, fidgeting with her necklace.

The last time she had her portrait taken, she'd been a senior in high school. No velvet drape or single red rose today, thank God. She'd swiped on her normal heavy red lipstick, wore a few necklaces of varying lengths, jeans, and a tank top. Oh, and of course, her boots.

Grier took additional readings at various points on her body. "We'll shoot a mix of close-ups as well as full body shots."

She scanned Zara and frowned.

"What's wrong? Do I have toothpaste on my face?"

"Shush. I need to adjust a few things. I'd rather eliminate imperfections now than cheat with Photoshop later." She moved her hands, hummingbird-fast, fiddling with Zara's hair, detangling necklaces, then adjusting the neckline of her tank. "There. Don't move. I'll deal with the garbage on the wall."

"Hey now. Those are potentially priceless works of art."

"I didn't mean *literal* garbage." She unplugged the sunlamps and shoved them into the corner. "Garbage, noise, junk, whatever. Clutter distracts from, rather than adds to, the aesthetics of the shot." Next, she unpinned warped sketches from the wall and laid them on the worktable next to the portrait miniatures. "Are these for birthday parties? You said you were done with face painting."

"I am. I keep meaning to pitch those, but..." She rolled the hem of her shirt.

"But what?" Grier situated the floral arrangement or the deep windowsill next to Zara.

"Last week, when Brendan was here—"

"When you hooked up," Grier sang and bopped her shoulders.

Zara sighed, and her cheeks heated. The snap of the camera's shutter echoed in the studio. "Are you taking pictures already? Why?"

"Because duh. Your flustered face is hot." Her friend swooped in and snapped pictures from different angles. "Sorry, I interrupted you. What were you saying?"

"He was way impressed with the miniatures. He said the one I painted of his daughter—"

Grier invaded Zara's personal space with the lens. "What's her name?"

"Emma." She rubbed her bicep. "He said it's his favorite picture of her ever. Maybe I could ply my trade through an online store."

"It's not a bad idea." She held her camera to the side. "Is he in the art community? Does he know what the market's like for portraits?"

"No. He's an IT guy."

"Oh. Then let's ask our good friend Google what kind of bank you could make." She fished her phone from her pocket, poked a few buttons. "The money's decent, I guess, but you couldn't make a living doing *only* portraits. There are artists on Etsy charging anywhere from sixty to a hundred dollars for postcard-sized paintings, but their work isn't as good as yours. Check it out."

Grier tossed her phone to Zara. Her friend's assessment was accurate—her miniatures had a different style, were a little more whimsical. But the market didn't look like it would bear steep price tags.

"I'd have to paint at least three portraits to earn the same money I earn playing Ravenna for ninety minutes." She glanced at the rooftops across the streets through the window's chicken wire glass. "That's depressing that a job I hate pays much better than my dream."

"Stay still. There's an awesome shadow on your face." Grier fired off another shot, then smiled at the back of her camera. "Nice one. Anyway, I'm not saying the portraits would land you a steady income. Just another way to supplement your bank account as you establish yourself, that's all."

"Not according to my agreement with Schwarz. I can't sell through any other dealer or venue. He was super clear about that. But if everything goes well, after 'Phoenix' launches, I won't have to scramble to make ends meet."

Or move to the shore and run the inn with my parents.

She couldn't bear to contemplate it. The show *had* to be a

success. But if it wasn't… She tunneled her fingers through her hair, stretched it over her shoulders, then let it fall like fringe.

"More of that, please. Sexpot artist with the bee stung lips." Grier hit the shutter release in such quick succession it sounded like her camera had a sneezing fit.

"This isn't a fashion shoot."

"Appearance always matters, and when you're hot, it helps." She scrolled through the images on her review pane. "We're done, by the way. I have a couple hundred shots."

"A couple hundred? Of me? From today?"

"Yep. They're good too. Which, of course they are, since I took them. Not sure how you'll narrow it down to one. When do you need to send it to the gallery?"

"Tonight. They're printing programs this week."

"Nothing like the last minute, huh?"

She shrugged. "What can I say? Deadlines inspire me."

"Speaking of, have you finished your paintings yet?"

Zara winced. More camera snapping. "You said the shoot was over."

"Your expression was too perfect But I promise, no more guerrilla shots. I should know better. I hate being the subject of them. Now what was that pained look about? Things not going well?"

"Opposite, actually. I finished the second one last night, which is bananas fast for me. I haven't even thought about the third one." She twisted her hair into a bun. "John Schwarz—he's the guy who runs the Schwarz Gallery—was happy with the first painting. I showed it to him yesterday."

"Wait. You let *another* person in here?" Grier thumped against the wall. "I may faint."

"Yeah, and he…he said…" She grinned. "He said it could be the highlight of the show."

"Squee!" Grier slid her camera behind her back and tackle-hugged her friend. When she released her, she asked, "How did you keep that to yourself for a whole day? I'd have bought a banner ad on the Sun's home page."

Zara twined her arms in front of her. "I didn't want to brag."

"There's a huge fucking chasm between bragging and reporting facts."

"I've been conditioned to expect a response that ruins my happiness. If I keep my news to myself, no one can deflate it." She tapped her temple. "Strategy."

"I swear, our parents should double-date and bond over the

crushing disappointments we are since we don't want to work for the family business."

"Can you call what your parents do a "family business" if it's a Fortune 500 company?"

"Yes. But let's only talk about happy and exciting things, like having three paintings in a major show."

"If I can get them done." Zara breathed in until her diaphragm protested. "I'm supposed to deliver them to the gallery by next Friday. The first two happened in a snap, but who knows if the third one will? I need to see Brendan, but things are weird since yesterday, and I'm having a small heart attack. My left arm is going numb."

She wobbled her arm. Wait, *was* it numb? That had been a joke but her fingers were tingly.

"Freaking out, huh?" Grier rested her palms on Zara's shoulders. "You've finished two of the three they contracted. That's huge. You have time to finish the third. You can blow off a date with Brendan. If he's a good guy, he'll understand you're on deadline."

"He's a good guy. A great guy, actually."

"I detect sappiness. Coming from you, this is disconcerting." She rested her hand on her hip. "By the way, why are things weird?"

"It's easier for me to show than tell." Zara crossed the room to the completed paintings. To keep herself from obsessively tweaking them, she'd hung them so they faced the wall. The beige backs of the huge canvases swayed on fishing wire she'd looped through eyehooks jammed in the ceiling.

"Ooh, am I getting a preview?"

"Yes." Zara caressed the edge of the first painting, the one that was her height. "Since the gallery's theme is 'Phoenix', I wanted to tell a story of new beginnings. Of *my* new beginning." Shifting her weight, she let go of the canvas, then clamped her hands around her neck.

My heart is going to explode. No one will ever see me the same way again.

"What are you waiting for?"

"These are kind of personal."

"If you're showing these in a gallery, you can't be precious about it."

"You're right. You're a hundred percent right." Zara lifted and flipped the painting. "The reason I have to see Brendan again, the reason things are weird, is he's my muse."

She shuffled backward to stand next to Grier, to view the painting from the same perspective.

A nude couple, depicted from the hip up, dominated the

canvas. Their upright, entwined figures surged from the lower left corner. The woman's back arched in ecstasy, and her banner of hair waved in surrender, dripping from her lolling head. Her purple-manicured fingertips hooked into his arm, clutching, making divots in his corded muscle. His torso curved into hers, and his head dipped to taste her breasts.

"I'm like some nineteenth century creeper, calling him my muse." Zara bracketed her arms across her belly. "These past few weeks have been a trip. My perspective on the world and the way I'm translating it into paint is crazy different."

Her heartbeat calmed. This was good. Thank God she could unburden herself to her friend.

"Maybe it started with the fire, or the offer from the Schwarz Gallery, or being with Brendan. Or maybe it's all of it happening at once? It's like a re-birth."

"Shhh." Grier waggled her hand. "Too much talky."

She bit the inside of her cheek to muzzle herself.

"Jesus. This is you. Isn't it? Both of you. In the middle of...of..." She glanced over her shoulder at Zara. "You've got a huge set of balls."

"You like it?"

"I love it. It's beautiful. The vibrant tones, and the way you leave some of it blurred. Reminds me of the effect of this vintage filter I have."

"Not so close. The paint's still kind of wet."

She backed away. "Sorry—checking out the detail. So, Brendan has a tattoo?"

"Several." Zara picked at her thumb.

"The background texture appears to be moving. Which, based on the pose of the figures, is making me a smidge uncomfortable."

"Wait'll you get a load of this, then." She rotated the second painting.

Grier gasped.

The second painting was smaller, horizontal. The style was the same. Big, bold strokes, photographic detail in some places, and a slight blur where the figures converged. A man's torso served as a fig leaf over the juncture of a woman's legs. Her thighs soared toward the upper corners of the painting, and her breasts gently sloped since she was lying on her back.

"You're showing this?" She hovered in front of the painting. "I mean, it's gorgeous. Intimate. And fucking sexy as hell."

"But..."

"It dances on the line between art and..." She flicked a glance at Zara. "Porn."

Her stomach dropped. If her best friend in the world thought these were trashy, she'd failed, no matter how enthusiastic Eleanor or Schwarz were about the work. "It's *not* porn."

"Obviously, but not everyone gets the difference." She pinched her chin. "People will talk about these, for sure. It's one thing to be aware a person is having sex, philosophically. For it to actually be in front of you like this? Whoa."

"I *know*." Zara hid her face in her hands, stifling her shaky laugh. "Trust me, it would have been easier if I'd been inspired by a bowl of fruit." Standing hip to hip with her friend, she contemplated the images.

"Can I take your picture with the paintings? Not for the Schwarz Gallery, but for you."

"Why?"

"Someone will buy these in a heartbeat. You should have a picture for posterity."

"You think they'll sell?"

"Without a doubt. Now, go stand in front of the blank space."

Zara stood under the empty third hook, and Grier scooted the worktable to the far side of the room. Her roommate backed all the way up to the wall-mounted easel across the room and rotated the barrel of her camera to zoom out.

"Okay, I can get everything in the frame. Oh, and hey, no need to look happy on the eve of your success. Glum chic is very on trend." She clicked off shots then glanced at the review pane. "Nice. You had a full-blown smile by the last frame. So, what's the third painting?"

Zara's newborn smile evaporated. "Excellent question. I envisioned the composition, the colors, the size of the canvas, all of it, before I even lifted a brush for these two. The final canvas is a mental blank and why I need to see Brendan again, because...muse."

"I get it. He's beautiful. And if this musculature is realistic, you're a lucky girl. So, Brendan's okay with these, then?"

"He..." she knotted her fingers.

"He what?" Grier narrowed her eyes. "Please tell me he's aware you've painted these pictures of him. These *very intimate* pictures."

She tucked her hands under her chin. "He knows I have a show, and I've been painting up a storm. But he doesn't know he's the subject."

"Oh, Zara. You've got to tell him. It would be cruel to surprise him."

"I don't know how."

"Maybe lead off with flattery? Tell him he inspired you at a critical time." She dropped the camera so it nestled against her belly. "Don't hint. Show him the paintings. He's bound to understand."

"I *could*." Zara scissored her legs. "I was also flirting with the idea of not telling him. At all."

She wrinkled her brow. "You're going to show nude—"

"You can't see everything."

"Semantics, but whatever. You're going to show *semi-nude* paintings of him without letting him know? And let him find out on his own, or worse, through someone else?"

Weaving her arms together, she protested. "You can't tell it's him."

"I've met the man *once*, and I can tell it's him. You're too good. The way he holds his head, the line of his jaw, it's all right there." Grier threw her hands toward the painting. "You've got to tell him."

"Why are you insistent?" She scraped her fingers through her hair and cupped the back of her head, elbows pointing to the walls. "You're *my* friend, not his. Just be happy for me and don't tell me how to handle this."

"I *am* happy for you, you crazy person. It's *because* I'm your friend that I'm *advising* you to tell him. It'll eat you up if you don't."

"I can't. Everything's at stake. I need a third painting. What if he freaks out or tries to keep me from showing them?"

"Is he like that?"

"No. At least, I don't think so." Zara scratched her inner arm. "My gut tells me the way to get what I want is to keep these a secret from him. It's easier to ask forgiveness than for permission, right?"

"Stop right there. That's shady, and you don't do shady."

"I don't?"

"Are you kidding? You're the most scrupulous person *ever*. Remember freshman year when you wouldn't take more than two slices of pizza because you'd only paid for two? I had to mash a slice into your face to make you eat more."

"I'm not sure what pizza has to do with this situation."

"I suck at analogies." Grier took a deep breath. "The inspiration for those paintings is a moment he shared with you. If you don't tell him about them, it'll bother you."

"I'm supposed to jeopardize my shot to beg for his permission?"

"No, of course not." She sighed. "I want this for you. I'm in your corner. He can't issue a cease and desist since his face isn't in them and you aren't calling him out by name, so you don't need his permission. You're the one who keeps bringing that up, not me. The right thing to do is to tell him before showing them to the general public. Trust me on this."

"What if he hates them?"

What if he hates me?

Grier packed her camera into her bag. "Then he hates them. That's the risk you took, that we all take when we put our real lives in our art. But he should know before they go on a gallery wall."

Her words coiled around Zara's brain and drifted to her heart. She tried to fend off their rightness, but it was no use. "Sometimes I hate having morals."

Fourteen

Wednesday night found Zara pacing the short hallway. She smoothed her hands down her waist, hoping the sheath would be appropriate for tonight's mystery destination. The suspense was killing her. Brendan had given her zero hints in the three days since she'd seen him.

Had it only been three days?

She wanted to hold his hand, catch the twinkle in his eyes, and ask him if Emma survived her first day back after being sick for a few days. None of which had anything to do with her next painting, so what the hell did that mean? As she checked her reflection, she nudged the question away.

"You look hot." Grier flowed behind Zara in the foyer and into the living room, joining Melinda and Brooke on the couch.

"Seconded," Melinda said, laying her tablet on her lap. "Edgy elegance suits you, sweetie. Nice job on her hair, Brooke."

She'd twisted Zara's hair into a romantic, side-swept chignon.

"Thanks. Nimble fingers. Where're you going tonight?"

Zara scooted the silver chain of her locket around until the clasp lay at the nape of her neck. "Not sure. He said it would be fancy."

Grier flopped on the couch. "Probably not crabs, then."

"That's what she said." Brooke punched the air.

"Brooke!" the roommates shouted in unison.

Melinda frowned. "Ladies, don't we have a rule we won't allude to STDs before a big date?"

"This isn't a big date." Zara's earrings jangled as she shook her head. She didn't normally wear chandelier earrings, hated the way they dragged her lobes down, but Brooke insisted she needed sparkle. "It's a third date. Or fourth, I guess. I'm not sure why he wanted to go big tonight."

Grier cleared her throat. "Is tonight the night you tell him?"

"I'm assuming you're all in the know?" She rested against the console table and crossed her legs.

Melinda clicked off her tablet. "Grier said your paintings are beautiful, and you're in them, and you're—"

"Naked." Brooke laughed. "Zar, if you need a life model in the future, you have a resident expert here."

"I'll file that away. About telling him... Tonight could be the night. Maybe. I'm trying to find the right time. I've got three weeks—"

"Two-and-a-half." Grier raised an eyebrow.

"Whatever. I might tell him tonight, but it won't be during appetizers. Can we stop talking about it? He'll be here any minute."

"Good." Brooke popped her feet on top of a stack of magazines on the coffee table. "I can't *wait* to lay eyes on the guy fueling your career with his magical—"

She groaned. "I will pay you to stop the dick talk."

The doorbell rang. Zara took a deep breath and pressed her hands to her belly to calm the thrills rocketing around inside. Would that always happen when Brendan arrived? If so, she'd have to explore ways to tranquilize herself. Maybe a hit of Melinda's sleepy herbal tea shit would help.

"Fine, no dick talk." Brooke's tone was hushed. "Only because I love you."

"Thanks." She twisted the deadbolt and eased the front door open. Even though she expected him, knew she would find Brendan on her stoop, electricity rocketed through her. The smiles he beamed at her made her feel seen and special.

"Hi, Princess. You're beautiful."

"And you're..."

Dressed to kill. Under a lux double-breasted overcoat, he wore a suit sharp enough to whittle a charcoal pencil. However, the man himself was ghost-pale and glassy-eyed. With him on the middle step, and with her in heels, she stared straight into his bloodshot brown-and-golds.

"You're sick, aren't you?" She fitted her palm to his forehead, her old caretaker reflexes taking over. No temperature but clammy.

"I *was* sick, but I'm much better now. Ready to hit the town?"

He slumped against the stoop's railing. Poor guy. She loved that he'd tried to rally, but the only thing he should hit is the hay. "You should be in bed."

"I was hoping that's where we'd end up."

"You, not we." She slipped on Grier's black dress coat, wrapped a scarf around her neck, then grabbed her overnight tote. Not that she'd be staying at Brendan's now, but her wallet was lost in its depths, and she needed to get him back home before he collapsed.

She turned to say goodbye to her roommates and bumped into Brooke. Zara jerked, heart thumping. "Jesus, could you wear a bell or something?"

"Hi," Brooke said to Brendan. "I'm Brooke Buras."

"Nice to meet you." Brendan's voice was watered down, and he didn't budge from the railing. He barely managed one of his dimpled smiles. Even at half the wattage, it stole Zara's breath. "I'm Brendan. Zara talks about you guys all the time."

"*O mój boże*," Brooke whispered. "Skip the restaurant. Have *him* for dinner."

"He's sick so I'm taking him home."

"Yeah you are." She winked as she fished Zara's keys from the bowl on the console and handed them to her. To Brendan, she said, "Have a nice night and don't be a stranger."

Zara joined Brendan on the stoop, and Brooke shut the door behind her. *Bet she's spying through the peephole.*

He touched her hip. "Ready for a fancy restaurant?"

"Don't be ridiculous," she said, brushing his hair from his eyes. "I'm taking you home."

"You keep calling me ridiculous. I could take offense."

"Well, stop *being* ridiculous. Did you drive or Uber?"

"I drove. I'm parked there." He gestured toward a silver Volkswagen Toureg parked a few doors down. "Sorry I'm late, by the way. Parking was a bitch."

"No problem. Give me your keys. I'll drive us home."

"You don't have to. I can drive." He pushed off the railing and wobbled.

"Yeah, into a lamppost," she said as she steadied him. She snagged his keys from his coat pocket then strapped her arm around his waist. "Let's go."

They walked across the empty street, and she opened the passenger door to his car.

"I like the body contact, but I'm not sick, I promise." Brendan slid onto the slate-colored leather and buckled up. "I'm sleep-deprived, that's all. We can go to the restaurant."

"So you can infect everyone there? No way." After closing his door, she circled around to the driver's side, then settled in behind the wheel. "I would have understood if you'd bailed tonight."

"I wanted to be with you. I like you."

"Flatterer." It took a minute for the seat adjuster to hum the seat forward. Once her feet touched the pedals, she tilted the mirrors, then hit the ignition. She revved the engine a few times, enjoying the power under her control. It'd had been ages since she'd been in a driver's seat.

"So what kind of plague are we dealing with?"

"Twenty-four-hour bug. Monday was rough. Between taking care of Emma, disinfecting the house, and fighting it myself, I was wiped out. Everything was fine by yesterday. I'm tired, but healthy."

His wan smile and the slight swelling under his eyes disagreed.

"Yeah, sure you are." Before she drove away from the curb, Zara flipped on the radio. A bubbly song featuring squeaky voices burst from the speakers. "What in God's name is this?"

"Emma's favorite station."

"Emma's not in the car."

"I forget to change it."

"Well, I can't take it." She punched a random preset on the console. Anything would be better than this song about yetis stomping. "I can't believe I'm driving a minivan."

"It is not a minivan." Brendan wiped his forehead.

A motorcyclist cut in front of her and she hit the brakes harder than she intended. Driving in heels was such a pain in the ass. "Station wagon?"

"It's a crossover."

"Sounds like a marketing ploy." She glanced in the review mirror before changing lanes in front of the Baltimore Plaza. "This is a family car. It's a *nice* family car, but it's still a family car."

He glanced at the floor in the back. "Well, at least I vacuumed up the Cheerios."

"It's quite the carriage. Much better than a pumpkin." At the red light, she touched his warm, clean-shaven cheek. "You're not feverish."

"I told you, I'm fine." He plucked her hand from his face and kissed it. Lightning bolts traveled from the spot his lips touched, up her arm, all the way to her heart. "It's run its course. If you stop driving like a grandmother, we'll have plenty of time to make our reservation at The Charleston."

"We were going to The Charleston?"

"Are. We *are* going to The Charleston. Make a left here."

"Nope." The light turned green, and she glided straight through the intersection. "We're going to your house. You should be in bed."

Maybe she could use the drive to tell him about the paintings. In this state, he wouldn't have the energy to get riled up.

"Now we're talking." Brendan lolled his head toward her and gave her a weak grin. In the short time they'd been in the car, he seemed to have crumpled in on himself.

No. She couldn't tell him tonight. He needed to be clear-minded. What a shitty person she was to consider taking advantage of the situation. "Slow down, cowboy. *You* need to be in bed, *asleep*."

They zipped past the Inner Harbor, the inky water mirroring the colorful neon lights decorating the waterfront buildings. Zara guided the big car through the narrow streets of Federal Hill and slipped it into an open spot near Brendan's house.

"C'mon, let's get you inside." She shut off the engine and minced to his side of the car. Stupid, impractical strappy heels. Never again.

"You were right," he said as she tugged him from the car. "I should be in bed."

"Smart man." She pulled his arm across her shoulders like a pashmina and wrapped her free arm around his waist. "Go ahead. Lean on me. Freakishly strong, remember?"

"Feisty, too." He unlocked the deadbolt and wobbled into his home, but left the door open. An invitation. Or an expectation? Inside, he wrestled his coat off and tried to slip it on a hanger but gave up and dropped it on the floor.

Zara stayed pinned to the front stoop, shifting on her spike-heeled feet. A couple of weeks ago, she would have said goodbye, closed the door, and headed to her studio. But he needed her, whether or not he wanted to admit it, and her paintings could wait. Today, instead of leaving him to fend for himself, she crossed the threshold and locked the door behind her.

"Does that mean you're staying?" He attempted to lean on the wall but thumped into it hard. God, he was so *exhausted*.

She kicked off her heels. "For now. Let's get you to bed." In his room, he dropped onto the comforter and wrapped an arm around the bedpost at the foot of the bed. "Maybe you should go. I don't think I'm contagious, but if I am, I don't want you to catch this."

"Too late." She laughed. "I'll be okay. I got a flu shot because I work with the elderly. If it isn't the flu, I've already been exposed."

"Sorry. Guess I'm not thinking straight."

"Don't worry about it." Now, where would she find clothes to change into? She opened his bureau drawers. Victory. Pajama bottoms for him and boxers for her. She dropped the pajamas into his lap. "Why don't you slip into something more comfortable?"

"This wasn't how I expected to undress this evening." He sloughed off his suit jacket and unknotted his tie. When he undid the first of his blue shirt's parade of buttons, Zara sighed. Even though tonight was supposed to provide more mind-blowing inspiration, she was surprisingly okay with the cozy, comfortable affection.

"When's the last time you ate?" she asked.

"Uh..." He furrowed his brow and ran a big thumb across his bottom lip, making it go crooked. "Breakfast? I had a lot to catch up on at work. I didn't stop for lunch."

"No wonder you're dead on your feet. Here." She fitted herself between his knees and presented her back to him. "Unzip me."

"Are you trying to torture me?" He held her hips and rested his forehead against her.

"No. I don't have elastic arms, and I'm not cooking in this dress."

"You're cooking?"

"Stop asking questions. If you get the zipper started, I can undo the rest."

"Fine. Someday, though, you'll wear this dress, and I'll get you out of it for the right reasons." Brendan fumbled for the tiny slider and pulled. The air was cool against her exposed shoulder blades.

"I look forward to it," she said, and bent to collect his discarded clothes. "I'll hang these up."

While she was in his closet she slipped Grier's dress off and hung it in the empty side. The gorgeous sheath was sad and lonely, a promise unfulfilled. In their glamorous gear, she and Brendan would have fit right in at the Charleston.

Maybe they really would do it another time. If they lasted that long. He didn't know about the paintings yet, after all.

No time to dwell. First, she needed a shirt. Ten dad-style short sleeve polos lined the upper rod. Hell no. On the shelf, Zara spied a stack of T-shirts. She rifled through them and squealed.

"What?" Brendan called. "Did you see a mouse?"

She slipped the shirt over her head. "Ew, do you have mice?"

"No, but we live in the city. I'm always on guard."

Zara emerged wearing his boxers and the faded Oasis T-shirt she'd unearthed.

"Oh, no you don't." He wagged his finger. "That shirt doesn't leave this house. I bought it at my first concert."

"I completely understand. I'll treasure the minutes it's on my body."

A shallow dimple pocked the surface of his cheek. "It looks good on you."

"Thanks. Now, you rest. I'll put together some dinner."

"You're an angel, Princess."

In the kitchen, she sifted through the contents of the fridge. Huh. Brendan was way better stocked with staples than she and her roommates were. The fridge at the townhouse was full of half-empty takeout containers, orange juice, pasta, and a single, dried-out lime.

Here, she had all the ingredients for homemade chicken soup, which she hadn't made in years. Didn't matter. The recipe was carved in her heart since she'd cooked it countless times. Toward the end, the soup had been one of the few things Gramma would reliably eat.

After raiding the fridge, she dumped the bundle of ingredients on the counter and got to chopping. She wielded the knife with confidence, and the motion eased tension in her neck.

Huh. Painting gave her the same reprieve. She hadn't cooked often enough in the past couple of years to notice the similar effect on her body, but the calm was impossible to ignore.

A half an hour later, she entered Brendan's bedroom carrying a cookie sheet laden with two steaming bowls of nourishment, tea, and juice. "I couldn't find a tray."

"That smells great. What is it?" Brendan had tunneled under the comforter. On *her* side.

"Medical grade chicken soup." She laid the cookie sheet on his lap. "What are you watching?"

"Nothing. I'm flipping channels."

She picked up her bowl and settled into the armchair on the other side of his nightstand. "I heard *Addams Family Values.*"

She shifted her ass a few times.

Were there bricks in this chair? Who would make a chair this uncomfortable?

"It might have been." He side-eyed her as he slurped more soup. "Thank you for this. I can't remember the last time I got TLC. I usually have to suck it up and power through."

"You're welcome." She blew on a spoonful of soup before swallowing it. "Would you mind changing it back to the Addams Family?"

He groaned.

She nudged him with her foot. "Come on. You'll love it. I swear."

"Fine." They ate as the images flickered across the screen, laughing at the one-liners. Thank God he wasn't one of those people who babbled through the whole thing.

After they finished, Zara stood to collect his dishes.

"You seem better," she said, brushing his hair away. The glassy sheen in his eyes had dissipated.

"I am." Brendan stretched, and his chest expanded to the size of the pillows stacked behind him.

"Good." She was pretty sleepy, herself. Late nights every night for weeks were starting to catch up to her. She held on to the bedpost to stop herself from falling into the bed.

He gestured toward the empty bowls. "Were there antibiotics in there?"

"Nah. Just lo—" She bit her tongue. She'd almost said *love*, like her gramma used to. "Chicken and vegetables."

"Well, if the art thing doesn't work out, you could be a kickass nurse." As he yawned, he closed his eyes. Good thing, too, because the color must have drained from her face. His joke was the actual nightmare she'd lived in high school. Nursing the sick, putting her life on pause to care for someone.

Phew, okay. A little bit of space was required right now.

Zara collected the makeshift tray. "Back in a few."

In the kitchen, she rinsed the dishes and stacked them in the dishwasher. On her way back up the stairs, she snagged her tote. She should leave now, after changing into the clothes she'd packed for tomorrow, but who can skip the second half of *Addams Family Values*?

Inside his room, she dropped her bag on the floor. "Need anything else?"

"You." He flashed her a dopey smile.

"*That* won't help you kick this bug."

"It's kicked. I swear I'm in the recovery stage." Brendan tapped the empty side of the bed. "Come on. That chair is awful. All I use it for is to hold the basket when I'm putting laundry away."

If she got into his bed after taking care of him, just to cuddle while watching a movie, it was as good as admitting she was kicking this relationship to a different level. Because all that? Was girlfriend shit.

He grinned, unaware of the seduction in his sweetness. "I promise I won't try anything."

"Fine," she said, and fluffed the pillow on the other side of the bed to make it a backrest. Brendan asked. Once she settled, he hit play on the movie resumed. As the movie progressed, he slid deeper and deeper under the comforter. Toward the end, she eased the remote from his grip and lowered the volume so the final action sequence didn't startle him.

By the time Wednesday smirked and the credits rolled, his eyes were closed.

Zara slipped off the bed and circled to his nightstand to turn the lamp off. Fumbling for the switch, she stole one last glance at Brendan. She *could* skulk away, and he'd understand. She knotted her hands together to keep from smoothing his tousled hair from his forehead.

"Hey, Princess," he mumbled.

"Shh. You're sleeping."

He caught her around the waist. "You're not going, right? Say you'll stay."

"I…" Inside, it was warm and comfortable. Out there? The cold, miserable, end-of-February. The wind whistled past his bedroom window. Sheesh, nature was as good as telling her to stay.

"Pancakes for breakfast," he said.

She turned the light off. "You know I'm powerless against your pancakes."

In the dark, she walked back around the bed and slipped under the comforter. "You only get to sleep on my side because you're sick, by the way."

"I'll share. C'mere." He opened his arm and made room for her on his chest.

She laid her head on the fleshy part between his shoulder and his collarbone.

"Where'd you learn to take care of people?" he asked.

Her lips puffed out as she exhaled. Since she had a whopper of a secret on lockdown, she could at least answer this. The only cost would be a crack in the wall she built around her heart.

"My gramma didn't want to go into a care facility when she was sick. I homeschooled myself and took care of her, drove her to chemo, and when it wasn't working, handled things at home. My parents and I had help. Nurses came a few times a week, but mostly, it was me."

He kissed her on the temple. "That must have been hard."

"It was." She draped an arm across his chest, her arm rising and falling with the drowsy rhythm of the breath beneath his muscle and bone. "Caring for her in those last few months was my privilege. I wouldn't change a thing. Well, except that she died. That kind of sucked."

Brendan wrapped his other arm around her, forming a warm net of tenderness. In this safe space, in the dark, she allowed a few tears to fall. Not for her grandmother. She'd exhausted her tears of mourning seven years ago.

No, these tears were for the girl she'd been *before* she'd lost her soft place to land.

The girl who let people take care of her and took care of them in return. And for the woman who was beginning to feel like that girl hadn't been lost forever.

Fifteen

Brendan woke to the snick of his bedroom door closing. Through his lashes, he spied Zara tiptoeing across his room. The bed bowed as she lay down.

She stayed over? As his muzzy brain cleared, last night came trickling back. He'd meant it when he said she might want to go. Not because he didn't want her company, but because he didn't want to overwhelm her and make her think she *had* to take care of him.

Jess used to get annoyed whenever he caught a cold, like he was inconveniencing her. So he'd fallen into his old pattern of pretending he was fine to avoid the hassle. It had never occurred to him Zara would see right through it and offer him tenderness. She'd been an angel.

A nugget of truth pelted him square between the eyes, and he opened them wide.

That's what your girlfriend *should* do. Help you up when you're down. Or lay next to you while you go through it. Not shake her head and check her e-mail.

Ah, shit. His girlfriend? They hadn't talked about it, but he'd already gone and bumped her from the 'potential' column to straight-up 'girlfriend'. Seems like information he should share with the woman in question. On second thought, he'd keep that to himself. She was sensitive about labels, and losing her was not on his To Do list.

He stretched and inched toward her. Bright mid-morning sun suffused the sheer curtains and lit the dips and hills of her body under the blankets.

"Good morning," he murmured and hooked his arm around her waist. Burying his face in her hair, he breathed deep. *God, that scent.* He hoped his pillows sponged it up again.

"Hi," she said. "Sorry for waking you."

"Don't be." He nuzzled her neck. "Did you sleep okay?"

"Yep, even though it was the wrong side." She arched her back against his chest. "How are you this morning?"

"Great." He fanned his fingers over her belly.

"How great?"

He pressed his hips to her ass so she could feel for herself.

"Well now." Zara wiggled against him, and his balls tightened in response. "Is this a smart move since you were at death's door yesterday?"

"I wasn't at death's door. I was exhausted. Now I'm well-rested and..."

Brendan skimmed the waistband of the boxers she'd borrowed. Christ, this woman in his clothes transformed a T-shirt and shorts into the Sexiest Lingerie on Earth.

"Well-rested and what?" Zara asked.

"Turned on."

He delved under the faded T-shirt to caress her waist. Her hidden skin was like soap in his hands, smooth and curved and...

Oh, delightful.

Zara didn't have a bra on. He closed his fingers around a soft mound, kneading. He was already hard, but in the wake of his discovery, rock had turned to diamond.

She twisted her head toward Brendan, blinking big blue eyes at him. "You sure you're better?"

He rose on his elbow and kissed her, deep, hard.

"I'll take that as a yes." She shifted to her back. "Do you have anywhere to be?"

"Nope. Already took the day off. I'm playing hooky."

Which was not exactly true. He'd coded like a beast the past couple of days to be able to take an office day off. The site redesign for Mike's shop was overdue, and he wanted to finish it up. Probably part of the reason he was wiped out last night. The side job wouldn't take all day, though, so right now?

This bed was the only place he had to be.

Zara swirled her fingers in his hair. "Good."

"I'd hoped you were a morning sex kind of woman."

"With you, I'm a sex any-time-of-day kind of woman. I'm using you for distraction, remember?" she asked. "To get my creativity flowing."

"I can think of other things I hope to get flowing," he growled and knelt between her knees.

He peeled the Oasis T-shirt off her and pitched it overboard. Her locket slipped over her shoulder and gleamed in the dark of her hair. His gaze traveled to her rosy nipples, already taut and begging for attention.

"You're gorgeous, Princess." He curled forward and dropped a kiss on the space above her heart.

"You always say that." She ran her hands through his hair, scratching at his scalp.

Pleasure shivered down his neck, his spine, and circled to his groin.

"Because it's true." Brendan licked the underside of her breasts, the smooth slopes where they met her ribs. His tongue skated around, teasing the buds of her nipples.

"Do that again," she gasped.

"I love making you hard," he said between kisses. "Love making you wet."

Love making love to you. Love you.

Thank God he had the sense to keep those last two thoughts to himself.

He eased off the bed and planted his feet on firm ground. "Come here." He gripped her hips, and shifted her until her legs hung off the bed.

Naked, except for boxers and a smile, she reached for him. He stilled, struck dumb by the picture she made in the rumple of his bed.

"Something wrong?" She raised an eyebrow. "If you're not up for it, that's okay."

He was beyond up for it. Body, soul, and heart. Not that he'd confess any of that yet. She'd run for the hills if he even hinted how hard he was falling for her.

"Couldn't be better," he said, tugging at the boxers she'd borrowed. "Time to return these."

"All yours." Zara arched her back and lifted her ass so he could slip the boxers free. She sat up on the bed. "Now you. Shirt first."

"Yes ma'am." He clenched the scruff of his T-shirt and dragged it over his head. As he dropped it on the floor, she kissed the triangle tattoo on his pelvis and licked the bumps and furrows of his abdominal muscles.

"You have a fine, fine body, Brendan Stewart."

"Nothing compared to you," he said.

She yanked down his pajama pants and freed his cock.

"Eager aren't—"

Zara swirled her tongue around the head and flicked its ridge.

He clutched the bedpost. "Jesus Christ, Princess."

She released him then licked her lips.

Her soft, cool fingers wrapped his raging heat. She stroked and spiraled his flesh. "Not a fan?"

"*President* of the fan club. I wasn't prepared, that's all."

He sucked in his breath as she molded her mouth to him. She was churning wet pressure, and he rode the waves. Much as he loved it, he needed her to stop. There were other things he wanted to explore first.

"Lay down," he said.

She let him slip from her mouth. "What are you going to do to me?"

"Everything."

His need for her, to claim her, to bury himself in the wondrous, creamy reality of her drove everything from his mind. He snatched a condom from the fresh stash in the nightstand drawer and tore it open with his teeth. He rolled it on his shaft, grateful the thin skin of latex would reduce his sensitivity. Otherwise he'd come in a minute flat.

He reached down and explored between Zara's legs. "Already wet for me."

"Always," she sighed and tweaked her nipples as he worked his fingers in her.

He wasn't sure how he earned enough karmic points to land this beautiful, responsive woman. He spread her legs, cradling a pearly thigh in each hand, and positioned his cock along her folds.

"You make me so hard." He ground against her. "I can't think straight when you're with me, and I think about you constantly when you're gone."

She bucked, encouraging him.

"You want it, don't you?" He teased her, dipping inside her, then swaying back. Then, tunneling further, repeating the move, careful not to give her everything until she asked, demanded, pleaded.

"Oh Brendan, please." She gasped and reached for him. "I need you now."

He slid forward, inch by slow inch. The heat of their mingled flesh was a balm and a delicious burn all at once. He withdrew as far as he dared, before gliding home again, and again, and again. The slap of his hips against her thighs sounded like slow, satisfied applause.

"Yes, yes, yes," Zara said, her breath hitching between the words.

He folded toward her, locked his mouth on hers, and searched for her hands in the sheets. When he found them, he laced his fingers with hers, holding tight. Her grip was fierce as he pinned her flat to the bed, rocking in and out of her.

She moaned in his mouth.

He needed to surround her, overwhelm her, possess her.

The wall. He needed her against the wall.

He broke their kiss, released her hands, and slipped his palms under her, like when he carried her a few nights earlier. With her legs wrapped around him, he lifted her free of the sheets, pivoted then pinned her against the plaster.

"Look at me," he growled.

She met his gaze, her blue eyes flashing.

"You're mine." Brendan buried himself in her core. His chest expanded with his breathing, flattening her breasts. "I want you all the time. You hear that? You. Are. Mine."

She nipped at his neck. "And you're mine."

Zara lowered one pale stem to the floor, and took back some of her weight. He kept a palm glued to her ass and hitched up the leg she hooked over his hip. Her glossy black and purple hair flowed down her shoulders, down her breasts, and half-hid her nipples. He clutched a fistful of it, tugged, and stared into her eyes as her climax began to carry her away.

"More," she said. "Like that. More. More. I'm going to—"

Her blissed out lips slackened with pleasure. As the rest of her went limp, like a marionette whose strings had been cut, she pulsed and throbbed around his cock. He buoyed her through the crashing waves of her orgasm, and after a few seconds, she kissed him. "Thank you."

"You're welcome."

He ran his palm down her face, neck, breast, waist, hip until he arrived at her thigh. Soft under his grip, he pulled it up, high and tight. The shift and the pressure on his cock was glorious.

"Keep your eyes on me while I come," he murmured. "I want you to see what you do to me."

"What do I do to you?" she asked, her eyes sparkling.

"You make me lose control." He thrust hard, fast. The friction between them sparked an inferno. It washed over him, burning, baptizing, blazing a trail right to his heart.

The orgasm hit him like a cannonball in the back, clouding his vision, thrumming blood in his ears. He clenched his muscles from his forehead to his feet and tightened his grip on Zara's wrists. A few spasms, and he was empty.

When his vision cleared, there, in front of him, was Zara.

He pressed his forehead in the crook of her neck. After a few breaths, he kissed her cheeks, her beard-burned lips. Laying his forearms on the wall on either side of Zara's head, he braced himself.

If she forced him to move in any way, he'd fall over like a newborn horse.

Zara rested her cheek against Brendan's bicep. Her thighs were jelly, her stomach quivered, and her dopey brain was defogging.

She was his? He was hers?

If he'd said that a week ago, she'd have laughed. Today was different. As soon as the words were out of his mouth, something low and primal tumbled into place within her. She'd painted the inexplicable *rightness* of how they fit together, big as life and just as bright. Essentially, she'd claimed him, and now he was doing the same.

"Can I make you breakfast?" he asked.

"I never refuse a meal."

He eased away, and the room was cold without his big body sheltering her. Zara slithered back into bed and wrapped herself in the cozy tangle of linens.

Not that he seemed to feel the chill. When he returned, he leaned on the bedpost, all flexed muscles and rough scruff. This man, he gleamed like a god. Her happy, satisfied gaze roved over him. The spark she thought they'd snuffed minutes ago bloomed to life again between her thighs.

Hooray for hooky days. She could have him again, if he was willing. Seemed like he was, too, if that growling was any indication.

"Princess? Your purse is buzzing."

"Oh. My phone." Zara knelt next to her tote and attempted a graceful pose as she rifled through her gigantic bag. "What time is it, anyway?"

Brendan glanced at his clock. "10:30."

The phone droned on. Where was the stupid thing? Ah—there. It had cozied into a ballet flat. Zara glanced at its cracked surface. Broken letters spelled 'The Sandcastle.'

Well, that'll kill a ladyboner.

She let the call slide to voice mail and pitched the phone back into her bag. Her stomach went oily. Mama and Dad probably wanted to remind her it would be a busy summer, interviews were starting soon, and they had her room ready...

Not happening. How could she live with them again? A simple phone call made her want to stab herself in the leg. Proof she had to go big, because she couldn't go home.

"Everything okay?" Brendan asked.

Ugh, gut twist.

When she put their intimate life on a gallery wall, he'd lose his mind. She knew it, but she had to go through with it. These were the paintings John Schwarz wanted. If she caved and withdrew from the show, she'd burn that bridge and make it exponentially harder to get another shot. At which point she might as well scoop out her soul, pack up her shit, and learn to love sand in every crevice of her body.

No choice at all.

Even though it meant hurting this innocent, lovely man.

She had to tell him. The sooner, the better.

But not now. Not while she was naked.

"Fine," she said, clearing her throat. "It was nothing."

"Are you sure? You looked like you wanted to strangle your phone."

"It's all good." Grateful for her pillowcase-sized bag, Zara stood. If she held it at an angle, it covered her nudity. It didn't seem right to bare herself to him when she wasn't willing to explain her sudden shift in mood. She needed a minute, or ten, to pull it together before breaking his trust. "Okay if I shower?"

He thumbed the stubble on his chin. "Be my guest. Extra towels are under the sink."

"Thanks."

She hustled past him, into the bathroom, then flipped the lock on the door. Alone, Zara cooled her forehead on painted white wood. The show was within weeks, and *her* work would be on the walls. Finally, *finally,* her grandmother's death wouldn't be the defining moment in her life, because she would achieve the dream she and Gramma had shared.

Still, doubt wormed its way through her brain.

What if she didn't sell? What if Eleanor and John were wrong and she ended up with her heart—not to mention her body—on display and no one understood the paintings? Brendan would hate her, and she'd have to move back to the shore where her bad memories lived, and her soul would shrivel and die.

No biggy, right?

~ * ~

Each creak on the stairs twisted her stomach. She dropped her tote bag on the landing. This conversation would suck, but it would be better if everything was out in the open. Grier had been *so* right. As much as Zara enjoyed the dark and gothic side of life, she couldn't be shady.

"Brendan?" She cupped her hands around her neck and followed the scent of pancakes and bacon toward the kitchen. "I need to talk to you."

Hello, broad-chested goodness. He'd pushed the sleeves of his snug green Henley up to his elbows, exposing a thick column of forearm. Plus the color was working for him. The thing working best was the happiness in the smile he flashed at her.

This truth bomb was going to suck.

"Sure thing. About what?" he asked and carried two plates stacked with food to the table, where steaming mugs of coffee already waited.

The whole picture echoed Sunday morning, except today she was wearing leggings, and Emma wasn't about to hurtle through the room. Still, everything inside her clenched. No way Zara'd be able to choke down breakfast.

She eased into the chair and chewed her thumbnail instead. "My paintings."

"Oh, good." He relaxed his shoulders and smiled. "You're not breaking up with me. After I went a little caveman this morning, I figured you'd head for the hills."

"No, I—" She tilted her head. "Wait—*can* we break up?"

"I'd prefer not to, but uh, yeah."

"But technically, we're not a thing."

"Officially, we're not a thing, but technically, we're very much a thing."

She scrubbed her forehead. "This is not what I wanted to talk about."

"Right. We'll table that." He sat across from her. "Which paintings? The ones for your show? Or the miniatures? Because I had brilliant idea."

Jesus, trying to direct this conversation was like herding ferrets. The rich aroma of the lumberjack quantities of bacon called to her. Might as well try to eat. Get some sustenance before hitting him with her reveal. His reveal too, come to think of it.

"Did you now?" she asked and drizzled syrup on the pancakes.

"Let me set up a site for you. I'll register a domain, create a digital portfolio and storefront, hook it to a PayPal account, and boom, you're in business. You've got a nice, clean, professional site, and you wouldn't have to cut in Etsy or eBay or whatever when you sell your own work."

She swallowed. "I have a site."

"A redesign, then. Unless you love your current site?"

"It's not that, I—"

"Because, I've gotta be honest, it's not doing anything for you. The freebie sites don't produce the clean design you need."

"Brendan Stewart, you have *got* to stop interrupting me."

"Sorry." He smiled. "Bad habit of mine when I'm excited.

What do you say? It'd take me a day. Not even. And today's relatively light, so I bet I could knock it out pretty fast."

"Do you always force your services on people?"

"Only people I like." He nudged her foot under the table. "Come on, Princess. Friends don't let friends use BlogPress."

She nudged back. It was the polite thing to do, right before you made someone angry. "Are we friends, or are we a thing? I'm having trouble keeping up."

"We're a thing," he said and winked.

Unfair. Here she was, trying to kick off a conversation bound to end in shouty recriminations, and he was flirting like a madman. It was working too, because now she wanted to lick the stubble peppering his face, could imagine the rough scrape against her tongue.

His helpful eagerness was refreshing…and kind of sexy.

If her gallery paintings didn't sell, this could be a Plan B. Then again, if she wasn't confident they would sell, should she show them at all? No matter which path she took, she'd be using him. God, when had she become such an avaricious bitch?

Her stomach grumbled against the pancakes. Apparently, underhanded shenanigans gave her indigestion. Twiddling her fork, she said, "I couldn't ask you to build a site for me."

"You didn't. I offered."

She gulped her coffee. Big mistake. It was lawsuit-level hot.

"I'd pay you," she wheezed. "I don't need charity. I can't pay in advance, because I'm kind of broke, but I if I sell—"

"*When* you sell."

Tears sprang to her eyes, and she blinked like she was staring straight into the noon sun on the beach. What the hell was *wrong* with her? She didn't cry. Not when people were being supportive and royally fluffing her ego.

This emotional roller coaster was the exact opposite of where she'd been for the past few years. Instead of seeing the world in dispassionate black and white and gray with occasional sparks of emotion, now everything was a brilliant, make-your-teeth vibrate, Richter-scale live wire.

She must be PMSing. Hard.

Swallowing past the guilty boulder in her throat, she croaked, "I can't establish a commerce site, anyway. My gallery contract says they sell everything."

"But don't they take a cut?" Brendan tapped his fingers on the table. "I don't understand why you're hung up on the gallery, anyway."

A lightning bolt of irritation spiked Zara's chest. Where did he get off questioning her chosen path? He'd admitted he didn't know much about art, or the art world. This was *her* profession, and she'd been learning the ropes since freshman year of college.

"Because, it's *everything*," she snapped.

"Princess, I didn't mean—"

"This contract validates me, Brendan. I've been working toward this for eight years, been rejected from dozens of shows, been struggling to find my motivation to keep going. And the fact that someone recognizes the quality in my work tells me, wants to work with me, believes he can make his livelihood through his association with me proves I'm not deluding myself. *That's* why."

He massaged her hand. "No need to come out swinging. All I'm saying is you don't need a gallery to tell you you're good. You know you are. That's why I want to help you sell it."

She blew out her lips. Overreact much? He was kind, trying to understand her point of view, and she'd behaved the same way she did when her parents told her to paint pastel seascapes.

Totally immature. She needed to calm down, and she sure as hell shouldn't tell him about the paintings right now. Not while she was in this frame of mind. If he said *one* thing she didn't want to hear, as entitled to it as he might be, she might explode into a million tiny shards.

Still, she owed him perspective, wanted to reward his desire to understand her with a peek into her past. Which made her want to hurl, because giving him this particular perspective meant she'd have to crack open her crusty heart and reveal more of the tender mush she preferred to keep hidden.

Whoops. She'd been gargoyling at him.

Blinking, she offered him a watery smile and hugged her legs to her chest. "That was a...big mood. Can I explain?"

"Always," he said.

Zara's blood drummed against her ears. "Hoo, okay. Calming breaths. So, I've told you about my grandmother. The thing is, she was a second mother to me. My parents worked twenty-hour days during tourist season and left me in her care. Gramma always told me I was her favorite person, which felt like sunshine. Do you know what I mean?"

"Yes," he said, and shifted his gaze toward the drawing of smiley stick figures on the refrigerator.

"Of course you do," she said and closed her eyes. "Losing her changed me. It...defined me. I was broken, flattened. Dead in the soul."

"I'm sorry." He rubbed his thumb on his chin.

"Thank you." She edged closer to him. "Making art is the one thing that helped. I connect to the way she made me feel—safe and celebrated. This gallery telling me I'm good, letting me through the gate…well, it's huge. If someone buys my paintings, then her belief in me wasn't in vain. I'm an artist. I know that beyond a shadow of a doubt, but other people need some proof I'm for real. If I sell my own work, without an expert's validation, people like my parents would say I couldn't hack it on my own."

"I get that," Brendan said. "But having other jobs, other sources of income, is smart. How many artists are big-time successful in their own lifetimes?"

"You sound like my parents." She pressed her forehead to her knees, closed her eyes to shut out the world, then said in a thick drawl, "It'll never work out. You need a safety net."

"Ouch," he said.

His chair scraped against the floor, and the air whooshed as he knelt next to her. He rubbed her back, big, soothing strokes, and said, "Let me build a site for you. If the gallery show works out then it never goes live. Otherwise, you've got it in your back pocket."

She twisted her head against her knees to stare at him. He was making sense.

A chime echoed Brendan's back pocket. "I'm sorry, Princess. This might be something to do with Emma."

"Go ahead," Zara said, and sucked in a deep breath.

He glanced at the screen and yanked his big warm hand from her back. "Are you kidding me?" he ground out. He locked gazes with her. Fire flashed in eyes.

Oh, shit. Had he found out about the paintings? How? For a thin slice of time, she lived with the heart-pounding reality of his fury.

"What is it?" she asked, tangling her fingers together.

"Jess needs to leave Emma with me tonight. The poor kid went there yesterday, and now she needs to bounce back to me. At this point, our arrangement is more eighty-twenty than fifty-fifty."

Zara's body flooded with relief, and then guilt slammed into her. Finding the upside in Jess abandoning Emma was wrong on every level.

"Can I help?" she asked.

"Nah, but it means the world that you offered," he said and riffled his hair. It made it puff up at weird angles, lending him a manic air. "There are a bunch of things I planned to do today for my freelance work. Since I'm picking up Emma after school, the deadlines just got tighter."

"When it comes to understanding deadlines, I'm your girl." Zara thumped her feet to the floor and rose from her chair. "I'll let you get a start on your day. I've got a class to teach at the Waxter Center in a half hour anyway."

He trailed her down the hallway. "Come over tonight? After Emma's in bed? We've already broken the seal on the three-month rule, but I don't think staying over is in the cards."

She pulled her jacket from the closet. "It's a Wine & Paint night. What about tomorrow?"

"Wide open, and Emma would be back with Jess. Come over, and we can talk about whatever you wanted to talk about before I hijacked the conversation. Your paintings, right?"

God, let him not notice the blood draining from my face.

"Yep," she said, nodding. "I'll bring dessert. Any special requests?"

"You. But if you mean food? Chocolate pie."

She kissed him. "I can do both."

He let go of her, scooped up her bag, then handed it over. "I hate saying goodbye to you."

"Me too," she said and slung her tote over her shoulder.

I'll hate it when it's for the last time.

Sixteen

The doorbell ejected Brendan from the coding zone. He yawned and pushed back from his desk, before heading to the door to let his brother in the house.

He'd spent the late morning and early afternoon finalizing Mike's site. Since he'd finished that job early, after picking Emma up from school, he'd gone balls to the wall on whipping up a site worthy of Zara's work. For the past twenty minutes, he'd been vetting the links on the published version of the site and checking the way it rendered on different devices. It was technically live, but when he finished, he'd throw the redirect to hide it from public view.

As disappointed as he was Zara wasn't coming over, he could use the time to catch up on day job work. He was in an okay spot, but this was a big client. Monday's demo had to be flawless.

Mike clumped into the house in his heavy work boots and shoved a plastic container at Brendan. "This is for you."

"What is it?" Brendan lifted the corner of the lid and sniffed.

"Banana muffins or some shit. Monica sent it." Mike unsnapped his coat and hung it on the newel post. "I ate one on the way over. They're pretty good."

"Tell her thank you."

Emma blurred past them, waving a foam ninja sword. "Hi, Uncle Mike!"

As soon as she was out of earshot, Mike asked, "How much notice did you get this time?"

Here we go. After the day he had, the last thing he needed was Mike busting his balls.

"A couple of hours before she had to jump on the train. It's cool. She'll be home tomorrow." Brendan loped toward his workstation in the kitchen. "Come review your site and give me a punch list."

"Man, no way she'd let you get away with the same thing."

"Much as I appreciate the sentiment, Mike, maybe save it?"

He jerked his head toward Emma, who skulked around the

living room, playing ninja. Jess had given her the sword as a memento from her last trip. Emma wouldn't be parted from it.

"Cool. I gotcha."

Brendan pulled a kitchen chair over to his workstation for Mike and flopped himself into his office chair. "I integrated the online scheduler, cleaned up a bunch of code, and shifted into HTML5 so the site is mobile-friendly. I had to create a couple of style sheets. Easy enough, but it'll make updates easier in the future."

Mike wiped his face with his palm. "This must be what it's like for you when I tell you how I rebuild a carburetor."

Brendan laughed. "Want me to show you instead?"

"Yup."

"Here goes." Brendan clicked around and loaded the site in his development environment. He rolled away from the monitors. "Ta-da."

"Bro." Mike squinted at the screen. "That's not an auto shop website. It's a bunch of little paintings of Em and a chick in costume."

"Shit." Brendan spun toward the monitor. "Sorry. Wrong URL. That's another side job I'm testing."

"For anyone I know?"

"Nah. Not yet. It's Zara's site." Brendan dragged the project to a peripheral monitor. He opened a new browser window and typed in the address for the development version of Stewart's Auto Service. "Here's yours."

"Nice. I like it." Mike invaded Brendan's space. "Okay if I check things out for myself?"

"Go for it."

Mike scooted in front of the keyboard. He built fake appointments with the scheduler and reviewed the sub-menus listing their services and prices. Half-moons of grit lived under his fingernails. That'd been true since he'd tinkered with his first engine twenty years ago.

Brendan's own nails were clean, but bitten to the quick.

"When can I start using it?" Mike asked.

"My freelance tester is hitting it now. If she doesn't find any bugs, I can launch it this weekend."

"Cool." Mike clicked on Zara's website and dragged it to the middle monitor.

"What are you doing?"

Mike swatted Brendan's hand away. "Shhh."

He magnified the website until the picture of Zara filled the screen. "This is the chick from Valentine's Day. And you're building a site for her."

"Yeah." Brendan fought not to list the dozens of things he liked about Zara. Mike would put him in a headlock if he did. "We've gone out a few times, now."

"Dude." Mike hooked his arm around the back of the chair and nailed Brendan with his patented 'you are so stupid, little brother' expression. Brendan had been on its receiving end for his entire life.

"What?" Of *course* he knew what.

"*Duuuuuude.*"

"*Whaaaaaat?*"

Mike shook his head. "Mom and Dad say you're the smart one."

"I am the smart one." He smiled.

"You must suck at history, then, since you're repeating it. You fall ass over head for a girl who gives it up to you. Check." Mike ticked off his fingers as he went. "Girl is creative. Check. Girl asks you for help and takes advantage of you. Check. Girl—"

Brendan T'd his hands in the classic "timeout" signal.

"No check. None check. Null check. At least for that last thing. Zara didn't ask me to do this." He gestured toward the screen. "I had to convince her it'd be a good idea."

"Points for her if she turned you down. Brend, for real—"

"Daddy!" Emma shouted from the living room. "I want apple juice."

"How do you ask?" Brendan's chair creaked as he rose from it.

"Please I want apple juice." Emma scampered into the kitchen.

Brendan grabbed the bottle from the fridge and sloshed a more-than-normal amount of juice into a plastic tumbler. He didn't want her to interrupt him to ask for more thirty seconds from now. "Here, sweetheart."

"Thanks." She wrapped two small hands around the cup and carried it to the living room.

He opened his mouth to call her back to the kitchen to sit at the table. Juice in the living room was a spill waiting to happen, but her little ears needed to scram while he set his brother straight about Zara.

He lowered his voice and said, "Ready to continue your lecture?"

"It's not a lecture." Mike sighed. "I've got one way to say this. It'd suck donkey balls if you get burned again, and you're marching straight toward a volcano. Nothing against this chick—"

"Her name's Zara."

"You're in a good place now, and you weren't for a real long time. Protect yourself, is all. You don't have to be-all and do-all for a girl because she f—"

Brendan punched Mike in the shoulder. Emma had snuck back into the kitchen, and the corona of her dark curls was visible past his brother's head. This ninja shit better end soon. She was getting too good at it.

"Boo." Emma giggled.

"Ah!" Mike clutched at his chest. "Where'd you come from?"

"From there." Emma pointed toward the living room. Her gaze drifted to Brendan's monitor and Zara's site, where he'd stubbed in thumbnails of Emma's portrait to illustrate the variety of sizes Zara could offer.

"There's me!" Emma thrust her overly full cup toward the screen. His keyboard and lap were drenched in a sea of apple juice.

"Emma!" Brendan leapt for the paper towels and unspooled half of it.

"I didn't mean to." Her bottom lip quivered the way it did when she was teetering on the edge of a complete meltdown.

"Shit." Brendan caught the flood before it hit the CPU tower under the desk. Jesus, how did this much juice fit into one plastic cup? His brother ripped off more paper towels and shoved them at him.

Brendan glanced at his daughter. Silent tears tracked down Emma's crumpled face.

"Em." He folded her into a hug with his free arm. "It was an accident. It's okay."

"Did I break your computer?"

"No, sweetheart. Hey, Mike, can you give me a fresh one?" Brendan dropped the sticky clump of paper towels onto the floor and took a dry square from Mike. He mopped Emma's face and pinched the paper towel over her nose. "Blow."

She honked into it. "I'm sorry."

"Thank you. Don't carry around juice, okay?" He tried hard not to yell at his kid for accidents. Being a kid was hard enough, and she learned as much from mistakes as she did from successes.

"Okay." She twisted her toe against the hardwoods. "Can I have some goldfish?"

"After I finish cleaning up," he said, sighing. "Go play in the living room, okay?"

Emma took off, and Brendan picked up her plastic cup from the apple juice puddle on the floor and tossed it in the sink.

"Sorry, Mike," he said as he yanked his spray mop from the broom closet.

"What, like I don't have kids? Zero days since the last

catastrophe at my house." Mike cleared out of his brother's way. "Anyways, like I was saying. Don't let this chick fuck with you like Jess did."

"Do you watch your language around your own kids?" Brendan glanced at Emma, who seemed lost enough in her own world that she might not have overheard his loudmouth brother.

"Tried, but it didn't take." Mike folded his arms over his chest. "Monica gives me seven kinds of shit about it, but I'm around mechanics all day. It's not a PG-rated environment."

"I can imagine."

"Now that the big brother talk's done, let me ask you about your girl." Mike stole another banana muffin from the container on the island.

Brendan shoved the mop back in the closet. "Zara."

"She's cute. She always dressed like that?"

"No." Brendan laughed. "These are the only pictures I had of her. They're from Emma's party. She's in costume."

Mike ate the muffin in three bites. "Good. 'Cause it'd be weird if she wore it to Easter dinner."

~ * ~

Late that night, Brendan's phone vibrated with an incoming call from an unknown number. Only one person he could think of might dial him from a mystery phone. "Hey, Princess."

"Oh, how *adorable*."

Wow, he couldn't have been more wrong. Jess's frosty tone iced him down. Brendan threw his arm over his eyes. "What's up, Jess?"

Manhattan traffic and car horn blasts overwhelmed the background.

"Jess?" he prompted.

"So, I need to stay here for the weekend. My publisher—"

"What?" he barked. "Jess, I've got plans."

This was Not Good. His day job project's go-live date was Monday. His stomach churned. There were hours and hours of code cleanup and unit testing to do. Between being sick and the day off yesterday, he'd lost ground on this latest project and planned on using the weekend to catch up. That wouldn't happen with Emma in the house.

"I'll bet you do. Sorry if our *daughter* is cramping your style. How's your—what's your cutesy nickname for her—Princess?"

"It's not her. I have *work* plans, Jess." Which was slightly not true. Zara was supposed to come for dinner tomorrow night, but the rest of the weekend was prep work for Monday's demo.

"Typical of you to assume I'm staying for fun. You *know* I hate this city. My publisher and I were working on a marketing plan for the book, and we wound up scrapping everything. Ask your parents to help you like you always do."

Her accent was in full effect. Good. Because he'd sailed past irritated and straight into pissed.

"They're at the cabin this weekend. But that's not the point," he said in a low, controlled voice. Every cell in his body begged him to shout, but he didn't want to wake Emma. "You can't keep doing this to her. Please. Come home. Emma needs to know she's a priority for you. She misses you."

"I miss her too. And I'm doing this *for* Emma. This book is a huge deal." She paused to take a breath. "I'm sure it'll pay better than whatever project *you're* working on."

Jesus Christ, did he hear a *smile* in her voice?

"Fine. Stay in New York. I'll handle things here, like always."

He ended the call then punched his pillow. It coughed up Zara's citrus and lavender scent. Great. His own bed was mocking him. Much as it made him clench his jaw, first thing tomorrow, he had to cancel his date with Zara. No way he could take a night off.

He threw back the covers and headed downstairs to brew some midnight coffee. He'd have to get the quiet, focused work done after Emma's bedtime to hit his deadline.

Fuck, it was gonna be a long weekend.

~ * ~

As sun broke over the city on Friday morning, a paint-smeared Zara huddled on the floor of her studio in the Tower.

The third and final canvas for her Phoenix series shimmered with wet paint, and she wouldn't touch another inch of it. Her masterstroke had been scraping away thin strips of paint with her thumbnail. The resulting negative space gave the piece the tension it needed.

It was perfect.

Tears pricked Zara's eyes and blurred her vision. The brush dropped, her heavy fingers unable to hold onto it anymore.

Tonight. I have to tell him tonight.

~ * ~

Brendan tapped the steering wheel while he waited at the red light. Was it too early to call Zara to cancel tonight? His parents had drilled the nine o'clock rule into his head as a kid. No calls before nine in the morning, no calls after nine at night. Otherwise, it better be an emergency.

Like Jess's call last night.

He couldn't prove it, but he'd bet last week's paycheck Jess had invented a reason to stay in New York, even though she hated it. Not him. Manhattan always made his blood pump faster. It was exciting to walk around the busy streets, to see the iconic structures that served as background to dozens of movies and television shows he loved. They'd gone together once for a getaway weekend, but Jess complained the city was too crowded, dirty, and smelly for her taste. That was another sign they hadn't been destined to go the distance. He'd even targeted the city for jobs his senior year, but Em happened, and moving back home to Baltimore seemed the right choice.

A horn blasted behind him. *Shit.* The light had turned green.

He'd dropped Em off at school a few minutes ago. He only had six hours before he needed to collect her again. Not enough time, not by a long shot. He'd made some headway last night, but he wasn't anywhere near where he wanted to be. There was at least twenty hours of work between now and eight a.m. on Monday.

Do-able, but barely have a chance to breathe. Then, Tuesday, it would all start back up again. Meetings, meetings, and more meetings to plan the next round of work. It's like he sprinted across the finish line for one project and jumped straight into the next marathon.

Was there anything worse than all-day planning sessions? They always ate up a fuckload of his productivity. On-site meetings especially sucked balls. He couldn't code while the team chattered about milestones and acceptance criteria for the next two-week chunk of work. He didn't see the point of it, anyway. He told them time and again, "Tell me what you want—even better, give me a picture of what you want—and I'll get it done."

It never went that way. They had to map out minimum viable products, scope creep, legacy data plans, and *blah blah blah.*

Day by day, Mike's suggestion to go into business for himself was more appealing. If his back was going to knot up like this in the face of a tough deadline, he'd rather it were for his own contracts and not someone else's. If it weren't for Em, he'd do it in a heartbeat, but he needed to have a stable gig since Jess's job was a total x-factor. Her income could evaporate the minute she wasn't 'on trend.'

Better to have something steady than shoot for the moon and crash back to Earth.

Speaking of people shooting for the moon... He glanced at the clock.

Yeah, 8:30 a.m. was too early. After all, she'd done the Wine

& Paint thing last night. He scratched his forehead and tried to remember if she planned to go to her studio after. Probably. By herself too, he'd bet.

His stomach clenched. Maybe he could make a standing offer to give her a ride on the nights he didn't have Em. Not that he would've been able to last night anyway.

Focus, Stewart.

He parked in front of his house, went inside, then typed a note to Zara. *Change of plans—I've got Em for the weekend. Need to cancel. Sorry, princess. Call me when you get this.*

No pulsing dots.

He squashed his disappointment and dropped into his chair

~ * ~

Zara rolled over in bed, hair damp from her morning shower. She'd come home from the studio, scrubbed up, and fell into a coma.

Hunger roused her.

She padded downstairs to rifle through the sparse contents of the refrigerator. Orange juice, bottled water, old bread, and grape jelly. She dropped the bread into the toaster and uncapped the jelly.

How sad. In Brendan's kitchen, she'd spontaneously cooked a magical elixir of chicken vegetable soup. Here, all she could whip up was stale toast.

She was such a fucking kid sometimes. Maybe growing up wasn't flipping calendar pages, but an actual choice to mature. Or, more accurately, a series of choices. Impossible ones, like telling Brendan about the paintings even though it would anger him.

Her stomach fluttered. At dinner, she'd tell him then show him the pictures. Depending on his reaction, maybe she'd take him to the Tower to inspect them in person.

Zara nibbled the crunchy corner of her breakfast and nudged the wake button on her phone to review the pictures of her paintings she'd taken last night.

Except, the phone stayed dark.

What the huh? She held the power button down, hoping she'd accidentally shut the whole thing off in her earlier sleep-deprived haze.

Nothing. The phone was dead. *Dammit.*

Her brain fizzed with the logistics. She needed to book an appointment to try to repair the phone, get herself to the store, and pay for a new phone if the store's savants couldn't fix it. Not like she could afford any of it—the time or the phone.

Head. Ache.

She needed help. Zara trudged up the stairs.

"Grier?" She knocked on her roommate's door. "Hey Grier?"

"Entres."

She cracked open the door and entered. How did Grier live in this jumble of clothes and books and cables? She tried not to come in here often because the chaotic mess ramped up her anxiety levels.

"My phone died. Can I borrow yours for a minute, and then use your car to go to the mall?"

"Yes to the phone. As for the car, can I come with? I haven't been to the mall in forever." She disconnected her phone from the charger and handed it over. "Much as I adore our boho city lifestyle, sometimes a girl needs to go to Nordstrom."

"Don't you have to pay them five bucks just to browse in there?" She entered Grier's code on the lock screen and a photo of a handsome black man smiled back. "Wait a second. Who's this?"

"Oh. Um." She sat up in bed and flushed a gorgeous shade of crimson. "His name's Quint. I went to high school with him. There's this thing my parents want me to go to, and I might run into him."

Zara ping-ponged her gaze from her fidgety friend to the phone.

"You're leaving out the part where you love him."

Grier folded her arms over her chest. "It's stupid to taunt the person granting you boons."

"Good point. Once I don't need anything from you, I'll resume taunting."

She swiped the photo away and searched for the phone company's number. While it rang, she asked, "What kind of a name is Quint, anyway?"

"He's the fifth John Kincaid, so they nicknamed him Quint to avoid confusion."

"He must be fancy."

"Nope, which is why we were friends." She flicked back the blankets and sat primly on the edge of her bed, legs crossed and hands folded in her lap.

Before Zara could pursue that delicious nugget of information, the employee on the other end answered, took down her info, and scheduled her repair appointment for ten o'clock the next morning.

"There's nothing for today?"

"No ma'am. As it happens, appointments are first-come, first-served. This is the last appointment for tomorrow. Do you want it?"

Shit.

"Yes, please." She gave him a few more details, hung up, and handed the phone back.

"So you're stuck without a phone today, huh?"

She nodded. "Which is ridiculous. I'm having dinner at Brendan's tonight, and I've been preparing myself to spill the beans about the paintings. I even took pictures of them last night with my dumb dead phone."

Grier fished around for a clean bra and panties in the laundry basket next to her bed. "If you want, I can print eight-by-tens of the ones I took the other day. You'll have the first two paintings, at least."

"You kick ass. Yes, please." She leaned against the bureau.

"How will you tell him?"

She picked at the red paint under her thumbnail. "I'd rather keep that between him and me."

"Oh, *that* you'd rather keep between the two of you. But the way his naked body looks, is up for the world to see?"

Zara rolled her eyes so hard she might've damaged her optic nerves. The truth was, she had no idea what to say. An apology implied wrongdoing. Nothing about these paintings was wrong.

He'd see that and eventually everything would turn out okay. At least, she hoped it would.

Seventeen

The church bell around the corner gonged seven times as Zara rang Brendan's doorbell. She balanced a chocolate silk pie and a hopeful overnight bag.

She jiggled her leg as she waited.

Tonight. Absolutely, definitely, one hundred percent, she would tell him about the paintings tonight. Not right away, though. Later. After dessert. Chocolate is a natural sedative, and she could use the calm provided by a full, contented belly. Please, please let him understand.

She straightened her shoulders, and her stressed vertebrae popped like corks.

The door inched open and a comforting aroma—chicken nuggets and French fries?—curled through the crack. Huh. There was no one at the door.

Spooky.

"Hi," a tiny voice said from below. A stripe of Emma's face stared through the gap in the door.

What was Emma doing here? Why wouldn't he have cancelled if...wait.

Zara scrunched up her nose.

Motherfucking phone.

"Hi, Emma." Zara knelt so she and the little girl were nose to nose. "Is your dad home?"

"Yes." Emma tilted her head, and her springy curls dangled to the side.

"Could you get him please?"

"Daddy!" Emma shouted into her face.

"Thanks." Zara winced.

"Em," Brendan said from behind his daughter. "You're not supposed to open the door, sweetheart."

"But it's her," Emma said.

Brendan pushed her down the hallway. "A rule's a rule. Go

play."

Emma scuffed away in her footie pajamas.

After a warm hello kiss, Brendan dragged Zara inside.

"I'm happy to see you, but didn't you get my text?" he asked. Stubble peppered his jaw and his hair puffed up like he'd been running his hands through it all day.

"No. My phone died this morning." She peeked past his shoulder. Emma struck a variety of ninja poses. "I can guess what it was about."

Brendan squared his shoulders. "If you want to bail, I get it. Staying over is, unfortunately, not on the itinerary. Emphasis on unfortunately."

"I'm happy to stay," she said. Much to her surprise, she meant it.

Emma's presence might even be an advantage vis-à-vis the whole confess-naked-paintings situation. The kid was a vaccine against shouting. As long as she was in the house, Brendan would stick with normal tones. All of which might help shape it into a rational conversation.

"I mean, I can't eat this whole thing by myself." Zara presented the dessert.

"Come to me, chocolate pie." He took the dish from her, and she took off her coat and shoes.

Before they ventured further into the house, he dragged her in close, almost lifting her, and planted a firm kiss on her lips. There was heat behind it—affectionate, cozy heat. One she liked as much as the inferno.

Dammit.

"Thank you for coming," he murmured. It's been a long day."

She rubbed her thumb along his cheek. "You're welcome. Don't drop that pie."

"Never."

Zara followed him to the kitchen, enjoying the way his muscles shifted under his V-neck T-shirt. He *had* to be okay with the paintings. It would *hurt* to lose the closeness they'd built up, and the opportunity to build the bonds further. There was a freedom in familiarity she hadn't expected. The more Brendan knew about her, and liked her, the less she had to worry about impressing him.

Now, she just had to worry about hurting him.

"Can I get you a drink?" he asked.

Zara's gaze slid to Emma, who skulked around the armchair. "I'll help myself to water."

She opened the cabinet where he kept the glasses and filled one from the sink. "What's for dinner, by the way?"

"Fish sticks and French fries." He shuffled his fridge's contents around to make room for the pie.

"I was close. I guessed chicken nuggets."

"Ordinarily, yes. It's Lent, so, fish." He rummaged around a bit more. "We've already eaten. I have leftovers, or I could offer you string cheese? Maybe some applesauce? Fruit snacks? Goldfish?"

Everything he mentioned made her queasy. "No thanks. I actually had a late lunch."

Does a fat cup of anxiety count as a late lunch?

"Daddy, let's play this." Emma ran into the kitchen and stopped on the other side of the island. She wielded Candy Land in front of her like a shield.

"I'm busy cleaning up dinner. Give me a couple of minutes?"

Poor guy. He acted exasperated. Single parenting must be exhausting.

"Can I play?" Zara asked, peering at the little girl.

Emma furrowed her brow. "I don't *want* to play with you."

"Emma," Brendan warned.

She squatted next to his daughter. "The thing is, I haven't played Candy Land since I was your age. You'll probably win, but if you don't want to play with me, that's okay."

"Fine." Emma shuffled into the living room, opened the box, then unfolded the board game in the middle of the floor.

"You don't have to," Brendan said.

"I want to," she said. Not because she legit loved Candy Land. No—she wanted to play so she could help Brendan. She slipped from her chair, gently whipped him with a dishtowel, then joined Emma in the living room.

The little girl lay on her belly and glanced up as Zara neared. "I'm the blue guy."

"I'll be yellow." She folded herself onto the floor next to Emma. "What are the rules?"

"Spin the spinner." Emma flicked her finger but missed the plastic arrow. She whiffed it twice more before she gave up and swept the arrow with her finger. "I'm not good at spinning. Oh. I got purple. Now I move my guy to purple."

She hopped her token to the purple square. "Your turn. Don't cheat."

"Never. You know I'm not Ravenna's evil sister, right?"

Emma narrowed her eyes. Wow, she really resembled Jess.

"I'm your dad's friend. You don't have to like me. Lots of people don't, actually." Zara was again grateful Grier, Melinda, and Brooke had seen past the gargoyle. "All I'm asking is for us not to be mean to each other, okay?"

Other people might interpret Emma's silence as a stubborn no, but she understood. The five-year-old was having a deep think. After all, Zara reacted the exact same way to new and important information.

While the little girl pondered, Zara twirled the spinner, and it landed on orange. Officially, that meant she was in second place. They volleyed turns until they were both within a few squares of King Candy.

Emma nudged the spinner, and the color took her straight to the goal.

"I win!" She pumped her fists in the air. "You lost."

"Congratulations." Zara thrust her hand toward the child.

They shook, and Emma said, "Winner cleans up. That's the rule."

"I like that rule, but I'll help."

As they tidied up the game, Brendan appeared in the living room. "Ready for beddy, Em?" To Zara, he said, "Then in fifteen or twenty minutes we can have P-I-E?"

"You spelled pie!" Emma shouted. "Can I have pie?"

Zara snorted.

"Wow, you're smart. But no pie. You already had dessert."

"Aw, fine." She batted thick eyelashes at Zara. "But I want *you* to do my bedtime story."

Goo. Her heart turned to goo. How had Zara not noticed before now? Not only had Emma had inherited Brendan's hair and eyes, but also dimples. If there was one thing she'd learned in the past few weeks, it's that she was powerless against Stewart family dimples.

"Em," he said. "Meet you upstairs in two minutes. Go put on pajamas, okay?"

"Okay," She skipped away, dragging her sword behind her.

"You don't have to read her story."

"I don't mind. What does bedtime involve?" Zara asked.

"Shot of whiskey," he said. "Knocks her right out."

"Me too. I knew she and I had something in common."

"Her actual routine is brushing her teeth, washing her face, brushing and braiding her hair, and a bedtime story. Whole thing takes maybe fifteen minutes. I'll do the bathroom stuff if you tackle a story. Her current favorite is about princesses."

Ugh. Princesses.

Why had she agreed to do this?

She stared at Brendan's back as she followed him upstairs. Oh, right, to help him. If playing Candy Land and reading a bedtime story to a moppet made his day easier, she'd do it. Especially since she was about to drop knowledge on him that might add to his frazzle.

"We'll be right back—you can hang out in here."

Brendan ushered her into an explosively purple bedroom.

Above the twin bed, multi-colored wooden letters spelled *Emma*. No doubt whose room this was. While she waited, she plopped into the comfy chair parked next to a prissy white bookcase. Its shelves smiled under the weight of dozens of books. From a soft storage crate in the corner, a hundred shiny black eyes stared at her. *Shiver.*

Stuffed animals were creepy.

A few minutes later, Emma bounded into the bedroom.

"I'll come kiss you good-night in a few minutes."

"Okay, Daddy." She extracted a book from the shelves and shoved it toward Zara. "I want you to read this to me."

"Princesses Can Do Anything, eh?"

Emma clambered in beside her. The girl smelled of minty bubblegum toothpaste and strawberry shampoo.

"Oh. Okay, then. Personal space, not a thing."

She opened the book, and Emma jabbed at a girl on the inside of the front cover. "That's me."

"She's awesome. I like—" she circled the page and found a girl with a paint brush, "—her."

"Me too. She's my second favorite."

As Zara read the book, Emma turned the pages. Judging by the number of wrinkles and tiny rips in the pages, this was a well-loved story. By the second to the last page, the little girl was rubbing her eyes and yawning. She'd relaxed all of her fifty pounds onto Zara, and the warmth and coziness had a soporific effect. If she didn't get out from under her in the next few minutes, she and the girl would fall asleep right here.

At the end of the story, she closed the book. "I'll get your dad."

"I'm here," Brendan said from the doorway.

She jumped. "Sh...ugar! You surprised me."

Her heart beat in her ears.

"Sorry," he said. "Didn't mean to startle you. Can I tuck you in?"

"Uh huh." Emma held her arms toward her father. He plucked her up, swooped her around, then plopped her into her bed. "Good night. I love you, and I'll see you in the morning."

"Good night, I love you, and I'll see you in the morning." She snuggled under the blankets, and Brendan tucked them in tight around her, then switched off the bedside lamp.

Out in the hallway, he murmured. "Thank you for being so sweet with her. Jess needed to go to New York for meetings, and—"

"No need to explain or thank me. She's a nice kid."

"But you don't like kids."

"I never said I don't like kids. Everyone misunderstands this." She followed him downstairs and into the kitchen. "I don't want to *have* kids, but I like Emma. She reminds me a lot of me."

"That's why you're good with her." Brendan offered her chair at the head of the kitchen table. He'd plated two fat wedges of pie and poured them each a glass of wine.

"How do you mean?" She snapped a napkin across her lap.

"You talk to her." He squeezed her knee under the table. "I heard you ask her about the family arts events at the BMA during your game."

"She has lots of interesting things to say. And she's totally right—safety scissors are terrible."

Emma was an unvarnished slice of personality. She said whatever came into her head, even if it was rude. It was refreshing. Plus, the little girl didn't try to cheat at Candy Land, not even once.

There was no artifice to her at all.

That was a thing you learned when becoming an adult, apparently.

Her heart leapt to her throat. Soon. She had to tell him soon. She flicked her gaze toward the clock. 7:45 p.m. Who could have predicted the most awkward conversation of her life would begin at such a mundane time?

"Everything okay?" he asked. "You haven't said much this evening. I just vented about work for ten minutes, and you didn't try to change the subject once. Coding is boring to non-coders. Hell, coding is boring to coders, too."

He grabbed the bottle of wine and tipped more into her empty glass. *Hmm.* She'd drunk that fast.

"I'm fine."

"Good." He whisked their dishes off to the sink.

She wouldn't get a more perfect segue into this conversation. This was it. She took a deep breath to calm her heart. When that didn't work she gulped her wine.

"Would you mind sitting down?" she asked.

"Uh oh. Serious talk time. Relax. I can guess what you're about to say."

"I doubt it," she muttered.

"Things are happening too fast, aren't they?" He pressed a hand to his chest. "That's all me. I've never done the casual dating thing."

"Brendan—"

He ran his thumb over her knuckles. "I hold hands, I buy flowers, I have your back, I say I love you. But I can chill, I promise. I don't want to ruin this."

Did he say I love you?

She tried to steady her heaving guts. "No, it's not your...zealousness."

"So you don't want to slow things down?"

Tears pricked at her eyes and guilt clogged her throat. Was there *any* chance she could explain this and not seem like a complete user?

Grazing his lips with her index finger, she said, "Brendan Stewart, hush. You're making it impossible to confess."

"Confess?" he mumbled behind her finger.

Zara closed her eyes, gulped, and plunged into her fear. "Remember on our first date, when you asked me why I agreed to go out with you? I had painter's block, so I was trying to live a little."

"You also said I was hot. Go on."

"Well... You've..." Her mouth went dry. "You've...unblocked me."

He raised an eyebrow. "Sounds vaguely dirty."

"Funny you should say that." Zara drained her wineglass. Two glasses in a half hour on an empty stomach was maybe not the best idea, but she'd take her courage where she could find it.

"I finished the paintings. Three of them. My mentor and Schwarz, the man who owns the gallery, love them. They say it's my best work, and I could be the hit of the show."

"That's awesome." He patted her knee. "Was one of them the space painting? Or the portraits? I bet they loved the portraits."

She fidgeted with the napkin still draped on her lap. "Uh, no. The ones they responded to the most were brand new...and inspired by you."

"Wow, I'm flattered. Can I see them? I could bring Em. She'd love your studio. She's into arts and crafts."

"Um, that wouldn't be a good idea." She bit her lip. Why couldn't she breathe? It was like she was sipping oxygen through a coffee straw.

He nodded. "There I go, rushing things again. Sorry."

"Stop saying you're sorry." Every one of his apologies was a red-hot poker of a reminder that she was such an asshole in comparison. "The paintings aren't appropriate for kids. They're of…us."

Her vision went hazy as she exhaled.

There, she'd said it.

"Cool." After a second, his face crinkled. "Wait. Why aren't portraits of us appropriate?"

Everything was heavy, unbearable. Had gravity cranked itself up a notch?

"They aren't portraits. The paintings…" If she was bold enough to paint them, she had to have the ovaries to talk to him about them. She locked in on his eyes. The flush crept from her chest and wrapped itself around her throat and face. "They're of you and me. Together. Nude."

He backed away. "I don't understand. Explain. Use simple terms."

Despite all the hours she'd spent memorizing his face, his features transformed into a brand new composition. One that made her heart hurt. His crinkle hunkered between the slashes of his brows, but the skin around his eyes tightened and blanched. Worst of all, the warmth drained from his brown-and-golds, leaving flat, inscrutable frozen puddles behind. Unless he relaxed his jaw, he'd crack his molars.

From her toes to her crown, her muscles cramped. The pie sat like lead in her stomach, and air refused to inflate her lungs. If she had a wish stashed in her pocket, she'd use it to melt the ice in his glare and gain his approval. Hell, she'd settle for his understanding, even if he didn't approve.

Judging by the way his nostrils flared, though, it would take a shit-ton of magic to get there. She sucked at words. Images were more her thing. But he wanted words, so she'd do her best.

Zara tucked her hair behind her ears, then took another deep breath. "After our first date, and the way we were together in my studio, you were all I could think about."

He remained a perfect, silent sculpture of hard lines.

"Beautiful, authentic, and persistent images came to me." She smoothed her hands along the length of her thighs. "I didn't want to paint them, because they put you on a pedestal and I didn't know you that well. But the ideas wouldn't go away, and they blocked other ideas. Every time I tried to sketch something else, my brain returned to you and me. So, to exorcise them, I had to paint them."

"You had to paint nude pictures of me?" Brendan's brittle voice ground out, "*Had to?*"

This was horrible. Why couldn't she be a poet? Then she could weave a glorious, mesmerizing explanation. Instead, she was stuck with this blundering tongue.

"The paintings are tasteful. You can't see any, um…" Zara fumbled for a more mature way of saying *private parts*. She came up short. "And you can't tell it's you and me—they aren't photo-realistic. They're more about shapes…and angles and… Words are failing me here. But I have a picture. Let me show you."

She started to rise from her chair, but his expression stilled her. Anger wafted from him.

"I don't want my private life on display. At all." Brendan pushed back further, away from the table, away from her. He crossed his ankle over his knee and clamped his hands on his shin. "I've been down that road before and have zero intention of repeating the trip."

"They aren't gossipy, like Jess's blog, I swear. They're honest, and celebrate life, and sex, and love, and…"

She was fucking this up. Zara's heart collapsed on itself. She stared at her fingers, at the crimson crescent under the thumbnail, then dug her nails into her palms. That tiny pain focused her to the point where she could hold back the tears pricking her eyes.

There had to be a way to make him understand.

"If you would just—"

"I don't care. I don't want any part of it." His chair creaked under his shifting weight. "You don't know what you're doing by exposing yourself like this. Exposing *me* like this. I've got a kid, Zara. I've gotta keep my name clean, because it's her name too."

Zara's head jerked up.

"Clean? My paintings aren't dirty." She wheeled her hand between them. "What's between us isn't dirty. This kind of thing should be celebrated. Not shamed."

"You're missing my point." Brendan scrubbed at his scalp. "You haven't thought this through. Can't you paint something, anything else? Like the portraits."

"Oh, my God, do not try to tell me my business. The portraits aren't on the level of the work I'm putting in the gallery. I've *tried* to paint something else. It'd be fabulous if I could Van Gogh the Harbor or something, but that's not me." She touched his knee. "I'm good at painting passion, and you are my passion."

They stared at each other, deadlocked.

210

"I'm not giving you my permission."

He'd given her a terrible gift by saying that. Now she understood there was no such thing as having her pie and eating it too. She could choose him, and bail on the show, or choose her career and break her own heart.

"I wasn't asking for permission. I—" Her voice broke. She swallowed, hoping to clear the lump blocking her words. "I wish I could say I'm sorry, but I'm not. What I've created, and what you inspired, is beautiful, and that's all there is to it."

"Have you even weighed the pros and cons of what this will do to *your* reputation? You'll be the naked chick in the paintings." Brendan scraped his chair backward. "Fuck. You know, Mike called it. He said I was repeating history. Getting in too deep, too fast. I thought he might be right about that, but I didn't care. But, I didn't think it meant making my private life available for the public consumption. A-fucking-gain."

Ouch.

"It's not the same." Zara jumped up from her chair, marched down the hallway, and yanked her coat from the closet. A hanger went flying. "You said the shit your ex wrote was a distortion. My paintings aren't. It's not the same thing at all."

"It is."

"Then you're being small-minded." Zara pulled a folder containing Grier's photo from her bag. "When you're ready to be rational, look at the picture."

She shoved it at him. He refused to uncross his arms and take it from her, so she dropped it on the chest of drawers in the foyer.

"I'm not changing my mind." He stared down his nose. "This is the one thing—*the one thing*—I told you got under my skin. I'm willing to share my life with people I love. Not with strangers."

"You've only known me for two weeks. I'm a stranger, remember?" She wrenched the door open. The cold night gusted inside, whipping her hair around her face. She snatched her tote and hurried away from the warmth, the food, and the coziness.

The door slammed shut behind her.

Eighteen

Brendan hadn't slept well. All weekend, he'd fumed and tried his damnedest not to take his foul mood out on Emma. It wasn't her fault he was trying to work and be her dad—and doing a half-assed job at both. She clearly thought his playmate skills sucked, because she asked every couple of hours when Zara would come back over. All he could say was he didn't know, which killed him. He'd had to do that enough to cover for Jess's absenteeism. Now he had *another* woman flitting in and out of his kid's life.

Epic fucking mistake.

This weekend drove it home that he could be everything for Emma. By mostly ignoring her, he'd made the deadline. Good for the job, but a total dad fail. He'd bring it up at today's marathon meeting—no more Monday deadlines. His adrenaline was still pumping from the volume of tasks he'd needed to finish to hit today's deliverable. It was hard to spin down from that kind of energy. Case in point—his eyes had flown open at four a.m. today for no good reason.

He'd tried to fall back asleep, until he caught Zara's scent on his pillow. Which, nope. He didn't have the bandwidth to think about her and her upcoming show. The only cure for going down that road was to distract himself with more work.

He'd flipped back the blankets then headed to the kitchen to tackle bonus items on the development task list and to prep for this meeting. Now he was raring to go, fueled by annoyance and black coffee. If all went well, he could be on his way home by pick-up time so his mom wouldn't have to do it like they'd planned.

The elevator doors opened onto the fifth floor of the office building. He entered the company's code on the cypher then depressed the door handle. Nothing happened.

Must've flubbed the code.

Brendan hit the buttons again in a different sequence, pressed again, and nothing. It'd been weeks since he'd been to HQ. Maybe they changed the codes and he ignored the e-mail?

He knocked on the company's plate glass door, trying to get the attention of a staffer in the Human Resources pod of cubicles.

A minute later, Drew, the beefy mailroom guy, let him in. "Hey, Brend. Good to see ya."

"Hey, Drew." Brendan switched to his work personality. "Thanks. They change the combination again?"

He laughed and held the door open. "We sure like to mess with you remote guys."

Brendan dropped his stuff into his cubicle. Most of the others were empty, the monitors dark. Shit, he must be late if everyone's already in the meeting. He double-checked his phone for the location and marched toward the Pratt Meeting Room.

The door was closed. Weird. He tapped a few times and entered.

Greg, the CEO, and Phyllis, the Director of Human Resources, sat at the table.

Oh, shit. This combo of people meant this meeting was going one of two ways. He was either getting a promotion, or fired.

Phyllis smiled like she was showing off new dental work. "Hi Brendan."

"What's going on?"

"If you'll sit, we can begin."

Brendan flicked a glance at her. "Not to be rude, Phyllis, but I'd prefer for Greg to tell me what's going on."

His boss broke eye contact with his omnipresent cell phone. It was a gigantic douchey one that might as well be a tablet. Christ, who was he constantly texting?

"It's pretty straightforward, bro," he said, and shrugged. "We've sold the company in a sweet, sweet deal. It's the dream."

Brendan dropped into the chair Phyllis nudged toward him. "Whose dream?"

"If I may." She side-eyed Greg. "I need to drive this meeting so we can be certain we've covered everything. Now, Brendan, you've worked for us for five years—"

"Six. Why didn't you talk to me?" He stared across the table. "This had to have been in the works for months."

"No offense bro, but you have zero risk appetite. I needed to keep your big brain focused on this last release. You'd have started looking for a job if you thought things were shaky. The buyers want to move the operations to Kansas City, and you and I both know you aren't moving. Not with your personal situation. Come on," Greg said, smiling. "Tell me I'm wrong."

Brendan's palms burst into swamps, and he rested them on his legs to dry his hands on his khakis. He needed a job, and he needed one *now*. His savings would keep him afloat for two months, three if he yanked Emma from private school. He'd have to talk to Jess about it first, but he'd rather eat glass.

"This is a shitty way to treat people. I busted my ass on this app."

"Which is why DigiTex wants to buy it. You rocked it, man."

"So by doing a great job, I screwed myself out of a job?"

"If we could get back to the agenda," Phyllis interrupted, "I'll explain the terms of the payout."

"What payout?"

"*Your* payout, bro. You got in early, so you get a payout and stock options."

Phyllis cleared her throat. "Which you can't sell for 180 days after the company goes public."

"The company's going public?"

Greg laced his hands behind his head. "I keep telling you—it's the dream."

This guy. How had he stomached work for him this long? He pinched the crinkle at the bridge of his nose. "Not my dream. I need to figure out insurance and where I'm going next."

"Baltimore's tech industry is booming. World's your oyster. You can go anywhere you want. My advice is you start your own gig. That's where the real money's to be made."

Or lost. Then he'd really be up a creek.

"What about you? What are you going to do?"

"Me? Sail my boat to the Caribbean, float for a few months, and come up my next big idea."

"Sounds about right." He blew out his lips and faced Phyllis. "You said there are details to discuss?"

She nattered on about the terms, and his eyes glazed over. The countless late nights developing software for this company had resulted in a golden parachute. Which bought him time to find a new job, but Christ. Hunting down a gig that gave him all the flex time and telework he needed would be a goddamn nightmare.

How was he going to tell his parents, his brother, Jess? Fuck that noise. None of them would get what it felt like to have the rug yanked out from under them like this.

His parents and brother would be sympathetic. Jess... No issue there, because he'd rather eat glass than tell her he'd been canned. Mike and Monica would throw beer and food at him until he was too

214

drunk, fat, and happy to worry about anything.

None of that was what he wanted. Truth was, he wanted commiseration. Someone who would flip off his old company, and then help him figure out his next move.

Zara.

She was the one person in this whole city he wanted to talk to. What with the fire, and the scrambling she'd done to hang on tight to her shot, she understood what it meant to have your security ripped away from you.

Except, he wasn't talking to her right now.

"Sign these." Phyllis twisted a sheaf of papers toward him. "To say you understand what we've covered, and that's it. You'll have time to clear out your desk."

Greg's phone rang. "Sorry bro, gotta take this. Good luck to you, and feel free to use me as a reference."

He jabbed his hand toward Brendan. He was supposed to shake this guy's hand? Fine, then. He wrapped his hand around Greg's and crushed it in an iron grip. When he let go, his ex-boss shook his hand and zipped from the room, already talking to whomever was on the other end of the phone.

In the hallway, Drew waited with a cardboard banker's box and an apologetic expression. Brendan didn't blame him. What do you say to a friend you're escorting from the building? They strolled toward Brendan's cube in silence. In five minutes flat, Brendan cleared the drawers and overhead cubbies and dumped it in the box without sorting through it.

~ * ~

At home, he dropped the box on the kitchen table and ripped off its lid. Expired cough drops, an old ColdFusion manual. Who programmed in ColdFusion anymore? Both went straight into the trash.

He smiled at Emma's stick figure drawing from last year's Take Your Daughters to Work Day. The office hadn't planned any activities for the daughters, and she'd kept herself entertained with a wad of sticky notes and a colorful assortment of pens. She was a pretty great little artist—the stick figure was in profile and was definitely him at his computer. Maybe Zara had been onto something when she said she understood his kid.

He started his "keep" pile with the drawing. The only additions were a portrait from her year in dance, a gel ink pen he'd always liked, and an Agile Development manual he'd marked up with notes.

That's all he had to show for six years of employment. Christ, what a six years it had been too. Marriage, house, kid, divorce… All he wanted was to keep life safe and predictable. Why the hell was that so hard?

Pacing the house, his frustration built until he couldn't take it anymore. He punched the wall in the foyer and knocked his crucifix from where it hung near the steps.

"Fuck." He shook his hand to staunch the immediate pain. Why did he keep doing that? Stupid, plain and simple. The wall always won.

He crouched and fished under the chest of drawers for the crucifix. His fingers scraped against something flatter, thinner. The photo of the paintings. Must've slipped there the night Zara stormed out. Might as well face the damage. His brain couldn't break any further today.

He sat with his back to the wall and his legs tented in front of him. Pinching the corner of the photo, he slid it out, then flipped it over. There was Zara, a shy smile playing on her lips. Even in miniature, she made him catch his breath. He missed that smile.

Behind her were two paintings. A bolt of heat hit him straight in the balls.

There they were. She and him. *In flagrante delicto.*

Sort of.

The bodies in the picture entwined with each other, moving together, swept up in the heavy brushstrokes. These images uncorked sense memories of her strong limbs wrapped around him, her warm body under his, her sweet taste. The way she melted against him and laughed in his arms. That one night, when she thought he was already asleep, and her tears had dampened his chest.

He studied the photo, bringing it closer, understanding threading through his body.

Zara had been right.

Somehow, she'd captured how things were between them. Not just the actions, but the emotions too. Bright, strong, and fast. They weren't exaggerated, or exploitative. They were... What did she call them? Authentic.

Racy as hell too. Mom and Dad could never see them. That was for goddamn sure. The real gut check was this—would he be embarrassed for Mike to see these?

Nope cudgeled him in the brain. Of course his brother wouldn't care. He'd probably clap him on the back and tell him Zara was a keeper.

Speaking of...

He woke his phone and scrolled, hovering his thumbs over her name. What was he planning to say? Sorry?

Yes and no. He wasn't sorry he'd lost his temper when she told him about the paintings. All things considered, he'd been pretty fucking restrained. The thing he was sorry for was not realizing all he needed was some time and space to understand these paintings for what they were.

Love letters.

His heart wanted to say, "Hi, I miss you. Your paintings are beautiful. Come over."

What a fucking loony thing to do after a bunch of petulant yelling.

"Agh." He riffled his hands through his hair.

When in doubt, follow Maslow's hierarchy. Food, shelter, safety, money. Then love and belonging. Much as he might like to go pound on her door, he had some other things to square away.

First, figure out the job. Then, apologize to Zara.

He examined the picture again. Damn, she was talented. She'd blended what he'd seen in the portraits—her ability to capture a person's essence—with her abstract stuff. These two paintings were better than the portraits by miles.

He furrowed his brow. Two paintings.

She said she was on the hook for three paintings.

Jesus Christ, Princess. He peered at the photo, searching for a hint. *If those are the first two, what's the third one?*

~ * ~

"The delivery entrance is somewhere over there." Zara pointed toward the driver's side of the road. "Schwarz's assistant said it's a bright red door on Lovegrove Street."

"This isn't a street." Grier white-knuckled the steering wheel. "This is a paved alley. A very narrow paved alley. I'm flashing back to my birth."

"There it is." Zara spied the red door a block away. Her belly flipped, and she turned to count her paintings for the fortieth time.

One, two, three.

No goblin had snatched them during the drive from the Tower.

They parked on the concrete swatch of the loading zone next to the gallery's delivery door.

She closed her eyes. This was the jumping off point. Once she let go of the rope and submitted these paintings to the gallery, there was no going back.

Deep breaths.

Grier flicked her on the shoulder. "Everything okay?"

"Peachy." Zara shifted her gaze from the delivery instructions gleaming from her shiny, new phone. It was encased in an industrial strength rubber.

"You don't look peachy. More like bloodshot and bruised."

"I haven't been sleeping." She slipped the phone into her bag and peered through the window. "I'm supposed to ring the buzzer."

"Brendan hasn't returned *any* of your texts?"

"No." She sighed. "I sent him a couple a day for the past week. Nothing."

"You're so…moony." Grier planted her elbow on the back of her seat and propped her head with her hand. "It's different. You've always shrugged guys off like shirts."

"Moony? Did you borrow that word from your mother?"

"Stop redirecting. You like him, don't you?"

Zara twisted her lips and tangled her fingers together. "I do. Or did? Should I use the past tense? I like him, but…" She buried her face in her hands. "This is nuts. We were only together for a couple weeks. I shouldn't be this…"

"What? Moony?"

"Gutted." She let her hands fall on her lap, palms up, fingers curled. "I should be dancing a jig about turning in these paintings. Instead, I want to throw up."

"Real talk." Grier squinted like she was peering through an invisible camera to inspect her friend. "Are you for sure not pregnant?"

She laughed. "A hundred percent not pregnant. I got my period on Saturday. Apparently, my heartsickness bears a striking resemblance to pregnancy. Glowy nausea."

"If you're interested, I have a theory."

"Do tell." Zara raised an eyebrow heavy with pencil. Her makeup was a little extra today, an attempt to arm herself against whatever the universe might throw at her. Completely ineffective, but it still made her feel better.

"Those couple of weeks with Brendan were *intense*. You opened yourself up to new possibilities. You're upset about what was, obviously, but maybe you're also mourning what might-have-been?"

"Nah." She waved off Grier's theory. "This whole thing had an expiration date from the beginning. How can I mourn something I never wanted?"

"Bullshit."

"Nope. No bullshit. He has a kid, and I'm busy, and—"

"Stop using his daughter as an excuse. You're enamored of her. I saw it with my own eyes at the party. And you've told me about reading her a bedtime story at least six times."

"I…" She could almost smell Emma's sweet, cozy scent.

"All the butterflies of flirting, of doing new things, and sex might've cleared the cobwebs from your creative side." Grier's hand cupped Zara's shoulder. "This thing you have with him, and the affection you have for his kid—it's feeding your soul in ways the rest of your life isn't."

Each word thudded into her heart. Their truth was undeniable. She was a different woman than she had been two weeks ago. How was that even possible?

"I'd expect hippie shit from Melinda, not you." She wiped at her eyes. Good thing she'd used waterproof mascara.

"Right? The scion of a long line of one-per centers would be touchy-feely, wouldn't they? And, on the topic of emotions—"

"Oh no. I can't handle any more."

"Too bad. Handle it you must. I'm proud of you for telling him about the paintings. It was the principled thing to do." Grier glanced behind her at the three paintings huddled together. "Are you sure these are worth the torment?"

"It's killing me, but I have to say yes. If I never see him again, it'll hurt like hell. But something good and permanent came from us." Zara wrapped her hand around the car door handle and cracked open the door, slid from the car, then hit the button on the silver box next to the garage door.

A garbled voice asked, "Can I help you?"

"Uh, hi. I'm Zara Kissette, delivering paintings for the Phoenix exhibit."

The door spooled upward, and a wiry bald man wearing jeans and a flannel shirt greeted Zara. "Hi hon, I'm AJ. You said your name was Sara?"

"Zara with a Z." She pumped AJ's outstretched hand.

"Nice to meet you, Zara with a Z. He peeked into the car. "This your first show?"

"It is. Do I give off a newbie vibe?" She crisscrossed her legs.

He pointed through the glass. "Well, your paintings are loose in there. Veterans are lots more precious than that, on account of suffering a busted frame or two."

"My studio's two miles away." She opened the rear car door. "Excessive packing seemed fussy."

"I gotcha." He gentled the first of the three canvases from the Mercedes. "But one fender bender, and your work would've been damaged. Your gamble."

"Good point."

"Slim chance of it, but no reason to take the risk." AJ slotted the art into a rack in the receiving area. "Just use heftier packaging next time."

Her heart shuddered. *Next time.*

As he collected the other paintings from the car, the inner door to the gallery opened. Schwarz hastened across the concrete to bear hug Zara. That was a welcome she could get addicted to.

"Well, this is a nice surprise." He released her and rocked on his heels, hands in his pockets. "I half-expected you to say you needed an extension."

"I honor my commitments." She was as serious as a medieval wedding vow when it came to her career, and she needed him to know that.

"A wonderful trait in a professional. While you're here, I have paperwork for you to fill out. It details the pricing, commission rate, and titles of your paintings."

"Oh, okay. Let me tell my ride."

Her footsteps pecked the concrete. She knocked on Grier's window and waited for her friend to roll down the glass. "I need to review paperwork about terms."

Grier laughed. "Of course you do, now that you're so fantastically adult."

"It might take some time, so you don't have to wait."

"Got it. Text me when you're done. Maybe we can grab a celebratory bite?"

"You sure?"

"Yes. Food will be my reward. I've got a boring stretch of PhotoShopping wedding photos. The bride had the most beautiful, dark skin, and the groom was as pale as Boo Radley." She started the car. "Lovely couple, but a ton of light metering."

"You said it's cheating to use Photoshop."

"Did I?" She wrinkled her nose. "Well, I stand by that, but we all need to cheat sometimes."

Zara let that roll around in her brain as she returned to Schwarz, who took her arm and steered her toward Schwarz's cozy loft office.

An hour later, she texted Grier. *Need food & booze. Am shaking. Meet me at the Stable in 10.*

~ * ~

Zara flagged down her friend as she clattered into the cool confines of the Mount Vernon Stable & Saloon.

"What happened?" Grier asked as she collapsed onto the

neighboring stool. She eyed the two glasses of champagne bubbling in the flutes on the bar. "Good things? What are we celebrating?"

"Did you run here?"

"Yes." She gasped. "You said you were shaking. I run to shaky people. Why? Why the shaking?"

"Schwarz priced the big painting at twenty-five hundred and the others at two thousand each." Her blood whooshed fast through her veins. "The gallery gets fifty percent in commission. He warned me buyers will haggle, and it might come in under the posted price. But I expected him to set them at four hundred at the absolute most. That he thinks he can get so much for a debut artist..."

"You're a debutante?"

"Hardly."

"Shit." Grier laughed. "I was hoping for a cotillion."

"Get this." Zara leaned in close. "He said for the next show, he'd be able to set my prices even higher. Once I have more of a brand name."

"Next show? That's fantastic!"

"Yes. He wants six pieces for the next show. In a month."

"Can you produce six more that fast?"

"Fuck yes." She pushed up her sleeves and laced her fingers together. "I finally, finally, *finally* locked in on my style, and my subject matter. The next paintings are sparking in my fingers. I'll need models to make sure the physicality is true, but that's the easiest part."

"Well, in that case..." Grier held her glass aloft. "A toast to perseverance. And sexy times."

They clinked and drank.

"I do love day drinking." Grier twisted the glass until it caught some of the dim light shining through the window. "Makes me nostalgic for my parents' fundraisers."

"What a naughty rebel, sneaking champagne in the garden. Lots of kids at the shore staved off boredom through sex, booze, and prescription pills. But they were more acquaintances than friends." Zara shivered and blew out an exhausted breath. "Thank God I don't have to move back."

Grier narrowed her eyes. "Was that a possibility?"

"Yes." She stared at the liquid in her glass. "Up until this morning."

"Explain, please. Why would you do that? You hate the shore."

"Remember how I freaked senior year because MICA cut my financial aid package?"

"Yes."

"My parents loaned me the difference."

"Loaned?"

"They weren't giving it to me outright because they thought it was a mistake that I went to art school in the first place. So, I cut a deal where I have until this June to repay them. If I don't, I promised to return to The Sandcastle to work it off."

Grier drained her glass. "How much do you owe them?"

"Ten thousand dollars."

"This is stupid." Grier yanked her checkbook from her purse. She flipped it open and scribbled Zara's name. "I'm not letting my best friend go to purgatory over ten thousand dollars." She ripped the check free and handed it over.

Zara tore it to pieces. "This is why I didn't tell you. You throw money at any problem—"

"Will you just let me be your fairy godmother?" She wrote another check and shoved it at her. "I'm throwing money at the problem because money *is* the problem here."

"No, it's not. The problem is my parents don't believe I can do this." She destroyed the second check and dropped the shreds on the bar. "They're convinced I can't survive on my own, find a good place to live, or fund my life through my chosen profession. If I give them *your* money, they'll be right."

"You don't have to tell them where it came from."

"But I'll know." The champagne bubbles burned Zara's throat as she drank. "It's a moot point. I stand to make three thousand dollars, maybe more. And then I could make more at the next show."

"*Coulds* and *maybes* are tenuous words to build your life around." Grier touched Zara's knee. "Can I be your Plan B if your paintings don't sell?"

"I already have a Plan B." She chewed on her thumbnail. Even if Brendan didn't create the site for her, his idea about selling her work herself could be the alternate route. "Sort of. But I'm full-throttle going for the gallery for now. Anything else is as good as saying I don't believe in myself."

"That's no guarantee…"

"Doesn't matter." Zara gestured at the bartender to order another round. "I'm not taking your money."

"What if I buy the Phoenix series from you at like, quintuple the asking price? I'd be investing in my favorite artist, and—"

The bartender left two full glasses of pale, effervescent wine in front of them.

"I love you, but please don't be my safety net. I need to do this my way."

Grier pursed her lips. "Your pride fucks with you, you know that?"

"There have been times when my pride is all I have."

Nineteen

A week after delivering the paintings, Zara and her roommates glided through the night toward the Schwarz Gallery for the show's opening. Her heart knocked against her sternum so hard she was surprised she wasn't shaking the whole car.

"We're getting close." Grier lowered the radio's volume. "There's valet parking, isn't there?"

"Yes. Street parking too." She couldn't quite tuck her curls behind her ear. Brooke had insisted long and loose was the way to go for a formal event, but the goddamn slippery spirals wouldn't stay put.

"You okay, Zar?" Brooke asked from the backseat. "You're fidgety."

"I'm nervous." Nervous? That was putting it mildly. Every part of her vibrated with apprehension, right down to the toes in her boots.

"Of course you are, sweetie." Melinda said from her spot behind Grier. "March 14th is finally here, the culmination of all the work leading up to your big debut tonight, and everyone will see your fabulous paintings for the first time…"

"This isn't helping," she said, hiding her face in her hands, careful not to crush the fake eyelashes she had applied an hour ago.

Melinda massaged Zara's shoulder. "Let me finish validating your feelings. You just have classic opening night jitters, that's all. Everything will be fine, I promise."

"Fuck street parking," Grier said as she pulled up to the valet stand. "I'm wearing six-inch heels, and we're five minutes late."

"My fault." Melinda sighed. "But I couldn't rush the makeup or I'd turn her into a clown."

Zara unzipped her wristlet to extract a couple of bills. "How much? Ten bucks?"

"Your money's no good." Grier smacked her hand away.

The valet opened the curbside doors, and the four women slid out to the sidewalk.

Brooke wolf-whistled. "You're definitely bringing the glamour for your big night."

With pin curls by Brooke, dramatic makeup by Melinda, and a body-hugging yellow sparkler of a gown on loan from Grier, Zara felt beautiful. Not pretty. Not 'I look good for me.'

Legit, head-turner beautiful.

"We all do," she said, searching the eyes of her three best friends.

They'd cheered her on and picked her up every step of the way. Having been there for so many of the valleys, she was thrilled to have them along for a peak. Just like she'd gone to the symphony for Brooke, or to the opening night of a play at Charm City Stage for Melinda, or any of Grier's family's fundraiser galas. These women were part of her team, her squad, her posse.

Her family.

As they formed a semi-circle around her, Zara stretched out her arms to wrap them in a group hug. "Thank you for coming with me tonight."

"Of course we'd come." Brooke hip-bumped her. "This is the biggest night of your life. Plus, free canapés and drinks."

"Not everyone understands." She blinked to clear the rising tide of tears. "You guys get it."

Melinda wagged her finger. "Uh, uh, uh, sweetie. No crying. It took me ten minutes to apply your smoky eye. Here."

She shoved a tissue at Zara.

"Thanks." After dabbing at the corners of her eyes, she took a deep breath, squared her shoulders, then marched through the front door of the Schwarz Gallery.

~ * ~

Brendan lingered at the rear of the long gallery and shifted his weight. The entrance at the opposite end was blocked by the sculptures in the middle of the room.

He jammed his fists into his pockets. How had he let all this time go by without talking to Zara?

Well, he *knew* how. No mystery there. He'd promised himself he'd call her as soon as he got his job situation straightened out. Problem was, the job situation was still pretty loose. Despite all his friends in the industry, no one was offering the immediate work-from-home flex he wanted so he could be at home with Emma before and after school.

No matter what, the looming equation was the same. Unless he could work from home, he'd have to send her to the on-site aftercare program or hire help. The little bit of time he had with her would be whittled to a sliver.

It made him sick.

Somewhere between the third and fourth nanny profile, he'd decided to bail on steady, structured work and go into business for himself. Risky, but do-able. Between his payout, his savings, and the couple of side-jobs he'd already booked, he had a financial cushion. So, he had to give it a shot. After crunching the numbers, he figured if he hustled for just a couple more clients, he could keep his home life at the status quo. Maybe even better.

Not how he planned to go into business for himself, but the best things in his life were unplanned. His kid, his house…

And Zara.

Meeting her had taught him to set his rigid blueprints on fire. If the old Brendan had planned to dive back into romance, he'd have put his faith in the almighty algorithm of a dating site. Result? A series of nice meals with women who were perfect matches to the version of himself he wanted the world to see. Not who he actually was.

Instead, fate, magic, or plain old dumb luck delivered him a princess.

The tall front door swished open, and there she was. Zara led a constellation of women through the entrance and toward the middle of the gallery. Was she walking on fairy dust? He could swear she glittered, and the delight in her eyes was unmistakable.

She scanned the art featured throughout the room. Looking for her work? When she turned on her heel, her bright yellow dress flared out, and a narrow slice of pale thigh winked at him through the side slit. On the surface, she was all bold sexiness. But underneath, you could feel the steady beats of a huge, tender heart.

Just like her paintings.

He had missed her these past couple of weeks. More than he could have predicted, given how betrayed he felt when she first told him about the paintings. The photos had helped open his eyes a little, but now that he'd seen them in person? They flattered him. Especially the third one.

Two entangled figures lay wrapped in sheets, blissed-out expressions on their sleepy profiles. Anyone could see it was him. Dimples, and even the patch where his beard scruff didn't quite grow in. He shouldn't stand next to it if he didn't want people to recognize him.

Thing is, he didn't care anymore.

This painting captured sex, yes, but also satisfied, comfortable happiness. Who in their right mind could be embarrassed by that? Zara must be so happy.

She hadn't been the last time he'd seen her. Had been downright distraught. What if... His knees almost buckled. What if his being here tonight spoiled her joy? Why hadn't he thought about that earlier? But it was too late now. Across the room, a bushy-bearded dude collected Zara in a hug. He guided her and her ladies-in-waiting toward her paintings.

Toward Brendan.

He swallowed the boulder in his throat and took a deep breath, waiting for Zara.

~ * ~

Zara allowed Schwarz to lead her by the elbow toward her section of the exhibit, and her friends trailed behind.

"We gave you the feature wall, kiddo. Lots of chatter about your work already. I wouldn't be surprised if we sell all three tonight."

"You're kidding." She pressed her wristlet to her belly, hoping to quell the bubbles within.

"I never joke about sales. I'll introduce you to the collectors who have expressed an interest."

Collectors. Schwarz said *collectorsssssssss!* As in multiple people who wanted to buy her stuff. Her inept heart was too small, too finite to contain the meaning of this moment. She wished she had an emotional DVR so she could replay this moment of joy and accomplishment for years to come.

She'd have to settle for the photos Grier had been taking.

"Zar, are those your paintings?" Brooke pointed toward her artwork. Only the top halves were visible over the heads of the crowd. "I like what I see so far."

"I'll give you a few minutes before bringing prospective buyers to you to chat." Schwarz clasped Zara's shoulder. "Artist in the house! Could we have some room, please?"

The gaggle of people clustered in front of the paintings drifted away.

All except for one man.

Clean-shaven and in his crisp suit, Brendan Stewart gave her James Bond vibes.

She wobbled in her boots. After the trouble she had getting Brendan into the house the night he was sick, she didn't trust herself in heels.

Wise choice.

"Hi Princess," he said. "Nice to see you."

She wanted to respond in kind, but her parched throat wouldn't cooperate. She offered inadequate blinks instead.

"These are...enchanting." He angled his face toward the paintings on the wall next to him, giving her his profile. He exposed the vulnerable spot of his neck, the one that bumped his satisfied heartbeat against her lips when they snuggled in his bed.

The word snagged her thoughts. He'd said *enchanting*. The same word he'd used to describe her art. That had to be a good sign.

Maybe he didn't hate her for the paintings after all?

She cleared her throat. "You aren't a man who uses 'enchanting' in everyday conversation."

"No, I'm not." His lips curved upward.

A light flashed in Zara's periphery. Grier lowered her phone and beamed.

"Seriously?" She furrowed her brow.

"For posterity," her friend whispered. "Also, he's hot in a suit."

"He's hottest in nothing," she whispered back.

"Clearly." Grier nodded at the paintings.

Heat crept up her cheeks.

"That's him, isn't it?" Melinda leaned forward, her lanky height augmented by her platform wedges. Her natural curls tickled Zara's shoulder. "Hot Daddy?"

"Oh my God, Zar." Brooke side-hugged her. "He *is* inspiring. I could write a concerto about those shoulders. He have a brother?"

"Yes. Married."

"Damn." Brooke pouted.

She had been whisper-chatting with her friends while Brendan stood there, dashing and obviously uncomfortable. Time to ease his anxiety. A little. She wasn't sure they were on totally friendly territory again. Closing the gap between them, she stopped as soon as she caught his familiar blended scent of soap, clean laundry, and man.

"Brendan," she said. "You remember Grier?"

Grier rippled her fingers at him.

"Of course. Are these your other roommates?"

"Yes. You met Brooke briefly the night you were sick, and Melinda." Zara touched each of her friends on the arm.

"Hello, ladies."

An eternity of thirty seconds clicked by before Brooke giggled. "I'm sorry, Zar, but I can't handle all this sexual tension. Ow!" She frowned at Melinda. "What was that for?"

"For making things more awkward," she said.

"We're going to the bar." Grier flicked her gaze between Zara and Brendan. "Do you want to go with or stay here?"

"Stay here." Zara raised an eyebrow at Brendan.

They had business to resolve.

~ * ~

The tension swelled and threatened to knock him backward. While she scoured him with her thorough gaze, he hoped she could see he wanted to make things right between them. Right didn't mean together, though he hoped that's where they ended up. No, right meant one thing and one thing only—a sincere apology for doubting her intentions.

Right now, right here in front of her brilliant paintings, he needed to ask for her forgiveness. He didn't care if they had an audience. His naked body was up there on the wall—no sense in keeping his heart under wraps.

He shuffled forward and curved toward her. Okay, this was it.

"I'm sorry," they both said.

What? Why was she apologizing?

"Jinx," she said and popped him on the shoulder. "Oops, there's the crinkle. You better go first or you're going to give yourself a headache."

He relaxed his face. "Where do I start? I'm sorry for a lot of things. For judging your paintings before I even saw them, for calling them dirty, for not responding to your texts."

Patrons meandered by them, widening their eyes, then cutting their gaze from the paintings, to him, and then back. Let 'em look. All that mattered was whether Zara forgave him

"Thank you," she said. "But I understood. After everything with…anyway, I understood. Don't get me wrong. I missed you and was desperate to hear from you, but I was giving you space."

She reached out to finger his tie, and her knuckles rubbed his abs. She kept touching the soft spot where his ribs butterflied out, and the contact fired electric bolts through his body. God, he'd missed her casual touch, missed talking to her, missed her humor. She thought of herself as this dark and gothic person, but to him she'd always shined bright like sunshine.

He took a fresh hit of her scent. "I would have called sooner, but I had an emergency."

Zara released his tie. "Is it Emma? Is everything okay?"

Brendan settled his hands on her soft shoulders. "She's great. It was a work thing. Everything's fine now. I got laid off a couple weeks ago."

"That's all?" She exhaled. "I was worried for a second. As long as nobody's sick or dying, you're still winning at life."

"Sage advice."

"But that sucks about the job."

"It's okay. Decided to set up my own shop. But I didn't come here to talk about me." Brendan kinked his knees to stand eye-to-eye with her. He needed her to hear him on this next part. "This is a big night for you, and I wanted to clear the air. I'm not mad about the paintings."

"You're not?" Zara's eyebrows shot up.

"Obviously, I was at a first. But I'm over it. You said from the get-go that you went out with me to shake things up. It should've occurred to me if I was the inspiration, I might end up a subject."

Zara stared at him, and he couldn't get a read on her expression.

"You're gargoyling."

"I am, aren't I?" She shifted her features into a smile, and her shoulders relaxed. "Thank you, Brendan Stewart. I needed to hear that."

"My pleasure. It helps that your interpretation of me is flattering."

"Not flattering—it's faithful to how I see you." Zara batted her thigh with her purse.

"I'd planned to buy one, until I saw the price tags." He poked her in the shoulder. "You're picking up the check next time we go out."

"Are you asking me out?"

"If you'll have me." The poke turned into a caress. Her skin was smooth and cool, vanilla ice cream he wanted to melt under his tongue. "I've missed you, Princess."

"It's been the worst, right?" She ran her hands through her curls. "I wanted to talk to you, but I didn't know how to break the ice…"

"Well, let's not do that again. If things get weird between us, let's use a code word to signal we're being awkward. Like pineapple, or yeti, or—"

Zara snapped her fingers. "*Gursha*? In honor of our first date?"

"Perfect." The past couple of weeks of scratchy discomfort, like he was wearing a steel wool shirt, evaporated. There *was* a deal breaker when it came to him in her paintings. "One more thing."

"What's that?"

"Never, and I mean *never*, any dick pics if it's been cold out. Got it?"

She laughed and kissed him. Everything that had been wrong was right again. He'd never thought he'd find this kind of playful passion again, and now that he had? He didn't ever want to let it go.

"Got it. While we're negotiating... Please don't talk to me like I'm a child. It makes flames shoot out of my face and conversation is not super productive when I have a face full of fire."

"Done."

A tiny camera noise erupted from Zara's purse. Her face broke out into questions.

"That's Grier texting me. Isn't she like, twenty feet away?" She swiveled her gaze around the room as she dug the phone from the tiny purse dangling from her wrist.

The color drained from her face.

"What?" Brendan asked. "What is it?"

"My parents." Zara's knuckles whitened around the phone. "They're *here*."

Twenty

Zara couldn't breathe.

Donna and Robert Kissette of Fenwick Island, Delaware, were yards away. Any second now, they could be face-to-waist with the more intimate parts of Zara's series of dissolute self-portraits.

"I need a drink." Zara tapped the cell phone against her sternum, keeping pace with her heartbeat. Grier had herded her parents over to the bar area as soon as she'd spied them, but neither of them indulged, so they wouldn't stay there long.

They were always going to see the paintings. Someday. Not here, tonight, where their unmistakably negative opinions would decorate their faces.

Stop that. She shook her head, clearing the self-doubt. Her work was stunning. If they couldn't appreciate that...well, it was no different than the past fifteen years.

"I've gotta go." Zara tucked her phone in her wristlet.

"Do you want me to come with you?" Brendan touched her shoulder. "Or hang back? Your choice. I don't want to crowd you."

"With me." No contest. Life was better with Brendan next to her. "Hope you don't mind meeting my parents."

Brendan traced a line along her jaw. "Not at all. One more thing, Princess."

"What's that?"

"I'm proud to have inspired your paintings."

Cozy warmth bubbled inside her. What a one-eighty. He'd gone from embarrassment to full-on pride, and exactly what she needed to hear to confidently greet her parents. If she could wrap herself in Brendan and wear him for the rest of the night, she would.

"Thank you." Zara pivoted toward the bar area before the shimmer in her eyes became too obvious. Fuzzy party noise filled the main gallery, and Grier was easy to spot in her stoplight-red dress. Its sequins beamed a million rosy dots of light over Brooke, Melinda, Mama, and Dad.

Under the gallery's bright halogens, her parents seemed...smaller. Zara squeezed Brendan's hand and towed him along as she threaded through the crowd. She approached her parents from behind and waved at her roommates.

"Zara." Grier gave her crazy eyes. "Your parents and I have been chatting while Brooke and Melinda tried to find you."

Her parents slowly turned toward her. The oily feeling in her belly oozed back. Like the drift of a Tilt-a-Whirl pod on the boardwalk, there was no telling which way things would go. All she knew for sure was she'd end up sick and hanging on for dear life.

Spinny rides sucked balls.

"Mama, Dad." She released Brendan. "I can't believe you came."

"Sweetheart, there you are." Her mother hugged her and stepped aside to allow her father space to kiss her on the cheek. "You look so fancy."

"Quite a variety on display, isn't there?" Her father's gaze danced over the dozens of paintings and sculptures lining the perimeter of the wall.

Nodding, her mother said, "When you're right, you're right Robert. This is certainly something."

Ah, yes. There it is.

On some level, their consistency was comforting. When they didn't love something, her parents offered simple, indisputable statements of fact in place of compliments. There was an art to it. In the moment they seemed supportive, but on reflection their vague comments were completely neutral.

"It *is* something, isn't it?" Grier locked arms with Zara. "She's the first person in our class to get a show on this level. She's the most determined person I know."

"Aren't you sweet?" Her mother firmed her lips. "Zara's always been a fool for painting. That's for certain."

Zara dug her nails into Grier's bicep. She'd apologize later but was confident Grier already understood.

"When did you get to Baltimore?" she asked.

"Just now," Dad said. "The Bay Bridge was gummed up, else we'd have gotten here an hour ago."

For once in her life, Zara was grateful for heavy traffic in the metro area. If her parents had been at the show from the start, the past ten minutes with Brendan never would have happened.

Brendan. Shit, where was he? She glanced over her shoulder. There he stood, arms loose and smiling at her parents. *How can he be so relaxed?*

Her father's gaze followed Zara's. No time like now to make the introductions.

"Dad, Mama." She tugged him toward her parents. "This is Brendan Stewart. He's my…"

They hadn't had this conversation with each other yet. Adding everything up, there was only one label that fit. "Boyfriend," she said. "He's my boyfriend."

She did her best to ignore Grier's wide-eyed grin.

"Boyfriend? You're dating someone?" Her mother frowned.

"Good to meet you, Brandon." Her father stuck out his hand.

"Brendan," he corrected and accepted her father's greeting. "Your daughter's a hell of an artist. You must be proud."

Affection for Brendan whooshed over her. Even though she and her parents didn't see eye to eye on the merit of her job, she loved him for trying to get them to change their perspective.

"We're certainly impressed with her stick-to-it-iveness," her mother said. "We'd no idea she'd stay with this art stuff for this long. Robert and I were sure she'd have grown out of it by now."

Brendan bristled. She glanced at him, and oh, and there was the crinkle. She had grown accustomed to her parents' pattern of talking down to her, but this was his first taste of it. He'd made it seem like his parents were his own personal cheerleaders and probably couldn't comprehend a parent being any other way. Small doses were best here. Time to give him a break.

Zara touched his wrist. "Would you mind getting me a drink? There's a bar in the corner."

"Sure thing." He circled his gaze around the group. "Anyone else need a drink?"

"Yes please," Grier said, but Zara's parents declined.

As Brendan wended his way across the room, her mother whispered, "He's a good-looking boy, sweetheart. Maybe we can talk about him later?"

"Okay, Mama." *If by later you mean never, then great.*

Her mother pulled her glasses from her purse. "Now which of these paintings are yours?"

A cluster of patrons hid the feature wall toward the back of the gallery.

Now or never.

"Follow me," she said. "I'll show you."

Long breath in, short breath out.

Her work was good. If the paintings sucked, she wouldn't be

featured in the 'Phoenix' show, now would she? Her parents' support would be amazing, but she wasn't expecting it. She stiffened her spine as she wove her way through the crowds.

No, she was a hundred percent certain they'd worry the series would reflect poorly on them. What would their neighbors think? The other business owners? Members of their congregation?

Zara loved them. Always would.

But this was her voice, her aesthetic, her passion, and if they didn't get it by now, she was done trying. She couldn't compromise it for anyone. Now that she was on the cusp of paying them back? She had no reason to toe whatever line they drew in the sand.

Their opinion didn't matter.

"Zara Jean," her mother said and entwined her arm with Zara's at the elbow. "I'd have lost a bet if anyone said you'd still be chasing this dream at twenty-five. Who knows what she wants to do for a living when she's ten years old?"

"Me, Mama." She unwound from her mother's arm, stopped in front of the feature wall, then faced her parents. "These are mine. But art isn't what I *do*. It's who I *am*."

Zara pressed a hand to her chest, and her grandmother's locket nudged the center of her palm.

"Oh my." Her mother covered her mouth with one hand and reached for Dad with the other. "You painted these? I was expecting…"

Dad cleared his throat. "Are you sure you want to put your name on this, Zara?"

"Why can't you do something like that?" Her mother threw her hand in the direction of a series of neo-pop culture portraits. "*Those* kinds of paintings I understand. They aren't far off from the caricatures my friend Bobbi does on the boards. She makes a good living off them too. Parks herself under an umbrella near the arcade and rakes it in all summer."

"Mama, stop."

Schwarz materialized next to them. "Kiddo, I need to talk to you." His lips were a slit in his beard. "Upstairs."

What was this angry body language about? *Oh, no.* Were they being too loud? Disturbing the other artists and patrons? Warmth fanned across Zara's chest and bloomed on her face. She couldn't fuck this up, not this close to the finish line.

"Okay." She followed him across the room and up the spiral staircase. The collection of attendees glittered below in their high fashion and dramatic makeup. Halfway up she spied Brendan making his way to her parents and Grier. Brooke and Melinda had found them too.

In his dark loft office, Schwarz snapped on his desk lamp. The noise from the party bubbled up to the ledge overlooking the gallery space below. "Have a seat."

Zara eased into the chrome and leather chair in front of his desk.

He perched on its edge. "Our terms state I have exclusive rights of representation, right?"

"Yes." She held herself as still as a statue. "My work is only with you."

"Then why is a client asking if she should purchase your paintings through me, or through your website?"

Her scalp prickled. "I have no idea, Mr. Schwarz."

Schwarz opened his laptop and typed. The glow of the screen reflected in his glasses, and he stroked his beard as he stared at the screen. "Hmm."

Air. She needed air.

"Hmm what?" she squeaked.

He spun the laptop toward her. "Is this you?"

She approached his desk, her dress shushing against the floor. "Zara Kissette" curled across the banner space at the top of the page. Below the banner were sub-menus for bio, works, and shows. She pulled the laptop closer and clicked on "works." Thumbnails of the portrait she painted of Emma dotted the screen.

"That's me, but I don't..." Her stomach lurched.

Brendan.

She rubbed her forehead, crunching through the memories of their conversation about websites. This was supposed to be hidden, a safety net. Not a fucking gillnet. In the struggle to free herself from the deal she made with her parents, she'd trapped herself further.

"My boyfriend—he's a web developer. He thought it would be helpful if he built a website for me. But I *swear* I told him not to. The site isn't supposed to exist. I don't know how or why he did this. Please, he's downstairs. Let me go get him, and he'll explain everything."

She edged toward the steps, chest heaving.

Schwarz twisted his lips. "Kiddo, stop. What do you think this is? An episode of 'Homicide?' I don't care how, or why this happened. This is business, and we're not dragging your boyfriend up here for an interrogation. Here's what I'll do. We've got a couple of interested collectors in the house tonight. I'll negotiate a good deal for you on the paintings in this show, but your contract is void. I'm not litigious, so I won't sue you for breach."

Her legs went numb, and she braced herself against his desk to keep from falling over.

"Mr. Schwarz, no, please," she shouted. "This isn't my fault. You can't do this."

She pounded his desk with her fist and a framed photo tumbled to the ground. The glass shattered, and lines spider-webbed across his family's faces.

"I can, and I will. Here's what it boils down to. I can't tell if you're telling the truth, but I know a tantrum when I see one. Problem artists are a dime a dozen, and I don't need another one. Eleanor seems to think you're a good kid, but I'm too old for drama."

"It's not a tantrum. It's passion." Had she really worked this hard, sacrificed sleep, steadier and better-paying jobs, and nights with her friends only to be dismissed?

Her dream was washing away like a sandcastle in a tidal wave.

"Whatever it is, I don't need it in my gallery." He stood. "It's best if you leave. I'll forward any sales commissions to you."

"That's it?"

"That's it."

That fast, she was done. Dreams gone. Poof.

Some other force animated her body. She pinched up her dress, gripping the railing as she descended the looping metal stairs. When her boots touched the hardwoods of the gallery, she searched for her friends. Where were they? Zara needed them to get her home before she collapsed and humiliated herself. The faces in the crowd blurred together.

There. There were a pair of eyes she recognized.

Brendan.

He proffered a glass of red.

She lowered her eyebrows, ready to charge him.

"Hey Princess," he said, his forehead cranked low and gaze searching hers. "What's wrong?"

Bile boiled in her gut and scalded her throat. His suggestion of a safety net had been her undoing. She should have trusted her gut and pursued only the path she wanted. Because of her lack of confidence, her career was officially down the shitter. Word spread fast, and she'd have a helluva time climbing out of this hole. She'd have to do triple the work to get into another gallery.

"Everything is fucked," she snarled.

"Whoa." He sat the wineglass on a tray on a nearby pedestal.

"How can I help?"

"You *can't* help." Zara jabbed him in the chest. "You're the problem."

"What? I don't follow…"

"Schwarz cut me loose. The terms of my agreement with the gallery have been voided because of a website selling my paintings. Want to tell me how that happened?"

He furrowed his brow. "Oh, shit. I was checking the links to make sure everything worked, and Emma spilled juice on my computer. I must have forgotten to go back and hide the site again."

"Fucking juice?" Zara shouted. The crowd quieted. "My career explodes on the launch pad because of *juice*?"

"It was an accident," he said. "I was distracted, and—look, where's Schwarz? Let me go talk to him."

"Do *not* try to fix this! I don't need you to save me."

Grier sidled next to her. "Zara, maybe we could…"

"Shut it, Grier."

"Okay. Shutting it." Grier slipped Brooke the valet ticket and a twenty, and she and Melinda flanked Zara. The crowd chatted among itself again.

With his hands into his pockets, sincerity dripped from Brendan. She didn't care. All it did was make her want to throttle him.

"I wanted to help. To give you options in case the gallery show didn't work out. I'm so sorry."

Zara took a deep breath. "Yeah, well, sorry doesn't fix it. Grier get me out of here before my parents find out."

"Zara, can we at least talk about this?" Brendan asked.

"Don't you get it? I've worked my whole life for this. I should be drinking champagne and swallowing compliments. Instead, I'm getting kicked to the curb because of you and your arrogant *help*. I can't even look at you."

Acid crept up the back of her throat. She needed to get out of here, now, or she would vomit.

"Tomorrow? Let's talk tomorrow."

She walked away from him, head dipped low. "No. We're done. Don't call me."

"I can fix this," Brendan called.

Grier and Melinda held her arms as they left the building and headed toward the street, where Brooke waited for them. Zara kept it together until the valet delivered the Mercedes to them. Once she was perched in the back between Melinda and Brooke, she dissolved into tears.

Grier's gaze flicked to her in the rearview, and Melinda rubbed small circles on her back as they drove home in silence. Brooke provided an unending supply of tissues from her tiny purse until it seemed like Zara was weeping into a meringue.

A train hooted nearby, heralding a departure. She blinked away tears as they passed Baltimore Penn Station. She read the time on the glowing clock nestled high in the building's facade.

Eight o'clock.

The fairy tales got it wrong. Everything goes to shit waaaaay before midnight.

Twenty-One

Zara chomped her way through the salad languishing in the plastic container resting on her mother's desk at The Sandcastle. She had a few minutes left in her break. She wouldn't finish lunch, which was fine. It wasn't like she was enjoying it. Food was just fuel since she ghosted from Baltimore a month ago, on the night of the show.

She sniffed at a wedge of tomato speared on the tines of her fork. Blah. Not as interesting as Ethiopian food. Argh. How had a *tomato* reminded her of *him*?

Despite latching memories to cinder blocks and shoving them into the deep waters of her mind, they insisted on breaking free and floating to the surface.

Talking to Emma with adoration shining in his smile.
His gratitude when he was sick and she brought him soup.
Reading to a sleepy-eyed Emma.
Scruff peppering his face in early morning sunshine.
Him, over the top of her, all hooded eyes and dimples.

A torrent of butterflies ripped through her belly at that last image.

Stop thinking about him. She mentally slapped herself and squeezed her knees together. *He cockblocked your shot. Don't give him brain space.*

She glanced at the quote-of-the-day calendar. April 15th's pearl of wisdom: *Seize the day and put the least possible trust in tomorrow.* *— Horace (December 8, 65 BCE — November 27, 8 BCE)*

The day-seizing would begin as soon as her shift ended at four. So, *carpe noctem?* Her fingers itched with anticipation. She'd finish her third midnight seascape tonight. Full moonlight playing on the rippling surface of the ocean took her breath away.

Finding inspiration here at the beach was a top five contender for Biggest Surprise Ever.

The night of the gallery show, she'd gone home, packed her bags, then called her parents to come get her. No point waiting to begin her indentured servitude. Grier, Brooke, and Melinda had pleaded with her to stay, but she explained she needed to leave town to clear her fucking head.

Clear her heart too.

She made her roommates promise not to tell Brendan where she'd gone. In the same couple of breaths, she told them she'd be in touch, but for her sanity, she was switching off her phone. If they needed to reach her in an emergency, they could get her at The Sandcastle.

Side note—no one had called.

After saying her goodbyes, she climbed into the back seat of her parents' sedan. On the way out of town, they passed the Bromo-Seltzer Arts Tower, and Zara had pressed her fingertips to the cold window and bid her studio a farewell.

She hoped she would return to Baltimore someday. But when that would be was anybody's guess. How long does it take to pay back ten thousand dollars on minimum wage? A year? Two years?

Her first night back at the shore, she swaddled herself in one of her Gramma's crocheted afghans and moped out to the veranda. She intended to embark on an angst-riddled hermitage for days, weeks, maybe even months.

Mostly, she wept many times in those first days. She was losing her edge. The last time she shed a typhoon of tears had been when they laid her Gramma to rest. Back then, she'd decided tears didn't do anything but puff up your face.

Except, she was wrong.

All the anxiety and upset and anger whipping around inside her had been purged through the tears, and she could think straight again. The occasional burst of tears didn't mean she was weak.

It meant she was human.

Sometime during the first week, as she drank in the sight of the midnight moon on the black ocean, she decided she would not sit on her ass in a funk. There was too much to do. Maybe this detour wasn't how she'd planned to build her portfolio back up. Hadn't expected she'd be able to—not while wearing khakis and a Hawaiian shirt. It all should have been her kryptonite.

Not anymore.

What she wore, where she lived, what people thought, none of it changed the fact she was an artist. She didn't need to fit anyone else's definition of the word.

~ * ~

Brendan threw his car into park and sighed. A huge cherry

blossom tree dominated the front of the property, and its petals carpeted the yard like snow.

This was the place, for sure.

He eased from his car, approached the inn, then yanked open the plate glass door of the lobby. Inside The Sandcastle, he had to stop for a second. Citrus and lavender. The whole place smelled like Zara, like a place he missed and needed to be.

His guts twisted. He could leave right now. She never had to know he'd figured out she'd moved back to the shore, and his already-busted heart had broken to dust for her when he dialed The Sandcastle's main number and she answered.

He could drop the envelope emblazoned with The Schwarz Gallery logo on the front desk and go.

No. He'd come all this way He had to take a chance. He inhaled, long and slow to steady the thrum in his blood, then rang the bell at the front desk.

Zara called from the office behind the front desk, "Be right there."

Then, true to her word, she appeared behind the counter. "How can I help…" Her smile dissolved, and she swallowed hard.

The purple streaks were gone, and her raven hair was bound in a French braid. Her clothes were wrong too. A floral Hawaiian shirt, khakis, and thick-soled sneakers.

"*Gursha.*" Brendan's thick forearms rested against the counter. "*Gursha, gursha, gursha.*"

Her eyes gleamed like sunshine on glaciers. God, he wanted to leap over this counter and fold her into his arms. Wouldn't be smart. The way she was glaring at him, she'd probably stab him with a pen.

Silence. Major gargoyle silence.

This wasn't going very well.

Zara lifted her chin. "Why are you here?"

"To apologize, and—"

"You can't apologize. It's too big." She crossed her arms over her chest.

He couldn't lose her. Not again. "I'll make amends, then."

"What amends?" She tilted her head.

"This kind." He slid the envelope across the table. "I have a delivery for you. From Schwarz. All three of your pieces sold on opening night."

Zara lifted the flap and removed a stapled packet of paper. She flipped through the pages, then flipped back to the beginning and read them a second time. "Holy shit," she said through her fingers.

Brendan smiled at the yellow splotches of paint on her hand. She hadn't given up.

She turned big eyes on him. "Do you know what this is?"

He nodded. "After you stormed out, I stayed. Your paintings sold for twice the listed price. There should be a check in there for $6,500."

"For my paintings." She fingered the chain of her necklace. "$6,500 for my three paintings? After Schwarz's cut and everything?"

"There was a bidding war. I might have goosed things a bit." Brendan leaned toward Zara, and the hard Formica bit into his stomach.

"That's cheating." She waved the papers at him.

"How? I would have paid and eaten Ramen for a month if I'd won."

"Well, it's like cheating. And Grier didn't buy them?"

"No, not unless she had secret agents in the crowd."

Zara folded the packet and tucked it back into the envelope. "Why did Schwarz give you this?"

"I was desperate to find you to apologize. Your friends are loyal, by the way. They wouldn't give me any clues about where you'd gone. The only other place I knew to check was the gallery. When I stopped in to ask Schwarz if he'd heard from you, it turned out he wanted to talk to you too. 'All good things,' he said. Then I called here to see if this is where you ended up, and you answered. I told him I was going to see you, and he asked me to deliver this."

She gripped the edge of her side of the counter, and her knuckles blanched.

Brendan dropped his fists to his sides to stop himself from gathering her hands and kissing the stress from each finger. "I also told Schwarz the site was my fault. I explained how it happened and that you didn't have any idea about it. He wants me to pass along an invitation to the show he's staging next month. There should be a letter in that packet."

~ * ~

This was everything she wanted. A huge chunk of what she owed her parents, another show, and Brendan standing in front of her. She wanted to strip off this awful shirt and vault into his strong arms.

Except pride and cold anger kept her feet glued to the sandy tiles.

"Schwarz wants me in another show?" Zara stared Brendan full in the face. He hadn't shaved for days, maybe weeks. His normal rakish scruff had matured into a full-on beard.

Wonder if his beard is rough?

Stop that.

Her gaze drifted to his eyes. Sleep-deprived, dark smudges lay under them. Zara frowned. Was he okay?

Stop that some more. You aren't allowed to worry about him.

"Yes." Brendan curved toward her, his face within kissing distance. "I can't remember the new theme."

All she had to do was lean forward and his lips would be back on hers.

Where they belonged.

First, a clarification.

Zara walked around the counter until there was nothing standing between them. Wow, so that was a mistake, because over here, the heat from his body kissed her skin and clouded her brain. Unfortunate, because she needed her wits about her.

"I told Schwarz you built the site without my knowledge, and I'd get it taken down. He booted me out anyway. Why'd he believe you? Some kind of man code?"

"No. It was all you. Whatever you said must have sunk in." Brendan drummed his fingers on the counter. "Or your phenomenal sales persuaded him to reconsider."

"Who asked you to get involved?"

"Nobody, but you dropped off the face of the earth. I wanted to help. Are you okay?"

"Oh, sure, totally fine. I sleep within twenty feet of where I took care of my dying grandmother. Everyone who knew me in high school thinks I'm a total weirdo, so I have no friends. And I have to wear this travesty." She gestured toward her Hawaiian shirt. "It's fine. I'm making the best of it."

As if *that* wasn't the biggest lie she'd told in the past month. She'd found inspiration in the nightscapes, but while her life on the shore was a great many things—temporary, humid, bearable, sandy—it wasn't *fine*.

"Oh, sweetheart." Her mother stood at the corridor leading to the beach patio. She'd come in from cleaning off the tables on the veranda. "Are you really unhappy here?"

Zara cringed. "Mama, I didn't mean for you to hear that."

Both her parents, but her mother especially, had been sweet to her since they got back to the shore. Maybe it was because it was the off-season and they weren't as distracted, or maybe it was because she'd been walking around like a zombie, but they seemed to want her to find her peace at the beach.

"Well, there's no unhearing it." Her mother pushed past

Brendan and circled behind Zara. "Excuse me…Brendan, right?"

"Yes ma'am."

"I need to talk to my daughter in private." Her mother pulled her into the back office and closed the door. "Now, sit. What did the young man say about selling your paintings?"

"It doesn't matter. I'm honoring our deal."

"Psht." Her mother waved her concern away and parked herself in her swivel chair. "Could you make a viable career with this art stuff? It's not a glorified hobby? Like what your grandmother did."

"Mom, art was more than a hobby to her, but she had to give it up when she got married and had a baby."

Her mother sat back in her chair. "Did she tell you that?"

"I put it together." Zara shrugged. "We talked a lot. She said she hadn't done much painting after Dad was born, and she was thrilled to get back to it in her retirement."

"I see." Her mother twisted the last button on her shirt. "I don't like to break confidences, sweetheart, but I s'pose it's for the best if I opened your eyes to some things. That's a really simple version of a very sad story."

Mama took a deep breath.

"Your gramma was desperate to have a child. After a string of miscarriages, she was convinced it wasn't in the cards. She prayed on it anyway. Your dad was born on his parents' tenth anniversary. And once he was here, well, the doctor said more babies could kill her."

Zara clapped her hand over her mouth.

"So Gramma decided she would devote herself to your father and support him in whatever he chose to do in life. When your grandfather died, we used the bit he'd left your dad to buy this place. You knew that part, right?"

"Yeah. She said she was your first employee."

Mama laughed. "As if she ever took order from me. She worked as hard as we did to get The Sandcastle on its feet. When we were in the black for a few years running, she retired and that's when she made time for painting."

"I didn't think you and Gramma were so close. She really told you all this?"

Her mother rolled her chair forward until their knees touched. "After I went through something similar."

All of the air whooshed from her body.

"Mama, I didn't know." She touched her mother's knee. "I thought you only wanted one child because you were busy with the inn."

"Oh, sweetheart, *no*. We didn't talk about it because I never wanted you to think you weren't enough for us." Her mother caressed her cheek. "We've been happy here and wanted the same kind of life for you."

"I know, but it's just not for me." She pressed into her mother's palm soaking up the comfort. "I haven't been happy here since high school."

"Back then, I thought you were grieving Gramma. And then when you moved home a month ago, I chalked your emotions up to missing your friends and your show going sideways. I didn't realize it was this place. You've always had such a poker face."

Gargoyling forever, apparently.

"Even now, to look at you, I'd think you were perfectly content. But if you're truly unhappy, we shouldn't keep you here. Now, I can't pretend to understand why painting makes you happy. Or say I approve of your subject matter, but if that's what you want to do, Dad and I won't stand in your way."

"You won't?" Her heart lifted.

"You haven't been yourself. I don't want to torture you with a life you don't want. If you ever want it back, we're here, but I won't force it on you. Dad will agree with me."

Zara burst into an ugly cry. "Mama, you have no idea how much that means to me. I promise I'll pay off the rest of the loan by the deadline."

"You don't need to." Her mother wrapped her in a fierce hug. "We were never going to keep that money. Making you pay it back was to build character, but we planned on putting all of it in a rainy day fund for you. Given these tears, I'd say it's today."

Zara cried harder and snuffled into her mother's shoulder.

Mama kissed her the top of her head. "I'm sorry about not reading you right. A mother should understand her child better than that."

~ * ~

Brendan stared at the office door. Was that sound Zara?

His heart hurt, and he wanted to soothe her tears away, not eavesdrop through a closed door.

She hadn't asked him to stay before disappearing with her mother. Hadn't even hinted he should. Unless he was a total masochist, he should spin on his heel and hit the road before she tossed him out on his ass.

Except the crying on the other side of the door shackled him to The Sandcastle. He needed to check on her then he could go. The door cracked open. Her mother led a puffy-faced Zara from the office. He tensed every muscle to keep himself from gathering her up to protect her from everything the world had to dish out.

"Are you okay?" he asked Zara.

She shrugged and pinched a tissue to her nose.

Her mother stepped out from behind the counter. "Brendan, is it?"

"Yes ma'am."

"When are you returning to Baltimore?"

Her dismissal flattened him. "If you're asking me to leave, ma'am—"

"Oh for Lord's sakes, call me Donna. Zara's moving back to Baltimore. Her dad and I can't take her until next week, but if you're headed back today, you could take her home."

"Mama." Zara tugged her mother's shirt. "He and I are fighting right now."

"Oh, well, don't be silly. The way you two are around each other? He came all this way to apologize. Have you accepted?"

"No."

Donna stared at her daughter. "Well why not?"

"We need privacy." Zara dabbed at her red-rimmed eyes.

"Go on, then. I'll mind the desk."

"Thanks," she said and crooked her finger at Brendan. "Follow me."

~ * ~

Zara toed one of the cherry blossom tree's thick roots, refusing to meet Brendan's eyes. She steadied herself against the tree's slender trunk, the bark rough under her palm. All she wanted was to lean into him, to let him wrap his strong arms around her.

How was it possible to crave a man who'd been in her life for like, a minute?

She wouldn't feed this craving. Couldn't, unless she wanted to deal with the interfering, backstabby woman he was attached to for the rest of his life. Schwarz never said who alerted him to the site that got her in trouble, but she was able to paint a portrait using negative space.

Jess. It had to have been her. That fact was as solid as a marble sculpture.

Brendan palmed the tree, laying his hand next to hers. "This is the tree, isn't it? From the tattoo on your back."

Small talk? He'd driven a hundred miles for small talk?

"I don't need to be rescued like some fairytale princess. I'm good."

"The crying, then—those are good tears?"

"Yes, as a matter of fact." She swiped at her drying eyes. "Why are you here? You could have called or mailed the news about the show to me."

His feet came into her field of vision. "Would you look at me? I'll tell you, but I want you to look at me while we talk."

A dangerous request because that was how this started. Looking matured into touching, which moved on to kissing, which proceeded to shedding every stitch of clothing and throwing herself at him. It could have ended there, but that's not what the universe had in mind. Oh, no, she had to go and fall for him and his daughter.

Losing all that had hurt more than she wanted to admit, and he'd see the truth of it in her eyes.

Zara tore her gaze from the ground and let it drift along the length of Brendan's body. The capable hands, the ropy forearms, the broad shoulders, the twinkling eyes that shone with happiness and affection for her.

She definitely wasn't sold on that scruffy face yet.

"That's better." He shoved his hands into his pockets. "I'm here because I messed things up for you, and for us. Sincere apologies need to happen in person. You knew what you were doing and didn't need any—" he scratched quotes into the air between them, "'help' from me."

He thought she knew what she was doing? She was making it up as she went along. The plans she had were gut instinct and dogged determination. Nothing strategic, not like the plans he had for his career.

The wind caught at his untucked shirttail, revealing the top edge of his tattoo. She licked her lips, remembering the heat of his skin under her kiss.

She settled her hand against the divot between his pecs, and his heart beat fast against her palm. "Thank you, but the website was an accident. I mean, don't get me wrong. I was furious. After a few weeks of beach therapy, I realized it wasn't on purpose. Intent matters more than anything."

He sheltered her hand with his, and oh, *no*. She sucked in her breath. His touch lit a fuse that wound its way through her body.

"Then why'd you shut me out?" He rubbed his thumb over the back of her hand, the way he had the first time they held hands.

"Because I thought your life was too complicated for me to deal with."

"What about now?"

"Now, I know what I need to do."

"What's that?" he asked, leaning in. His clean linen scent wafted over her, invading her. When did detergent become such a turn-on? She couldn't tell anyone, or she'd have to give up her angsty Goth status posthaste.

"I need to talk to Jess without you there."

He let go of her. "Why, exactly?"

"I know she was the one who found the site and talked to Schwarz. Who else would it have been? She's going to be a part of your life forever, and if I'm going to be in the mix, we've got to work this out. I fight my own battles, remember? Even though she's your ex, you can't be there because you'll get in the way of an honest conversation, which is what she and I need."

"I don't like it."

She hooked her fingers into his pocket and pulled him close. "I'm pretty sure the relationship bubble you wanted to keep us in popped ages ago."

Brendan hesitated, searching her eyes, then snaked a hand around her waist. Something in her, some cord that had been stretched to the point of breaking, finally relaxed.

"I don't know, Princess."

She'd never admit this to another soul, but her knees buckled when he used her nickname. "I need to, Brendan. I don't want to fight with her. In unexpected way, I kind of understand where she's coming from."

Hair escaped her braid, and he tucked it behind her ear. "That scares me."

"No need to be scared." She rose on tiptoe and tightened her arms around his neck. "Nothing's scary if you and I are together."

"Are we? Together?" He held her face and searched her eyes.

Oh, there was the dimple.

"Yes, please."

Their lips touched, sparking, and melting, and welding the fractures in Zara's heart.

Twenty-Two

Zara knocked on the stately door. On the other side, Jess yelled, "Emma, Daddy's here."

Then the door was thrown open, and Zara was face to face with the Messy Jess. Who was, in fact, a bit messy. Her hair stuck up in different directions, and she hadn't yet changed from her workout gear. Also of note—Jess didn't sweat sexy.

"Hi, Jess. Hi, Emma," Zara said, peeking under Jess's elbow. Zara pointed toward Brendan's car waiting curbside. "Your daddy's here, and I need to talk to your mom for a sec."

"You do? I can't imagine what you have to say." She knelt next to her daughter and smoothed the folds of the little girl's skirt. "I'll miss you, Emma Bear. Have fun at Grammy and Pop Pop's."

"'Bye, Mommy." Emma hugged her mother around the neck, turned, then bounded toward Brendan. He swooped her up, swirled her around, then set her back on her white patent leather Mary Janes.

"Is there something I can help you with?" Jess asked Zara.

"I hope so." Zara glanced past Jess and into the chaotic swirl of the inside of the house. "There's something I've been meaning to ask you."

Jess folded her arms over her chest. "I'm listening."

"You called John Schwarz to tell him about my website, right? The one with a storefront, I mean. Not the face painter one."

"Well, I *so* love to support local artists, and I needed to know how to buy your work." Jess narrowed her eyes at Zara. "Especially when it features images of my daughter."

Zara's brain buzzed in the same satisfied way it did when she nailed a composition. Most people would be angry, but all Jess had done was take advantage of someone else's mistake. Not exactly noble, but well within the bounds of the rules of the game.

Plus, this was confirmation that Zara understood Jess on one level. Pretty good odds she understood her on another more primitive level, which would make things easier.

"I'm sure you know Brendan and I are dating." Zara fingered the poky leaves of one of the tall potted bushes flanking the door.

"Best of luck to you."

Wow, Jess was throwing shade. Zara was above it, though, especially when it came from an insecure place. She plucked a leaf from the bush. "I'm not trying to creep in on your territory. At all."

"Duly noted, but I was over Brendan before Emma was even born."

"I'm not talking about Brendan. I'm talking about Emma."

Jess furrowed her brow. "I don't know what you mean."

"I like Emma. You guys are doing a great job with her. The thing is, I want to be her friend, not her mother. So, can we chill with crashing at weird times and telling Emma I'm Ravenna's evil sister? It's making things weird."

"I don't know where you get off—"

"Here. I'm getting off right here." Zara stuck out her hand. "C'mon, let's be grown-ups together. You don't talk smack about me, I won't talk smack about you, and Emma gets to be surrounded by happy, healthy adults."

Jess inspected her fingernails.

Well, at least she could say she'd tried. She turned to leave Jess behind.

"Brendan doesn't know what he's gotten himself into with you, does he?"

Zara chose to take that in the best spirit it could have been intended. "Nope."

"You're going to the Stewarts' for dinner?" Jess asked.

She nodded. "First time I'm meeting the family. Any advice?"

"Did you bring earplugs?" Jess smoothed down her hair. "It's a lot of noise. There are two conversations going for every three people. Half of them are named Mike. Most of them are conservatives, so keep political chitchat to a minimum unless you want to get a headache. Last, if you compliment Robin's cooking, she'll love you for life."

Zara offered Brendan's ex a wide smile. "Thank you."

"Good luck. If there's any hint you're trying to brainwash my daughter, prepare for a reckoning."

"I'd expect nothing less. 'Til next time."

"If there is one," Jess rolled her eyes and shut the door.

That went as well as could be expected. Zara dropped the leaf in the soil of the potted plants and walked toward the two people who made her heart smile.

~ * ~

Brendan rested his hand on Zara's knee and steadied her nervous jiggling.

"Are you sure this dress is okay?" She smoothed her skirt down over her thighs. "I didn't bring all my clothes when you drove me home yesterday. This was the best I could do."

"You're beautiful, Princess."

Emma ignored them as she shouted along with a tame kid's cover of a bubblegum pop tune.

"So," Brendan said, "I'm scared to ask, but what did you say to Jess?"

"Nothing much. Mostly that I'm not here to take her place. She's jealous."

Brendan frowned. Jealous? He and Jess weren't in that space. At all. Unless he was beyond clueless at reading women. "No way. She and I—"

She laughed and nudged his arm. "Not of you and me. She's jealous of me and—" Zara jerked her head over her shoulder toward Emma. "I assured her I have no interest in taking that job."

He caressed the curly tendrils lying against the nape of her neck. She'd worn her hair up, and it had taken all of his willpower to keep from dragging her to bed for a third time this morning.

"She also wished me luck meeting your family." She rubbed her hands on her biceps. "What am I walking into? I'm not used to big gatherings. Didn't you say your cousins, aunts, and uncles will be here too? I've been working on the whole gargoyle thing, but I can't promise I won't stone face your father or ask your mother something weird, or—"

She jiggled her knees again.

"You'll be great, Princess. Don't worry about inappropriate questions. The Stewarts ask plenty of those. Their favorite activity is busting ba—" He glanced in the backseat and substituted a word. "They tease. If you need to, use the safe word, and I'll rescue you."

"I don't need rescuing, remember?"

"I remember."

Brendan parallel-parked in the gap near his parents' townhouse. Zara slipped from the car and waited for him on the sidewalk. Her re-purpled hair gleamed in the Easter sun, and the wind flirted with her sundress, offering him flashes of thigh.

Jesus, this would be a long family party.

He opened the door to let Emma out. She'd recently mastered the art of unbuckling herself and wanted no help in the matter, *thankyouverymuch.*

The three of them walked hand in hand in hand, with Brendan as the center link. With each step toward his parents' house, his stomach fizzed. He hadn't been this eager to show off a girl since they'd brought Emma home from the hospital. It was important that his family embrace Zara. He wasn't worried. Not really. How could they not embrace her?

She was wonderful.

Before he could knock, Mike flung the door wide.

"Hey, Mike," he greeted his brother.

"I'm the welcoming committee." He held out a meaty hand toward Zara. "Zara, right?"

"Yep," she said. "You're Brendan's brother, right?"

Mike's hand enveloped hers. "The one and only. Come on in. Everyone's in the backyard. They're doing the Easter egg hunt soon."

"Yay!" Emma took off into the house. "Come on, Zara!"

She shrugged and chased his daughter into his parents' home.

Brendan climbed the steps and paused next to his brother.

"I kind of wish she'd worn the princess get-up." Mike punched him in the shoulder. "Looks like she's a keeper, eh?"

"More than you know. Hey, before I forget." Brendan removed his wallet from his suit jacket pocket. "Here she is at Easter dinner to meet the family, like you predicted."

"Keep your money. It's a win for me if you're happy."

"That I am, big brother." Brendan glanced down the hallway, tracking the way Zara's dress swayed as she walked toward his family. She paused, glanced over her shoulder and flashed him a full-lipped smile. He'd enjoy that view for the rest of his life, if she'd let him.

~ * ~

We hope you enjoyed *The Reluctant Princess*, book 1 of *The Charm City Hearts* series. If you did, please write a review, tell your friends, or check out the other offerings from the authors at Champagne Book Group.

Acknowledgment

This book is my love letter to Baltimore, a.k.a., Charm City. It's the biggest small town you'll ever visit—wonderful and weird, heartbreaking and hopeful—a place I'm proud to call my home.

I owe a lot of people for helping me churn this baby out and make it sparkle. First Cassiel Knight and Franny Armstrong—your collective input has been invaluable. Thank you from the bottom of my heart.

Next, I need to thank my Pitch Wars mentor and conference buddy, Lynnette Novak. She has the eagliest of eagle eyes, and completely immersed herself in this world. After her encouragement and careful commentary, my characters do more than furrow their eyebrows to express themselves. And to the entire Pitch Wars community, especially the 2015 cohort, sharing our collective ups, downs, and in-betweens has been a joy and a comfort. I am so grateful to be a part of it.

To my critique partners—Stoni Alexander, Andy Palmer, and Magda Alexander—your support and critique helped shape these characters and this story. Thank you for the conversations and the coffee as we hashed out the plot twists and hooks in our books! My friend and fellow author Christi Barth also deserves a shout-out for the Panera writing dates that helped get the next book in the series written and for the publishing consultation that goes on in between the sprints. You're an absolute gem. And to the Maryland Romance Writers—you are an amazing chapter full of generous writers, and I am lucky to be among you.

I also want to thank Barbara Collins Rosenberg for her tireless efforts championing of my work, her cheerleading, mentoring me through this process, and for being an all-around lovely person.

These acknowledgements would not be complete without a heartfelt thank you to friends, my enormous family, my incredibly supportive husband, David, and my children. I couldn't carry on with this career without their love, laughter, and encouragement. Thank you for being wonderful.

About the Author

M.C. Vaughan is a Baltimore-based author of contemporary romance riddled with humor and local flavor. So, if you want to giggle throughout your sexy stories, welcome! You'll root for her characters as they fall for their perfect people...and simultaneously want to throttle them for being big dummies about love.

She grew up in a house crowded with family, friends, books, music, and the occasional ghost. After graduating from Georgetown University with a degree in English literature (and an unofficial major in student-run theatre), she worked in sports marketing, higher education, toy production, and software development.

Currently, she lives in Maryland with her husband and three delightful kids.

M.C. loves to connect with her readers. You can find her at:

Website/Blog: https://mcvaughan.blogspot.com/
Twitter: @MC_Vaughan
Facebook: https://www.facebook.com/mcvaughanauthor/
Pinterest: https://www.pinterest.com/MC_Vaughan/
Instagram: https://www.instagram.com/mc_vaughan/

Now, read on to sneak a peek at the opening of *Pictures of You*, book 2 in *The Charm City Hearts* series.

Pictures of You
The Charm City Hearts, book 2

One

Grier Cushman ducked behind a marble column in the Four Seasons' ballroom. Hiding here wasn't brave, exactly, but she needed to calm the hell down before traipsing across an elegant minefield of people she'd avoided since high school.

Ha. What she *really* needed was a cocktail.

She smoothed the skirt of her Marchesa mini-dress and breathed deeply, once, twice, three times. This was silly. She had nothing to be embarrassed about. As a sample-sized woman with flawless makeup, a fresh blowout, and designer clothes, she was the polar opposite of her frumptastic teenaged self.

Who cared what they thought, anyway? High school was years ago, and honestly, only one of her former classmates could truly spin her up. No chance Quint would be here, though. He lived in New York, but even if he were local, he couldn't stand this crowd.

Throwing back her shoulders, Grier swished out among Baltimore's wealthy glitterati.

"Pumpkin, here we are." *Dad.*

Her parents sat at one of the smaller tables overlooking the Inner Harbor. Grier picked her way through the two hundred-strong crowd, avoiding eye contact. Halfway across the room, a photographer blocked her path and raised his camera.

"Smile!" he prompted, and a pop of diamond-white light blinded her.

"Wow, that's a lot of flash," she said, blinking away the spots.

By the time they cleared, the photographer had targeted fresh quarry. As he scurried around the room, he machine-gun shot pictures and startled guests. *So* not her style when she was behind the lens.

Except she hadn't worked her camera much lately, since serving time as a socialite consumed enormous wedges of the clock. She needed to change things up. Right after this lunch. Oh, and the Gala, and the Preakness. When was the Historical Society's fundraiser again?

"Hi!" she said, and perched in the empty chair. "Have you been here long?"

Mom fixed her with a steady gaze. "Please explain the fifteen thousand dollars."

"Uh," Grier said. "The what?"

She wanted to hide in her menu. *Those elocution lessons paid off, huh Mom?*

"Donna," Dad said, his expression flickering. "We agreed to wait until after we ordered."

"You're right." Mom signaled their waitress.

Grier peered at the luncheon choices, but the words blurred together as blood pounded in her ears. Confrontations sucked in general, but parental pop-up fights were the worst. The minute she'd written the fat check to the gallery, she'd known she'd crossed the money line. She was proud of her artist friend, though. What else could she do but buy out the show?

The waitress poured water from a crystal pitcher and asked, "Have we decided?"

Mom nodded. "We'll all have the *petit filet*, medium rare."

"Excellent choice. And to drink?"

"Water's fine."

"A glass of pinot grigio, please," Grier chirped.

Mom's lips thinned, but Grier didn't budge.

After the waitress disappeared from the table, Mom returned her attention to Grier. "Now, the fifteen thousand dollars?"

Honesty was the only way forward on this one. "I bought paintings from Zara."

Mom choked on her water and coughed into her napkin. "Good God. Couldn't you buy a Gustav Klimt lithograph like everyone else?"

"Her art is an investment," Grier said. "She's amazing."

Tinkling stemware and dull chatter droned in the background. Mom and Dad stared at her. What was going on? They'd never quizzed her about money before. Granted, the paintings were more expensive than her usual impulse-buy, but they'd barely blinked when she dropped the same amount to build her darkroom.

"I can afford it," Grier said.

The waitress delivered a pale glass of wine to Grier and pivoted away from the table. She didn't blame her. The heated expression on Mom's face could melt plastic.

"That's what we're here to talk about. Your father and I..." Mom paused, taking a deep breath. "We're cutting the financial cord."

Grier spluttered, and the pinot burned in her nose. "Wait,

what?"

She eyed the two of them. Were they joking? But, that was impossible because they never joked. Mom and Dad were all business, all day long. Even at parties, like today, they donned power suits and neutral expressions. Like you sacrifice your integrity if you wear a fun frock and a berry lip.

"Frowning will age you, Pumpkin." Mom's Mona Lisa lips were a lighter shade of pink than normal. She was probably trying to soften her brusque, lean-in demeanor. Except the sharp points of Mom's lacquered bob undercut the attempt.

Grier massaged her temple. "It's a lot of money, but it's not everything."

"Your allowance was supposed to last you through the end of the quarter. We're not in a position to replenish it. Our liquid resources have been devoted to the Foundation's launch next month."

Grier moaned under her breath. Why hadn't she seen this coming? She was a *photographer*. Seeing reality and putting it in its best light was kind of the point.

"Dad, what about the trust?"

Mom shook her head. "No. Your grandfather set it up in a Kiss Trust. Until you're forty, it can only be used for tuition, purchasing a home, or health expenses. Not rent and groceries."

Cold trickled from her skull and wound its way down, around her neck, her arms, her waist, her legs. She felt footless, unable to walk away from this.

Dad patted his mouth with his napkin. "If you need money, Pumpkin, we have an idea. You're an ideal candidate for a fundraising position at the Foundation."

Mom appraised Grier. "Of course, you'll need proper attire and a haircut."

Grier hugged her middle. Haircut? What she needed was a Nexium, *tout de suite*.

Many people would be thrilled if the CEO and Chairman of the Board of the region's biggest real estate development company tapped them for job. She was not one of them.

"You don't need to get me a job."

"How else will you pay your bills, Grier?"

"I'll handle it, Mom."

"Don't be silly, Pumpkin. I'll schedule an interview after Dad and I return from our trip." Mom reached for her omnipresent cell phone. "Better yet, I'll do it now."

Grier gently rubbed her fingertip along the serrated edge of her steak knife. "Mom, stop. We shouldn't work together. It would be you and Gramps all over again."

"My father and I were different people. Whereas you and I are cut from the same cloth."

Ugh. Grier's stomach roiled. If she didn't have to hurl before, she sure did now.

Work for Mom? There was no chance Grier could maintain her composure for forty hours a week around her nitpicky mother. Exploding into a frazzled bundle of nerves by Day 5 would kind of ruin the capable, polished vibe Grier had been cultivating since she was seventeen.

"We've been considering this for some time." Mom tucked a stiff lock of chestnut hair behind her diamond-studded ear. "Even if we didn't need to divert funds, after this near tragedy with your friend Oliver—"

Grier held her palms up. "Hold on. That wasn't a *tragedy.* When the cops busted him, he and his friends were wired on pills and launching each other into the Harbor in a shopping cart. He's lucky he didn't drown."

"Lower your voice please," Mom hissed.

Grier bit down on the inside of her lips. She hadn't meant to get that loud. Even though the crowd noise and classy string quartet created a sense of privacy, shrill tones would draw the focus of other guests.

One thing Grier Cushman would not, could not do was attract negative attention.

Dad swirled the ice in his water glass. "Let's not gossip. We're here to celebrate Oliver's successful completion of rehab."

"With an open bar?"

Mom ignored Grier to thank the waitress, who slid their artfully plated meals on the table. Delectable aromas wafted from the steak and slender, roasted vegetables. When would she eat like this again? In the minutes since Mom made their selections, Grier had tumbled from a one-per center to a well-coiffed panhandler.

Mom snapped her napkin across her lap. "This event underscores an unfortunate trend among your friends."

"Can you stop referring to them that way? None of these people are my friends. They're *your* friends' children. I'm glad Oliver got help, and I wrote a nice note in his card." Grier flapped a stiff pastel envelope at them. "But I'm only here because you told me to come."

"So we could talk to you about your direction, Grier." Dad peered down his nose at her. "Oliver's not the first among your *peers* to go to rehab. Many of our friends' adult children live at home or depend on their parents for everything. The papers call it 'affluenza.'"

"I'm not like that. I barely even drink."

Grier pretended not to see the way her mother cut her gaze toward the sweaty glass of pinot. Whatever. It was medicinal, to take the edge off. Good thing, because this conversation was full of edges.

Sheesh. If they were coming for her like this, wonder what life was like at the homestead for her little brother?

"Have you put the *kibosh* on Hunter's senior week? Yachting in Santorini is expensive."

Dad cleared his throat. "No. Not yet."

Mom drummed her fingers on the table. "This is off-topic, but could you take him for his prospective tour at Hopkins next week? I tried to reschedule since we'll still be in Europe, but they are firm on their dates. He can't miss it—the school is *very* interested in recruiting him, given his 4.0 and his lacrosse statistics."

When was the last time they'd hung out? A few months ago, at dinner maybe? Unbelievable. She only lived ten miles away. These last few months had been busy with her parents' requests she attend various soirées, the street photography, and the odd gigs she'd booked.

Grier missed the goof. "Sure, but can we back up? To this whole "you're not giving me money anymore" situation? Because I honestly don't understand what I've done wrong."

Dad reached across the table to pat her on the hand. "It's not you, Pumpkin. It's us. We should have shifted this paradigm ages ago. You're a Cushman. That name comes with responsibility in this city. You need to find your feet, contribute to society."

Grier twiddled her fork. "I shot a wedding two weeks ago."

"You can't build a life on itinerant work. You're nearly twenty-five. It's time to stop drifting and playing around with this hobby of yours. You need a career. At your age I'd earned my MBA and was already a vice president."

"I didn't realize there was a timer."

Mom pushed her lunch plate away and folded her hands on the table. "We've been hinting at this for years, but we've indulged you anyway, hoping you would launch yourself. That hasn't happened, so, here it is, loud and clear—this month's allowance is the last of it. From now on, your bills will come directly to you."

"But... I don't..." Grier gulped. What was happening? She couldn't form a coherent sentence, much less an argument against her parents' decision.

"Have a plan? I assumed as much." Mom woke her cell phone. "I'll email you the resume I've drafted for you. Review before I send it to HR, if you'd like."

The world swirled, and Grier clutched the edge of the table. *No, no, no.* She could not work for, with, or near her mother. Even if— huge, gigantic, galaxy-sized *if*—Grier enjoyed the work, Donna the CEO would hover, instructing her on every detail and taking charge of every task.

There was one respectable option to escape this.

Lie.

Grier straightened her spine. "It's funny we're having this conversation now because I have some interviews lined up. For photography jobs."

She hated lying, and was normally terrible at it. This wasn't a lie, though. More like as a pre-truth. As soon as she left this stupid party, she'd be on a job hunt.

Mom rearranged her features into a blank stare and nudged Dad. "Bryce, isn't that a coincidence?"

"It's marvelous. You'll keep us apprised?"

Grier nodded, not trusting her voice to keep up the act.

Mom put the phone down. "Steady work will be good for you. You won't have time for Oliver's kind of nonsense."

Stupid Oliver Adams. She'd left the Preston crew behind years ago, yet they managed to blow up parts of her life anyway. The mature, gracious side of her applauded Oliver's recovery efforts. The rest of her wanted to throttle his tattooed neck.

Grier looked past her parents to level Oliver with an epic stink-eye, but she couldn't get a clear shot. His table was filled with fellow graduates of The Preston School.

Preston. Such a fishbowl. She couldn't shake off her mistakes while was a student there. Forever and always, she was the kindergartner who'd been afraid of Santa Claus, the fifth grader who'd hyperventilated while dissecting the frog, and the awkward twelfth grader who'd—

Wait. She hit the brakes on a destructive stomp down memory lane. She sucked in her breath. Oliver was talking to someone whose shape fit her life like a missing puzzle piece.

She squinted. It couldn't be him. Could it?

Come on, contacts, don't fail me now.

Her stomach fluttered. There'd been one boy at Preston who had triggered this uncertain, happy, glittery reaction in her body.

No. No, absolutely no. That cannot be…

When the mystery man in a killer suit eased into the chair next to Oliver, the flutter in her stomach erupted into a traitorous flock. John Aloysius Kincaid V, a.k.a Quint. Taller and broader and more delicious in every way. She'd hoped never to encounter him again, but that particular hope popped and settled in her gut like a ruined balloon.

What was he *doing* here?

She couldn't wrap her brain around it any more than she could an original Ansel Adams in a bathroom. Grier clenched her cutlery, and her manicured fingernails bit into her palms.

With Quint in the room, she wasn't the polished photographer who'd studied abroad in Paris and interned at a magazine in D.C. No, she was reduced to the itchy-in-her-own-skin teenager who wore clothes her mother chose for her and titled her broody self-portraits "Solitude."

Mom's voice cut through the fog. "It's paramount you have a plan, Grier. You need to be able to stand on your own feet. There's no foster care for adults."

As her mother listed banal business advice, Grier tracked Quint. She had to leave before he noticed her.

Her fork and knife clattered against the plate. "Excuse me." She snatched her purse from where she'd slung it on the chair. "I need to run to the ladies'."

Two

According to the sharp-edged place card in Quint Kincaid's palm, he was assigned to Oliver's table. Every muscle in his neck tensed. Was he doing this?

Yeah, of course he was. He'd promised his parents.

Quint had been in the middle of a venture capital pitch book when they called. Pop didn't have enough energy for an outing today, and Mama couldn't leave him. They asked Quint to go and wish Oliver well, and the whole point of his return to Baltimore was to make life easier for them. End result? He'd taken a deep breath, suited up, then Ubered to the Four Seasons.

"Need any help finding your table, sir?" a passing waitress asked.

He flashed a tired smile. "No thanks. I'm avoiding the inevitable for a minute."

He could do this. Suck it up and chat like they'd been friends. Because that was the strategic thing to do. Like it had been the right choice not to make waves back in the day. After all, Quint's parents had rearranged their whole lives to enroll him and his sister at Preston. They'd called it the opportunity of a lifetime.

The jury was out on that one.

Quint strode toward the table where Oliver sat alone. Jackets and purses dangled from the other chairs. Probably other Preston classmates. Maybe she was here? Quint's heart skipped a beat, and he fought the urge to scope out the guests.

Nah. He squashed that hope. She'd never come to this.

Would've been better if he'd listened to his gut and stayed away too. The financial grunt work waiting back at the office nagged at him. He was ambivalent about investment banking, but he was good at it, and the generous salary was too important to his family.

An hour. He'd bullshit about jobs and the weather, then head back to work.

"This seat taken?" He unbuttoned his suit coat and claimed the chair next to the guest of honor.

Oliver peered at him through a flop of messy black hair. "Quint

Kincaid! Never in a million expected you to be here."

"I'm a proxy for my parents. They send their best." Quint glanced at his watch. One minute down, fifty-nine to go.

"They were always my favorite teachers."

Quint sipped his water. "I hear that a lot."

"How the hell are you, anyway?"

"Better question is, how are *you*?"

Oliver twisted the ring on his thumb. "Enjoying my sobriety. You in town for the weekend, or something? I thought you'd escaped to New York."

Quint half-shrugged. "I did, but I'm back in Baltimore for a while."

"That's awesome." Oliver clapped a hand to his shoulder and squeezed. "So dude, before we get into anything else, I'm sorry for the shitty things I said back in school."

Quint arched a brow. Was Oliver high?

"One of the steps in my recovery process is to apologize to people I've wronged." As Oliver ran a hand through his hair, an intricate tattoo peeped out from his shirtsleeve. "And, man, I was an epic asshole to you."

"No need to dig up old news." Quint lifted his palms. "But I won't argue."

"There's no excuse for how I behaved, but I can explain, if you're interested?" Oliver drummed his thumbs on the table.

"If you must," Quint said.

"Okay, here we go. This is a total over share, but here it is— I'm bi, and I didn't know how to handle it in high school. Or get that it didn't *need* to be handled, and that I'm just me. I didn't want to be different."

Was he supposed to console this guy? Quint reached for a dinner roll instead. "I doubt anyone would've cared."

He shook his head. "Attitudes were different. I numbed myself with vodka and pills and tried to bring everyone else down."

"I remember." Oliver's taunts had been the earworms of Quint's adolescence, slithering around his brain and under his skin.

He'd drowned out some comments with music and laughed off others with Grier. Not all of them. Some of the snide observations about his discount clothes, secondhand books, and needing financial aid stuck like burrs.

Oliver steepled his fingertips together in some Namaste bullshit. "I'm truly sorry, dude."

His apology shaved the edge off Quint's bad mood. It didn't

erase the, "Come on, can't you take a joke?" gaslighting or wipe the slate clean. But, given the right circumstances, some people could change for the better. Took work, though. He eyed Oliver.

"Thanks," Quint said. "I appreciate it."

Oliver grinned. "Wanna get together sometime?"

Psht. Sure. Oliver might not be high, but he was definitely delusional.

Quint wouldn't call him out at his own party. Not when half of Baltimore's wealthiest families were in the room. They were financially incestuous, serving on each other's Boards, employing each other's children. He couldn't lob a truth bomb in here without becoming his own collateral damage.

Quint dragged his bottom lip between his teeth. "Nope. I don't let shit slide anymore."

"Perfect," Oliver said. "I need that in my life."

This guy couldn't take a hint. No surprise. Oliver'd never been a straight-A student. "I don't have much free time."

His excuse had the benefit of being true. As the new guy at his firm, Quint worked twice as hard as everyone else. The rest of his waking hours were devoted to Mama's honey-do list.

"Hey, how about this? Come with me to Violet's wedding. It's in two weeks."

Quint fought the urge to frown. The only person he wanted to socialize with less than Oliver was Violet Summerville. "I'm flattered you asked, but I'm a ladies' man."

Oliver laughed. "No offense dude, but you're not my type. Too tall. It's way too early in my recovery to date, but I don't want to go alone. Come on. Be my plus one."

The bread sat like concrete in Quint's stomach. Prestonites dredged up the old less-than, have-not feelings from back in the day. But, this could be a golden business opportunity. Rich kids have rich parents, and rich parents invest.

Solid move for an investment banker.

Quint crunched an ice cube. "Black tie, I'm assuming?"

"Probably. Violet's here somewhere. You can ask her."

Damn, he could not catch a break. He lifted his glass, wishing it contained something amber-colored and at least 100 proof.

"So where are you living these days?" Oliver asked.

"Fell's Point."

"Hey, Alberto lives in Fell's too."

"British guy, right?"

"British*ish*. His parents emigrated to the States when he was fourteen. Anyway, he has a sick voice. Plays guitar, too. Me, I'm unparalleled on the skins, as you know." Oliver beat rhythm on the centerpiece with his fork and knife. "We're starting a band, and as it happens, we have an opening for a bassist. What do you say?"

"I don't play much anymore." Much as it pained him to say that out loud, it was true. Six months ago, Quint had flirted with quitting finance and getting back into music. That daydream died as soon as Pop got his diagnosis.

"What?" Oliver smacked the table, rattling the glasses. "Unacceptable. You need to be in this band. It's fate."

This guy has some balls, right here. He might be on his way to forgiving Oliver, but joining his band? Bands were an intimate, hardworking brotherhood. They required talent, dedication, and trust. Oliver possessed the first trait on that list, but was beyond lacking in the others.

Quint side-eyed him. "No can do."

"Sure you can. We were great in Jazz Band. Plus we already have a name." Oliver spread his hands. "We. Are. Balt-Rock."

"That's a terrible name." Quint groaned.

"It'll be fun. Plus, it's a good way to meet girls."

Quint ran his hand over his close-cropped hair. "Not a selling point. I don't have time to do laundry, let alone date."

"Who said anything about dating? I'm talking groupies."

Across the room, a redhead popped up from a table, and Quint's world hushed. As she slipped through the crowd, she was the only crystal clear thing in his sights.

Grier Cushman.

His former best friend's curve-hugging green dress revealed she'd slimmed down since high school. Not that she'd needed to. She'd also tamed her crazy red curls into a sleek, tight, upswept style. She was sexy no matter what, but he'd loved wild hair. They used to joke that they both had Afros. Guess it made sense she'd try a different style—even he'd played around with mini-dreads and short twists before settling on a short buzz cut.

One thing she hadn't altered was her stride. She hustled like someone fired a starting pistol and she was striving for gold.

Oliver followed his gaze. "Whoa, is that Grier? I had a massive crush on her during senior year."

Didn't we all? Quint's tie was too tight, and his whole body itched. A seething mix of lust, regret, and curiosity shot through his veins. What was she like these days? He hoped life was treating her well. She deserved nothing but the best.

"I was such a dick to her. I owe her an apology too." Oliver shoved his chair back from the table, but Quint beat him to his feet.

"Sit tight. It's been a minute since she and I have spoken."

He crossed the lush room toward her. Pride and deadlines could go to hell for today. This might be his one chance to say hello and to make everything between them right again.

~ * ~

For notice of sales and special deals, visit Champagne Book Group at (http://www.champagnebooks.com) and sign up for our newsletter, including chances to get advance copies of releases before the general reader public does.